OCTOBERLAND

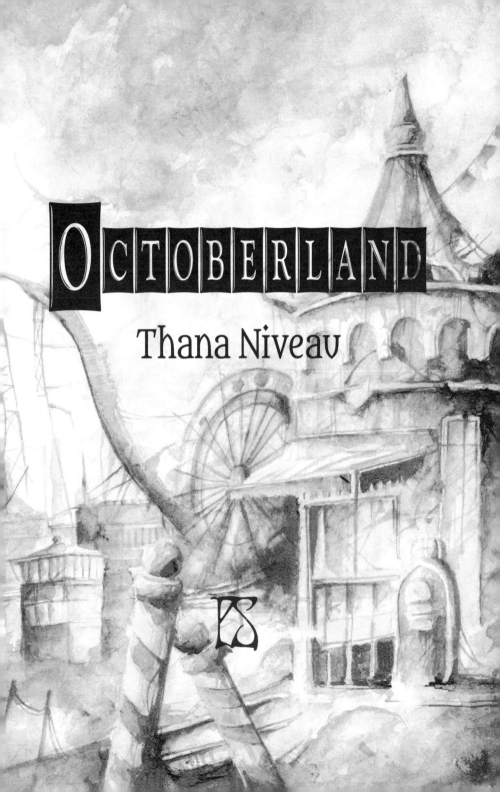

OCTOBERLAND

Thana Niveau

PS Publishing Ltd
Grosvenor House
1 New Road
Hornsea, HU18 1PG
England

editor@pspublishing.co.uk
www.pspublishing.co.uk

CONTENTS

INTRODUCTION

I T'S A GENUINE PLEASURE AND AN HONOUR TO INTRODUCE these stories. The first thing to know about Thana Niveau is—she's a huge talent! If you've already purchased this volume, you're in for a treat. If you're leafing through and wondering if you should, don't hesitate.

I could trot out that well-worn phrase, 'never a word wasted'. But of course that's the case, because Thana Niveau can *write*. She dances with words, building pictures in the reader's mind that are vivid and exotic and gloriously real. She is mistress of the telling detail, her descriptions ranging from the sensuous to the visceral before gleaming with gleeful delight. We feel every emotion—indeed, we can hardly fail to do so, when Thana Niveau gives them bones and flesh.

I've been aware of Thana—and her alter-ego Kate Probert, if I may—for some time, through various publications and genre-related events. The magazines and anthologies in which these stories appeared are like a roll-call of those I've read and enjoyed over the last few years, and Thana's have always been among the most memorable.

The work included here is wide ranging, taking us across the world from Wales to Cornwall, from North America to Mexico. They cover the present day, childhood memories and a past more distant still. There is a range of themes: J-horror videos give rise to new and unspeakable visions; a dolphin dosed with LSD lends us insight into human destructiveness. There is pure horror and eroticism, folklore and magic, subtle disquiet and creeping fear. There are nods to Ray Bradbury and Lovecraft, an homage to Arthur Machen, and a story written from the notes left behind by a mutual friend, Joel Lane (a thoroughly beautiful and fitting tribute to his memory).

There is unity within these pages too. This book offers us a journey into wild places and wilder seasons, where characters find themselves in the grip of something larger and more powerful and infinitely more mysterious than they can understand. Indeed, some of Thana's finest work is concerned with nature. Here we have strange creatures born of earth or water, snow with a mind of its own and flowers that are subtly... *wrong*. The author shows us the wonder and fascination of the living world, but as she says, 'Nature isn't always kind.' She revels in the idea of immersing ourselves, but lurking not far away is the horror of truly becoming one with nature and losing what it is to be human. There are cities in this collection too, though they are possessed of a more overt and pernicious evil, liable to rot your soul from the inside.

It is easy to gain the impression that Kate loves the genre, relishes the genre, lives the genre—as, indeed, I know she does. It came as no surprise to see, in the story notes, that *Octoberland* is full of Kate's own memories. It's easy to picture her hanging effigies outside her house and scaring the local kids—or indeed enjoying a present day Halloween with her husband, Lord P, he no doubt dressed as a mad surgeon holding a scalpel to her throat, or she as a vampire, biting his neck...

There is a delightful theatricality in their lives, which brings me to *Two Five Seven*, my favourite piece in this collection. I have vivid memories of Kate reading—and singing—this story late one night at World Fantasy 2013, with the wind howling around the turret room that was the setting for the event. Kate and Lord P invited me to read that night too, and it's the first reading I've ever done from beneath a bloody veil, but then, such is their influence. And my nerves I'm sure showed through quite plainly, though Kate, as ever, performed as well as she writes. She read this spooky, eerie, and rather sad story in magnificent style, curled up in a chair as if she was the little girl in the tale, and the audience was rapt. It was wonderful to see, and when re-reading it I can hear her again, recounting that sequence of ten numbers just waiting to be decoded.

And in the spirit of theatre, all that remains now is to recommend to you these mysterious, unsettling and hugely enjoyable stories. A drumroll, please . . . Thana Niveau, the stage is yours!

—Alison Littlewood
Deepest darkest Yorkshire
4322562018

For my brother
I hope these stories don't damage your calm

Going to the Sun Mountain

W E BURIED THE FIRST BODY IN THE WOODS BEHIND A bar called the "Nite Owl". I don't like when they do that—make the spelling of words wrong on purpose. It shouldn't be allowed. Glacia bought the shovels at a hardware store and no one asked her what she wanted them for even though it was almost dark outside. She was going to say we had to dig up a tree stump if anyone asked. But no one did. Nobody cared.

We didn't make the hole very deep because it was hard work and we got tired quickly. No one would suspect us anyway. There were probably fights every night at that bar, so anyone there could have killed him.

Afterwards Glacia said we should get back on the road, so we did. We crossed the border into Colorado and found a motel. The first one we saw was a Super 8, but Glacia knew I wouldn't want to stop there. 8 is a bad number. So she kept driving and the next one was called Vagabond Inn, which was better.

It was almost 2 a.m. and the desk clerk was asleep in the back room when we got there. We had to ring the little bell for ages to wake him up. Even then he barely even looked at us, which was good because we were filthy. Glacia wrote down made-up names for us and handed him the money. He yawned as he took it and gave us the key to room 10. The worst number of all.

"Not that one," I cried. Then, at his startled expression, I added "please."

He looked blearily at the other keys hanging on the pegboard behind him and picked up the next one along, number 11.

I relaxed and gave him my sweetest smile. "Thank you."

In the room we helped each other wash off the dirt, grass and blood, then we crawled into bed. There were two beds in the room but I didn't want to sleep by myself. I could still hear the noises he'd made.

"Where will we go now?" I asked.

Glacia sighed and said she didn't know. She didn't say anything for a long time but I knew she wasn't asleep. She does that sometimes—goes quiet for a long time. I have to push my mind into hers to see what she's thinking. Most people don't notice when I do it but Glacia can always tell.

"I know you're there, Lys," she said.

"I just want to know what our story is now."

She thought for a moment. "If anyone asks, we're urban explorers."

My skin went cold. "But that's what *he* said he was."

Glacia nodded.

I didn't like it. I didn't want to be the same thing as the body was before we killed him. But I was curious about the words. "What *is* an urban explorer?"

"Someone who explores abandoned buildings," Glacia said. "Usually they take pictures."

"We don't have a camera."

"Then we'll say we're artists."

"We don't have anything to draw or paint with."

She laughed softly. "We take pictures in our minds," she said, tapping my forehead in the dark. "Then we go home and draw them from memory."

That sounded better. I have a very good memory. The way I see things in my head, they're almost like photographs.

"Pictures in our minds," I said. I liked the way that sounded. I was also glad we could be explorers because words with an X in them are good.

We fell asleep at the same time and I had the dream again, the one where I was made of snow.

The next body wasn't as messy. We pushed him off a bridge. It was also easier because this time I was really angry. He'd *touched* me.

Afterwards I sat in the dust by the side of the road scrubbing at my skin with a rock to get rid of the feel of him. My flesh crawled just at the memory of it. I wanted to scream.

Glacia heard it in my head and told me to stay calm. "We'll wash him off, don't worry," she said. "At the next motel."

"What did he mean?" I asked her.

"He doesn't matter. It's just you and me now."

"I know, but what did he mean?"

But Glacia just sighed and started the car. She looked at the rock I was using like a sponge. I had raked open my leg, and blood and muscle gleamed against the white of my skin. The dust was making it burn.

"You're not the same as other people, Lys. You don't even look like them."

"I know. But why did he say that about me?"

"You shouldn't have taken your sunglasses off."

That was all Glacia wanted to say and when I tried to push into her mind it was like she had closed a door. She gave me a warning look and I stopped trying. So I tried to go into *his* mind but of course there was nothing there at all. He was just an empty piece of meat at the bottom of a ravine. I didn't like the thought that he had the touch of my skin with him. But it wouldn't be long before animals chewed him up. I'd be safe with them.

The engine purred as we drove away and I went through his rucksack. He had $944. I had to count it three times to be sure. Then I slipped one dollar bill into the glove box to make it an odd number. I'd wanted to keep his guitar but Glacia said it wasn't a good idea so we threw it off the bridge after him. It made a sound like a broken song when it hit the rocks. There was nothing else we could use in the rucksack so I tossed it in the back seat of the car. We could get rid of it later.

"That's a lot of money," Glacia said, smiling. "We can stay somewhere nice tonight if you like."

I didn't care. I just wanted to wash myself. Even though I had taken off all the skin he'd touched, it was like his ghost was still there, pressing his hand against my leg, trying to slide it up under my skirt. He'd thought he was the one robbing *us* until Glacia slit his throat. He didn't even notice at first. I pushed him away and he called me ugly things. Then he saw the blood and forgot all about me. Until we dragged him to the bridge. That's when he looked in my eyes and said I was a demon.

I was silent while Glacia drove, thinking my own thoughts. I must have fallen asleep because the next thing I knew, the car was stopped and Glacia was shaking me.

"Come on. We're here."

I looked up at the buzzing neon sign. TRAVELLERS REST, it said. I liked the name. It had lots of sharp letters.

Our room was actually a cabin, one of many. They were all set apart from each other like a little neighbourhood. There was even a small kitchen inside ours. It was number 3, which made me happy. It's my favourite number.

"We can stay here for a couple of days if you want to," Glacia said, "get our bearings and decide what to do next, where to go."

I wasn't listening to her. I was in the bathroom trying to get the shower to work. It sputtered into life and I hissed with pain as the spray hit the wound on my leg. But pain was better than the feel of that body. He'd even tried to touch my hair but I'd pulled away in time.

The TV came on and I heard Glacia searching the channels. Looking for news. But we were a long way away from the first body and I didn't see how anyone could ever find the second one. That bridge was high up over a canyon and the dust covered everything like a blanket.

The towel was soaked with blood. I didn't know what to do with it so I stuffed it in the wastebasket. I came out of the bathroom naked and Glacia stared at my leg, frowning.

"Oh, Lys," she said. "You mustn't do that."

"I had to get rid of him."

"Now you'll have a scar."

I had other scars but this one would be the biggest. "I don't care about scars. I care about not being touched."

She wasn't upset with me, not really. She tore one of her shirts into strips to tie around my leg so it would stop bleeding. Glacia was the only one who could touch me.

"There," she said. "We'll get some alcohol and clean it out if it gets infected."

"It won't."

"I know. But just in case."

She turned back to the TV, where a pretty reporter was standing in front of the Nite Owl. I glared at the misspelled sign. It made me think of the one that says NO THRU TRUCKS. That's the worst one of all.

"Once again," the reporter was saying, "police are asking anyone with any information to please get in touch." A phone number appeared on the screen beneath her.

Glacia frowned. "We should have buried him deeper."

"It wouldn't have mattered. You know that. Animals would just dig him up anyway."

The story on the TV changed to a commercial for used cars but Glacia was just staring blankly at the screen. I went over and turned it off, clicking the button three times to be sure. I could see the room reflected in the black screen, Glacia sitting there, still watching. Finally she turned to me.

"What are we going to do now?"

For a moment I didn't know why she was asking me. But then I guessed it must be because of the first body. Because he was mine. I didn't know what to say. "Can't we just keep driving like we always have? No one will ever find us. We can see the whole country."

But she looked sad and shook her head. Her long dark hair looked dirty in the yellow motel light and her face was tired. "I didn't want it to be like this," she said. "I didn't want any of this to happen."

I pushed inside and she didn't resist me. Her thoughts were all red and going in circles. I didn't like the way she felt sad about the first body but at least she wasn't upset with me. The second one had happened out of her control, because there was a hole inside her that had to be filled. I didn't want to think about the hole it would leave in me if she had done what she was thinking of with the first body. The hole I would then have to fill.

So I turned my thoughts to all the places we could see instead, all the different states. I pictured deserts, forests, swamps, mountains. Then I remembered my dream and that made me happy. "Glacia! Do you think we could go all the way to Alaska?"

I saw snow flash inside her mind and she smiled. It was tiny and weak, but still a smile. "I think so," she said at last. "We'll have to get to Canada first."

"But Alaska's a state."

"Yes, but it's way up north, past Canada."

I didn't understand why part of one country was in a different country, but I trusted Glacia. She'd been to school for a little while so she knew more than I did.

"Is Canada a long way away?"

"I don't think so. We're pretty far north already."

I smiled, thinking about Alaska. It was made of snow, like Antarctica but not at the bottom of the world. I'd seen snow way up high on mountains, but I'd never touched it before. Even so, part of me knew how it would feel, how it would taste. Like hard-frozen ice cream, so cold it was chewy. I could feel the happiness in Glacia's mind as she looked at me.

"You belong in the snow," she said.

She reached out to stroke my hair, admiring the white strands as they passed through her fingers like silk. Usually I liked for Glacia to touch my hair but this time it reminded me of the second body and I pulled away from her. I was still confused by what he had said.

"Why would he say I was a demon if he thought my hair was pretty?"

"Because of your eyes," Glacia said.

"But why?"

"Because he'd never seen eyes like yours. Or probably hair like yours. Or skin like yours."

My skin was paler than most people's, and my hair was too. But I didn't understand how my eyes could upset anyone. Most people had brown eyes. Some had blue ones. Or green, like Glacia. Mine were pink and to me that was a lot nicer than brown. Brown was a big round word like earth and mud. Pink was for living things like flowers and worms.

"You mustn't let people see your eyes," Glacia was saying. "They don't understand. They get scared. But most of all, it makes them remember you."

Yes, they did remember me. And I remembered them.

I thought back to my only day at school, when I was very little. The other kids had been staring at me all day. But then a boy called Davy pointed at me and said I was a freak. I didn't know what the word meant. All I knew was the ugly thought in his head. The "Yuck" he said in there and the face he made when he thought it.

It didn't hurt. It was just confusing. I stared at him and he said it again. A girl next to him giggled, and then, from somewhere near the back of the group, another kid said it too.

"Freak!"

I didn't even think about what I was doing. I picked up the newly sharpened pencil from the teacher's desk and plunged it like a stinger into his hand. I made a little twisting motion and the pencil broke off inside his skin with a soft click.

He screamed and screamed and then the other kids were screaming too. The teacher just stood there, looking shocked. I didn't feel anything at all. I stared at the blood spilling from his hand onto the floor like black honey. After that I never went back to school.

Our father had to pay a lot of money to the boy's family and Glacia said our mother was worried about him losing his job because of what I'd done. He worked at the university. Glacia said he was a scientist, but she didn't know exactly what he did. Sometimes he would take us to the lab with him, but we hated it there. It was full of evil smells and there were lots of animals screaming in cages. It made us hurt inside.

I didn't like to think about that. I didn't like to think of any time when it wasn't just Glacia and me. We had each other and that was all we needed. She had a licence so we moved around, driving from place to place. Sometimes Glacia got small jobs that paid cash, but other times we stole. Sometimes she simply persuaded people to help us or give us money. And everything had been fine.

Until the first body. I still don't even know why I did it. It was like something had been sleeping inside me and he'd made it wake up. Maybe it was the way he looked at Glacia, like her legs were something just for him. Like he was the only person she had ever smiled at.

Glacia had only asked him if there was a road that went through the mountains. He looked her up and down and smiled back at her. There was a leap of excitement in his mind that made me feel funny, so I didn't push all the way inside him.

He asked if she wanted to go the fast way or the scenic way. I wasn't sure what he meant, but Glacia seemed to understand. She was acting different, like she was suddenly shy. She told him she wanted the scenic route and he said if she gave him a ride, he'd show her a good time.

It was like I wasn't there at all, not even for Glacia. I didn't care if *he* saw me or thought about me, but I hated feeling so far away from Glacia. Her thoughts were so confusing, and when she sensed me in there, she pushed me out. I didn't want him in the car at all, especially not in my seat, but Glacia said I should ride in the back so he could show her the way.

"I'll be the navigator," he said. Then he saluted Glacia and called her Captain and she laughed. A real laugh too, not a being-nice one.

I didn't say anything. I just moved into the seat behind Glacia and curled away as far from him as I could get. It felt like I was in a cage, cut off from Glacia. He didn't even look at me. All he did was talk to her. But I didn't like the way he was looking at her. His eyes crawled all over her like ants. One time he touched her hand on the steering wheel and she didn't pull away.

After a while we stopped at a scenic overlook and they got out. We were surrounded by weird stripy hills and rocks that looked like demolished sandcastles. There was no one else around. Glacia tried to get me to come too, to see the view. But I didn't want to see it with him there. He was making everything bad.

I don't even remember picking up the tyre iron. Or getting out of the car. But I remember his arm going around Glacia's shoulders and her not fighting back. The heat haze made everything look like it was underwater and she seemed to be dancing like a charmed snake, moving right up against him. I wanted her to bite him the way a snake would, the way *I* would. When she didn't, I knew I had to save her. So I shoved the pointed end of the tyre iron into his back.

He made a gulping, grunting noise and fell to his knees with the metal sticking out of him. His hands flailed at his sides like he was falling and then there was a big splash of blood on the ground. He coughed and choked and spat, but he didn't scream. Neither did Glacia. She wasn't even looking at him; she was looking at me. I'd never seen such a look in her eyes. Tears shone there.

We watched the body flopping around in the dust like a landed fish. It took him a long time to die. He even managed to pull the spike out at one point but that only made the blood spurt faster. It came out in rhythmic gouts, thick and dark. His skin was almost as pale as mine by the time he was finally still.

Glacia closed her eyes and lowered her head, like she was praying. That's when I knew something was wrong, that I'd *done* something wrong. But it was just the two of us now, like it should be. How could that be wrong?

It was a long time before she spoke. "Come on, Lys," she said. "Help me get him into the trunk."

Then we drove into the next town where we found the roadhouse with the bad name and the hardware store where they weren't even curious about us.

We were a long way from that place now, and getting further away all the time.

We drove for another day, through forests and mountains and wide dusty plains. Glacia bought a road atlas at a gas station and I looked for Alaska. She was right. It was a million miles away.

"Don't worry, Lys. There are other places where we can find snow."

I hadn't really understood just how big the world was until I looked at the map, trying to find somewhere for us to go. It was full of numbers. They looked different written down than they did on road signs. In my head I could see them changing, adding up like a calculator and going down like a bomb counter in a movie.

And there were so many cities and towns! Even the biggest ones we drove through were like specks of dust on the map. I had never felt so small. I wondered, if you had a giant magnifying glass, could you see the even tinier specks of dust that would be us, slowly making our way along all those twisting roads? Could you zoom in like on a computer screen and keep going down, down, down until you saw the tiniest ants and grains of sand, down to the molecules and atoms?

"Where should we go?" I asked.

Glacia shrugged. "Anywhere we want. Pick someplace that sounds nice."

We were close to Yellowstone National Park, which was a place I'd heard of. On the map it looked like someone had spilled green paint across the borders of three states, like a child who couldn't colour inside the lines.

Near the top of the spill was a town called Big Sky. Sky was a good word and at first I thought we should go there. But there was another one called Pray close by and that made me think of the second body calling me a demon.

Glacia sensed my discomfort. "Read some of the names out," she said, and I did.

Places like Wise River and Spirit Lake made it seem like the country was a living thing, something that would protect us. But there were some really weird names too. Soon we'd made a game out of it.

"There's a town called Sourdough," I said. "And one called Fishtail."

Glacia giggled. "That's the stinky part of the country."

"There's another one called Squirrel."

"Wow. Some really unimaginative settlers there. Maybe that's all they could find to eat."

"What about—" my finger scanned the map "—Atomic City?"

Her eyes went wide and she looked frightened for a moment. "No! That one's full of radioactive mannequins. They were poisoned by bombs and if we go there they'll cover us in ash and keep us with them forever."

I stared at her for a long time. I'd never heard her say anything like that before. She was trembling.

"Find somewhere else, Lys. Please."

I turned my eyes back to the map and quickly found another place. "Bear Dance?"

She thought for a moment. "City of strippers," she said at last. Her voice sounded sad, but she was smiling, so I knew it was meant to be a joke. Still, I didn't like it that she thought of things like that. It reminded me of the way the first body had put his arm around her and she hadn't done anything to stop him. I pictured her killing the second one instead.

"Here's a good place," I said. "Craters of the Moon."

Now her smile was bright and there was no trace of her dark mood from before. "Oh, I like that. I wish we could live there."

"Me too."

But it wasn't actually a place to live, just a park with a dormant volcano. I knew the word from the "*Dormez-vous*" song. That meant it was sleeping. Like I was before the first body. I could see it in my head—a field of charred, blackened ground from the lava flow, the volcano sitting in the middle like a hollow mountain. I bet if you buried something there, no one would ever find it. But then I realised something that made me sigh in frustration.

"It's the opposite of snow."

Glacia reached over to stroke my hair, soothing me. "So go farther north."

I traced the line of the road with my finger, following numbers I liked. 15, 287, 89. Then I saw it. Just on the border between Montana and Canada. "Glacia!"

"What?"

"It's your name. Well, *almost* your name. Glacier National Park. *That's* where we have to go!"

She glanced over at the map. "Is there a real glacier there?"

"I don't know. It's all green on the map and there are lots of lakes and mountains. Look—there's a city called Rising Sun! It's perfect!"

It was perfect because sunrises were like cold fire. All icy white sharp colours, and they happened when most people wanted to be asleep. Dormant. I liked being awake when others weren't. It made me feel like the world was mine, even if only for a short time.

Rising Sun was next to the Blackfeet Indian Reservation, and I wondered if they had walked through the lava field to get there. Blackfeet was a good word. I pointed to it on the map for Glacia and she said we could probably reach the park by nightfall. She even let me drive for a while to make sure we would. I didn't have a licence but the roads were mostly empty, so it wasn't likely we'd get caught.

We had to pay to go inside the park, but we still had plenty of money left over from the second body. At the booth they gave us a special guidebook with a map.

"There's *definitely* a glacier," I said, scanning the pages of the book. "More than one."

"But can we live here? In the park, I mean?"

I didn't know. The area was so huge I couldn't see why not. Maybe we could live off the land like the Indians used to. It would be just like when we were kids and pretended we were animals that had escaped from cages. I liked foxes best. Fox had an X in it. Together we could be fast and clever, swift and cunning. We could just run away or hide from anyone who told us we couldn't stay there. I was so lost in my daydreams that Glacia had to nudge me to ask which way to go.

Mountains rose up all around us, and one had the best name in the world: Going-to-the-Sun Mountain. I didn't even think about the letters or the words; for once I just saw the meaning. The name made me feel calm, the way I felt in my dream where I was snow. It was Glacia's park, *our* park, and all the names were safe. All the words were good.

The sun was low in the sky, turning the heavens into a blaze of fiery colours as we drove along the winding road through the park. The next sign we saw was for a motor inn, which sounded like a motel just for cars. We stopped and a woman told us there weren't any rooms left, but she said there were other places to stay farther down the road.

As we drove, I looked at the map and tried to match the names to the mountains we saw around us, but I had to give up. It was too hard to tell which peak was which. The area was full of U-shaped valleys that had been carved by advancing glaciers and I was awed by the power that suggested. Ice was only water, after all. Glacia said the whole planet had once been covered with ice, like a giant frozen marble. It must have been beautiful. Our bodies are mostly water, so ice is like another kind of life.

It was almost dark by the time we found somewhere to stay. It was another motor inn, this one with a campsite beside it. It wasn't as nice as the first one we'd seen, but we were exhausted by then. It was called the Siyeh Inn, for the mountain it was near. Glacia looked to me for approval, even though we didn't really have another option. The guidebook said the name meant Mad Wolf. I smiled.

The guy at the front desk wore a name tag that said BOBBY. It looked like his name was full of holes. I could tell he liked Glacia from the way he kept looking at her when he thought she didn't know. He smiled at me too, but that was just to be nice. Glacia was the one he wanted to like him. I wished we hadn't thrown the tyre iron over the railing.

She gave him cash for the room and I looked out the window at Mount Siyeh while they talked and Glacia signed the register. It was too dark to see anything but a huge silhouette.

"I'll give you girls number nineteen," he said, handing her a key. It hung from a blue plastic disc printed with the number. "It's the nicest room we have."

I wanted to ask what made it nicer than the others but I didn't because 19 was Glacia's age, a *safe* number.

And the room *was* nice. It was all made of wood and there were pictures of glaciers on the walls. I always thought they would be like gigantic ice cubes, smooth and white. But they were all crumbly and jagged and blue.

"They look like teeth," I said.

But Glacia only glanced at the pictures. "Mm-hmm," she murmured. Then she said she was going to get cleaned up.

She sang in the shower and took a long time to come out. When she did, her lips were red and her eyes were rimmed in black, like she was going somewhere.

At my questioning look she said, "Bobby invited us for drinks at the campsite."

My skin felt cold, like a tiny glacier was sliding over my bones. "Why?"

"He's probably lonely. He said we're the only ones here tonight. Anyway, he said he's got beer."

I made a face.

"You don't have to drink any," she said.

I tried to see her thoughts but she wouldn't let me. She seemed distracted and nervous. Also a little sad, like she wasn't sure where she was or what she was doing. Outside the moon was shining like a fang.

"Okay," I said, and followed her out. I made her lock the door three times.

"So what's your name?"

It was the first time he'd spoken to me. For twenty minutes he'd just sat on the log next to Glacia and their voices were like the hum of mosquitoes in the chilly night air. But Glacia had gone to get more drinks and now I was alone with him.

"Lys," I said.

He made a puzzled face and poked at the campfire with a stick. Sparks rose into the air like fireflies. The licking flames made me think of fox tails. "That's a weird name," he said. "Is it short for something?"

"It means lily," I explained. But his expression didn't change. "I like it because it's sharp."

"What do you mean, sharp?"

"It's not round," I said, trying to be patient. I didn't know why he wanted to know my name anyway when he was just going to die. "There aren't any round letters in it. Not like your name."

He stared at me like he couldn't understand what I was saying at all. Finally he shrugged. "Suit yourself, kid," he said, taking a big drink of his beer. He held the bottle out to me and I recoiled.

He laughed. I didn't know why it was funny to him but he didn't offer again. He finished the bottle and tossed it aside and I caught him staring at me.

"Is that a fashion statement or something?"

"What?"

"The shades." He laughed, a harsh, ugly sound. "I mean, it's pitch black out here." He squinted at me, as if seeing me properly for the first time. "And Jesus, girl, you need to get some fucking sun."

"We are," I said. And when he just stared at me I added, "We're going to the sun."

But I might as well have been speaking another language. He didn't say anything at all after that so I didn't either. I was just glad he had stopped talking to me. Soon there was the sound of footsteps and Glacia returned with the drinks. A Coke for me and more beer for them.

I shuddered at her nearness to him as she sat down. They looked all strange and wavy through the flames, like the mirages Glacia and I had seen on the roads in hot places. Something about the fire unnerved me, so I pictured a glacier sliding over it until it fizzled out.

Then he put his arm around Glacia and kissed her neck. He said something to her that I couldn't hear and she laughed even though I knew whatever he'd said wasn't funny. It made my stomach feel rotten and I tried to think about other things.

"We're urban explorers," I said.

He looked over at me, confused and annoyed. "Huh?"

"We take pictures in our minds. Don't we, Glacia?"

She smiled. "Yes, we do."

He didn't say anything for a while. He just stared at me. Then he frowned and shook his head. "Whatever."

Then he went back to smiling and trying to charm Glacia. She sipped her drink and listened, pretending he was interesting.

When he kissed her I felt my skin prickle, and when his hand crept inside her shirt, I felt it. He was touching *me*. My insides churned sickly and I felt all my scars burn, like there were ants inside me, biting. The feeling was familiar and horrible and I pushed it into Glacia's mind. She made a sound and he looked up, but it was me he glared at. He jerked his chin at me.

"She gonna watch or what?"

Glacia shook her head. "Don't worry," she told him in a low whispery voice, "she won't see a thing."

I turned away so that wouldn't be a lie and I listened as she raked the knife through his skin and the blood began to spatter on the dusty ground. He made some throaty choking noises but it wasn't like a voice at all. Soon he was quiet. Shapes danced in the licking flames and the fire crackled like laughter.

Glacia didn't say a word as we dragged him into the woods behind the campsite. We went back to the fire and I teased the flames with a long stick while Glacia kicked dirt over the dark stain on the ground.

"I wish we had marshmallows," I said.

"Mmm."

After a while we heard sounds coming from the woods. Branches snapped and there was the heavy tread of a large animal. I thought it might be a bear. I wanted to stay and see it but Glacia said we should leave it alone.

"Let's just go to sleep," she said.

The dream came as soon as I closed my eyes. I was high up in the clouds, standing on top of a mountain, and below me was a valley full of sharp rocks and spiky trees. My skin was liquid, cold and white. It rippled like the surface of a lake, crusting with ice. The cold seeped into my bones, hardening all the muscle and veins and blood inside. It didn't hurt, but I couldn't move. All I could do was feel. Then I began to melt.

It was the best part of the dream. As I melted, I became snow, spreading across the top of the mountain and down its slopes, moving like frozen lava from a volcano made of ice. All the warm things inside me turned to cold. The valley was mine to shape and carve as I moved down the slope, flattening the land beneath me. I had no skin, but the sensation of movement was thrilling. I felt everything in my atoms, in every tiny particle.

A crisp wind was blowing, sending flurries of ice crystals up into the sky. They danced like frozen butterflies, circling the frosty landscape. There were patches of deep red beneath me, but I kept them buried and hidden.

Gradually I became aware of a black smell, but it took a long time for me to leave my snowy form. When I realised I had eyes, I opened them and swam up out of the dream. Something was burning.

Glacia stood in the open doorway, her arms wrapped around herself. It was just getting light outside and a freezing wind blew into the room. Her thoughts were wide open and full of confusion and fear. And memories. She sensed me there and turned around.

"What's wrong?" I asked.

She didn't say anything for a long time. Then she tried to smile, but her lips couldn't seem to make the right shape. "Everything. Lys, what did we do?"

I sat up and swung my legs out of bed. The room was frigid. I could see Mount Siyeh in the pale light. A mad wolf watching over us. A wolf no one could ever cage. Smoke billowed from somewhere outside.

"We did what we had to," I said. "Like before. Like always."

"You were in my head. Did you make me do something?"

I didn't know what to tell her. I didn't know why she couldn't remember. "It's just you and me," I reminded her.

But she still didn't seem happy. I got up and went to see what she was staring at. It wasn't morning at all; the campsite was on fire. Flames crawled up the scattering of picnic tables and the little circle of trees where we had sat last night. Where the body had been. A thin column of smoke rose into the wintry sky. I imagined I could hear sirens and that made me think of the other time. I knew Glacia was thinking of it too even though she didn't want to remember. She was *haunted* by it.

"Ashes," she whispered. "They covered us in their ashes."

"No they didn't," I said. "No one knew we were there."

"What have we done, Lys?"

"They hated us! They did things to us in the lab."

I could see in her head that she was remembering it. Room 10. The wires and chemicals and electrodes. The cages. And his hands. Our father's hands.

"No," Glacia said, sounding confused. "That wasn't us. That was . . ."

But she knew it was us. Just like she knew she'd had to let it happen sometimes because he liked her better. Because she was pretty. Because then he would leave me alone. The freak. The demon.

"You always protected me," I said. "So I protected you. Don't you remember?"

She gazed out at the dancing flames, reliving the night we'd opened the cages and let the animals out. They were mad with fear and rage, and some of them had been—changed. Just like we had been changed. There were teeth and claws, screams and blood. I was the one who had opened the cage doors, but it was Glacia who started the fire at home, just as she'd started the one that blazed around us now.

"We escaped the fire before," I told her, "because we were made of snow. We can do it again."

But she still looked confused and afraid. Even worse—she looked lost. Tears trembled in her eyes and I wished for them to turn to ice. She stared at the flames for a long time and I saw the past in her mind. I didn't want to be in there with her but she was holding on to me, making me see. I could hear the animals crying, howling, *screaming*.

"Make it stop," I begged. "Please, Glacia, make him stop!"

It was like I was lost inside her thoughts, trapped and caged. The animals sounded wrong. Finally, I pushed her away very hard and opened my eyes, blinking in the smoke. And I realised what the sounds were. Sirens. Someone was coming.

I shook her out of her daze. "Come on," I said. "We have to go!"

There was no time to get our things. We just ran for the car and then we were on our way. Behind us we heard the sirens stop and I imagined firefighters battling the flames, just like they had at the house all those years ago. But that was over now. We were back in our world again, just the two of us.

The sun was just beginning to rise and the trees were alive with birdsong. And as the cold pale colours arched across the sky, I thought of the glaciers all around us, making their slow, relentless way down the mountains, crushing everything that lay in their path, making the world theirs.

THE FACE

Pistyll Rhaeadr and Wrexham steeple,
Snowdon's mountain without its people,
Overton yew trees, St Winefride's well,
Llangollen bridge and Gresford bells.
    "The Seven Wonders of Wales" (anonymous)

HARRIE PAGED THROUGH THE LATEST BATCH OF DIGITAL photos, tagging her friends and family when prompted by the software. It was funny how the computer sometimes mixed people up. True, Owain and Gareth looked a lot alike. As brothers, they ought to. But surely she looked nothing like *her* brother. Gwilym was much taller, with longer, darker hair. She was short and blonde.

IS THIS GWILYM? the pop-up window asked.

Harrie shook her head and ticked "no". Then she entered her own name. ANGHARAD. She was the only "A" in there so all she had to do was type the first letter for her full name to appear.

She'd gone through all the pics from their hike through Snowdonia and then the Berwyn Mountains in September. Most of the landscape photos didn't have people in them to tag but she and Owain always took a few pictures of each other, and Gareth when he came along.

Gareth was slightly younger than Owain but he'd seen and done some incredible things in his twenty-four years. He was a thrill seeker who'd started climbing the local mountains as a kid and progressed to extreme sports as soon as he was old enough to defy his and Owain's overprotective parents. He'd been skydiving, whitewater canoeing and he'd even gone swimming with great white sharks in South Africa. More than anything he loved climbing and he talked about someday going to the Himalayas. Owain didn't share his brother's lust for adventure but he and Harrie benefited from it, as he was always a great subject for dramatic photos.

"No, that's not Owain," Harrie chuckled, correcting the computer when it misidentified the bloke abseiling down a slate wall.

She was quite proud of some of the shots she'd taken of Snowdon shrouded in fog and there was one particularly striking image of a hawk cutting down through the mist like an arrow. Just a happy accident, really. She never could have captured that if she'd tried. The hawk was lightning-fast and after a sharp piercing cry it snatched a mouse from the ground. It soared back up into the sky, only to drop its prey a few seconds later. The mouse fell like a stone but the photo showed only a tiny grey blur. A shame, but at least she had the first shot.

After that there was a beautifully atmospheric series of castles too but, if she was honest, Owain's shots were better than hers. He had a great eye for interesting architectural details and features most people probably didn't even notice. He'd won a prize when he was a teenager for a photo of Llangollen Bridge and it had been used in a "Beautiful Wales" ad campaign. His parents had it framed in the front room. Harrie hoped that someday one of her pics might garner some acclaim too. A great photo was 10% skill and 90% luck. Well, maybe she'd enter the hawk photo in the next competition.

It was always fun retracing their steps this way. All the Seven Wonders were there, along with several other sights that hadn't made the rhyme. Then, from the old East Llangynog silver mine to craggy Craig y Mwn, the images led up to their favourite place of all to photograph: the stunning waterfall Pistyll Rhaeadr.

In full flood it was an awesome sight, plunging over the cliff in three cascades to the valley below. That was how Owain and Gareth liked it—a raging torrent, mighty and ferocious, thundering down the rock face and threatening to sweep away the fairy bridge—the natural stone arch that spanned the rushing water. But Harrie liked it best when the river was low. When there hadn't been much rain the water would spill gently over the rocks like silk, delicate and ghostly.

She tagged two photos of Gareth and Owain standing together at the base of the falls, their faces showing clear disappointment that the water wasn't more exciting. Harrie softened the focus in some of the images, blurring the movement of the water to make it look even more ethereal, like a mystical wedding veil. Owain wouldn't approve. He didn't like Photoshopped images. He was a purist, he said, and preferred purely natural shots. Harrie suspected he was just lazy when it came to processing.

In her opinion, no photo was ever complete straight off the camera. Just as every face, however lovely, needed makeup, so every image needed adjusting. She almost always tweaked the contrast to make her shots a little more dramatic and sometimes she played with coloured filters for an otherworldly effect. And whereas Owain wasn't bothered by evidence of the modern world, Harrie always cloned out unsightly fences and telephone poles and stray tourists. "Middle Earth pics," Owain teasingly called them, although he had let her erase a litter bin from one of his castle shots.

She paged through some more pictures, surprised at how many she had taken. Owain probably had even more, since her memory card had run out that day and she'd forgotten to bring a spare.

WHO IS THIS?

Harrie blinked at the screen. It was a detail of the top of the falls and the area highlighted by the box showed nothing but water.

"No one I know," she said with a laugh and closed the window. But the programme flagged the next photo as well with the same question.

She peered at the box, trying to see whatever the computer was seeing. But she couldn't make out a face anywhere in the swirling currents and frothy spray.

"Sorry, but no," she said, moving on.

A few shots later the computer prompted her again. This time she felt a little unnerved. Surely the pattern of the water was different in every picture, so how could it keep zeroing in on the exact same spot? Sometimes a clutch of shadows or branches might form the elements of a rudimentary face and confuse the software but this was different. The tagging box was in the same place every time. The computer was adamant that there was a face there.

Too intrigued to ignore it, she dragged one of the photos into the editing suite to try and isolate the face. She played with the brightness and the contrast, hoping to tease out any rocks behind the water that could be responsible for the confusion. There was nothing. But the more she stared at it, the more she started to think she could see a pair of eyes. Maybe it was like those holographic images that were so popular in the '90s. You had to let your eyes go out of focus to see the 3D picture buried inside the pattern.

She tried that. She relaxed her eyes and the waterfall went blurry as she tried to look beneath the swarming pixels. And then she saw it. The face.

It looked wrong. Like some kind of alien, all sharp lines and angles. A long gash for a mouth. And what she'd taken for eyes were two bright smears, as though it—whatever *it* might be—were blind. Or seeing through a different kind of eyes. Staring.

Harrie shuddered and looked away. Her eyes immediately refocused and when she turned back to the computer she expected the face to have vanished. But it was still there. She couldn't un-see it now. In fact, it was so obvious that she wondered why she'd never seen it before.

That evening she showed the sequence to Owain. "Do you see anything strange?" she asked.

He studied the pictures and she imagined he was probably looking for some evidence of Photoshopping, like a fairy she might have superimposed onto the background.

"No," he said after a while. "Nothing at all. Why? What have you done to it?"

"I haven't done anything. It's something that's there in the picture. Look closer. Cross your eyes."

He frowned, looking puzzled, but he did it. After a few seconds she heard a sharp intake of breath.

"What the—?"

"You see it?"

"That's weird!"

Harrie felt inexplicable relief. A part of her had been worried that he wouldn't see the face at all, that she'd only seen it herself because the computer had put the idea in her mind. She didn't like the thought that she was that suggestible.

"So what causes that, then?" Owain mused, enlarging the area with the mouse.

"I don't know. I wouldn't have seen it at all if the computer hadn't flagged it up. It's creepy, huh?"

"Yeah. I wonder if anyone else has noticed it?"

Harrie ousted him from her chair and navigated to the web browser. She typed "Pistyll Rhaeadr" and "face" into the search engine and the first hit was a blog called "Rhaeadr Wyneb". It was Welsh for "waterfall face". And it was filled with photographs showing the same thing Harrie and Owain had seen. Everything from professional high-res photos to grainy mobile phone pics, but every image showed the same staring face, the same blind eyes.

"That is seriously creepy," Owain said, exchanging a haunted look with her.

They'd been up there hundreds of times, separately and together, ever since they were kids. How was it possible they'd never seen the face before?

Gareth was less impressed when they showed him the photos and the blog. "Underlying rock formation" was his predictable response. That had been Harrie's first thought as well, and it certainly made sense. The fact that they couldn't see what was forming the strange features didn't matter. It was there under the water. It had to be.

"Nature's full of weird stuff," Gareth assured them. "You ought to come climbing with me sometime. I'll show you some proper weirdness!"

"No thanks," Harrie laughed. "I'm happy to keep a respectful distance. My camera can take all the risks for me."

Owain likewise refused the offer. "I don't mind a bit of hillwalking but mountaineering is too much like hard work."

"Please yourselves," Gareth said. "But you don't know what you're missing."

Winter came early, a biting, snarling thing that kept Harrie and Owain huddling indoors. They promised to brave the mountains again once it snowed, however. Nothing transformed a landscape like snow and ice. Winter was a horrible season to live through but a spectacular one to photograph. And picturesque snowscapes were easy to sell.

Owain's phone jolted them awake one bitterly cold morning. It was Gareth.

"Bloody hell, mate," Owain grumbled. "What time is it?" He flailed sleepily at the bedside clock but only succeeded in knocking it to the floor.

Harrie cried out as he turned the lamp on, flooding the room with unwelcome light. She buried her head under the pillow as she listened to the one-sided conversation.

"Snow? Yeah, we know. It's not going to melt before noon, is it? Can't you let us—"

There was a pause. Harrie could hear the tinny voice on the other end of the line but only a few words came through: ice, frozen, climb.

Whatever Gareth was saying was clearly interesting because Owain sat up, fully alert. "Absolutely! Yeah. Of course, mate. We'll be right over."

"We will?" Harrie mumbled from beneath the warm refuge of the duvet.

Owain cruelly whipped it away and she hissed like a vampire exposed to sunlight.

"The waterfall's frozen solid!"

It took a few seconds for the words to penetrate her sleepy brain but once they did she was wide awake. "Seriously?"

Owain was already out of bed and getting dressed. "Gareth wants to climb it. It's a once-in-a-lifetime photo op. But we've got to get there before anyone else does."

Harrie scrambled out of bed and began pulling on layers of winter clothes. It was dark outside and probably still would be when they got to Pistyll Rhaeadr. She made sure she had both memory cards this time.

The frozen waterfall was a breathtaking sight, absolutely magical. The sun was just coming up, tinting the sky with delicate pink and gold as they arrived at the base of the falls. In places the ice was thick and blue and frozen solidly to the cliff face, resembling diminutive glaciers. In others it hung suspended in long jagged shards like the fangs of some crystal monster.

"Incredible," Harrie breathed.

She'd never seen anything like it in her life. Of course they'd experienced Pistyll Rhaeadr in snow before, and it was an exquisite sight. The spray from the falls gathered in the trees like glass ornaments, turning the surrounding area into a crystalline wonderland. But for the entire river and the waterfall itself to freeze solid... She could almost believe that the fairies had been responsible. It was so still and silent the whole world might be holding its breath.

Gareth gazed up at the columns of ice, his eyes shining with excitement. "I've only ever climbed one frozen waterfall," he told Harrie, "when Owain and I were in Norway. I never dreamed the one in my own back garden would look like this."

The two lower cascades looked challenging enough but the top one—the tallest—looked positively daunting. The entire waterfall was around 240 feet tall and more than half of that height was the top cascade. While some of the ice was attached to the rock, the majority of it hung free, a single giant icicle about twenty feet wide. It was thinner where it connected to the pool below, just a thread, really. Harrie saw several chunks of ice scattered nearby from where it must have broken. Her stomach fluttered.

She hated to ask such a boring question but it came out anyway. "Is it safe?"

Gareth smiled at her. "Oh yes. It's just like climbing rock."

Harrie had never climbed either rock or ice in her life but even she knew that that couldn't be true. Doubtless he was just trying to placate her so she wouldn't fret. Not that she could have talked him out of it anyway. Gareth was nothing if not tenacious.

"You're worried about that thin patch, aren't you? Well, don't be. If it breaks I'll fall all of ten feet, but if it holds I'll know the rest is strong enough."

"He'll be fine," Owain said lightly, shouldering the rucksack with his camera equipment. "I'll head up to the top and meet you when you get there. Harrie, why don't you follow him up the side as far as you're comfortable going?"

She nodded, happy with the plan. Owain knew her so well. She didn't have a great head for heights and had never even been to the top of the falls. She much preferred the perspective of looking *up* at majestic sights. The path wasn't that steep and there were plenty of little plateaus where she could stop and take pictures, but she had no desire to go much further than about halfway up.

Owain crossed the iron bridge at the bottom and set out along the footpath. Harrie watched until he disappeared into the woodlands. While Gareth sorted out his gear she took a few shots of the pristine ice. It was bizarre to be looking at a waterfall without the accompanying sound of rushing water. It wasn't entirely silent, though. Occasionally the ice would creak and groan, as though the mountain were mumbling in its sleep.

Gareth strapped crampons onto his climbing boots, equipping his feet with vicious spikes for what he called "front-pointing". In each hand he carried an ice axe, the pick end hooked downward at a slight angle. He chopped into the ice at the base of the falls to show Harrie how they worked and when she saw how well they stuck she felt a little more secure. But only a little.

"Cool," he said. "I'm off!"

Good luck, Harrie thought but didn't say.

Gareth swung one axe into the ice and then kicked the spikes of one foot in, pulling himself up a few inches. He swung the other axe and followed with the opposite foot. It looked like a slow and laborious process and she could already hear him panting with the effort. How long would it take him to reach the top?

He scaled the two lower cascades in just under an hour, leaving behind a trail of rope looped through ice screws. Harrie busied herself with pictures of the snowscape around her and the occasional shot of Gareth as she made her own way up alongside the column of ice. As he'd said it would, the thin ice held and he was soon onto the wide part of the main cascade. Harrie got used to the sound of his measured chops and after a while she stopped jumping every time he dislodged a brittle chunk of ice. She'd had to bite back a scream the first time an icicle had come loose and crashed to the frozen water below.

"Hey down there!"

She looked up, shielding her eyes from the glare of the white sun. A tiny silhouette stood at the top of the falls, waving to her. She waved back and then took a few shots of Owain up there, standing on the frozen river as though it were solid ground.

"Too bad we don't have ice skates," she called up to him.

When she passed the fairy bridge she considered staying put, but the scenery was just too magnificent. Besides, Gareth was already well into his assault on the final cascade and she'd dawdled so much she wasn't even level with him yet. For once she felt a twinge of competition with Owain. He would get some great vertiginous shots of Gareth from high above but Harrie was in a better position for the kind of "right there in the moment" images that graced the covers of adventure magazines. She was perfectly safe on the snow-covered hill; Gareth was the one taking all the risks. She told herself she could go higher.

Gareth chopped, kicked and hauled himself up, inch by slow, agonising inch. From her vantage point down below he looked like some strange insect-human hybrid, crawling up the icicle with long mantis arms. She raised her camera and zoomed in, just in time to capture him shearing off a long shard of ice with one axe. He ducked as it fell past, just missing him, and she watched it shatter like glass against the mirrored surface of the pool beneath.

If Gareth was worried he showed no sign of it. He was calm and cool, pausing to catch his breath before anchoring himself with a length of rope and continuing on up. Harrie released the breath she'd been holding and looked up towards the top of the falls. And froze. The face was watching her.

She'd forgotten all about it in the excitement over the snow but the sudden unwelcome idea came to her that she'd been *made* to forget.

Stop it, she told herself. What had Gareth said? Underlying rock formation. That's all it was.

Nature's full of weird stuff.

It was indeed. And those blind, staring eyes were among the weirdest. But how could she be seeing it now? She'd only seen it in photos, like everyone else who had contributed pictures to the blog they'd found. Nobody had ever seen the face in person, as it were.

Was it her imagination or had it got even colder? The ice seemed sharper and more brittle, hanging like knives in the trees. Harrie felt the deep chill penetrate to her bones. Her gloved hands trembled on the camera as she realised that Gareth was heading straight towards the face. She tried to tell herself there was no reason that should disturb her, that she was only worried about the stability of the ice and projecting irrational fears onto a convenient scapegoat—in this case an imagined presence.

She turned away and hiked a little higher up the path. Best just to focus on taking pictures. That was why they were here. Gareth knew what he was doing and he knew more about the mountains and waterfalls than she could ever hope to. So did Owain, for that matter. She looked up at the top of the cascade and there he was, lying on his belly, camera aimed down at his brother. She thought of her hawk photo and the one of the little grey blur that followed. Her stomach swooped.

She shook her head to banish the vision that was trying to form in her mind. Owain had shown her the ice screws Gareth gave him to anchor himself up there, the rope to fasten to them. He wasn't going to fall.

Teeth.

The word came into her mind as a whispered picture: sharp glistening fangs, frayed nylon rope, a death plunge.

What the hell was wrong with her? The world was so still and quiet she could hear Owain's camera clicking away some hundred feet above. There was nothing scuttling around up there with him, least of all something that would eat through rope.

Harrie pushed herself up the path, her boots sinking deep into the crisp snow. Her legs were quivering with the effort and she could only imagine how Gareth must feel. How could he keep at it? She'd have been exhausted after the first little cascade.

It's waiting for him.

"Nothing's waiting for anyone," she growled. It was just her fear of heights, intensifying the further she went. She was already higher than she'd ever climbed up the path before. No wonder her mind was feeding her little snacks of panic. She was determined now to make it all the way to the top, to prove to herself that there was nothing to fear, either from the height or from a nonexistent apparition behind the ice.

When at last she drew level with where the face was, she took a deep, icy breath and looked straight at it. There was nothing there. Nothing but frozen water.

She looked up at Owain and waved. He gave a whoop and called down to her.

"I can't believe how high you've come! Are you scared?"

"No," she lied.

"Brave girl!"

She was delighted to have made him proud of her. Gareth was probably too winded to add anything to the conversation and that was OK. She didn't want him to lose his focus. He was two thirds of the way up the ice now. Just below the face.

There is no face.

As if in response, the ice creaked and there was a splintering sound far down below. The bottom of the pillar had broken away. The waterfall hung freely now, an enormous dangling icicle.

This time Gareth didn't look so calm. He stared for a long time at the place where the ice had come away and Harrie saw that his next axe placement was gentler than previous efforts. He tapped gingerly at the ice above him, testing it before letting the pick sink in. He quickly twisted in another ice screw and looped his rope through it, tugging it and seeming satisfied that it was secure. He was soaked through, covered in chipped ice and snow. Harrie didn't like the thought that he was being consumed by it.

She told herself angrily not to fret and she focused on her own task, zooming in for close-ups, zooming out for context. She turned the camera sideways to capture the whole length of the ice in portrait mode. Gareth was just a speck on the expanse of deep blue crystal. Insignificant to the fearsome majesty of nature.

As he continued doggedly on his way Harrie told herself that the ice sounded no different up here than it had at the base. It still groaned and creaked but it was only her imagination that made it sound like a voice. It was just rocks and water, that was all.

Gareth was right underneath the face now, just where the mouth would be. And now that he was so close to it she could see the strange features again. They emerged from the jagged pattern like something rising from a deep lake. The eyes seemed to shine beneath the ice, burning with malevolent white heat.

Gareth's axe was poised to strike the dark blur of the mouth but something made him hesitate. He stared up at the shadow, his eyes widening at whatever he saw there. The ice cracked. His hand wavered.

Harrie opened her mouth to call his name, to tell him to move away, that it wasn't safe. But the words froze in her throat. All she could do was watch helplessly as the shadowy mouth grew wider. The ice was splitting.

Gareth tried to scramble away to the side, kicking his feet in as he inched away from the unstable area, but it was already starting to crumble. Several shards broke away and seemed to fall forever before they smashed into the glassy pool below. Harrie felt the vibration from the impact all the way up on the hill and a little cry escaped her as she saw the waterfall tremble and sway.

Her stomach plunged as Gareth lost his footing. He hung by one arm, legs kicking wildly as he searched for the ice with his feet. A clump of snow fell from directly above him, knocking his axe loose. He fell several feet before the rope jerked him to a stop. Dazed, he hung there, swinging back and forth for several seconds, his face bloodied from where he'd struck the ice. He looked like a bug caught in a spider's web. At last he steadied himself against the ice and began to haul himself back up.

Up above she could faintly hear Owain calling out and she might have heard Gareth say he was OK. But the sounds coming from the ice were too loud. Now there was no mistaking it. It was a voice.

And as she stared at the face behind the waterfall, the mouth gaped even wider, revealing rows of jagged crystal teeth. Greenish water oozed from between them like drool and the air steamed as if with hot breath. There was a hiss as the liquid slithered over the ice, melting it.

Gareth only had time to look up and see what was happening before the ice cracked and split and the waterfall broke away, snapping like a toothpick. He didn't make a sound as the huge mass of ice fell, carrying him all the way to the bottom, to the unyielding surface of the frozen pool. The impact shattered the silence and set the ice jingling on all the surrounding trees.

Like bells, Harrie thought crazily. *Or laughter.*

Owain was screaming his brother's name over and over but even his maddened cries couldn't drown out the sound of the ice. It grated together like teeth. Harrie turned her eyes to the terrible face and there was no mistaking it this time. It was smiling.

Xibalba

LONDON COULD BE SO TEDIOUS; ONE SIMPLY HAD TO escape sometimes. We had a year to kill before making up our minds what we wanted to study at university. So Rosamund invited us to Cancun.

You simply MUST come, Camille, her email gushed, its cartoonish font not unlike the loopy girlish handwriting she'd used in school. *I'm DYING for you to meet Zeke!*

Ezequiel was the latest in a long line of what her mother termed "unsuitable" boys. By which she meant penniless. Mrs Langford-Brooke seemed to think that Victoria was still queen and her daughter was destined to marry a duke and rule the empire.

Rosie's parents had taken her with them on holiday to Cancun and she had fallen in love with the place. The Caribbean sun had seduced her. And so, apparently, had Zeke.

"What do you think, Seb?" I asked, showing the email to my brother. Although we were twins, you'd be hard pressed to spot any resemblance—to each other or to anyone else in the Somerleyton family. Our minds were another story, however. We had the sort of telepathic bond that made us function as a single person sometimes. And we were inseparable.

Sebastian was lolling in the window seat, gazing out over Hyde Park and looking quite bored. I gave him my phone and he scrolled through Rosie's message and looked at the photos she had attached. Dazzling white sand beaches. Vibrant nightclubs. Yucateco cuisine. Lush tropical forests. She'd proposed camping out in the ruins of Tulum, a Mayan ghost town on the Yucatán coast.

The more I looked at the pictures, the more invested I became in the idea. I had originally been hoping to convince Rosie and Sebastian to go with me to Japan, but the thought of roughing it in the wilds of Mexico for a few days was working its magic on me. Besides, I hadn't seen Rosie in months and I missed her terribly. She was family. The three of us had grown up together and in that time Sebastian had been Rosie's friend, brother and occasional lover.

"Come on," I pressed. "You can bring Phoebe and we'll make it a fivesome."

He considered. "Yeah," he said at last. "Why not?"

"You don't sound thrilled. What's wrong? You and Phoebe on the rocks?"

He shrugged. "I'm just not sure where it's going. Sometimes I think she likes those bloody ponies more than me."

I laughed. Phoebe Anstruther was a show jumper. And it was true, she did spend more time with her horses. But then, my brother wasn't exactly ideal boyfriend material. With his long dark hair and pseudo rock star image he pulled groupies without even trying. Fortunately, Phoebe wasn't the jealous or possessive type and she didn't seem to mind his outrageous flirting. And if he wasn't entirely faithful at times, well, she either didn't notice or didn't care. She was quiet without being precisely shy and I liked her without knowing precisely why.

"I'm sure that's not true," I lied. "And anyway, there won't be any horses in Mexico. At least not ones she'd be prepared to ride." I pictured mules and swaybacked old nags hauling fat sunburnt tourists up trails and along beaches. "It won't be the same without you."

He smiled and I knew he was thinking the same thing. We'd always done everything together. *Nothing* was the same by ourselves. "I know. And we haven't really had a proper beach holiday since that bloody awful trip to Mykonos."

We both shuddered at the memory. Our parents had been such frightful bores throughout the trip that we'd both feigned food poisoning so they'd leave us alone in our rooms at the hotel one night. Then we'd sneaked off to a club, only going our separate ways once we found partners for the night. We'd compared notes in the morning and agreed that Sebastian had found the hotter date, but the girl refused to leave him alone afterwards. She followed him around the island for days and it wasn't until I dared him to kiss a boy in the hotel bar—which he did—that she finally got the hint and left him alone.

In case he was worrying I added, "Rosie and I will deal with any stalkers you attract."

"OK," he laughed. "You talked me into it. Let me see if I can tear Phoebe away from the show ring."

"You made it!" Rosie exclaimed, rushing into my arms as though she hadn't believed we'd actually come. She kissed me on both cheeks and then threw her arms around Sebastian and then Phoebe, whom she'd only met once before. Phoebe returned her hug as warmly as if they were sisters.

"You look great," I said, taking in Rosie's sun-kissed appearance.

She smiled, doing a little spin for us to show off her long brown legs in designer cutoffs. "Thanks! And you lot look so *pale*!" She laughed, ruffling my pixie-cut hair. "But we'll soon sort that. Margaritas by the pool— swimsuits optional!" She winked at us, then gestured to a porter to take our bags as she led us into the hotel.

Phoebe had been anxious on the flight but once we were slathered in sunscreen and baking by the pool she began to relax. She wound her long hair into a bun and executed a graceful dive into the water.

"Where's Zeke?" I asked.

"*Siesta*," Rosie said with a giggle. "Poor thing was *so* tired after last night."

Sebastian and I rolled our eyes at each other.

"So what's the name of this place we're going to again?" Sebastian asked, pouring himself another drink from the pitcher sweating on the table. He was already ahead of Rosie and me.

"Tulum. It's about an hour south of here along the coast road. I've hired a Range Rover and it's all packed and ready to go, so we can leave whenever you're ready tomorrow."

"Sounds great," I said.

"I got the hotel to sort out air beds and camping gear for us so you don't have to worry about a thing. And I told them to get us a big family-sized tent so Camille wouldn't have to sleep alone."

"Thanks. I definitely don't fancy being left to the elements and the mozzies by myself."

"Although," she added with a coy grin, "I expect we'll have to kick each other out on occasion . . . "

Sebastian gave a hearty laugh at that. "If the Mayans want a virgin sacrifice I think we'll all be safe."

"They didn't sacrifice virgins."

We all looked up to see Phoebe climbing out of the pool She patted herself dry with a towel and stretched out in one of the loungers, shielding her eyes behind a pair of oversized sunglasses.

"Who did they sacrifice, then?" Sebastian demanded.

"Children."

Rosie blanched and looked at Sebastian and me.

"And prisoners from rival tribes, of course. They've discovered mass graves over the years and there are records of bodies being thrown into sinkholes as offerings. Like the sacred cenote at Chichen Itza: they called it the 'Well of Sacrifice'." She took a sip from her margarita and stretched languorously, oblivious to our surprise.

"How do you know all this?" Sebastian asked. "Is it from that Mel Gibson film?"

She eyed him reprovingly over the frames of her sunglasses like a bikini-clad librarian. "Please. If you believe everything you see in films then it's possible to rip a still-beating heart out of someone's chest. Or for people to die with their faces contorted in fear."

Rosie glanced at me as though seeking confirmation of what Phoebe had said. I gave her a "How should I know?" look.

Phoebe lay back down and crossed her arms behind her head. "The Mayan stuff is all in the guidebook," she said coolly.

That silenced us all. I'd merely looked at some of the pictures and as far as I knew Sebastian hadn't even glanced at those. It was highly unlikely that

Rosie had done any research either. None of us were what you'd call the intellectual type and it was an unexpected revelation that Phoebe apparently was.

"Zeke!"

We looked up at Rosie's cry to see a Mexican guy about our age standing there. It was obvious what Rosie saw in him; he was gorgeous.

Rosie leapt to her feet and gave him a deep, passionate kiss. "You're up!"

He glanced shyly around at us as Rosie introduced us one by one. She told the waiter to keep the drinks coming and Zeke took his place beside her in the adjacent lounger.

"Does he talk?" Sebastian asked after a minute, draining his third glass.

Rosie blushed. "He doesn't really speak English," she admitted.

I peered at the bronzed athletic boy toy and stifled a giggle. "And you don't speak Spanish," I said. "Sounds like a perfect relationship."

No photos could ever have done justice to Tulum. The picturesque ruins were interspersed with palm trees and bright green grass, wound about with crumbling walls and limestone paths. The turquoise sea was beyond, its waves lapping gently at the soft pale sand of the beach below the cliffs on which the city was perched. But I didn't like the way the palm trees tossed their heads as though they were laughing. Or the way the darkened openings of temples seemed to watch us like eyes. The entire city was encircled by a massive stone wall that made me feel claustrophobic despite the sprawling openness of the site.

Even though the ruins were swarming with tourists, it wasn't difficult to imagine them sitting empty and abandoned on the cliffs. No one knew what had happened to the Mayan civilisation. Like the dinosaurs, they had simply vanished. One day Tulum had been a thriving city filled with people and the next it was deserted. All dead.

El Castillo sat like a fortress on the highest cliff, overlooking the sea. A series of wide steps led to a temple at the top of the squat, four-sided structure. The columns of the temple were shaped like snakes, their fanged mouths open, and the entrance was cloaked in forbidding shadow. To our disappointment, the stairs were roped off at the bottom, preventing us from climbing them.

"Oh, we'll just wait until dark," Sebastian said, cocky as ever.

His presumption made me uneasy. I was curious to see inside but I didn't fancy sneaking in there at night. And as Zeke led us around, chattering happily to us in Spanish we couldn't understand, I found myself oddly disturbed by the ancient carvings of jaguars and eagles and hearts being torn from the chests of still-living sacrifices.

Most of all I disliked the faces. Stylised and unreal as they were, there was something horribly malevolent about them. The expressions made me think of tribal war masks, something one would put on to terrify an enemy. But I got the feeling that the figures in the carvings weren't wearing masks, that the ugly, snarling expressions were meant to be actual faces.

"*Y esto es Templo del Dios Descendente*," Zeke said, taking us around the side of the structure. He pointed to a carving above the doorway into a lopsided and jagged temple. "Kukulcan. The descending god."

The stone had eroded considerably and it took me a moment to make out its features. The figure was upside-down, as though it were diving down from the sky. I'd seen similar images already. Sometimes Kukulcan was depicted with what looked like horns, and his slitted eyes and grimacing mouth made him look even more sinister. In this carving his hands were almost completely worn away and I didn't like the idea it suggested to me— that he was crawling through the stone into the temple.

I pressed close to Rosie with a shiver despite the blazing sun overhead.

"You okay, Camille?" she asked.

"Yeah. Just—maybe a bit jet-lagged."

"Do you want to get something to eat? Or drink? Here, have some water."

Everyone was watching me as Rosie fished a bottle of water out of her bag and I suddenly felt silly and self-conscious. "Don't make a fuss."

Zeke looked puzzled but I didn't know how to tell him it wasn't his fault.

"I know what you need," Rosie said confidently. "Let's go down to the beach. There's a reef we can snorkel around and sometimes there are sea turtles. Or we can work on our tans while we watch the boys set up the tent."

She was trying so desperately to cheer me up that I couldn't help but smile.

"Mmm, sea turtles," I said. "Yes, please."

By the time our temporary home was erected and we were all snorkelling along the reef, I'd completely forgotten the weird feeling that had come over me.

That night we sat around the little fire we'd built, drinking margaritas from plastic goblets. The stars were brighter than we ever saw in London and Zeke pointed out constellations to us in Spanish while we tried to guess their English equivalents. "*La estrella de avispa*" left us shaking our heads, though.

"Does *anyone* know *any* Spanish?" Rosie asked, exasperated.

"Sorry," Sebastian said, topping up our glasses. "A-level Greek."

"Japanese," I said, thinking wistfully of my original plan to go there.

Phoebe shrugged. "Enough Latin to make out occasional words but that's all."

Zeke seemed oblivious to our confusion and continued to indicate the bright star hovering above the tracery of palm trees. He kept repeating a word that made no sense before finally writing it in the sand: *Xux Ek*. He indicated the star again.

"Must be a Mayan name," Phoebe said.

"Isn't that Venus?" I asked.

"*Si, si*, Venus!" Zeke said, happy that we'd caught on at last. "*Muy importante* to Mayas."

He drew a crude picture which we managed to interpret as a wasp. "*Avispa*," he said emphatically and we finally caught on. Venus was the "Wasp Star".

There came another burst of Spanish from which Phoebe was able to extract the words "worship", "fear" and "harm", since they were close enough to Latin. But the rest meant nothing to us. He tried the English tourist trick of talking louder, as if that would get the meaning through our thick skulls, but it didn't work any better on us than it did when we tried it on foreigners.

"Like a zombie," Zeke added in English, as though that cleared everything up. He pointed up at Venus again. "Kukulcan. *El dios descendente*."

"Zombie star," Sebastian said, grinning. "I've no idea what he's on about but it sounds brilliant. The Mayans were a bunch of bloody loonies."

Phoebe smiled indulgently. "I think he probably just means the gods couldn't die."

The disquiet I'd felt earlier returned. I felt exposed under the stars, watched. There was something in Zeke's untranslatable description that was bothering me. Something I'd already seen enacted in the carvings in one of the temples.

Out in the darkness, the waves hissed restlessly on the shore and the rustling palm leaves sounded like the beating of wings.

The next day we wasted no time. We packed our rucksacks and headed off into the jungle behind the ruins. The trees were alive with the noise of shrieking birds and insects, but at least it was cool in the shade. By midday the humidity would probably make it unbearable, but Rosie had said there were cenotes scattered all through the area—natural wells with fresh, cool water we could swim in. Swimsuits *genuinely* optional this time.

"Not the same ones they chucked bodies into, I hope," Sebastian said.

But Rosie was fretting about other things today. Every little sound in the undergrowth made her start and I glanced at Zeke, who was grinning after her latest little squeal.

"*Serpientes*," he explained, suppressing a laugh as he pulled up his shirt to show us the coiling rattlesnake tattooed on his back.

"I hate snakes," Rosie whimpered.

Sebastian admired the tattoo, nodding appreciatively. "Good job it's not on your chest, mate," he said, giving Rosie a theatrical wink.

She rolled her eyes, "Real ones, you knob. I know they're out there."

"Your screaming probably scared them off."

Her response to that was a withering look and he backed away, hands upraised in surrender. I was usually the object of my brother's teasing but Rosie was easier prey.

I was a little nervous myself about what might be lurking all around us in the prehistoric forest. I'd seen carvings of things I didn't want to encounter either, namely scorpions and wasps. The foliage was so dense it could be hiding any number of unpleasant creatures.

We passed through a cluster of huge plants with curling fronds and emerged into a little clearing. Sunlight streamed through the trees overhead and colourful birds burst into flight around us. Something chattered scoldingly from the canopy and Phoebe pointed up at a group of monkeys racing along the maze of branches and vines. Although they were far above us, they still seemed perturbed by our presence. They twitched their long tails like irritable cats and pelted us with nuts.

"They're so cute!" Rosie squealed, aiming her camera up at them and tutting when they wouldn't hold still for her.

Phoebe picked leaves out of her hair from the shower of shaking branches. "I see, so the quiet, peaceful snakes are horrid and the noisy, chavvy monkeys are cute."

"Monkeys aren't poisonous," Rosie declared primly.

She'd barely got the words out when there was the loud crunch of something breaking and Rosie dropped out of sight. We froze, listening in horror to her rapidly fading scream until it was broken by a distant splash.

Zeke called her name and ran to the spot where she had disappeared. She'd fallen through a hole in the forest floor. We smoothed away the leaves around the jagged and crumbled edges.

"It's a cenote," Phoebe said. "The limestone must have given way beneath her."

We lay on our bellies around the opening, peering down through the shaft of light into a deep well of greenish water.

"Rosie!" I cried, jumping at the resounding echo of my voice.

There was no answer for several seconds and I wondered whether I'd be able to hear anything at all over the hammering of my heart. But finally she called up to us.

"I think I'm OK," she said in a tremulous voice, "but I'm a long way down."

"How far?" Sebastian shouted.

"I have no idea. A hundred feet, a mile, how should I know?" She burst into tears and I felt my heart twist in sympathy. I clutched at Sebastian's hand but the look of alarm in his eyes didn't reassure me at all.

"Swim into the light," Phoebe said.

There was some splashing and I felt limp with relief when Rosie appeared, a tiny figure spotlit against the flickering water so far below.

"What can you see around you?" Phoebe called.

"It's a huge cave. There's a ledge that goes all the way around the lake." Her voice cracked. "But there's no way up. There's nothing but spikes pointing down at me."

Phoebe drew back from the hole. "Does anyone have any rope?"

We all shook our heads.

"What about these?" Sebastian asked. He jumped to his feet and ran to the nearest tree, where he yanked and pulled at several coiling vines. The monkeys screeched above him and the vines refused to budge. "Maybe if we could cut them?"

"I don't have a knife," I said. "Do you?"

There was no need to answer. None of us had been prepared for anything more than a little hiking, swimming and snorkelling. One by one we looked back down at the hole.

"Someone should go get help," Phoebe said, calm and reasonable as ever. "This sort of thing must happen all the time."

"Yeah," Sebastian said, returning to the edge of the cenote. "Probably best if Zeke goes. He can explain it better in case they don't speak English."

Zeke hadn't moved from the hole but he looked up at the mention of his name and seemed to understand the plan. He nodded and got to his feet.

"I'll go with him," Phoebe said. "You two stay with Rosie."

Sebastian shouted our plan down to Rosie, who had stopped crying and was splashing around again, treading water in the light.

"OK," she said bravely. "But please hurry—it's dark in here!"

Phoebe and Zeke headed off, back the way we'd come, and the monkeys began shrieking again. Clearly we were in their territory and they wanted us out. I hoped their aggression only went as far as throwing nuts and branches down at us.

I heard splashes below and I looked back down into the cenote. Rosie was swimming away from the shaft of light.

"Where are you going?" I asked, losing sight of her.

"Just climbing out onto the ledge," she called back. "The water's bloody cold. Don't fancy jumping in here to keep me company, do you?"

I gave an uneasy laugh. "Not really, no." I tried not to think what would have happened if there hadn't been any water down there. Or if it had been too shallow.

Sebastian, meanwhile, was picking his way around the clearing, as though he expected to find a ladder someone had left behind.

"I wish these bloody monkeys would give it a rest," he grumbled. He picked up a chunk of limestone rock and threw it up into the trees. The monkeys screamed and scattered, only to return in force.

"Leave them alone," I said. "You're only pissing them off more."

"Hey, this is weird!" Rosie shouted.

I turned my attention back to the hole. "What is?"

"There are carvings all over the walls. Just like we saw in the temples. But it's too dark to see it clearly."

Phoebe's words about the "Well of Sacrifice" echoed in my mind and a chill slithered up my back. I couldn't help but think of what might be resting at the bottom of the cenote and I was selfishly glad I hadn't been the one to fall in.

"My torch still works," Rosie said with a note of triumph. "And there's a massive carving down here. I think it's that 'cuckoo' guy Zeke was talking about. The descending god. It looks just like the one we saw on that temple. This place is enormous!"

I tried to share her excitement as I listened to her moving around and exclaiming over her discovery.

Sebastian had moved closer and he called down to her to sing something.

She obliged with a few notes of a song and laughed at the booming reverberation of her voice. Just as the echo faded, we heard the first scream.

It silenced the monkeys and I edged closer to Sebastian. There was the sound of someone running, crashing through the trees. Then another scream, high and chilling. Phoebe.

The scream came again and this time it was cut short with an awful abruptness that could only mean one thing. I stumbled to my knees.

Zeke burst into the clearing, his shirt torn and his arms and legs streaked with blood. His eyes were wild and he was shouting something in Spanish.

"What happened?" Sebastian asked, grabbing him by the arms and shaking him. "Where's Phoebe?"

"*Está muerta*!" he cried over and over. But of course we'd already known she was dead.

There wasn't even time for the shock of it to register before we heard something else, a sound like no animal could ever make. And it was followed by the crash of something coming our way.

Zeke panicked, looking frantically around the clearing and shouting a string of words we couldn't understand. Not that we needed to. Whatever had killed Phoebe and chased him back into the jungle was coming for us now. And it was obviously big. We huddled together by the edge of the cenote as the thing came closer and closer.

What finally spurred us into action was the almighty crack of a tree splitting apart. We saw a spray of green palm leaves begin to shake as the tree was torn away from the canopy and then the ground shook like an earthquake as it fell.

And the thing was still coming.

"Into the hole," Sebastian hissed. "Go!"

I didn't hesitate. I let him push me in and my stomach swooped as I fell the long distance to the lake below. I hit the water and went under, flailing around before struggling back to the surface to gasp for air. My body ached from the impact and at first I couldn't move. Then Sebastian splashed into the water just beside me, jolting me back into the moment. I swam to the ledge where Rosie was reaching out to me.

There was another awful roar and the roof of the cave trembled as the creature moved overhead. Stalactites fell like spears into the water, just missing Zeke, who was the last to dive in. The shaft of light vanished and we froze, dripping and trembling on the ledge. A huge gleaming eye peered in, searching for us. Rosie screamed and Zeke immediately covered her mouth with his hands.

But it had heard us. The eye swivelled in our direction and we slowly backed away from the edge of the water, until we felt the wall of the cave against our backs.

I held my breath as the eye scanned the cave, hunting us. Then it drew away from the hole and the beam of light penetrated the gloom once more. A moment later something reached through. In the darkness it was mostly a silhouette, but it was still enough to make me sick with horror. It was long and thin, like an insect's leg. It seemed to have far too many joints and each segment bristled with fibrous black hairs. It twitched back and forth, sweeping just above the surface of the lake. If we had still been in the water it might have touched our heads. We pressed tightly together, all of us trembling and staring in silent terror as it tried in vain to reach us.

After a while the creature seemed to grow bored and the arm slid back out of the hole. It was quiet for a few moments and then the cave rumbled again as the thing finally moved off, hopefully in search of other prey.

Sebastian and I released the breath we had both been holding. Zeke collapsed onto his back and I heard Rosie being sick behind me. Sebastian slowly removed his rucksack and began pawing through its soaked contents. I put my arm around him and he whispered Phoebe's name.

There was nothing I could say. Her screams were still echoing in my head. I didn't even want to imagine what the rest of the monster looked like. Our glimpses had been enough.

Rosie had recovered and she knelt over Zeke, asking him what had happened. The water had washed away the blood but some of his cuts were starting to ooze again. None of them looked serious but I felt my stomach lurch at the thought of him having been touched by that creature.

He was murmuring in short little bursts, Spanish mixed with random bits of English. But I heard the word "wasp" and turned away.

Sebastian had taken a bottle of tequila from his rucksack and he took a healthy swig before passing it around to the rest of us. His eyes were dry and staring vacantly and I felt his shock as acutely as if I'd been the one to lose my partner to such a hideous fate. I gulped a burning mouthful of tequila to quell the nausea.

"*Templo*," Zeke whispered, gazing up at the wall of the cave.

Rosie nodded. "Yeah." She shone her torch up onto the wall. "I bet no one's seen this in hundreds of years."

Zeke seemed fascinated and he clambered to his feet, leaning on Rosie as she showed him the elaborate mural. It was nothing like the ones we'd seen in Tulum, which had been weathered by time. In here all the colours and details had been perfectly preserved. Zeke followed the images with a finger, muttering to himself as he presumably pieced together some kind of storyline.

The mural was a catalogue of cruelty and death. There was a man being stabbed, another one swollen to grotesque proportions, another one coughing up his intestines. In amongst the mayhem, a group of demons seemed to be dancing around the people they were tormenting.

I recoiled when the beam came to rest on the carving she'd described earlier. It was uglier than any of the ones we'd already seen and it seemed more menacing. The play of light and shadow animated the figure's baleful grin, and when I saw the enormous wasp-like creature beside it I turned away with a shudder.

Zeke saw it too and gasped. He glanced nervously around the cave. "*La entrada*," he said, looking lost in thought.

That was a word we knew: entrance.

"Entrance to where?" Rosie asked.

He took Rosie's torch and ran it over the mural again. Then he said something none of us understood.

"Write it," Rosie said, indicating the floor of the cave.

He dipped his finger in a puddle and scrawled a strange word on a dry patch of limestone. *Xibalba*.

"What's that?" I asked.

There was a haunted look in his eyes. "*El Inframundo*," he said. Then he pointed to the water. "Here."

"He said that word last night," I said. "Any idea what it means?"

Sebastian closed his eyes and I knew he was hearing Phoebe translate it in his head.

Rosie dug inside her rucksack. "Phoebe said all the Mayan stuff was in the guidebook, right? I took it this morning to look at the map." She removed the book and tried to turn its wet pages. They stuck together and tore like soggy bread in her trembling hands. "Damn!"

"It's OK," I said. "Just be gentle."

She took a deep breath and carefully levered a fingernail between the pages, easing them apart slowly. The process was laborious but she finally made it to the chapter on Mayan history. There were pictures of Tulum and other sites, along with details of various temple carvings. Underneath a photo of a cenote was the caption "*Xibalba*".

"The Underworld," she read in a hushed voice. "It was called 'the place of fear'." She looked up at us with wide, frightened eyes before continuing. "'The Mayan Underworld was a great city ruled by twelve Lords of Death, who terrified and humiliated travellers with a series of deadly tests. If they failed these tests, they could not enter'."

I recalled an image I had seen in Tulum of a river teeming with scorpions. Suddenly the cave seemed very cold.

"Is that all?" Sebastian asked bitterly.

"No, listen to this: 'The Mayans believed that there were three entrances to the Underworld and one was through the bottom of a sacred cenote. Through sacrifice they communicated with the gods to allow them passage'."

Sebastian snorted. "What a load of primitive rubbish!"

I rounded on him. "Did you not see that thing up there?"

He was silent, angry, glaring at the mural.

"It's real," I said quietly. "I don't want it to be but it is."

Zeke seemed to understand our exchange. He nodded gravely, his injuries and the stricken look in his eyes confirming that it was very real indeed. I didn't want to imagine the full horror of what he and Phoebe had seen. I'd merely felt the presence of something that didn't want us here; they had actually been attacked by it.

Sebastian heaved a long shuddering sigh and lowered his head. "I know," he said at last. "I just . . . Phoebe."

There was nothing I could say. I put my arms around him and held him.

After a while Rosie broke the silence. "Are we going to die down here?"

Sebastian moved to the edge of the lake and splashed his face with water. The light from above was piercingly bright, illuminating the spiky stalagmites under the water. He turned back to the wall, his brow furrowed.

"Who carved all this?" he asked. "I mean, how?"

I shook my head in confusion.

"What I mean is—how did *they* get in here?"

The penny dropped.

"There's another way in," Rosie said, a note of hope creeping into her voice.

We spread out, making our separate ways around the ledge, looking for another entrance. But the limestone was solid and unyielding. It looked as if it hadn't changed in millions of years. There was no chance that a boulder had simply fallen to block the way in. There *was* no way in. Or out.

But Sebastian still looked deep in thought. He gazed at the water. Then he fished his mask and snorkel out of his rucksack and dived into the pool. He made a careful circuit of the lake, dipping down from time to time to explore nooks and crannies before coming back up for air. And then he disappeared.

I held my breath when I saw his snorkel dip beneath the water and I kept holding it until my lungs began to ache with the need for breath. All we could do was wait. Rosie squeezed my hand and finally I gasped for air. I kept my eyes on the water, not daring to blink as I felt the minutes crawl by, each one only further cementing the fact that if Sebastian was still down there, he wasn't coming back.

"Oh Camille," Rosie said softly.

I had just begun to cry when my brother broke the surface of the water with a triumphant shout. We stared at him in wide-eyed amazement.

"There's another cave," he said excitedly. "It's smaller than this one but I found these." He dropped a handful of seashells onto the ledge at our feet and smiled.

Zeke realised their significance at once and Rosie and I caught on a second later. The caves led to the sea. We found our snorkels and strapped our rucksacks back on. If we were lucky we wouldn't be coming back here.

We slipped into the chilly water and followed Sebastian to the far side of the lake. He took a deep breath and dived in and we followed one by one. The cenote was immense. Underwater we could see that it was even larger than the cave. It was hard not to be awestruck by the subterranean cathedral with its limestone spires. The light filtered down through the turquoise water, lighting our way. No wonder the Mayans believed these places were sacred.

I was just starting to feel the need to breathe when we reached the opening to the second cave. We swam through a little tunnel and emerged, gasping, in a smaller chamber. The floor sloped upwards for some distance into the cave, forming a natural ramp out of the water. Pinprick beams of light shone from above and the walls glowed with some kind of phosphorescence. There was just enough light to see what was on the walls.

"Oh, Jesus," Rosie said.

The mural displayed very little skill or artistry. It was crude and functional. But what it depicted was unmistakable. The city perched on the cliff was Tulum and the people its ancient inhabitants. Etched into their faces were rough expressions of terror and misery, their mouths open and screaming as they tumbled into the gaping maw of the insect-like creature clinging to the side of the cliff. Bodies littered the beach beneath it, and several more were impaled on the thing's spiny legs. Out on the rolling waves of the sea, the demons danced in celebration.

We were witnessing a survivor's testimony, the solution to an ancient riddle.

"*Sacrificio*," Zeke whispered.

Yes, I thought. But not just individual people this time. In the end the gods had demanded more. And in the case of Tulum they had wanted the whole city.

"Someone escaped," Rosie said softly. "They made it here and drew this so someone would know."

"It's not real," Sebastian growled. "It's just ignorant mythology."

But I could hear the quaver in his voice and I shared his fear. "If that thing was around back then," I said, "where has it been all this time?"

No one responded. I already knew the answer. It had been right here, waiting. And as the cave floor began to rumble beneath us I saw that the others knew too.

We raced along the passageway and turned a corner. And stopped short. There was nothing there. Just a smooth blank wall glowing greenly. We were trapped.

My heart pounded like a drum and I felt dizzy. The cave was still vibrating, shaking bits of limestone and small stalactites loose, but I couldn't hear the creature itself.

"The passage is underwater," Sebastian said, putting his swim mask back on. "We have to go back."

Rosie's eyes went wide. "But what if it's in there?"

I swallowed my own terror at the idea and fitted my mask as well.

Sebastian grabbed my hand and took off. I heard Rosie scream and then she was behind me, with Zeke behind her. We made it back to the little cave and Sebastian plunged straight into the water without hesitation. I didn't give myself time to worry about what might be beneath the surface before following him in.

We spread out in the pool, diving down to look for a way out. I got excited when I found an opening until I realised it was the way we'd come in. Finally I heard Rosie shouting at the surface and I came up.

"There's a tunnel," she said breathlessly, "just below this overhang."

The water sloshed with the trembling of the cave and we swam over to Rosie. We held on to a jutting shard of limestone, panting for breath. We knew we had to move, but we also knew that there was no guarantee the passage was an escape route. Even if it did lead to another cave, and from there on to the sea, cave diving was a sport for those with scuba gear, not snorkels. The passage might run for hundreds of feet under water, with nowhere for us to come up for air. Or it might narrow too much for us to fit through. There were a thousand things that could go wrong. All we could do was hope.

"I'll go first," Sebastian said. And just like that he was gone. This time we couldn't afford to wait for him to report back.

Rosie clung to Zeke but he pushed her away, indicating that she should go next. She looked pleadingly at me before following Sebastian. I took a deep breath, dived in and swam after her just as the cave began to shudder again. Bubbles rose around me like smoke, tickling my legs as I propelled myself into the tunnel.

The passageway narrowed alarmingly and I crawled through, terrified that at any moment I would reach the logjam of bodies that meant my brother and best friend were dead. But the tunnel soon widened enough for me to look back over my shoulder. Zeke was close behind me.

The water was crystal clear, lit from within by the phosphorescent glow, and I was dazzled by the refracted light. It was like swimming through a diamond. Under other circumstances it would have been a transcendent experience. Now, however, the beauty seemed merely cruel, as though mocking our helplessness. It had only been a few seconds but I was winded and frightened and I felt myself needing air already.

When the creature roared I didn't recognise the sound at first for what it was. The water distorted everything. But the sudden curtain of bubbles told me there was something beneath me and when I looked down into the endless blue void I screamed. A huge dark shape was rising up towards me.

I kicked as hard and as fast as I could, my chest bursting for breath. I could see light overhead and I forced my arms wide apart and then back again, scooping them through water that felt as thick as mud. It was all I could do not to breathe in. My head pounded in rhythm with my heart and I felt something hard brush against my bare leg. I tried to tell myself it was just limestone, but I knew better.

Its next grab snagged my rucksack and I hung there, trapped. Without even thinking, I slithered out of the straps and kept swimming. There came another sound, a strangled watery cry. And before I could stop myself I looked down to see Zeke struggling in the monster's grasp. His mouth opened in a gaping scream that emitted only a cloud of blood and then a pair of gleaming black mandibles cut him in two.

I couldn't help it. I gasped. Pain gripped my chest at once and I thrashed wildly, thinking the creature had me in its jaws. I screamed and kicked and clawed at the water with no idea where I was or what was happening. All I could feel was the terrible pressure as water flooded my lungs. Then the pain quickly began to fade and I felt dazed and almost sleepy. For a moment I dared to hope it had all been a bad dream, that I was simply ill and locked in a feverish nightmare. But the nightmare was winning. The hands pulling me out of the water might have been the hands of angels. I was ready to go to them.

Then something raked across my back and I realised it was the floor of the cave. I knew it must have hurt but I was too detached to feel it. There was the blur of faces and echoing voices. I smelled blood, tasted bile, someone was hitting me, and then I rolled over, coughing and gasping as water splashed from my mouth in scalding bursts. The pain was so intense it blinded me and I barely had time to register that I hadn't drowned when Sebastian heaved me over his shoulder in a fireman's carry and we were off and running down another limestone corridor.

I watched the mottled floor go past and saw my blood dripping behind us like a trail of grisly breadcrumbs. Sebastian and Rosie were shouting to each other but their words were lost to me. All I could think of was my last sight of Zeke, of the spiny, insect feel of the creature's leg as it reached for me that first time. Tears blinded me but breaking down was a luxury none of us could afford.

The monster—demon, god, whatever it was—wanted its sacrifices. All of the Mayan civilisation hadn't been enough for it. Something had woken it from centuries of sleep and it was here, now. Alive and hungry and wholly evil.

At last the dry corridor came to an end and we were faced with another pool. Sebastian eased me onto my feet.

"Are you OK?" he panted.

I stood shakily and nodded. "I think so." My chest burned with every inhalation and my back felt as though I'd been dragged behind a car but at least I could walk. And over the smell of blood I could smell the sea. Rosie clung to me, sobbing and calling Zeke's name.

"This could be it," Sebastian said, a hopeful note creeping into his voice. He peered down into the water. It was murky and dark, completely unlike the crystal clear water of the cenotes. "The tide must be out or this whole place would be flooded."

Rosie looked up, her eyes streaming with tears. "What if it doesn't . . ."

Sebastian shook his head fiercely. "Don't think about it."

"But what if we—"

"There's nowhere else to go."

His voice echoed in the damp, dripping cave and I closed my eyes for a moment, shutting out the hundreds of other what-ifs that crowded my mind. The cave had stopped rumbling but we didn't dare hope that was the end of it. The crude mural had shown more than one demon dancing in the sea.

Sebastian slicked his hair away from his face and adjusted his mask. "Ready?"

Breathing deeply was an effort but I told myself I only needed to do it once. When that breath ran out we would either be saved or dead. Rosie squeezed my hand and we both nodded.

We slid into the water and fitted our snorkels while we looked around for an opening. Our torches lasted a few seconds before finally shorting out and I tried not to take it as an omen.

We found an opening after several dives. It was deeper than the others had been and I had to force a few slow, painful breaths to quell the panic that threatened to take over. We'd waste half our escape time just diving down to the passageway. But I couldn't think about that. Instead I thought of Japan, of rolling green hills and serene Buddhist temples.

"This is it," Sebastian said.

As if in response to his words, the water trembled around us and my heart gave a frightened leap. *Stay calm*, I told myself. *Slow, deep breaths.*

"OK," I said.

Sebastian dived and I waited a few seconds before gulping in a huge breath and following him. It was a narrow tunnel but not a long one and soon we were in another underwater cave. Stalactites and stalagmites rose and descended all around us like the bars of a cage and we looked around frantically, not knowing which way to go. My lungs were already pleading for more air.

Then Rosie pointed and we turned to look. Light was streaming down into the water some distance away. It could only mean one thing. We kicked towards it, pulling ourselves along the bars of our limestone prison. A flickering school of fish rocked from side to side in the current and I ignored my body's desperate need to breathe as I made my way towards them.

Sebastian was just in front of me and he kept glancing back to make sure I was following. I could see Rosie to my left, but I looked back as well to make sure we were alone. Slowly I began releasing the air in my lungs. The bubbles scurried to the surface and I followed them. When I ran out of bubbles I began to feel dizzy, but we were almost there.

At last Sebastian reached the light and he soared up towards the indigo sky. Rosie and I were right behind him and we broke the surface together, gasping and panting as we breathed in the wonderful Caribbean air.

"We did it!" Rosie cried. She gave an hysterical little laugh that chilled me. And then she vanished.

Something thrashed in the water, something big, and we caught a glimpse of a long jointed tail with a vicious barb at its end as it dragged Rosie down. The sea turned red. I screamed and reached for her but Sebastian grabbed me and began hauling me towards the beach.

"Come on!" he cried.

For a moment I struggled against him, calling Rosie's name as the water churned where she had been. Then the surface settled and became smooth again. And something began moving towards us.

We kicked for the shore without looking back. My ears rang with wild, mad screams and my frenzied heart felt like it would split with both the effort of beating and breaking. But there was no time to grieve. Over the sounds of our splashing we could hear the water parting behind us, hear the silky wake of the creature pursuing us.

We gained the beach and clambered up onto the sand, kicking up pale clouds behind us as we ran blindly up the sloping cliff. Tulum was up there. Hundreds of tourists were up there. Safety was up there. Surely whatever was after us couldn't—

But we were wrong. Whatever had attacked us had already been here. The little paths and patches of grass were scattered with bodies, the ruins splashed with blood. And from behind us came the scratching sound of something gaining purchase on the stone.

"There!" Sebastian shouted, pointing up at El Castillo. "Run!"

We scrambled over the rope and up the long flight of stone steps to the temple, neither of us looking back. When we reached the top we plunged into the cool dark shadows, cowering and trembling and waiting to die.

Nothing happened.

Minutes passed like an eternity and finally we inched towards the columns and peered out at the carnage. Night was falling and Tulum lay below us in the moonlight like a wasteland, its buildings reduced to rubble. Bodies lay strewn across the site, sprawled over fallen trees, crushed beneath stones, some whole, some dismembered, some barely even recognisable as human. And creeping through the devastation were the things we'd seen in the crude carvings of that hidden underground chamber. Armies of them. They had some of the attributes of creatures familiar to us—wasps, scorpions—but were entirely alien. Hellish.

"Oh my God," Sebastian breathed.

I covered my mouth. It was tempting to scream but I knew that if I did I would never stop.

El Castillo seemed to be the only building still intact, and Sebastian and me the only survivors. We were both wondering the same thing: why us?

As we shared the thought the creatures stirred. They turned slowly, mandibles clicking rhythmically. They regarded us with cold insect eyes. And we understood.

There had been sacrifices but we had escaped. We had passed the tests.

As we emerged from the temple the creatures made no move to attack us. Antennae waved and wings buzzed as we slowly descended the stairs, hand in hand. High above us in the sky the Wasp Star glinted. Several corpses sat up, turning mangled heads on broken necks to regard us as we passed, reaching out to us like supplicants. The creatures began to hum, their terrible voices coalescing into one.

"Kukulcan," they seemed to be saying.

As we surveyed the kingdom they had created for us, and then saw how we ourselves were beginning to change, we wondered how long it would take to get used to our new bodies. And our new purpose.

The Things That Aren't There

I'M NOT GOOD WITH KIDS. I TOLD MRS PEARCE THIS BUT she said not to be silly, that everyone loved children, especially girls like me who would be mummies too someday.

"Not me," I said, making a face.

"Nonsense, Emma! You're only twelve. Believe me, you'll feel differently when you're older."

"No I won't."

The year before, my mother had shown me the video of my own birth. But the magical, beautiful event I'd been promised was more like a nightmare. I couldn't believe the wild-eyed screaming woman was my mother and I *refused* to believe that the bloody, slimy thing that split her open down there was me. The room started to spin and then I was sick all down the front of my new jumper.

"I'm *never* having kids," I said, swallowing the horrible memory.

"Oh, you just wait and see." Mrs Pearce ruffled my hair and smiled the way grown-ups do when they think they know everything. Then she went right back to telling me all I needed to know about watching Chloe while she was out.

I grumbled and said OK I would but that I hadn't wanted to do babysitting at all and Chloe could be really annoying and it was only because my parents had *made* me...

I didn't really say any of that. I just thought it at her really hard. Maybe if I made her feel guilty enough she'd never ask me again.

"It's only for a couple of hours," she said, as though she'd simply asked me to post a letter for her, "and you know how Chloe looks up to you."

Did I ever. Chloe was the most annoying kid in the world. The whiny six-year-old got dragged along whenever my mum and Mrs Pearce wanted to have tea and chat in our kitchen for hours and hours and hours. I always got stuck having to "entertain" her. Sometimes we pretended I was a famous movie star and Chloe was my biggest fan. I made her follow me around begging for my autograph while I ignored her or ran from her like she was the paparazzi. No matter how mean I was to her, she only seemed to worship me more.

"Well, I'll be off, then. Have fun, you two."

I was expecting Chloe to be overjoyed to see me. Normally she would have raced down the stairs shouting my name if she knew I was in the house. But this time she didn't appear until her mother had gone. I closed the front door and turned to see her on the landing, clutching a stuffed pony. It was blue and missing an eye and for some reason it made me feel sad for her.

"Hi Chloe."

She mumbled hello and came slowly down the stairs, where she stood staring up at me, her big eyes like melting chocolate.

I sighed. "Well, looks like I'm stuck here with you."

"For the whole night?"

"No, just a couple of hours. Didn't your mum tell you?"

"She's going on a *date*." She made it sound so important I had to laugh. No doubt her mother had told her it was her big chance to land another man. I'd overheard some of the desperate conversations she had with my mum.

"Yeah," I said. "A big date."

Chloe nodded solemnly. "So she won't be back tonight."

"What are you talking about? It's only seven now and you'll be asleep by the time she gets back."

"Last time she didn't come home," Chloe said. "Or the time before."

I stared at her while this sunk in. Mrs Pearce had lied to me! On the one hand it was rotten because you shouldn't lie to people—especially kids—but on the other hand, now I *definitely* wouldn't have to babysit for her ever again. My parents would be furious at her for lying to me.

Chloe was looking worried. "Emma? You won't leave me all by myself, will you?"

"No, of course not. Don't be stupid."

She stared at me, her eyes wide and searching. "You promise? *Really* promise?"

Her intensity made me uneasy and I smiled to reassure her. "I promise."

Chloe heaved a huge sigh of relief and squeezed my hand and I found myself actually feeling sorry for her. The poor kid was probably so used to her mum tricking her that she didn't trust anyone—not even me. So I promised again.

"Does your mum do that a lot?" I asked. "Leave you by yourself?"

Chloe pursed her lips and looked away, twisting her body from side to side. The legs of the stuffed pony in her arms swung like they were broken, reminding me of the time I found my cat Ivan dead in the garden. I'd carried his limp body around for hours, feeling like he'd abandoned me.

"Sometimes," Chloe mumbled. "I don't like it here by myself. It's scary."

I felt a sudden surge of big-sisterly protectiveness towards her and I imagined ringing the police. I could just see the SWAT team surrounding a posh restaurant on the TV, all spotlights and slow motion while a helicopter went chop-chop-chop overhead. As they dragged Mrs Pearce out and forced her into a police car, she saw me in the crowd and cried in her deep slowed-down voice that she was sorry, so very, very sorry. I stood shielding Chloe in my arms, unmoved by her pleas.

"Well, there's nothing to be afraid of," I said, but I was trying to convince myself too. I didn't like the idea of being alone in the house all night any more than Chloe did. I still slept with a night-light on in my bedroom. Not that I'd ever want anyone to know that.

Chloe glanced nervously at the darkened front windows, at the night that pressed against the glass like a giant pair of hands. She climbed up on a chair to reach the switch to turn on the porch light. A warm glow shone through the windows and she gave me a shy smile as she clambered back down.

I wasn't about to tell her off for wasting electricity; I was tempted to go through the house switching *all* the lights on.

"Are you afraid of them too?" Chloe asked as though reading my mind.

"Afraid of who?"

"The things that aren't there."

I didn't like the way she said it. The weight she gave to the words made me feel like we were being watched. "What things?"

She peered up the darkened staircase and my gaze followed hers. There was a patch of deep shadow where the stairs branched off from the landing. Anything could be lurking there unseen. I thought of the time I had reached inside a cupboard only to have a spider scuttle up my bare arm. I felt its tiny legs for weeks afterwards. With a shudder I turned back to Chloe. "There's nothing there. Stop trying to freak me out."

"I'm not," she said, looking fearful herself. "My mum says they're not there but they are. She just can't see them."

"See what?"

Chloe frowned as she tried to find the right words. "At first you can only see them when you're not looking. Like if you have to go to the loo at night and it's dark. They're right behind you but if you turn around to look, they slide back into the shadows. They live in the places where you've just been."

As she spoke I saw myself tiptoeing down a long dark hallway, sensing something behind me and whirling to confront it, only for it to vanish. I didn't want her to know how much she was scaring me. I particularly disliked her use of the word *slide*. It was too vivid, too specific.

"How do you know you aren't just imagining things?"

She looked wounded. "I'm not!" she cried. "They're real!"

"OK, so what happens if you do see them? If you look right at them?"

Chloe squeezed her pony tighter and turned to face the stairs. "I'm looking at one right now."

I felt my skin crawl as I stared into the shadows. "I can't see anything," I whispered, still straining to see. I yearned for the courage to stalk boldly up the stairs and prove there was nothing there. "Where is it?"

"It's halfway down."

Now I knew she was just trying to scare me. The first flight of steps was well lit and there was clearly nothing there. Determined to show her it was all in her head, I marched over to the stairs.

"Emma, don't—"

Chloe reached for me but I shook her off. I went up three steps and sure enough, the staircase was empty. The patch of shadows on the landing was empty too. Even so, I didn't want to go any further up. I turned back to her and spread my arms. "See?"

But Chloe was crouching on the floor, clinging to her stuffed toy and staring in wide-eyed terror. "It's *right there*," she hissed, pointing just to my left.

The space beside me was definitely empty. I waved my arm around where the thing was supposed to be and shook my head. "Nothing at all."

"You can't see them," she whispered fearfully, "but I can."

She was starting to scare me again. I glanced behind me and for a second I thought I'd seen something dart back into the shadows. Something long and thin. Something that would *slide*. I turned back to Chloe but I could sense it was still there. My heart started to beat faster and I told myself it was just my imagination. It was what my parents always said when I was scared. There was no long-armed man under the bed, no staring eye in my closet. Just my imagination. And Chloe's.

"Look," I said, heading back down the stairs, "no more monsters, OK? Let's watch a movie."

But as I reached the floor and turned towards the lounge I caught a flicker of movement out of the corner of my eye. A long slinky shape paced along behind me, like a shadow that was somehow heavy and real. Like something I would *feel* if it reached out to touch me. I stopped and spun around to see it, but it was too fast.

Chloe saw me and clutched at my hand. "You *do* see them!" she cried, sounding relieved and dismayed at the same time.

I wasn't comforted by the sudden thought that they were making themselves visible now that I knew they were there. From the stairs came a creak, like the sound a wolf might make sneaking up on its prey.

"You believe me now, don't you, Emma?"

I didn't want to admit it. What if admitting it made them even more real? I stared hard into the shadows beneath the hall table, the shadows along the wall, the shadows that swarmed like ants in every empty room. And I listened, straining to hear over the banging of my heart in my ears.

"They're getting closer," Chloe whimpered, her eyes filling with tears.

"Stop it! There's nothing there. You're just making it all up." I felt weird and a little sick as I said it and a strange thought came to me. Did grown-ups say things like that because there really *was* something there in the dark? Were they just as afraid? Mrs Pearce had lied to me. What if my parents had lied too? Did believing in lies make them real?

Chloe was clinging to me, soaking the leg of my jeans with tears as she begged and pleaded with me to make them go away. It wasn't fair. I was just a kid too.

I grabbed Chloe by the arms and shook her. "Look," I said, "they're not there. They're all in your head. Trust me. They're in your head and they can't get out."

And again I had that weird feeling. Like something was getting stronger with everything I said. Then I heard the laughter. So soft it might only have been in my mind. It sounded pleased, as though I'd done exactly what someone—or something—had wanted.

Chloe wasn't crying any more, but the look on her face was worse than tears. She looked empty. Her eyes were dark, like shadows. She stared at me, not seeing me. Not seeing anything. I let go of her and she slumped to the floor in a heap.

I shook her and called her name. "Chloe? Stop it; it isn't funny! Chloe, wake up!"

But she didn't respond. She didn't even blink as I waved my hands in front of her eyes. I crumpled to the floor as I realised what I'd done, what I'd said. *They're in your head and they can't get out.* She had believed me. Behind those blank eyes she was screaming but there was no way I could reach her. I cried and called to her for a while but I knew it was no use. She was gone.

Chloe had dropped her pony on the floor. I picked it up and held it but it only made me feel worse. I crept under the hall table where I couldn't see her vacant, staring eyes. The shadows wrapped themselves around me like arms but I knew they wouldn't hurt me. They'd got what they came for.

No one would believe me if I told them what really happened. But Mrs Pearce had lied to me, so I would lie to her too. What else could I do? I'd told her I wasn't good with kids.

WORM CASTS

NICOLE EYED THE FLOWERS UNEASILY. THEY WERE unpleasant bulbous things, sprouting like snakes from the grass, their heavy heads bobbing in the soft breeze. She'd never seen them before. The lawn reliably produced simple flowers and weeds. Daisies, buttercups, dandelions, the occasional daffodil. Once a trio of vivid pink lilies had sprung up by the fence, flashing their showy blooms for a week before dying back, never to be seen again. It was as though they had tested her garden and found it wanting.

These new invaders weren't showy but they were . . . different. The flowers were bell-shaped and partly open, like little mouths. Nicole wouldn't have been surprised to see a forked tongue flick out. She had never seen anything like them. And certainly never *there*.

Nothing grew beneath the raintree. She had always assumed that the poison from its dangling yellow blossoms had soured the ground below for anything but grass. It was why she'd chosen the spot. But now these ugly flowers had appeared there, concentrated in an area about two feet square. They were the colour of fresh bruises, purple-grey flecked with sickly yellow, and they just looked *wrong*. The flower heads nodded as though mocking her apprehension, quivering as if with laughter. As though daring her to uproot them.

Cool air teased the back of her neck and she shivered, wrapping her arms around herself. Suddenly the morning seemed impossibly silent, the world withholding itself from her. She felt watched.

Her skin crawled as she imagined the worst. Someone knew. Someone had sneaked into the garden to plant these flowers as a warning. *I saw you*, the message read. *I know what you did.*

For a moment she couldn't move. The silence swelled in her ears and she closed her eyes, feeling nauseated. She strained both to listen and not to hear. If she listened too closely to the roaring silence she could almost make out whispers. And if she focused on the actual words...

She shook her head, clearing it. From somewhere in the trees a bird chirped and soon it was joined by another. The spell was broken. In no time at all the sky was alive with noise as creatures shouted and sang to each other in their tiny secret languages. With a sigh of relief Nicole looked at the flowers again. They were just a sprinkling of ugly dark blooms growing in the shadow of a little tree. Nothing threatening, nothing meaningful. Nothing to worry about. If the ground there *was* blighted, the flowers would soon be dead.

She turned her back on them and returned to the house, locking the door carefully behind her.

That night she found herself drawn back to the garden. The moon was high and swollen, getting bigger as it neared fullness. Growing. Things were always growing. There was really no such thing as death, for even dead things grew. They swelled and changed. They fed the worms and soil as they grew, dispersed, mutated.

And the flowers. They also fed the flowers.

In the moonlight they looked unnervingly like tightly closed fists reaching up through the ground. Nicole didn't like to think of them opening, didn't like to imagine what they might be clutching.

She turned away with a shudder, telling herself she was being silly. Then she noticed the claw marks. All across the lawn were tiny curling furrows, like a child's manic scribbling. As though thousands of worms were boiling up to the surface.

The moonlight lent a bluish glow to the scarred lawn and the scent of earth was fresh in the chilly night air. The smell made her queasy. She remembered it all too well, had scrubbed for days to get rid of it. She'd pared her nails down to the quick but still they reeked of earth. Even now the scent felt trapped inside her nostrils, staining her senses.

She stared in horror at the gouges in the grass, at the patterns they seemed to form. There was such a sense of menace in them. In some places she could make out letters and in others, almost full words. In the centre of the garden, unobscured by the shadows of trees, she was sure there was a picture. A face. An angry, screaming face.

At once her knees began to tremble and her legs felt too weak to hold her up. The flowers weren't enough. Someone had come in here and done this, carved these furrows into the ground. But why? To frighten her? To warn her? She looked around at the silent bulk of the house, the lines and angles of the fence, the trees silhouetted against the flaring sky. From somewhere out in the dark a fox sent forth its high unearthly scream and from far off in the trees an owl twittered and was answered by another.

The sounds of the night bloomed around her, belying the stillness of the garden. Above her she was sure she could hear the leathery fluttering of bats as they feasted on insects she could neither see nor hear. Life thrived everywhere, hidden, secretive. Beneath her feet were worms and beetles and slugs and other things she didn't know the names of. Creatures that outnumbered her by the millions. Creatures that had been around longer than her kind and which would eventually feast on her bones as well.

Unnerved by the thought, she hurried back to the house, feeling overwhelmed. She slammed the door behind her, locked it and dragged the kitchen table in front of it. The world was filled with alien creatures but surely they weren't her real enemy. No. Out there amongst the crawling things was a *person*. Someone who meant her harm. Someone who must have spent hours watching and waiting and then desecrating her garden with calculated spite.

Her heart hammered in her chest as she peered out between the curtains at the lawn. From the sanctuary of the house the purposeful etching looked more natural than she had first imagined, the patterns less obvious. The sense of writing, of *language*, was gone. Now the tiny lumps looked like nothing more than the scratching of foxes or hedgehogs. But she could still see the shapes of the flowers.

Nicole climbed up onto the table and sat staring out into the night, watching for her tormentor and waiting for them to make another move. But nothing happened. When she couldn't keep her eyes open any longer she trudged up the stairs and climbed into bed, where she dreamt of coiling vines and thorns and creatures that squirmed and shrieked and tore her open from within. She woke with a cry and stared into the darkness of the room, alert for the slightest sound. But she was alone.

She lay awake until the first pastel rays of morning began to illuminate the sky.

The dawn chorus was boisterous and cheerful, banishing all sense of malignancy. The riot of birds greeted the sunrise like pagan worshippers rejoicing that another night had passed and the life-giving rays had returned at last. From somewhere down the lane a dog was barking. It was followed by the shouts and laughter of children. Normality had returned.

Nicole pushed the barricade away and unlocked the back door. A faint mist hung low over the valley out beyond the fence and the grass was heavy with dew. By all accounts it was a lovely morning and Nicole saw at once that her paranoia had been entirely misplaced. The scrawled messages in the lawn were nothing but worm casts. Tiny regurgitated tunnels left by creatures hard at work. They busily munched away underground and cast the undigested soil to the surface where it lay in tiny curls and furrows.

She stared hard at the worm casts and tried to see them as she had in the night, full of threat and warning. But the irrational fear had passed.

She remembered once as a child seeing a bright light moving vertically in the sky very far away and coming gradually closer. When she'd pointed it out to her father in terror he'd explained that it was simply an airplane. They were directly in the flight path as it landed. Sure enough, they soon heard the roar of jet engines as it passed overhead. She'd been both relieved and perversely disappointed, as though for a moment she'd inhabited a different world, one where anything was possible.

This time she felt only relief. Whatever world of delusion she'd entered last night, she didn't want to go back. No one had seen her. No one knew. Anyone peeking over the fence would merely have seen a woman planting something beneath a tree. Those weird flowers, perhaps.

The thought of them gave her a little shudder and she glanced over at the raintree. The flowers had doubled in size.

Her legs trembled as she crossed the lawn, muddying it with her passage through the worm casts. She knew enough about flowers to know that no species grew that fast. They had appeared overnight and in twenty-four hours swollen like tumours. The monstrous heads were too heavy for their stems and they lay along the grass as though sleeping. But their appearance wasn't the worst thing.

What made Nicole's stomach lurch was the smell.

She pressed a hand over her nose and mouth and stared in horror at the lolling flowers. The stench was absolutely vile, like rotting meat and raw sewage. At first she thought some animal must have died nearby but she quickly banished the idea. She knew what dead animals smelled like and it was nothing like this. The smell seemed to clog her throat and she had the sudden wild thought that it was trapped inside her now, that she'd never be free of it, never be able *not* to smell it. It had traumatised her senses.

She backed away as her insides began to clench and contract and then she was sick on the grass. She fell to her knees as her stomach heaved, over and over, expelling everything she'd eaten. The smell of vomit mingled with the smell of the flowers and her insides twisted again. When the violent episode finally passed she got shakily to her feet and looked over at the flowers. Their half-open mouths appeared to be smiling.

Worse than the putrescent smell was the thought that she might not be the only one to smell it. The stench would waft into her neighbours' gardens and someone was bound to complain. Possibly even call the police. She had to uproot the flowers and get rid of them.

Nicole ran inside and pawed through the cupboards until she found a length of cheesecloth. She doused it with perfume and wound it around her face. It did little to combat the smell still lodged in her nose but at least it gave her another scent to focus on. She grabbed a bin bag, a box of salt and the thick rubber gloves she wore to clean the toilet. Then she headed for the garden shed to get the spade.

The cramped space was wreathed in cobwebs and the spade hung where she'd left it on its peg, conspicuously clean compared to the tools on either side. The sight struck her at once and she made a note to sweep it all out after she was done. She couldn't risk throwing all the gardening implements away; that might draw attention.

Digging up the hideous flowers was the work of minutes. The roots were long and thick but she severed them with the spade and churned the soil as deeply as she dared before opening the box of salt. Then she hesitated. If she salted the area it would kill the grass. Then nothing would ever cover the guilty patch. It would stick out like a signpost. With a muttered curse she closed the box and grafted the patch of turf back into place. She'd carefully cut it out by hand two days ago when she'd first dug the hole and the grass hadn't had time to take root yet. It was a little paler than the surrounding grass. She pressed the turf down with the spade but she didn't like the thought of treading on it to pack it down.

She didn't know what else to do. Should she just leave it and hope the awful flowers didn't return? Plant something else there and pray it would grow to cover the conspicuously dug patch? Or would that look too much like a grave? If the ground was truly hostile surely nothing ought to grow there anyway.

She tied the bin bag tightly closed and gave the spade a cursory clean by dragging it over the lawn. It smeared the worm casts into a muddy path and she frowned, hoping it didn't look obvious. But then, what was suspicious about a woman digging in her back garden? She didn't follow the thought to its natural conclusion because she knew full well what was suspicious about it. She closed and locked the shed and drove the evil flowers all the way to the tip to get rid of them. They rustled unpleasantly in the bag as she tossed it into the skip.

By the time she got back the sky had darkened and the air was pregnant with the threat of rain. Good. That would wash away her muddy tracks in the lawn and pack the earth down beneath the tree. It felt like nature was on her side for a change.

Then the doorbell rang.

She jumped as though she'd been electrocuted and it took her a few moments to compose herself. A quick glance in the mirror showed her a harried and wild-eyed version of herself, with unkempt hair and dark circles beneath her eyes. That was just as well. No one expected her to look like a glamour model after what she'd been through.

She took a deep breath and went to the door but she got another jolt when she looked out through the spyhole. It was the police.

It's OK, she told herself. *Deep breath. They* expect *you to look frantic and desperate.*

She threw open the door before she lost her nerve and turned a hopeful, pleading expression on the two men.

"Is there any news?" she asked breathlessly.

The older of the two officers had a kind, round face and streaks of grey at his temples. He shook his head sadly, his eyes full of pity. "I'm sorry, Mrs Seward."

Nicole blinked away tears as she offered them a brave little nod to show she understood.

"We're still searching," he continued, "but we need something from you."

"Anything," she was quick to gasp.

The older cop glanced at his younger partner as though steeling himself. Both men looked uncomfortable. For a moment Nicole thought it might be a trap and she held her breath for what felt like interminable minutes until he spoke again.

"Do you have something that Ashleigh might have worn recently?"

Nicole knew how she was meant to react. The implication of the question was that they didn't expect to find her alive, that they needed something for the dogs to use to find her body. The thought was horrifying and she didn't need to pretend it was anything else. She took a step back, one hand fluttering to cover her mouth.

"Oh God..."

The cop was quick to reassure her. "Now, Mrs Seward, don't lose hope. We're simply trying everything we can to find her. It's only been two days, after all."

Nicole nodded her head, her eyes closed. "I know, I know. I keep telling myself that. Please come in. I haven't washed anything since... Yes, come in. Sit down. I'll just go and see what I can find."

Her legs felt like rubber as she let the cops in and hurried upstairs to the nursery. She took her time looking through drawers at the baby's things. Soft pastel blankets, romper suits, a knitted hoodie, tiny socks, mittens, a snow hat. She snatched up a girly pink romper with Disney princesses on it. Ashleigh had worn it only once and it was clean now. Surely it retained no trace of her scent. Not that it really mattered. The police would be searching the woods, the parks, the beach. Anywhere a kidnapper might dispose of a tiny body.

"Will this do?" she asked in a tremulous voice. Her hand shook as she passed the tiny pink scrap of clothing to the officers.

They both offered her sympathetic smiles as they rose and the younger man held the romper suit as delicately as he would the child it had once clothed.

"I have a little girl the same age," he said sadly and Nicole heard the promise he wished he could make in his voice. "We'll keep looking" was all he could reasonably say.

"Thank you," Nicole said. At least no one expected her to play hostess. There was no need to offer tea and biscuits and entertain polite chat about the weather. She was exempt from all such social obligations now and it was a bizarre sense of freedom. "Please let me know if—well, if..."

"We will, Mrs Seward. Just stay strong and let us know if you think of anything or if you remember anything else about that day."

They meant the day she said she'd turned her back for a single moment in the park and found that her baby had been taken. That was the day she'd put nothing but a baby-shaped bundle of blankets into the pram. The day she'd dug her very first grave. The day she'd accused Roger of kidnapping their daughter. Unfortunately, he had an ironclad alibi—the tart he'd left her for—and although Nicole had done her best to suggest that both he and his new girlfriend were involved, too many people had seen them together that day for it to be plausible. The police had searched Roger's new apartment, of course, but found no evidence of a baby.

"I'll try," Nicole said bravely, forcing a pained little smile as she saw them to the door. She closed it behind them and sagged against it, her heart pounding so hard she thought it would deafen her.

But it was OK. Nobody suspected her. Two different families remembered seeing her in the park, pushing the pram up and down between the rows of tulips, bending down to coo at the baby and tuck the blankets around her as she slept. No one would ever ask them if they'd seen the actual *baby*.

Nicole had never wanted a child in the first place. But Roger had. He'd *said* he had anyway. He'd said a lot of things. Promised he'd always be there for her. And Ashleigh. Promised he'd never leave her. But he'd had his fill after six months. He couldn't cope with the crying, the chaos, the responsibility. He hated being tied down. The sleepless nights. The lack of sex. Oh, Nicole knew he'd been shagging around and she thought she could forgive him for that. But his little fling quickly blossomed into something more serious and one morning she came back from shopping with Ashleigh to find Roger gone. He hadn't even left a note.

Angry tears pricked her eyes as she remembered the desolate days that had followed. She didn't try to find him and beg him to come back. No, she had more dignity than that. And in truth she couldn't really blame him. The reality of childbirth and the mutilation of her body had been worse than she ever could have imagined. But the daily reality of the baby surpassed even that.

Nicole's needs were completely subsumed by the little screaming horror that demanded her attention every moment of the day. Oh, she was cute, yes—on the rare occasions when she was quiet—but any affection Nicole had had for her went with Roger. Soon the baby was nothing but a bitter reminder of how she'd been used and abused and left with an impossible burden. A burden that would only grow and become needier and more demanding every single day of her life.

Ashleigh never slept. At least that was how it seemed to Nicole. And she was never silent. If she wasn't splitting Nicole's ears with full-throated screams she was uttering piercing little staccato shrieks. No doubt it was fun to make loud noises and watch her mother jump. But even in the dead of night, with all the doors between them closed, Nicole could hear Ashleigh babbling, kicking the plastic sides of the cot, yanking at the mobile above her that played mindless, repetitive children's songs. Crying, coughing, squealing, screaming.

The noise was endless and Nicole had felt her mind begin to unravel under the sensory assault.

Nicole pushed the memories away. She didn't have to think about such things any more. It was over now and her life was her own again. And if she hadn't been able to implicate Roger, well, at least she'd planted the seed in his own mind that his baby had been kidnapped because he hadn't been there to protect her.

She smiled as she made her way to the kitchen and looked out the window. The rain had started in earnest and it was sprinkling down on the lawn, washing away the worm casts and compressing the soil over Ashleigh's grave. Soon there would be nothing left to worry about.

The next morning the worm casts had returned. And this time they were bigger.

Nicole's stomach fluttered at the sight. Just like the hideous flowers, the worm casts had grown. They were as thick as fingers now, spreading out from the raintree and snaking their way towards the house. They covered half the lawn already.

When she opened the door she immediately smelled the rich and pungent reek of wet earth. It wasn't as terrible as the rotting stench of the flowers had been but it was overpowering. Perhaps the rain had driven the worms mad. They'd gone crazy digging tunnels in the wet night. She could think of any number of excuses for the phenomenon. Anything to avoid the possibility that there was something else at work.

If she stared too long at the wild loops and scrawls she would start to see words again and hear voices, see that screaming face carved into the ground. But no matter how strange they seemed, they were just worm casts. She was determined to believe that.

One thought kept nudging at her mind. That the worms had tasted the delicacy she'd planted by the tree, that it had driven them mad. Or perhaps they weren't worms at all. Her heart tumbled a little at that idea and she reluctantly turned towards the tree.

To her relief she saw that the flowers hadn't returned. The turf looked undisturbed, if still a little pale, and the surrounding lawn was riddled with worm casts. However, there were none on the grave itself.

It was the turf, she reasoned. Perhaps it was still too loose for the worms to wriggle up through it from the churned soil beneath. But that didn't explain why the new casts seemed to radiate out from the grave. Or why they were so much bigger now. Or why they seemed to be advancing on the house.

Enough. Her head was splitting. She couldn't think about this now, couldn't allow herself to get worked up over nothing or her guilt would be written on her face the next time the nice policemen came to reassure her that they were doing their best to find her baby. Best just to stay inside, away from the windows, take a couple of pills and sleep. She could face the next day with a clear head and the knowledge that every day brought her closer to the end of the whole ordeal.

The sound reached her slowly. A weak and feeble knocking. She bolted upright in bed, her heart leaping. She waited for the sound to recede with the remnants of her dream but it did not. It was faint, but steady and determined.

It took Nicole some time to realise there was someone at the door. It was 2.57 a.m. No one but the police would call so late. But why? Her blood turned to ice water at the thought. With a curse she pulled on her dressing gown and hurried down the stairs.

She looked through the spyhole but there was no one there. Nothing but shadow.

But the knocking continued.

It was soft, more an irregular thumping than a proper knock. And it sounded like it was coming from the base of the door. Something about that wasn't right. It showed no sign of stopping and she was terrified of waking the neighbours.

Slowly she unlocked the door and inched it open to peer outside. There was no one on the porch. But there was something there, in the shadows. Had someone left her a parcel?

She knelt down to look and recoiled when she saw what it was. A bin bag. Just like the one she'd thrown into the skip the day before. Her hands trembled as she reached for it, not wanting to open it, not wanting to see, but unable to prevent it. The knot was undone and she peeled the bag open. And bit back a scream.

Lying in a bed of damp earth were the flowers. At least she thought they were the flowers. As her eyes adjusted to the gloom she realised it was nothing of the kind. It was a hand. A tiny hand about the size and colour of a baked fig. The hand was attached to a tiny arm that ended in a ragged dark stump. Below that was a leg. And beyond it was a bigger shape, shrouded in the shadow of the bag. Nicole thought she could see the gleam of two piercing points of light.

She scrambled to her feet and slammed the door, frantically pawing at the locks. The wet thumping began again and Nicole backed away into the house, shaking her head.

"I'm sorry," she whispered, again and again.

When she slipped and fell she cried out. Her head struck the hard floor and she saw sparks for several seconds. Dazed, she sat up. Her vision was swimming and the smell of earth was heavy in the air. She must have tracked mud into the house.

Then she heard the scratching. It sounded like thousands of tiny creatures picking at the floorboards with tiny claws. *Scritch, scritch, scritch*. No, actually it was more like teeth. Like needle-sharp teeth gnawing at wood.

She levered herself up and clutched the back of a chair for support as she struggled to her feet. The room swam and for a moment she was afraid she was going to pass out. Bile rose in her throat at the sweet stink of rot and wet earth.

When the first barb stung her bare foot she gasped and swatted at it. The motion made her dizzy and she fell heavily on her hip. She cried out as whatever had bitten her struck again, this time between the toes of her other foot. The pain was astonishing and she flailed in the dark at whatever it was. Wasps? Rats? A snake?

Suddenly her legs were alive with pain, as though she had been pierced by several needles all at once. She screamed, pinwheeling her arms desperately at the shadows. She tried to get to her feet but her legs had got tangled in something and she couldn't move.

Light flared brightly in the room as a lorry trundled by outside, illuminating her surroundings. What she saw in that moment was impossible. It looked as though the worms had burrowed up through the floorboards into the house, filling the room with muddy casts. Except it wasn't worms that were attacking her. From each of the little furrows stretched thin black tendrils, tipped with vicious barbs. Several were already wound tightly around her lower legs, coiling and cutting deeply into her skin. They burned like the stinging tentacles of a jellyfish and she could smell the scorched skin as her flesh began to dissolve under their grinding acid touch.

Frozen in horror and pain, Nicole was helpless to move. Her final scream was cut off as a gleaming black filament slithered down her throat. She thrashed and struggled as the tendrils swarmed over her body, cocooning her as a spider might before squeezing her into stillness.

From somewhere uncomfortably close she thought she could hear a baby crying.

THE LANGUAGE OF THE CITY

IT WAS JUST AFTER THE FUNERAL THAT THE CITIES BEGAN to call to me. I remembered their voices from years before and I had hoped never to hear them again. I have always been afraid of cities. It's not the noise or the pollution, the crowds or the crime. It's the cities themselves. They terrify me. They're alive. And they hate us.

I was six years old when I first realised they were aware of me. My parents had taken me to London for the weekend, a million miles from our tiny village in Dorset. I felt like we were on another planet. I had never seen so many people, so many buildings, so much traffic. Everything was freakishly huge. And the noise!

The first day passed by in a blur. On the second day we went to Westminster Abbey. The gothic behemoth towered over us, its jagged spires threatening to skewer the birds. The building was intimidating enough, but then, as I stared up at those monstrous towers, I suddenly felt a presence. Although the sun was shining brightly, it was as though I'd stepped into a deep pool of shadow. Something pierced my feet, slithered up my body and made me begin to shiver uncontrollably. My parents had no idea that anything was wrong, and they just kept walking, pulling me along with them. But behind me I sensed an icy malevolence, as though the city were coiling like a serpent at my back, poised to strike. I could almost hear it hissing.

I didn't dare look back. I clutched my father's hand as we made our way through the crowded street. We queued with what seemed like the population of the whole world to get into the abbey. I didn't like the claustrophobic press of strangers but the lurking city behind me felt like a much greater threat, a gathering storm or an impending earthquake. I kept expecting the ground to rumble and open up beneath my feet like a mouth.

The feeling stayed with me all that day and lingered long after we'd returned home. My parents knew something was wrong. It was obvious that I hadn't enjoyed the visit, but I remained tight-lipped about why. Eventually, they stopped asking.

But even if I had wanted to keep that awful experience to myself, it was too late. My subconscious had been infected. I would wake screaming from nightmares, plagued by voices that whispered to me while I slept. My parents worried about schizophrenia, but a battery of tests proved that I was as sane as they were. And over time I almost began to believe it.

Years passed. Village life settled into its familiar, uneventful routines and eventually the echo of the city began to fade. My parents never brought it up again and neither did I. Even so, I refused to believe that it had just been an hallucination. The dreams, while less frequent and less traumatic, never went away completely.

Many years later I found myself going back to London. I had to face my fear, to prove to myself that I hadn't just imagined the whole thing.

I hadn't.

I visited other cities to see if they had the same effect on me. Plymouth, Southampton, Portsmouth, Brighton—all left me feeling anxious and slightly ill. But none of them filled me with terror the way London had. I wondered whether it would be safe to venture further afield. I was loath to leave the safety of my rural surroundings, but I needed to pursue a career, and they don't build universities in tiny villages.

York seemed like a good compromise. It was still a city, but nothing approaching the seething metropolises of places like London or Birmingham or Manchester. I lived there for three years, studying art and interactive media, honing the skills that would allow me to work from the safety of the home I longed to return to, a place where I could live well beyond the reach of any city.

Three years. It wasn't easy. Not a day passed without my sensing the restless shifting of the cobbled streets, the lurching and grinding of enclosing walls. I was the one who thought I was moving freely, and yet I felt stalked by my very surroundings. It was as though I were walking across a frozen lake, the spectre of the city dogging my steps beneath me, under the ice. I suffered terrible headaches and nausea, which I attributed to the endless looping nightmares the city gave me.

In these dreams I imagined myself seeing through the veneer of the familiar to the structure beneath. Solid objects broke apart, separating like oil from water. I could see beyond form to the molecular components within, visualise each single particle with agonising clarity. Atoms scurried visibly across the spectrum of my dreams, so horribly acute it burned my eyes to see.

These visions persisted into my waking hours, laid like lenses over my eyes, forcing me to see what others couldn't. I would look at the curve of a street and see a malicious sneer. The cornerstones of buildings were claws embedded in the pavement. Sometimes I saw them move, ready to score and rend the flesh of their foundations, to uproot themselves and creep along behind me. Even the air around me took on a sense of menace, as though I were inhaling poisonous gas with every breath.

I succumbed to periods of black despair. Fantasies of blinding myself began to pervade my thoughts, even though the visions were only a fraction of the horror. I couldn't shut out the insidious whispering, or protect myself from the rancid taste of the air. I was convinced that my mind would shatter like glass.

Early one morning I woke feeling dizzy. Gradually I opened my eyes, expecting to see the familiar surroundings of my bedroom. Instead, I found myself perched on the city wall, gazing down at the steeply sloping hill. I had one leg up on the stone, as though I were mounting a horse. I cried out and pushed myself back, instantly wide awake. I had no way of knowing whether the fall would have killed me or not, but I didn't care. I had had enough. I left that day and fled home to Dorset. With every mile I travelled away from York, I felt better. Away from the urban jungle, normality at last returned.

I hadn't finished my degree, but it didn't matter. I knew enough to get myself started, and soon I was designing websites for small businesses in the area, many of whom were as fearful of the Internet as I was of cities.

But the Internet made sense. Computers and code made sense. There were patterns in everything, patterns like the ones I had always seen in the city. But these were patterns I could control. Web design was neither science nor art, although it drew from both. I enjoyed manipulating data to create structure, found comfort in the knowledge that numbers were at the root of everything. Numbers could be understood. Numbers could be controlled. I was an architect of information and the only traffic I had to negotiate was virtual.

Beyond the reach of cities, I began to feel safe once more. I was no longer plagued by nightmares or visions. People regarded me as reclusive, perhaps a bit eccentric, but there was no suggestion that they knew I had only narrowly escaped madness and death. To them I was just a fellow villager, not one of those *city folk*.

And then I met Edward. He was the first person I had ever loved, and the only one I ever fully trusted. He even trusted me enough to love me back. After a couple of years, we got married and lived like ordinary people.

Until a city took him from me.

For twenty years the headquarters of the high street shop he managed had been in Bournemouth. Then the company was bought out by a large corporation, and they were based in London. A promotion followed, with one catch: Edward would have to relocate.

My heart pounded with terror at the prospect and all my worst dreams came back to me. I saw myself strangled by ropes of winding streets, crushed by looming buildings, smothered by the oppressive atmosphere. So I gave him a choice: London or me. He chose London.

Some weeks later his body was found by a group of urban explorers in a disused passageway at Moorgate Station. They had already taken a series of photographs prominently featuring what they'd assumed was just a pile of filthy rags. Then they moved closer and realised the truth.

Edward was mangled beyond recognition, and only dental records confirmed his identity. No one could explain what he was doing there, or indeed, how he had even found the place, especially as the photographers themselves had needed bolt cutters to access a service door that led them into the tunnels. Foul play was suggested and, naturally, I was the first and most likely suspect. But enough people had seen me around the village at the time, many miles from London, that it was obvious I couldn't have had anything to do with it.

Eventually the police pieced together a series of events that added up to "death by misadventure". Edward had apparently fallen down an abandoned lift shaft and then crawled into the passageway to die of his injuries. A tragic accident.

But I knew better. I knew the city had killed him.

I let his family handle the arrangements and I stayed well away from the funeral. Nobody missed me. I kept my head down and buried myself in work, finding reassurance in the predictability of code, the security of numbers.

That was when I began to hear them again. The cities. At first they only spoke to me in dreams, in visions of such harrowing clarity and strangeness that I thought I must finally be losing my mind. In sleep I found myself in a London that didn't exist, that couldn't possibly exist. I climbed long flights of crumbling stairs and wandered lost through dank, misshapen corridors and rotting alleyways. Once again I saw the secret design beneath the manmade constructs. The canted walls and impossible angles tormented me. I woke in a cold sweat night after night, my mouth forming meaningless words, my voice uttering meaningless syllables.

More than once I was woken by the sound of neighbours pounding on my door. They said I had been screaming. They said it sounded like I was being tortured. I reassured them on each occasion that it was just bad dreams. Someone suggested it was the shock of Edward's death, and I gratefully seized on the excuse. People are always happier with explanations they can understand.

The nightmares were bad enough. But then I began to see other things. Like the mould.

It began as a small downy patch of greenish grey on the wall, and at first I assumed it was just some dampness inside the wallpaper. But the longer I stared at it, the more I began to realise it was some kind of fungus, black and spongy, like rotten fruit. I scrubbed and scraped at it, but it was persistent. Determined.

Soon the wall became prickly with fibres and I peeled the ruined paper away, only to reveal more of the ugly stain behind it. The mould grew day by day, spreading rapidly, bubbling out from behind what remained of the paper. Now it covers an area the size of a door.

Every day it gets bigger, spreading like a disease. And as it takes hold in the wall, so the voices take hold in my mind.

It's a festering chorus, a city's discourse. The sound is somewhere between noise and music, simultaneously seductive and repellent. It beckons me even as I fight to resist its lure. I don't know how much longer I can hold out.

The wall is rotting away, and my sanity rots with it. What I see through the cracks terrifies me. I don't see into the next room; I see into *cities*. Like the effect of one mirror reflecting another into infinity, I see the endless propagation of their hellish particles, malignant spores that flicker and buzz like a faulty fluorescent light, creeping from my nightmares into my waking life. I hear their voices constantly. And I can understand at last what they are saying.

I thought I knew all about underlying structure and hidden meaning. It's the very essence of my job. Codes and ciphers. Interfaces. But the language of a city is something else entirely. It has no words, no grammar, nothing you can even comprehend as language. Yet still, it speaks. More than that— it *suggests*.

I feel the loathing, the cold, coiling malice in every tone, every nuance. It's the voice that lured Edward to his death. It opened the way for him into a hidden part of London and he had no choice but to follow. Now it wants me there. It wants me to *see*.

I must step through, into the rotting tunnel.

Into the city.

There is no way to climb through without touching the mould. I anticipate something wet and soggy, but when I brush against it, I find that it is curiously dry, like chalk. Some of it crumbles to dust at my feet. I am barely moving, yet it seems as though I have already travelled a long way, much farther than the actual physical distance between two places. The passage makes me think uncomfortably of a womb. A crisply burnt womb.

Fear takes root in my mind and soon it begins to blossom into panic, but the emotions don't reach my body. I am not alone. Something is controlling me from within, something that refuses to let me run away.

All around me I hear the humming voice of the city, the voice it shares with *all* cities. It throbs and pulses with menace. Trains rumble beneath the streets and I sense the pattern of their branching tunnels, their many levels and dead-ends. I can see the terrible design behind the system. All throughout the city people scurry like ants, entirely ignorant of the monstrous presence that surrounds them.

I emerge onto the platform of a derelict station, one where trains never come. The chipped tiles along the curved walls and ceiling are thickly furred with mould, blackened like a gangrenous wound. Fibrous tendrils spread out in every direction, strangling the ancient rails and taking root in the cavernous space beneath them. The threads reach for me like questing antennae, stinging where they touch my skin, breaking off to burrow inside. A distant part of me registers the pain, but I cannot make a sound.

I gaze down at the writhing coils. The tendrils part like fleshy hair as I peer through the rifts in the mould, looking further into the city. The understructure goes deep, deeper than my eyes can see. There is motion there, far in the distance. Shadows flow past like a river, maddeningly dark, but my vision is more acute than ever. The world is melting away.

There are so many layers. Layers upon layers. A building stands where a previous one was demolished, and before that, another. The city erases and rewrites itself constantly, a living palimpsest. Frenzied particles swarm throughout its boundless iterations, teeming like an infinite sequence of numbers, reflecting back onto itself without end. Part of me knows what I am seeing while another part tries to shield me from the revelation.

We are only creatures at the very edge of life, creatures who know nothing of what lies beyond our limited range of sensation. Dizziness overwhelms me at the thought that I am seeing beyond anything ever known or imagined.

I close my eyes, but it makes no difference. The mould is there behind my lids, undulating like a spill of ink into water, into the liquid of my eyes. My vision is infected, and all the more acute for it. Lines criss-cross one another, forming a mesh, a living network that connects me to everything I can see or perceive. Everything is moving, changing, shifting with a terrible speed that is too much for me to process. Except that something *forces* me to process it. The city. It is moving through me.

The knowledge is colonising my mind. I am the city's interface. It speaks. It screams. And I hear.

The fluid in my veins has changed, transmuted, and I know the mould for what it is—the blood of the city. My heart is a husk inside my chest, no longer performing any human function. All that remains is a dreadful awareness, too horrifying to contain within the remnants of my mind. I know why I was called. My madness is reshaping the city, clawing it apart to reveal its true face.

It is both unfathomably old and impossibly new. I stare into the heart of it, simultaneously into its far distant past and the infinite possibilities of its future, as it peels itself open, layer upon layer. Death, life, destruction, rebirth.

Soon there is only a barren stretch of ground, an empty wasteland devoid of life. A foetid wind stirs the powdery sand. Even the sky is sour, heavy with noxious spores. I feel them twitch inside my cold veins as the city awakens inside me.

I am seeing what will be. It's not the death of civilisation, because there is no civilisation. There is only the city. We delude ourselves into thinking we built all this, that we conceived it and designed it to serve our needs. But that's not true. *We're* the constructs. *We're* the ones who were built.

Through me, the city begins to speak. I feel cleansed by its presence and I let go, giving myself to it completely. I perceive with senses beyond mortal ones the changes beginning in other places. I see the spores drifting, the mould taking root.

The future is leaking through the crumbling edifices of the city, giving me glimpses of what is to come. It only needed one person to hear its voice, to open the way for it. Soon others will hear the voices too. They will open other doors, step through into other cities.

In Tokyo, a little girl picks at a scab of fungus on the wall of her school. In Paris, a bookseller spots a damp patch on the ceiling of his shop. In San Francisco, a hotel maid moves a chair to hide a discoloured spot on the carpet.

Everywhere, the city is opening the way to our ruin, decomposing from another time, a virus devouring the past. It rots backwards, into our hollow existence. Brick by brick, stone by stone, it will unmake itself. It will unmake *us*.

The Call of the Dreaming Moon

G HOSTLY PLUMES OF SMOKE ROSE FROM THE PEAKS OF the mountains as Sunoyi climbed to reach them, losing her way among the thinning trees and unfamiliar spiny plants. At last she came to an immense deep lake. It too was strange. It was wider than any lake she had ever seen and its waters boiled as if a great flame heated them from far beneath.

Through the waves she saw the darting silhouettes of terrible fish, their bodies huge and ungainly, as though the water was not their natural home. The creatures seemed to sense her nearness and she watched nervously as their movements began to slow. Soon they had stopped swimming entirely. The bulky shapes turned beneath the water and countless heads rose black and dripping above the surface, each with a gulping mouth that appeared to be trying to form words.

Sunoyi stepped back, her flesh crawling at the sight. The eyes of the fish were cold and empty and she knew they could see every dark thing in the world. They could see deep inside her and they knew her thoughts, her fears. She stared, unable to look away. Her eyes burned for want of blinking but she was transfixed. Soon her vision began to darken, as though someone were pouring black paint into her eyes. And then she saw beyond the darkness.

She stood now at the crest of the mountain, staring down with her new black eyes at the world below. The cold plateau was the grey of ashes and bones, the colour of eyes when all sight has gone from them. And swarming across its pale expanse were strange animals, so many more creatures than the Great Spirit could have made. So many more trees and plants. And in the impossible distance, so many more mountains. Mountains so vast they might reach all the way to the Upper World. Or perhaps to an even higher world above it, one her tribe knew nothing of.

In the centre of the dead plateau one creature stood apart from the others. At first it seemed human and she took it for a warrior of another tribe. But the unknown colours it wore could not be paint for they seemed to pour from the body of the creature itself, staining the ground beneath it. Inhuman sounds escaped its mouth, a mouth far too wide for its thin face. As she watched, it unfolded great dusty wings like those of a moth and turned to look at her, waving a multitude of spiky, jointed legs. Its eyes were the most terrible things she had ever seen. They were of an even deeper black than those of the gulping fish, a swallowing, bottomless black that threatened to reduce her mind to dust with the horror of its emptiness.

She trembled, wanting to run but unable to find the will. Her own eyes were burning with the sight, the visions becoming unbearable. In terror she clawed at her face, her fingers splitting and lengthening into vicious talons as she pierced the softness of her eyes. The pain was agony and she screamed. And then, as the fear-sickness spread through her mind, she began to laugh—a wild, hysterical and somehow liberating sound.

She woke violently, with Tawodi shaking her and calling her name. For several moments she glanced around blindly, in terror, before realising it had only been a dream. Gingerly she pressed her fingertips to her eyelids, relieved to discover that her eyes were whole and uninjured.

"What is it?" her husband asked with concern, gathering her in his arms.

"It was terrible," she gasped, but could think of no way to describe the awful visions. Worst of all was the terrifying sense of freedom she had felt at the end of the dream, when her mind had fully gone.

The sound of running feet reached her, along with concerned voices. The whole tribe was soon clustered around her, demanding to know what she had seen. The elders seemed to know something she didn't, as though it had been more than just a dream. At first she could only shake her head in bewilderment as she tried to remember, but gradually the images began to return.

"There was a lake," she said. "A very long and deep lake with black fish. And I stood on the highest mountain. Below there were . . . other creatures. One of them watched me with eyes as black as forever."

Ta'li Ajina, the medicine man, looked uneasily at the others before turning back to her. "You have been to the Edge of the World, my child," he said gravely. "You have seen forbidden sights."

Tawodi held his wife close, as though to shield her from what she had seen. "But Father, she has broken no law, done no wrong. Who has done this evil to her?"

Ta'li Ajina shook his head sadly. "No one. This is not witchcraft. It is the will of the Dreaming Moon." He clasped Sunoyi's hands and looked deeply into her eyes. "He has chosen you, my child. The place in your dream is real. You must go there. You must see what they wish you to see."

She clung to Tawodi, frightened and uncertain. "But I felt lost and separated from the world. From myself." She touched her forehead, indicating. "What if I can't come back?"

The old man's face creased with sorrow. "It is the risk you must take. The Edge of the World calls you."

The next night the moon rose high and full, painting the village blue with its fantastic light. Crickets sang in the whispering grass and from somewhere up in the mountains a golden panther screamed. The voice was so much like a woman's and Sunoyi shuddered to hear it. She couldn't help but wonder if her own screams would be heard tonight.

The tribe had gathered to wish her well. They sang and danced round the crackling fire but only Sunoyi was given the Black Drink. It would hasten her return to the dream. She drank, wincing at its bitter taste. Soon her body was contorted with pain and she fell to her knees, heaving and purging herself of the foul liquid. The magic poison it left behind in her body would protect her.

In her trembling hands she clutched two small stones, given to her by the chief. Animals were painted on their smooth surfaces. One would give her the courage of Wahya, the wolf, the other the swiftness of Ahwi, the deer. As the sickness passed her eyes grew heavy and the dancing feet around her began to blur and spin into multiple images of swirling colour. The fire leapt higher, the sparks soaring like tiny birds set alight and the beat of tribal drums became the beating of wings. She heard her husband's voice, praying for her safe return. She felt his kiss and then all was darkness.

She opened her eyes in cold silence. The fire had faded to glowing embers and the tribe lay sleeping all around it in deep pools of liquid shadow. Confused, she raised her head and clambered to her feet. As her eyes adjusted to the moonlit scene she realised with horror that they were not asleep. They were dead. Her husband, the medicine man, the chief. All dead.

Tears welled in her eyes and she lowered her head. Then she gave a little cry at what she saw at her feet. She knew the young woman well, had seen her many times before, reflected back at her in the clear waters of the pond and in her husband's eyes. The totem stones lay beside Sunoyi's silent body, released from her limp hands. She must be dead herself to be seeing her own body. Had the visions killed her?

A piercing animal cry shook her out of her confusion and her thoughts cleared at once. What she was seeing was not the world of flesh and blood. She had returned to the dream.

Her heart pounding, she took her first uncertain steps away from the dying fire and the bodies of her companions. She hoped they only appeared dead to her sleeping mind. She had to believe that or grief and fear would destroy her. Above her the moon shone like a glaring eye, cold and cruel, as she left the safety of the camp. The mountain was calling.

The winding path was hidden in shadow and she heard the scurrying of creatures beyond. Some sounded tiny and fearful and she wondered what was making them run. There were other sounds too. Large shifting noises, like the shuffling of immense feet, the snapping of huge mouths. Something shrieked then, close by, and she whirled round with a cry, clutching the little flint dagger Tawodi had made for her. She was a hunter but not a warrior and she was terrified of the things she knew were lying in wait for her.

The crash of rolling waves reached her ears and she pressed on, guided by the sound of the water. The vast lake lay up ahead and she heard the voice of the terrible fish, calling as one, calling *her*. She couldn't see them against the blackness of the water but she could feel their eyes on her.

With a shudder she turned away, towards the Edge of the World. Chaos had come. The sky churned, blood-red in the unnatural night. Shards of light split the darkness with a terrifying crash, illuminating the living things all around her. Baleful eyes turned to her, gleaming with hatred, but she could not see the one who had summoned her, the black-eyed creature with the moth wings.

She heard the damp step of something behind her and knew that the fish had crept out of the lake. They stood whispering behind her, reaching out to touch her with their dripping fins. Her fingers trembled on the handle of her dagger as she turned to see. They stood upright, large as bears, their slick mouths gulping, their hideous pink gills flaring.

"What are you?" she forced herself to ask. "What am I here to see?"

But they only continued to gulp, turning their awful heads to look upon the scene below. Then they inched towards her.

She recoiled from the slimy wet slap of their fins against the ground but there was nowhere to go. They had herded her to the edge. Below lay the cold plateau, strewn with creatures she didn't want to face, indescribable creatures that called her, speaking her name in guttural tones. The dagger wavered in her hand as she brandished it but the fish were not deterred. They shuffled forwards, their intention horrifyingly clear. She could never hope to kill them all.

There was only one place to go. She closed her eyes and jumped.

It took her endless moments to realise that she had reached the bottom and that the fall had not killed her.

She lay in the dust of the ash-grey plateau and all around her was the sound of hissing, slithering things as they came towards her. She had dropped the dagger.

Backing away, she clawed frantically at her back, feeling for her bow. Her arrows lay scattered around her and she snatched one up and slipped it into the notch of the bow, raised it and aimed. Her fingers trembled and she loosed the arrow quickly. Still, it struck one of the creatures, a toad-like thing with pincers and scores of tiny red eyes.

The beast screamed, rearing back in rage and pain. It flailed at the wound and Sunoyi gasped as she saw its skin flicker, changing colour like the shell of a beetle in the sunlight. Blood seeped into the dust at its feet and it lurched towards her, its flesh like mud, soft and shifting.

Sunoyi lifted the bow again but the creature gave another howl and scuttled away. She carefully got to her feet, turning in a circle to see how many more there were. They were monstrous to look at but it seemed they were easily wounded and easily frightened. She spied the dagger lying a few feet away and she inched towards it until she was able to drop to her knees and grab it. The creatures parted for her, clacking insectoid jaws she couldn't see but only hear.

She slung her bow over her arm and held the dagger out in front of her as she advanced along the plateau. A foetid mist was rolling down from the mountains all around her and Sunoyi felt dizzy looking up at it. How could she have fallen so far and survived? For a moment her confusion threatened to disorientate her and she reminded herself that this was all a dream.

But hadn't the medicine man told her that the Edge of the World was real? She looked up at the Dreaming Moon but the churning red eye offered no guidance. What if she never woke from the dream? Worse still, what if all the creatures around her were dreaming too? What happened if they woke alongside her?

She shuddered and continued on. She had no idea where she was going but she felt pulled in the direction of the descending mist. The creatures quivered as they moved aside for her, giving strange voice to their fear. The one she had wounded stayed closest, burbling like a leaf-choked stream. She felt lulled by the sounds they made, as though they were honouring her in their alien language, changing her name to one of their own.

The fog made her wary. She didn't like the idea of being lost in it. But the creatures had begun to hang back. They seemed unwilling to follow her any further. Sunoyi took a deep breath and plunged forwards, into the swirling arms of the mist.

It enveloped her like smoke, writhing around her like the ghosts of a thousand snakes. It smelled of colours and tasted of sound and almost immediately she found herself yielding to its seductive embrace. The vapour seeped into her mouth, her nose, her eyes. She gasped as it slipped beneath her deerskin tunic, teasing her skin with a powdery touch that was unnervingly pleasant. She felt as though she were drowning in the air.

And then he was there. The black-eyed moth.

He rose on four of his many legs, his great wings unfolding above her. Light streamed through jagged rents in his wings and she saw that his body was little more than a husk, a papery shell like the cicadas left behind when they woke from the strange sleep during which they grew wings. Sunoyi sensed that this creature was very old. Older than the wisest chief, the oldest tribe, older even than the world and all the living things that had ever walked upon it.

She met his black eyes and her mouth opened as if to scream although she herself felt no fear. There was something human in the face that peered down at her, something of remembered movement in the spiky legs it wrapped around her.

Without thinking Sunoyi raised the dagger and plunged it into the creature's body. It sank with a solid crunch, disappearing inside. But there was no cry of fury, no spasm of pain. Instead the creature clutched her tightly and drew her close. Now she did scream, as her body pressed against the brittle husk. Her hands crushed its outer shell and she felt something soft and sticky within it, like sap inside a tree. Uncountable legs enfolded her and she struggled desperately but to no avail.

It was then that she realised the creature was singing. Its voice was so alien she thought her ears would burst from the sound of it. Each whispered exhalation was like a knife slitting the threads of her mind one by one. She felt the nearness of death and something beyond, something distinctly *other*. She dug inside the monster's body, searching for her dagger.

All at once her back was alive with searing pain. Time seemed to slow as she struggled to see anything but the clutching legs and crumbling husk of the creature holding her tightly in its grasp. Its wings began to beat. Slowly, purposefully. The fog swirled around them and the pale dust of the plateau rose into the sky like a swarm of tiny insects, and they rose with it.

Sunoyi cried out again but no sound came. She was past believing any of this was a dream and she knew that if she woke now she would fall and die. Far below she could see the hideous forms of the creatures that had first tested her and then led her to the monster that held her now.

It carried her higher and higher, up to where only the mighty condor flew, and then it flew higher. The world below was a writhing mass of insignificance, of tiny lives that were of no consequence to the terrible world in which she now found herself. But all the while her captor continued to sing, its voice transforming her like slow, delicious poison.

At last she found the dagger. She pulled it free and began to hack at the creature's left wing as it carried her over the range of jagged mountains. It seemed to feel no pain as she chopped and sawed through the papery skin and crumbling bone. For a moment she even thought she heard it laugh.

When the creature dropped her she screamed. She fell and fell and fell, her arms and legs flailing in the air as she tumbled towards the grey expanse that was rushing to meet her. She was ready to die, ready to hit the ground and be torn from life forever. It took her a long time to realise that she was no longer falling; she was flying.

Extending to either side of her were large powdery wings, like those of a moth. And as she fluttered to the floor of the ash-grey plateau she realised with a dawning sense of terrible joy why she had been chosen. The creature who had transformed her lay in the dust a few feet away, its sole wing thumping uselessly on the ground.

It was not the Dreaming Moon that had brought her here but the creature itself, the one with wings like hers and eyes like the end of everything.

And as she flexed her wings she began to smile. All around her were voices raised in strange song. The toad-like creatures, the fish, the hidden monsters in the trees and mountains and the crawling things beneath the dead earth. They all sang for her, praising her, welcoming her.

And the creature that had once been Sunoyi raised her head and gazed with wild black eyes at the sleeping sky. Soon the tribe would wake her and she would lead the dream-creatures out, into the waking world.

Guinea Pig Girl

S HE WAS BEAUTIFUL. QUITE THE MOST BEAUTIFUL woman Alex had ever seen. But it wasn't just her beauty. What he loved most about her was the way she suffered.

He had been horrified the first time. He'd felt the stirring in his loins and then the growing hardness in his trousers. A sidelong glance at his mate Josh, whose film it was, then some uncomfortable shifting.

"Holy shit," Josh said with a laugh as the freak in the lab coat cut off one of Yuki's fingers.

She screamed, her beautiful mouth stretched open, her slanted eyes as wide as they would go. She screamed. Josh laughed. Alex got hard.

"Yeah," he said, to say something. Then he squirmed as Yuki's torture continued and his erection grew.

Oh, how she suffered.

That night he'd wanked himself silly over the image of her terrified, pleading face. He didn't dare go as far as imagining himself pinning her down on the filthy mattress in the basement room, fisting a hand in her long black hair and telling her how he would take her to bits, piece by piece. No, he didn't dare. The image flickered in the background of his thoughts but he shied away from it. Pictured himself instead as the guy who came to tend her wounds, give her water and a bit of food, hold her and reassure her that he would help her escape if he could, honest, but they were watching him too...

It was sick.

He felt ashamed and disgusted once the last throbs of pleasure had faded and he'd cleaned himself up and thrown the handful of tissues in the bin, wishing he could incinerate them. He felt as filthy as the room she'd been imprisoned in throughout the film. He'd let himself go this time but that was it. He didn't get off on stuff like that, no way. In junior school some bullies had once tried to make him join in with torturing old Mrs Webber's cat and he hadn't been able to do it. *He'd* suffered then, suffered their ridicule and taunting, them calling him a pussy. But he wasn't like them, couldn't bring himself to hurt something else, something helpless.

So why did Yuki make him feel like this?

Days later he still couldn't get some of the imagery out of his head. It was just some dodgy Japanese torture porn film he couldn't even remember the name of but he remembered every moment of every scene Yuki was in. She was tiny and fragile, the way so many Japanese girls were. Sexy and girlish, slutty and innocent all at the same time. An intoxicating package in any context but seeing her so helpless and vulnerable had done something to Alex. That wounded expression, her eyes streaming with tears, her hands clasped as she pleaded in words he couldn't understand... It got under his skin.

He'd wanted to dive into the film and save her, protect her, and yet that wasn't where his fantasies steered him afterwards. On the way to work his hands had clenched on the steering wheel as he sat in traffic and he imagined them wrapped around Yuki's slender throat. If he closed his eyes he could hear her gasping for breath. He could smell her urine as she pissed herself in terror.

Sick.

And yet every night his hand slipped down between his legs and all it took was the thought of her wide eyes and high-pitched cries to make him unbearably aroused. He couldn't banish the images. All he could do was let them wash over him as he came so hard his ears rang. Again and again.

✦ ✦ ✦

Yuki Hayashi. Actress. Born 13 April 1989 in Hokkaido, Japan. Filmography: *Victim Factory 1 & 2*, *Love Hotel of the Damned* and *Aesthetic Paranoia* (filming).

Alex clicked on each film and read the synopses. They were all low-budget rip-offs of the notorious "guinea pig" films from the '80s. Girls got kidnapped and tortured and that was basically it. Sometimes they also got raped.

The fourth one in the filmography wasn't finished yet and *Love Hotel of the Damned* didn't seem to be available anywhere, not even on Josh's pirate site. But Alex ordered the others.

Like all rip-offs, *Victim Factory* aspired to take things a step further than its inspiration. The gore was over the top, even by Alex's standards, and it was made worse by the homemade feel of the production. They looked like snuff films shot on someone's home video camera.

Yuki's debut was as "2nd victim" in an unpleasant scene where she was grabbed off the street and taken to an abandoned asylum. There she was stripped naked and thrown into a room stained with the blood of previous victims. To wait. After listening in terror to the screams and cries of another girl, Yuki was dragged off to the torture chamber next door for her turn. The killer bound her wrists tightly with rope and looped them over a large hook. He turned a crank that noisily hoisted her off the ground while she screamed and wept and kicked her pretty legs. Even her slight weight looked as though it was dislocating her shoulders and Alex winced. How could you fake *that*?

Finally, in a bizarre moment of artistry, the killer carved a series of Japanese characters into Yuki's skin with the jagged edge of a broken samurai sword. The subtitles only translated the spoken dialogue so Alex had no idea what the words inscribed on her flesh meant.

It drove him mad.

The exotic swashes and flourishes streamed with blood that looked disturbingly real, a striking contrast to Yuki's pale skin. Alex could almost believe that the mutilation had actually happened but for the fact that in the second film, the one Josh had shown him, she was unmarked. Pristine and ready for more. Ready to have her fingers and toes snipped off one by one, her mouth forced open with a metal dentist's gag and her tongue cut out.

He searched the Net for more information but the films didn't appear to be widely known. There was the occasional mention on a message board but Alex couldn't find any translation for the characters in the carving scene. Nor was there much information about Yuki. He found one screen grab from the first film, which he immediately stored on his phone. Her eyes pleaded with him through the image and he felt obscurely guilty, as though he'd imprisoned her in a tiny digital cage. But he didn't delete the picture.

The films made him feel uncomfortable, almost sick at times. And truthfully, he didn't enjoy the violence. When he played the DVDs again he only watched the scenes with Yuki and even then he felt funny afterwards. But he couldn't get her out of his head. The very thought of her was enough to make him hard and even though he tried to picture her whole and undamaged, the images of torture would quickly take over. He tried to imagine her voice, cheerful and sweet as she chattered on her phone before being abducted in each film, but the musical sounds always devolved into screams of pain and madness.

Her anguish was so excruciatingly *real*. He couldn't tune it out, couldn't un-see it. And he couldn't help the effect it had on him.

She was there behind his eyes every night, pleading with him to stop, her tiny body struggling helplessly against ropes and rusty chains. And no matter how much he tried to transform the images in his head, he always saw himself wielding the blades, the needles, the bolt cutters. Her blood ran like wine over his hands and he was drunk on the taste of her.

"Hey, mate, you know that DVD you were after?"

Alex froze, staring at his phone with apprehension. Then he took a deep breath before forcing himself to ask calmly, "Which one?"

"*Love Hotel of the Damned*. I found it."

"Oh, cool," he replied, as nonchalantly as he could manage.

"Yeah, some guy up in Leeds has it and he said he'd burn me a copy for a tenner."

"Thanks, mate. I'll pay you back."

"No problem!" Josh sounded pleased, no doubt proud of himself for tracking down the obscure film. If he had any suspicions about Alex's obsession it wasn't obvious. "I'll drop it by your place next week."

Next week. Alex felt his insides churn hungrily at the thought of seeing Yuki again, seeing her suffer and die in new and terrible ways.

The synopsis of *Love Hotel* made it sound like the worst of the lot. Same "guinea pig" concept but this time set in one of those weird Japanese hotels he'd read about online. The kind where you could fuck a manga character on a spaceship or grope a schoolgirl in a room designed like a train carriage. He'd found the trailer for the film on a J-horror fan site and it looked seriously reprehensible. Even some of the hardcore gorehounds said the level of sexual violence was too much for them.

Alex slid down in his chair as his cock began to stir.

The film was even worse than he'd anticipated. Murky and grainy, as though someone had simply held up a cheap camera and filmed it playing on a TV. The poor quality actually made the gore seem more realistic.

Yuki didn't appear until halfway through and Alex almost didn't recognise her. She was thinner and paler and she seemed even more fragile. But she was still beautiful. She wore an elaborate gothic Lolita dress with frilly petticoats and a lacy apron and mop cap. But not for long. Her "customer" cut the flimsy costume away with a pair of shears. From the way Yuki yelped and twisted, it was clear he was cutting her too. Blood trickled down one arm and over her belly and she stared straight into the camera for one heart-stopping moment. Alex had the uncomfortable sense that he was watching a genuine victim this time and not an actress.

His thumb hovered over the STOP button for a few seconds before he reminded himself that there was a fourth film on the list. *Aesthetic Paranoia*, which she was apparently still shooting. If this was real, surely she wouldn't have made another such film. Surely she'd be shouting "Police!" or "Help!" He was sure he'd recognise that level of distress even in a language he couldn't speak. No, it was just that weird sense of authenticity you sometimes got with ultra low-budget films.

Yuki cried and begged in plaintive Japanese while the man stripped the mattress off the bed and threw her onto the bare springs. He bound her, spread-eagled, with wire that Alex could see biting into her delicate wrists and ankles. Then he threw a bucket of water over her and she screamed again and again, writhing on the springs.

The man lifted the head of the bed and propped it against the wall so that it rested at an angle. The camera zoomed in and around Yuki's naked, shivering body, shooting from underneath the bed to show the mesh pressing painfully into her back, the wires cutting into her skin. In close-up the springs looked rusty and Yuki was bleeding in several places. The detail was too subtle not to be real and Alex began to feel lightheaded again. But he couldn't tear his eyes away.

The man held up a series of huge fishhooks with what looked like electrodes attached and Yuki screamed herself hoarse as the hooks were threaded through her skin one by one in a scene that went on for nearly ten minutes. When he was done, the man connected the trailing wires to a machine at his feet. He pressed a button and there was a terrible buzzing sound, followed by another piercing scream. Yuki leapt and bucked against the springs for what felt like an eternity before the current stopped. Wisps of smoke began to rise from the contact points and Alex thought he could smell something burning. Blood ran from Yuki's eyes like tears as she gasped and panted, too breathless to scream. The camera zoomed in on her face and she stared directly out of the screen again, as though she were looking through a window right at Alex.

When the buzzing sound began again Yuki tensed and started to plead frantically, this time with whoever was behind the camera. Alex closed his eyes against her screams and the metallic rattle of the springs and the zap of electricity. He held his breath as it went on and on, wishing it would end.

At last there was silence. Silence and the smell of scorched meat. He shut the film off and ran for the bathroom. He almost made it.

It was several days before Yuki came back.

Alex had put the three DVDs in a carrier bag, knotted it and pushed it to the back of the bathroom cupboard. When Josh had asked how he liked the film he'd forced a laugh and said it was rubbish, with crappy effects. And if his voice had trembled when he'd said it, Josh didn't seem to notice. Yuki's picture was gone from his phone and the J-horror sites he'd bookmarked were erased from his browsing history.

As disturbing as it had been, he knew it was fake. That was part of the point of films like that—to trick the viewer into thinking it was real. Actual snuff films were an urban legend. None had ever been found and they certainly wouldn't be readily available online in any case. People had been fooled by special effects before. And while it was a compliment to the makers of Yuki's films, Alex had seen enough.

He was in bed, almost asleep, when he first heard the sound. A soft rustle, as though someone were reading a newspaper in the next room. He froze. He had the mad urge to call out "Who's there?" even though there was no one else in the flat. Unless someone had broken in. It was that kind of neighbourhood but the flat was too small for a burglar to hide in without Alex knowing. A rat, then? It would have to be an awfully big one.

His heart hammered in his chest, drowning out any sounds that might be coming from the other room. Seconds passed like hours as he sat staring towards the open doorway, feeling like a child who'd woken from a nightmare. He should get up and switch on all the lights but the thought of putting his feet on the floor, exposing them to the empty space under the bed, was too frightening.

"Get a grip," he mouthed, trying to spur himself into action. But still he didn't move.

There was another sound. A soft slap, like a bare foot on the hard floor. Then another. And another.

His blood turned to ice water as the footsteps came closer and closer. A thin shape was emerging from the darkness of the corridor. Then he heard the dripping. He could almost believe it was some girl he'd brought home from a club and forgotten about. She'd just got out of the shower without drying off and now...

Except it wasn't. It was Yuki.

When she reached the bedroom Alex bit back a scream. She stood in the doorway, naked and dripping with blood. Her arms hung loose at her sides and Alex's stomach clenched as he saw the symbols carved into her body. The calligraphy was more extensive than he remembered from the scene in the film. The cuts ran from the base of her throat, across her small breasts and down her torso.

A strangled sound escaped his throat and Yuki's head turned towards him. It was a careful, deliberate movement, as though she had only located him by the sound and was trying to fix his exact position. She turned and took a step into the room. Alex stared at her in horror, desperate to run but unable to move.

It wasn't real. It *couldn't* be real. It was a dream or a hallucination, just like the images in his head he hadn't been able to get rid of. But worst of all, he felt himself responding as he always had. Hot desire pulsed in his groin even as bile rose in his throat.

Each step she took opened the cuts further. Blood flowed over her body like water, pooling on the floor. What was almost worse was the residual grace in her movements. She didn't shuffle or sway drunkenly. Rather, she moved with the precision of a dancer, each movement full of purpose. Blood gleamed in the light from the window, shining on her mutilated skin like a wet carapace, and Alex shuddered as he felt himself growing hard.

"No," he managed to whisper. "No, please."

Yuki responded to his voice, reaching out for him. Her eyes were empty pools of black but her lips seemed to be forming a smile.

It took all his courage to shut his eyes and wish the sight away.

He counted to three before his eyes flew open again in fright. Yuki was gone.

It was some time before he was able to get up off the bed and even then his legs threatened to buckle with each step he took towards the doorway. There was no blood on the floor, no evidence that anything had ever been there.

It was the middle of the night but Alex got dressed and drove all the way to work to throw the DVDs away. He snapped the disks in half and scattered them, along with the packaging, into the three large industrial bins behind the office building. He wondered if he ought to say something, but what? A prayer? He wasn't religious so he didn't imagine it would do any good. But surely it couldn't do any harm.

"Goodbye, Yuki," he whispered, and her name felt like an obscenity on his lips. "Please don't come back."

But she did.

It was four nights later and Alex was asleep. He was deep inside a pleasant childhood dream when his eyes fluttered open with a start and there she was, standing over him.

He screamed and scrambled away until he was cowering on the floor against the wall. Yuki cocked her head as if in confusion, her eyes streaming with black, bloody tears, her temples scorched and pierced by fishhooks. She looked thinner, more wasted.

Yuki raised one pale arm and reached for him. He could see the gleam of bone through the cuts on her chest. The wounds gaped like tiny mouths with each movement, as though trying to speak the words they represented. Alex shuddered with revulsion as Yuki drew her hand down over his torso. Her touch was gentle as she took hold of his cock. He stiffened in her grasp, unable to move, unable to resist as she stroked him like a lover. She pressed her blackened lips to his and he closed his eyes with a sickened moan as he came.

Then he crumpled to his knees on the floor, crying.

"Mate, you look like hell."
Alex had been tempted not to answer the door but Josh had kept pounding, shouting that he knew Alex was home.

"Yeah," he mumbled. "Got some bloody bug."

"I've been ringing you for days. The guys at work thought you'd died or something. You didn't even call in sick."

Alex managed a rueful smile. "Too sick to."

"Well, is there anything I can do for you? You need food? Booze? Drugs?"

"No, I'm fine."

But his assurances didn't get rid of Josh. His friend muttered about how stuffy it was in the flat before planting himself on the battered sofa where they'd watched so many DVDs together. He shrugged out of his leather jacket, revealing a black *Faces of Death* T-shirt. Alex stared at the grinning skull and spiky red lettering for several seconds before looking away. Josh didn't seem to notice his uneasiness.

An awkward silence stretched between them but Alex couldn't think of anything to say. He couldn't tell Josh he was seeing ghosts, much less the specifics of the encounters. But Yuki's presence hung in the air in spite of his silence. He could still smell her blood and burnt flesh, still feel the slick touch of her fingers on his skin.

He'd scrubbed himself raw in the shower after the first time but it hadn't changed anything. She'd returned the next night, and the next. She looked worse with each visit but each time Alex's own body had betrayed him, succumbing to her touch even as he choked back the sickness welling in his throat. He couldn't resist or escape and each violation only seemed to excite him more.

He was pretty sure he understood what the symbols were now. Hours of online searching had led him to a website about curses. He didn't need to read Japanese to know that one of the characters represented "desire" and another "obsession". He hadn't dared to search further to see if "love" was also among them.

Josh was talking, telling him about some new film he'd just seen, one his girlfriend hadn't been able to stomach.

Alex felt his own stomach churn queasily.

"Anyway," Josh continued, oblivious to his friend's discomfort, "pretty weird about that actress, huh?"

Alex blinked. "What are you talking about?"

"Didn't you get my email?"

"What email?"

"The one I sent you last week. About that Japanese girl. The one in the film you had me track down?"

Alex felt a crawling sensation in his guts. So his fixation on Yuki hadn't been lost on Josh after all. "What about her?"

"She's dead."

The words seemed to come from a long way away, like a transmission he'd already heard. He couldn't speak. The skull on Josh's shirt seemed to be laughing now.

"Alex? You OK?"

He nodded weakly. "Yeah, I think so." Some part of him had already known, of course.

Josh went on. "I figured you liked her since you wanted all her films and I was trying to find a copy of that last one for you—*Aesthetic Paranoia*. She died on the set. Some kind of freak accident."

"When?" Alex managed to ask.

"That's what's so weird, mate. It was only a few weeks ago, before I even showed you *Victim Factory 2*. She was dead the whole time we've been watching her films. Hey, are you sure you're OK? You're white as a fucking sheet."

That night Alex lay in bed listening for the familiar sticky wet slap of her feet. There was no point in trying to resist. Yuki would come for him, would *keep* coming for him, until there was nothing left of either of them. He'd met her eyes through the screen and she had chosen him. He was special.

He hadn't liked the way Josh had said *we*. *We've* been watching her films. He didn't like the thought of Josh seeing Yuki the way he did.

She was no longer able to stand upright but she could crawl. Her hair hung in matted clumps around her face as she pushed herself towards him on rotting hands and knees. Her skin was peeling away from the bone in places, hanging like strips of charred, wet paper.

"I'm here," Alex said softly, tapping the floor to guide her.

Before she could reach the source of the sound, she stopped. A heavy obstacle was in the way. She reached out a tentative bony hand to touch it. Her fingers moved over the grinning skull and the red letters that were smeared with blood, then found the tear in the material. She prodded the gaping wound in Josh's chest, gingerly touching the bloody edge of the kitchen knife while Josh stared vacantly up at the ceiling.

Yuki frowned, looking lost for a moment before recoiling from the unfamiliar body. Hurt by the deception, she raised her head and a feeble sound emerged from what remained of her throat. Alex could see the glistening strings of muscle trying to work to form words. His heart twisted.

"I'm sorry," he said. "But I had to know I was the only one."

She responded to his voice, turning her head towards him and then making her way to the bed with painful care. Too weak to climb up, she raised her thin arms like a child. Alex ignored the crunch of disintegrating bone as he lifted her up and sat her in his lap, his cock already swelling hungrily. Her lips hung in bloody tatters and he smoothed them into the semblance of a pout as he kissed her.

"I love you too," he whispered. Then he slid his hand between her ruined legs.

The Queen

IT WAS APRIL, AND WARM, AND SHE WAS THERE TO SEE the horses. She had apples and sugar lumps for them. The path led from the little wooded area behind the house to the field where the horses were kept. She'd been watching them for weeks, promising herself she'd go and say hello to them one day. She didn't think their owner would mind.

The horses certainly didn't. They came right over to the fence and Angie hoped they were just as delighted to make a new friend as they were to nibble on the treats she had brought. She stroked their velvety noses and sleek muscular necks, talking to them as they snuffled and munched and nickered softly.

She had never been good with people, but with animals she had no such difficulty. Jake was the only person she'd ever been completely comfortable with and she still hadn't grown accustomed to his absence. His friends had tried to comfort her but she wasn't capable of maintaining the relationships. True, no one expected much socialising from a widow, but it had been more than a year now. People had finally stopped coming by to look in on her and she could feel their disapproval, as though there were some unwritten law that said she was supposed to be over it by now.

Time had done nothing to ease the pain or make sense of the attack.

Jake had been minding his own business, heading back to his car with the new toner cartridge he had just bought for their printer. It wasn't the middle of the night. He wasn't in a bad part of town. He had nothing valuable and he wasn't even wearing his wedding ring. None of it mattered. Three teenagers had jumped out at him from behind a battered van and stabbed him to death in broad daylight. They stole his phone and the thirty-two dollars he had in his wallet. They left the toner cartridge.

The big white horse tossed his head, demanding another apple. He had already nudged away two other horses and Angie refused to let him boss them—or her—around. She ignored the bully and moved away, coaxing the other horses over one by one for their fair share.

That was when she heard it.

At first she thought it was a distant lawnmower. The low, rumbling hum was comfortingly familiar and, even though it might be miles away, she was sure she could smell the bright, sharp scent of freshly cut grass. She closed her eyes, transported to lazy summer days as a child, her father mowing the lawn, her mother weeding the flower beds. She remembered the sunflowers, their giant faces towering over her, raining their golden petals down on her when she shook their stalks like the trunks of trees.

The bumble of the mower seemed to fill the air, the sound made tactile by its vibrations. The horses heard it too and they didn't like it. They flicked their tails, looking around nervously, snorting and pawing at the ground.

Angie also looked around but she couldn't see anything. One of the horses, a chestnut mare, had wandered along the fence a little way. She had stretched her long neck through the wooden slats to get at some flowers that were growing in the shade of a huge sycamore. Suddenly the mare pulled back from the fence with a strangled neigh. She tossed her head frantically, rearing back and stamping her feet. Her panic set the others off and they galloped away like a wild herd, vanishing over the rise.

Angie stared after the animals, wondering what could have frightened them. Horses were easily spooked, so it could have been almost anything. But as the hum swelled in the hot air she recognised the sound at last. Buzzing. What she'd taken for a lawnmower was nothing of the kind. And what she'd taken for a dark patch of shade in the branches of the tree was an enormous cloud of bees.

The mass of black and gold insects hung from the tree like a giant pendulum, the writhing shape easily two feet in diameter. There must be thousands of bees there, possibly even tens of thousands. Angie had never seen an actual swarm before and, while she was curious, she knew enough to be cautious. She inched along the line of the fence to see the cluster in more detail.

She had never in her life been stung. Not by a bee or a wasp or any other insect that she could recall. Had she ever even been bitten by a mosquito? She didn't think so. Bugs had always left her alone, going after other (presumably tastier) people instead. Still, there was always a first time and she kept a safe distance as she observed the swarm.

It wasn't the vortex of dangerous fury she'd seen depicted in movies. If anything, the bees seemed sluggish, as though they'd been drugged. They clambered languidly over one another, maintaining the shape of the ball. The occasional solitary one strayed from the others in a long, looping flight path, only to return a few seconds later to rejoin its companions and reform the thrumming whole.

Angie remembered a teacher describing the process once when she was little. These were insect pioneers. It was time for the colony to reproduce, so most of the bees had left the hive with the queen to find a new home. This spot was a way station for them, a place to rest, waiting, until one of the scouts returned with news of a suitable location. Then they would mate and move on.

Intrigued, she crept closer. The bees seemed so placid she couldn't imagine them suddenly becoming angry. Certainly she was no threat to them. She just wanted to look.

She was now directly beneath the swarm. If she reached up, she could touch them. One bee circled her head before dropping down to land on her arm. She watched it, captivated by its twitching antennae and tiny transparent wings. It explored her skin for a moment, tickling her as it wandered across her wrist. It crept into her hand like a miniature pet and when she raised her hand up, the bee flew off.

The bees overhead were just as docile. She wondered what they were saying to each other in their tiny voices. Their buzzing might be the murmuring of a leisurely garden party or the contented purring of a cat.

The sight of so many tightly-packed bodies was mesmerising, and they moved as though they were one creature. Those at the centre must be half-smothered, Angie thought as she marvelled at the strength of the ones holding the weight of the giant ball. But then that was part of the genius of the hive mind. Each individual bee had its purpose but together the hive functioned as a perfect whole.

Even so, there was one bee that was special and unique. She was nestled deep inside the swarm, hidden and protected. The queen.

Before Angie even knew what she was doing, she had reached up into the cluster of bees. They parted like water for her as she slipped her fingers into their midst, and then flowed back into place just as swiftly. They were surrounding the queen, shielding her. Every single bee was under her spell. They would die to keep her safe, especially while they were away from the nest, exposed and vulnerable. A few bees clambered over Angie's hand and crept down her arm, but none of them seemed concerned as she pushed her fingers deeper, searching for the queen.

She closed her eyes, listening to the hypnotic drone of their buzzing and enjoying the sensation of their fuzzy bodies as her hand sank deeper and deeper into the swarm, as though into quicksand. When her arm was buried almost to the shoulder, she finally found what she was looking for.

The queen was easily three times the size of any other bee and Angie read the shape of her with her fingers. She stroked the long, tapered body, forming an image of the queen in her mind the way a blind person might read the features of a person's face. All around her, the bees hummed steadily. The sound was thick and their bodies were like velvet against her skin. As she caressed the hidden queen, bees streamed down her arm and across her face and body, creeping, buzzing.

Angie had no concept of how long she stood there, covered in bees. But suddenly the sound of the humming took on a different quality. It swelled in volume, grew urgent and excited.

She opened her eyes to see several scouts wheeling above the rest of the swarm. They landed on the backs of their comrades and waved their antennae excitedly. Angie suspected it was an exhortation to fly.

Moments later, the buzzing cluster began to split in two, hingeing open like a mouth. And Angie saw the queen at last, nestling at the very core. She was alien and beautiful and strange, only barely matching the image Angie had created in her mind. Her body was shaped like a long teardrop, but she lacked the characteristic black stripes and shaggy thorax of her retinue.

Attendants surrounded her, grooming her with their tiny jointed legs, caressing her with insectoid reverence. Angie's breath caught in her throat as she gazed upon the privileged sight.

The queen could hardly move for the bodies packed in tightly around her but after a moment she fluttered her wings. The other bees froze in their movements, responding to the signal. She raised her head like a sleeper waking from a dream. Her wings flickered again and then, slowly, she lifted away from the swarm. While her body was larger than that of the rest of the colony, her wings were not, and it seemed a real effort for her to take flight. She hovered around the other bees for a few seconds before at last swooping up and away. As soon as she was off, the swarm broke apart like a silent explosion, dispersing like dust into the air in a mad dance around her. The sky was alive with the music of their buzzing.

They swarmed in the air above Angie's head, pulsing like a giant heart made of smoke. Again and again the bees came together, packing themselves in tightly against one another, then bursting apart. Angie knew the queen was at the centre of that cloud, inspiring her subjects in the magnificent display.

Then, from somewhere high in the sky, there came another sound. A predatory cry. Angie shielded her eyes and peered up into the clouds. A bird was circling above the swarm, calling out in a high, piercing voice. It was answered immediately by its flock-mates. Angie had never heard such a terrible sound before. Even if she could have somehow alerted the swarm, there wasn't time. A split second later the horrible birds were everywhere, diving into the cloud of bees, their sharp little beaks snapping hungrily.

Angie cried out, helpless to do anything against the attack. She hadn't been there when Jake was killed but her mind had been perfectly capable of supplying her with endless images of knives plunging into soft, vulnerable flesh. She couldn't help but think of that now, watching the slaughter. The birds swooped and dived, stabbing and piercing, showering her with dead bees.

Abruptly the tone of the buzzing changed. There was something of horror in it now, and also something of grief. Angie knew at once that the queen had been killed. The rest of the bees flew in wild, aimless loops, like planes that had lost their pilots. Angie's heart twisted. They were lost. They could do nothing without their queen. They would all die.

Her skin still tingled from the sensation of crawling bees as she turned away, unable to watch any longer as the birds continued to dive remorselessly into the scattered swarm, their wings beating a violent tattoo on the still spring air.

Angie woke the next morning feeling desolate and missing Jake more than ever. The birds had brought it all back. She pulled herself out of bed and sat staring down at her bare feet, trying to find the strength to move. After a while she managed to drag herself downstairs to the kitchen. She stared at the coffee pot, unable to remember how to work it. With Jake gone she had no one to take care of her, no one to help her when she felt lost.

The silence was eventually broken by a demanding neigh and when she looked out the window she saw the horses. They were lined up along the fence, waiting for her. Their appearance cheered her a little and she moved as though in a dream, gliding through the door and out into the yard. Halfway to the paddock, she realised that she'd forgotten her shoes, but the grass felt pleasant and cool against her feet.

The horses stamped their hooves and whinnied at her approach, but when they saw she had no more treats for them they lost interest and moved away. Normally such a rejection would have wounded her deeply, but she was still in shock over what had happened to the swarm. Had it been like that for Jake? Had he suffered? Or had it been mercifully quick?

She made her way back to the sycamore tree, dreading what she would find. Quite a few bees had escaped the massacre. They flew in erratic circles, staying close to the tree. It was as if they hoped the queen would reappear and tell them what to do.

She could hear the lost bees buzzing. The sound came in fits and starts, the way a fly sounded when it was caught in a spider's web. Then a sudden pain made her yelp and she lifted her left foot to find she had stepped on a dead bee. The barb of its stinger protruded from the ball of her foot, the skin already bright red and swelling fast. She never would have imagined a single honey bee could have such powerful venom or that it could hurt so much.

The sky was a blur of pale blue smeared with clouds and the horses looked monstrous as she swept her gaze dizzily along the line of the fence.

The bossy white one gave a shrill whinny and the others snorted and tossed their heads. Then, as one, they spun and galloped away, afraid of something Angie couldn't see.

Her throat felt full, and for a moment she was convinced she could taste something sweet. But when she raised her hand to her mouth she saw that she was bleeding. Her tongue ached. She must have bitten it. Above her the colours ran together like paint and she closed her eyes as the sky dripped down on her, coating her like rain, like honey.

It was warm and the air was filled with the soothing murmur of bees. She could feel them crawling over her body, soft as fur. They tunnelled through her hair, wandered across her face, caressed her throat, their touch like the touch of a lover. She was suddenly too tired to stand. She sank to her knees in the grass, not even flinching as she came down on another dead bee. This time the sting didn't hurt. It only brought with it another infusion of warmth, and all she could hear around her was the droning buzz.

She lay down in the grass and gazed up into the kaleidoscopic branches of the tree. She could still see the swarm as it had been the day before, the massive pendulum suspended from a branch and held together by the perfect unity of the hive mind. Then the image began to melt away and her eyes grew heavy. When she could no longer keep them open, she let the darkness in and slept.

There was no more pain when she woke. Only comfort and the lullaby of buzzing. She felt cushioned on all sides. When she tried to move her arms she found that she was trapped. Softness pressed in on her from every angle, as though she were in an elevator stuffed with cotton balls. The sensation was slightly claustrophobic but the constant hum kept her fear at bay.

She felt fingers at her lips, gently coaxing her mouth open. She obeyed the unspoken command and was rewarded with a sweetness so sensual it made her head swim. Whatever the drug was, it reached every part of her body and she felt herself vibrating in time with the humming all around her.

The world had shrunk, and Angie with it. She might be tucked inside a thimble, drowning in sweet liqueur. She didn't care. All she wanted to do was sleep, but she couldn't seem to make her eyes close. And when she reached up to press her eyelids shut with her fingers, she gave a little cry at what she saw. That is, she tried to cry out. The only sound she could produce was a sharp buzz.

Instantly the downy softness around her was in motion, stroking and soothing her. But she had seen her hands—or what had become of them. Waving before her face were what looked like two thin black sticks, jointed and bristling with tiny hairs. She tasted more sweetness and at last recognised the taste as honey. But it was a honey unlike any she had ever known. It reached every part of her, nourishing her, rejuvenating her.

The movement around her increased and the buzzing began to sound frenzied. She felt herself being pulled. At first she resisted, but the undulating golden bodies before her were impossible to fight. As she emerged from her constriction she saw at last where she was. But she had no voice with which to scream.

All around her, as far as her new eyes could see, were bees. Giant bees. They climbed over one another to get close to her, to touch her with their long spiny legs, to gaze at her with their enormous compound eyes. With a shock she realised that she could understand what they were saying. It wasn't a language as such, but a series of images and feelings. And she understood at last where she was.

She turned to look behind her, at the waxy cell from which she had just emerged, at the sticky residue of the special honey the others had been feeding her. For a moment she cowered with fear, but her trembling transmitted through her body, causing her to vibrate and buzz. Her fear infected the bees around her and they crowded in to hold her still until she was calm again.

The buzzing attendants soothed her and she stopped trying to move. She flexed her body and her wings shivered on her back like leaves. The movement excited the others and a few of them began to lift away. They returned to stroke and touch her before taking wing again. She knew what they were telling her, but she was afraid. Her thoughts were becoming murky and clouded.

Several bees nosed themselves underneath her, raising her up. They were insisting that she fly. And there was a corresponding urge within her to fly as well. Flying was important somehow. Vital. The urgency of the bees convinced her and soon her wings began to beat and then she was in the air.

The other bees dispersed around her in a cloud, keeping her at the centre. She was high above the tree now, gazing down at the world. Everything had changed. The colours, the perspective, everything. There were towering creatures over the fence that made strange noises and fled at the sight of the bees, and all around and below were flowers of such vivid hues and exquisite scent that she could hardly believe they were real. But the flowers were not her responsibility. What was required of her was something altogether different, something only she could do.

When the first drone hit her, she lost her balance and began plunging towards the earth. But then the bee caught her in its sharp legs and held her in midair as they flew together. Sudden pain flooded her body, but with it came pleasure, a sweetness that was almost more than she could bear. It was excruciating, exhilarating, harrowing, intoxicating.

The drone released her and for a moment she fell, forgetting her wings. As soon as she found them again, another bee was there, clutching her, penetrating her. There was more pain, more intoxication, and then another partner. Drone after drone sought her and took her, filling her, feeding her. The mating went on for hours.

When at last it was over, the bees led her away, exhausted. She followed the diminished swarm in flight until they came to another tree, one with wide, sheltering branches. She had the sense of having travelled a great distance.

Her thoughts were confused and for a moment she thought of a warm place with soft things inside. Somewhere she could sleep and wake from this peculiar dream. But her comprehension was dissolving. The words made no sense and they fled from her mind like wisps of smoke. She thought now in pictures, in moods and tastes. Sensations.

The wax was smooth beneath her six legs as she was escorted to the centre of the hive, where the other bees immediately surrounded her. She was safe now and so were they. The chamber echoed with the low, pleasant hum of their buzzing as they pressed tightly against her, once more under her spell. She had fulfilled her obligation, but she would be allowed no rest.

Day after day they attended her, never leaving her alone for a second. She grew used to the crowded chamber, its waxen walls resonating with the constant hum of activity. With single-minded devotion they fed her and groomed her, waiting for her to give them what they needed. What the *hive* needed.

When the urge came she felt the tiny spasms in her long abdomen and she began to squeeze, depositing eggs which the waiting attendants carried away. The work was painful and exhausting. A part of her wanted to leave, to fly away and enjoy the glorious new world she had glimpsed in her single short flight. But each time the urge came, another bee was there to feed her the sweet nectar and her desires would fade.

Perhaps once she had given them enough eggs they would release her.

Hours passed. Days. Lifetimes. There was no way to measure the passage of time. There were only the eggs, the endless contractions of her body and the tireless attentions of her retinue. She found she could no longer move. She could barely even turn around, so tightly packed were they against her. Her senses had diminished, giving priority to the business of laying thousands upon thousands of eggs. She found that she could no longer process colours and the only sound she heard now was buzzing. There was the sweetness of honey and the softness of bodies, but nothing else. Nothing at all.

Outside the world was changing and the smell of pollen from returning workers changed with it. Soon they began to return empty. The air grew cooler and the bees pressed together more tightly inside the hive for warmth. The crush of bodies was oppressive.

At times she felt on the verge of awareness, so close to remembering something important, something from another time and place. She had fallen between worlds. Occasionally a word would appear in her mind and she could just about remember what it meant. Home. Jake. Help. Her antennae quested in the air, searching aimlessly as she tried to recall the images and thoughts of her previous existence. Then the buzzing around her would rise in concert with her anxiety and the honey would grow sweeter until she forgot again.

Her body contracted. She produced more eggs. She wished she could close her eyes.

The cold days passed until her strange memories began to seem like a dream. The sun warmed the hive and the bees flew off again to forage. New bees began to emerge from their cells but the colony still needed eggs. She hardly noticed the sensation of laying them any more.

She could feel the liberation of the bees outside, flying and gathering, returning and leaving again. She knew the mind of each single one, knew its precise function and location, knew its thoughts and moods. As simple as most of these were, certain feelings went beyond blind instinct. Fear was the most powerful.

One day the entire colony screamed. Their linked mind pulsed with raw terror. A deadly threat was coming. It was close, so close. It was here.

The new creatures buzzed too, but their sound was so much louder than that of the bees, so much angrier. They smelled of death.

The attendants formed tighter ranks around her to protect her, but they were no match for the wasps that forced their way into the hive, their huge gleaming bodies filling and overwhelming the small space. The bees fought back, sacrificing themselves as they stung the invaders and tried to push them back with their tiny legs, but the wasps were stronger and more vicious than the bees could ever hope to be. Wasps could sting again and again. They crushed the helpless bees in their powerful jaws as they plundered the hive, killing everything in their way.

The royal chamber was littered with bodies as a single wasp approached the queen. It hesitated for just a moment, captivated. It stretched out a tentative leg to touch her and its wings vibrated as it processed her scent. The queen sat immobile, terrified. She had forgotten how to move.

When the wasp pierced her swollen body with its stinger, the pain was terrible. Her mind screamed even as her mouth could not and, while death was swift, oblivion was not.

Awareness continued even as the wasp closed its jaws around her. In her mind she saw the hungry wasp larvae, newly hatched and writhing in their own cells, in their own nest, eagerly waiting to be fed.

As her mind at last began to go blissfully dark, a single word came to her. Angie. She had no idea what it meant.

CAERDROIA

AND AGAIN HE BRINGS HER ROSES, NOT KNOWING, NOT realising.

Ione smiles and gathers them in her arms, careless of the thorns. His eyes shine with fascination, with enchantment and hopeless devotion. So rapturous, so reckless. Something in her stirs at the way he looks at her and she wonders what he sees there, how she appears to his eyes.

The afternoon is spent like so many others, forming words and pretty smiles, batting her lashes and pressing catlike against him with sweet assurances and promises she will never keep. He is blind to all but his naïve fantasy of her, the beautiful yet attainable village girl he presumes her to be. But she has learnt the art of flattery through the long lonely years and she knows that a woman's eyes are the most deceitful of mirrors. It is the cruellest trick, and the easiest. And in trickery her kind have no equal.

Time passes slowly. Overhead the clouds congeal, thickening like scabs over the bleeding gash of the sun. Shadows crawl across the hills as though fleeing the dark woods. Ione sweeps the long dark hair from her face and gazes up at the emerging stars, the flicker of other worlds far away, worlds now long since dead.

Her lover speaks to her of beauty, of music and poetry and wonder. He tells her they belong together, forever. She pretends to be moved by his passion. It's such bitter irony. If she could show him something truly wondrous he would shudder with a horrible dread. His eyes would go wide with terror if he were to encounter real magic. Then her beauty would take on a terrible aspect for him and he would hurl words like stones: witch, harlot, demon. For then he would see her only as something to be feared and hated, something to be destroyed.

Her heart quivers with this tiny imagined hurt and she wonders that she should care at all what he might think. By the time he learns the truth it will be too late. His love for her will die an awful death but the pain he feels will fade with time if he has the courage to despise her. It gives her no pleasure; it is simply what must be done. It is all she knows.

When at last she is alone again she returns to the garden. His roses tremble in her arms like frightened animals as she slips them one by one into the sprawling tangle of thorns climbing the walls of the *caerdroia*. His people would call it a Troy Town, or more simply, a hedge maze. An excited murmur runs through the wild roses at her offering, as though they might devour their plain, domesticated cousins.

For a moment she is paralysed by the beauty around her, by the furled scarlet blossoms and their exhilarating perfume on the crisp night air. They whisper, rubbing their jagged leaves together, brandishing their thorns like smiling teeth.

If only he knew, they seem to say with cruel delight. *Poor fool.*

And she sighs as she strokes their velvet petals, some as dark as wine, some as pale as bone. Each one is a tiny stolen heart, forsaken and defiled. *Soon.*

Ione moves through the first passage of the maze, flowers and thorns brushing against her like teasing fingers. Each bloom is still possessed by a terrible love for her, even if they don't quite forgive her. The labyrinth is sevenfold, each turn leading deeper inside, winding towards the raised centre. She carved the pattern into the grass with her bare hands, staining the soil with her blood. Over time she planted the clawing vines to contain the strange roses.

It has taken her many years but at last she is nearing completion. When it is finished she will lead him inside. There will be no more roses then, only the one she plucks from his fragile heart to adorn the centre. There it will throb and bleed and nourish the earth beneath. But most importantly, it will open the way back for her. Back to where she belongs, whence she never should have strayed.

Around her the roses twine, hundreds of them, like splashes of blood beneath the sickle moon. They writhe in their prison of turns, mourning their memory of humanity, desolate with all the intricacies of grief. And yet still they mock. Their jealousy allows them to delight in each new addition to the maze, in each new ruined lover. It is a symphony of despair.

Ione is no part of this world. It is as much a prison for her as the maze is for them. Her kind are different. Wild and unknowable, full of magic and mischief. One by one she lured her lovers here with her fey beauty, her silken touch, her sweet promises. And one by one she harvested their hearts, ensnaring them within the thorny confines, there to wait until at last she had enough to appease her keepers. A pitiless means to an end, but a ritual older than time. If they knew the sinister origins of love they would go mad.

She closes her eyes and listens to the night. Bats dance in the sky above, their tiny songs inaudible to any ears but hers. Mice scurry in the grass, watched by hungry creatures from the trees at the edge of the deep woods. From the roof of her cottage comes the trill of an owl and from further away, the scream of a fox. All around her the world seethes with life, unnoticed and unremarked by the people of the village. All around them there is magic and beauty and yet all they choose to see are the simple things, the mundane and commonplace. It is all they *want* to see, all they want to know.

But close by, so close she can almost see them, are the watching eyes of her sisters. The veil between worlds is so thin and she is struck by the horrible fancy that she could touch them if only she reached through in the right place. Sometimes she thinks she does touch them, that a pale hand grips hers and pulls, to no avail. She hears them calling to her, crying for her loss over the great stretch of time.

How she came to be trapped here she has long forgotten. Some careless trick that went wrong perhaps, stranding her. Whatever the case, a door opened somewhere in the black night and she passed through.

The roses shudder in the breeze and Ione trails her long fingers through them as she follows the twining path to the heart of the *caerdroia*. The little raised hill shines iridescent in the moonlight. A solitary thorny bramble sprouts from the centre, its branching twigs poised like a bony grasping hand. Waiting.

Ione breathes in the lush perfume around her, feeling strangely content for the moment in her exile. For the captive roses bewitch her too. And the night's insidious beauty weakens her. She has been so long among their kind that she occasionally loses sight of her purpose. Sometimes she even feels their pain.

But she shakes herself awake. She must never get too close, never lose herself in them. For then she might be trapped forever.

"It's time," she tells him. "I have something I want you to see."

He follows willingly, eagerly, as they all have. She takes his hand, leading him into the labyrinth. Around them the roses hiss and whisper and she can see that her lover senses there is something different about her tonight. His eyes widen with fear and wonder and she smiles to reassure him.

"Come."

From deep within his breast she can hear the soft throb of his heart and she pushes to one side the thought of the pain she will cause him, the death he will likely choose for himself when she is done. For he is sensitive, his emotions raw and fragile. It is the work of nothing to break his heart.

"What is this place?" he asks when they reach the centre.

She turns, her eyes cold as the moon, her face expressionless. "This is where I bring all my lovers when I am done with them," she says simply.

The effect is not immediate. First he frowns, looking puzzled, then his lips twitch as though he is trying on an unfamiliar smile. He can't believe she is serious and yet neither can he fully believe it is a joke.

"Ione..."

She bristles slightly at the use of her name. She never likes hearing it from their lips; it seems to her a kind of blasphemy.

"It's over," she says with a shrug. "It was amusing while it lasted but I've grown bored."

He stares at her in shock, unable to comprehend this sudden shift. It is necessary to demolish his entire world. Behind her the roses shudder with perverse joy at his misfortune, the misfortune they all shared and yet delight seeing in others. She strokes them like dangerous pets.

His eyes fill with tears and she feels the first pang of his torture. His hand flutters to his chest, as though he might shield his poor heart from her cruel words. They penetrate like worms, devouring him like so much rotting fruit. There is nothing to say. He stares at her, bewildered and frightened by the hellish creature she has suddenly become. His legs tremble and he crumples to his knees, as they all do. Tears flow freely down his face. Behind him the bare thorny branch begins to bend, clutching, hungry for its prize.

In anguish, he says the words they all say, calls her the names they all call her.

She listens, unable to offer him any comfort. Their anger doesn't make it any easier for her.

"That's just how it is," she says.

Behind her the roses rustle, laughing.

And when his suffering is at its greatest, when he clutches at his head as though it will burst, she moves forward. She crouches before him and presses her hand against his chest, his skin such an insubstantial barrier.

Her palm begins to tingle, the sensation spreading to an itch, then to a searing pain as the pulsing organ is drawn to her hand, pushing through his flesh like pulp through a sieve. He doesn't even know she is there; all he knows is the misery of heartbreak. It is his whole world.

The process takes only moments although for both it feels like a lifetime. Afterwards Ione rises shakily, catching her breath. In her hand lies a crumpled rosebud, its petals bent and crushed like the wings of a newly hatched butterfly. Gently she strokes each one, teasing it into an exquisite blossom.

"There, now," she says admiringly. It is magnificent, this one, shaming the others with its exceptional splendour, its majesty.

At her feet her lover lies convulsing, oblivious to anything but the poisonous words she has spoken, the hollow agony in his breast. For the simple human organ will go on beating, sending blood through his veins. It will keep him alive for as long as he chooses to live. But he will never love again.

It is a terrible fate, but he is none of her concern any longer. With infinite care Ione sets the bloom in its place. The thorny branch clutches it tight and the petals begin to unfold even wider, splaying themselves open for the grinning moon.

She watches, waiting.

Mist drifts across the bruised sky, distorting the clawing brambles of the labyrinth. The vines sway like the tendrils of undersea flora, like the hair of the drowned, but they do not peel open the barrier.

On its spindly branch the new rose shudders at some horror she cannot perceive. The petals begin to break apart, blackening like paper in a fire. Before her eyes the rose withers and dies. A cry breaks from her lips and she clutches desperately at the fallen petals. They crumble to dust in her hands.

Above her the mist is clearing and the sky becomes ordinary once again. All around her on the vines the other roses are silent, perhaps dreading the same fate. But the world has returned to normal. All that is missing is the centrepiece of the maze.

Beyond the silence Ione can hear her lover groping his way along the passageway, his sobs growing fainter as he makes his way out of the trap, back to civilisation and the world where he belongs.

Desiccated thorns and leaves lie strewn at her feet. She stares at them, wondering at this betrayal. She has played her part, just as others have before her. Why is she still trapped here?

Above her the moon seems to gloat, as though secretly pleased she should be condemned to remain. She sinks to her knees on the cold ground. Tears shimmer in her eyes, blurring the roses into smears of garish colour all around her. They might be the faces of revellers at a masquerade, delighting in her misfortune. The walls of the *caerdroia* press inwards, making her feel tiny and insignificant. She feels the separation from her world more acutely than ever, like a blade at her breast.

And all at once it comes to her.

Trickery. All of it. The maze, the roses, the countless lovers. But she herself has been played the cruellest trick of all.

A sob escapes her lips and she scrubs away her tears, casting a rueful smile up into the cold churning stars, the indifferent sky. Then she turns and begins making her slow way out. Out of the maze and back into to the mundane world of simple people, where she must find someone to love. Someone cruel enough to use her and discard her. Someone who will cause her unimaginable pain.

Someone who will break her cursed heart.

Tentacular Spectacular

SENSATIONAL! The WONDER of the Century! A DREAM of Figure Perfection!

L UCY FOUND THE SHOP ON THE SOUTH BANK OF THE Piccadilly River on her way to Leicester Square. Ever since the Great Quake of '71, shops had been springing up along the banks of the newly formed Thames tributaries and Madame Hadal's was one she had not seen before.

She peered at the corset on display in the window. An exquisite garment of green silk trimmed with lace, it was gradually constricting the mannequin's waist as she watched. The laces trailed out to either side in back, where a pair of mechanical arms wound them round and round by means of an automated crank, drawing the corset tighter with each turn. When the gears finally stopped Lucy noted the measurement on the tape looped around the corset. Eleven inches. Impossible! But the tape couldn't lie. She stood admiring the result for several minutes before deciding to venture inside.

As the door closed behind her she became aware of a dank and pervasive smell. The interior of the shop was entirely at odds with the beautiful corsetry on display. The surfaces were furred with dust and the walls were spotted with ichorous yellow stains and tufts of fungus. Lucy pressed a lace handkerchief to her face and was just turning to leave when she saw the book.

On a battered lectern in one corner, a large volume lay open. Curious, Lucy inched closer, realising as she did so that the book was the source of the stench. Its crumbling pages were warped and stained and the stand beneath it dripped with foul water. But although she was repulsed, Lucy found herself peering closer at the open pages. The spiky text was presumably some foreign language but it was the drawing that really intrigued her. A peculiar multi-legged creature hovered midway down the page, its single monstrous eye seeming to stare directly at her from the depths of some awful abyss.

The oppressive smell was making her lightheaded and she backed away slowly, determined to get away from the book. As she watched, the creature's legs seemed to wave like fingers. Was it levering itself up out of the page? Surely it couldn't—

"Welcome!"

Lucy jumped at the sound of the voice and turned to see a woman, presumably the shop proprietress. She was of indeterminate age, unremarkable appearance, and her manner was both imposing and oddly alluring. Her deep-set eyes gleamed as she assessed Lucy with a jerk of her head.

"How may I help you?"

Lucy blinked as though emerging from a heavy sleep. She couldn't place the woman's accent and for a moment she wasn't sure she'd heard correctly at all. For a moment she was sure the woman had spoken in a completely unfamiliar language.

"Madame Hadal?" she ventured. When the proprietress nodded Lucy relaxed. "Forgive me. I must be tired. For a moment I thought . . . "

Her thought vanished as she saw that Madame Hadal was wearing the same type of corset she had just been admiring in the window, and that her figure was every bit as enviable as that of the wasp-waisted mannequin. Lucy was sure she could have fitted her hands all the way around the lady's tiny waist. The garment didn't just minimise her waist; it exaggerated dramatically the swell of her breasts and hips. But despite the daring cut of the décolletage, it was clearly not a corset to be hidden beneath one's clothes. It was a corset to wear boldly, proudly, on its own.

"You like, yes? It is very beautiful?"

"Oh yes," Lucy breathed, quite overcome. "But I fear I shall never be able to lace myself as tight as that. I am only down to sixteen inches."

Madame Hadal cocked her head and gave her customer a conspiratorial smile. "It is my secret, this special corset. For you I think it will be a—how do you say?—revelation. But come! You must try."

With that she whisked Lucy into the large fitting room at the back of the shop before she could protest. Here the dampness and the smell were less pronounced and Lucy dismissed the picture in the book as a figment of her imagination. Madame soon helped her out of her bustle dress and petticoats, laying them safely over the back of a chair. The triptych mirror showed Lucy from three angles as she stood in her plain cream corset and pantalets.

Her sixteen-inch figure was striking, as was the figure of every girl who danced at the Arabesque. Her legs were long and muscular, her face as fair as that of any lady. Whilst shunned by polite society, Lucy and her friends still enjoyed most of the privileges of respectable ladies when out dining or walking with their rich patrons. In fact, the dancing girls enjoyed rather more, for they were never expected to sit stiffly indoors with their embroidery, protected from all manner of stimulating things outside. They were not prisoners of the oppressive rules of etiquette which governed the wives of gentlemen, nor did they have any reputation to protect.

However, their freedom came at a price. With the new marvels of the Steam Age their special talents were fast becoming obsolete. Music halls that were once filled with appreciative audiences were now closing their doors as rival machine arenas took over, tempting the public away with acts like Professor Peaslee's Pistons and Petticoats, a show that featured a variety of motorised dancing dolls.

Lucy and some of her friends had sneaked in to see it one night, expecting cheap gimmicks and amateur puppetry. But they had been properly amazed by some of the "Professor's" creations and they were particularly struck by the finale. A stylised clockwork ballerina danced with all her gears and cogs on display, balancing en pointe in spite of the full-length pendulum swinging from her overlong neck. After executing a series of jumps so high it seemed she would take flight, she twirled in place and then one by one drew her arms and legs in to her chest. Then she curled her body into a perfect metal ball. She rolled offstage to thunderous applause.

The girls were, quite frankly, astounded. And not a little envious.

"If only we could do that!" Nettie had said wistfully.

But Vesta had snorted with derision. "Ha! Those wind-up dolls can't sell what we sell! What man in his right mind would take one of those toys to bed when he can have a warm flesh and blood woman?"

The girls had murmured agreement but, although Vesta had a point, there was no denying the popularity of such shows. Even the Arabesque was preparing to add the Marvellous Mechanical Menagerie to its repertoire. The prancing steam ponies and other engine-driven animals had even seduced Albert, who had signed them to open the show the following week. He claimed it was to give the girls a break but they knew the real reason. The increasing number of empty seats each night told them their days were numbered. If only there were some way that living, breathing girls could compete . . .

Madame Hadal unlaced Lucy's corset and eased it off and Lucy adjusted her chemise against her slim figure, smoothing away the wrinkles.

"No, no, my dear, it must come off. There must be nothing between the corset and your body."

Lucy blinked in surprise for a moment, then did as she was told. Perhaps the removal of the extra layer was the trick.

She held still as Madame wrapped the beautiful green corset around her and she braced herself against the mirror as the laces were pulled taut. The garment clasped her like a glove, cinching her waist tighter and smaller with each brisk tug. The bodice cupped her breasts like a lover's hands, moulding them into a flattering display of cleavage while the high-cut hips showed off her legs to their best advantage. At the Arabesque the girls had much more flamboyant costumes but the green silk was striking enough that Lucy hoped she might be allowed to wear it onstage for one of her solo numbers.

As Madame continued to draw the laces tighter Lucy expelled all the air in her lungs to allow the maximum shrinkage of her waist. It hardly seemed necessary. The garment felt as though it had been made to her exact shape, clinging to her like the lightest of gowns. It felt as much a part of her as her own skin.

But the most striking feature was the boning. Lucy's body was well accustomed to the bruising whalebone of most corsets, the stiff ridges that held one firmly in place, compressing the ribs and whittling the waist. She was used to the incidental pain of bruised ribs and chafed skin, the shortness of breath that came with the practice of tight-lacing. Such things certainly weren't the "torture" decried by those who abhorred the practice—merely the commonplace discomfort of any fashionable trend. But this corset was like nothing Lucy had ever worn. What she had at first taken to be silk was actually nothing of the kind. She'd never seen or felt anything like it. It was as soft as a baby's skin, as light as a breeze.

"There!"

Lucy stared in wonderment at her trio of reflections. She could tell at a glance that her waist was now even smaller and when Madame measured it at fourteen inches she gasped.

"Fourteen! But how?"

Madame smiled, looking pleased with herself. "It is comfortable, no?"

Lucy nodded, unable to put her emotions into words. A powerful feeling of euphoria overwhelmed her and she sighed with pleasure as she turned this way and that, bending and twisting. She kicked up one leg, then the other, astonished by the freedom of movement the corset allowed. Even the most comfortable of corsets was restrictive to some degree but Lucy had never experienced anything like the freedom of movement afforded by Madame's creation.

Without even enquiring about the price she said, "I'll take it."

"It's incredible, Luce! Wherever did you get it?"

Lucy beamed proudly as she showed off her find. The other five girls flocked around her, stroking the strange material and exclaiming over her tiny waist. Lotte had already measured it twice, unable to believe her eyes.

"Do you think it might help the show if we all wore them?" Nettie asked hopefully.

Vesta snorted. "Those steel tarts in the perpetual motion parade can lace down to nothing."

"Yes, yes," Nettie said, rolling her eyes, "but they don't have bones or organs to get in the way, do they? Where did you say you got it, Luce?"

Lucy told them.

"How odd," Vesta said. "I passed that way just last night but I never saw any shop."

"Perhaps it only opened this morning. Besides, it's in a strange spot, sloping almost right down to the water."

The word "water" had an unpleasant resonance in Lucy's mind, but she couldn't understand why it should make her feel uneasy. She found she could barely even remember the shop. All she could focus on was the beauty of her new corset.

"Well, I'm going straight there tomorrow!" said Lotte.

"Me too!" chimed the twins, Daisy and Claire.

"I hope Madame Hadal can keep up with us," Nettie said with a giggle. "Perhaps we should ask Albert to hire her to be our exclusive costume designer."

"If the Arabesque doesn't go under. Remember we're competing with electric elephants."

Nettie gave Vesta a fierce shove. "Enough of your doom and gloom, missy! Are you going to help us or not?"

Lucy ignored the others as she arched her back before the mirror, marvelling at her flexibility within the corset. She hadn't even warmed up for the show yet but her body felt as lithe and liquid as when she was clad only in the sheerest of garments. One by one the girls quieted down, watching her, their eyes shining covetously.

Finally Vesta began to smile. "You might be on to something after all, Luce," she said.

Even Albert noticed the difference in Lucy, complimenting her backstage for a particularly rousing performance. He even succumbed, without too much persuading, to their pleas for an advance so they could all buy one of the miracle corsets in time for the show the next night.

"It's simply the most comfortable corset I've ever worn," Vesta enthused, displaying her tight-laced body, encased in golden yellow.

"The most comfortable garment full stop," Lotte corrected. Hers was the blushing pink of a new bride and suited her less curvaceous figure perfectly. "I can't even feel the bones."

"I wonder how she makes them?" Nettie said, stroking the bold scarlet fabric. The touch of her fingers seemed to alter the colour slightly, a shift almost too subtle to notice. But then it was back to its original hue. Lucy had noticed the same effect with hers.

The girls were a riot of colour and their show that night had the audience hammering the floorboards with their feet and demanding a second, then a third encore. Over the following nights they performed feats they had never imagined possible, moving effortlessly through their dances, as lissome as cats. And each night the audience grew until finally the show sold out for the first time in months. They noted with triumph several empty seats during the steam ponies' routine.

It was a few weeks later that Lucy confessed to the others that she had never actually taken the corset off. She had worn it every day since purchasing it, danced in it, slept in it. She had even bathed in it. The one time she had tried to remove it, she had experienced such intense pain that she instantly regretted her efforts.

"It's as though the corset itself doesn't want to come off," she said with a sense of disquiet. "It's as though it's . . . become a part of me."

Uneasy glances passed back and forth among the other girls and it was obvious that they hadn't removed theirs either. Perhaps they too had tried and failed.

Nettie gave a nervous laugh. "It's more comfortable than being naked," she admitted. "Why should I ever want to take it off?"

MARTYRS to fashion! Ladies BEWARE! You are DESTROYING yourselves!

The leaflets had begun to proliferate with the renewed success of the Arabesque, which was due entirely to the popularity of the dancers. They astounded audiences with their flexibility and death-defying acrobatics. Word of their unparalleled acts of contortion quickly spread, as did Madame Hadal's popularity when it was revealed that the dancing girls all wore her special corsets to maintain their exquisitely pinched figures. Now even proper ladies were flocking to the little shop, much to the consternation of their husbands, who were torn between a duty to disapprove of a craze with its roots in the coarse music hall and the undeniably alluring result.

Doctors warned of the dangers of tight-lacing, claiming that the practice led to insanity and even death. Clergymen, meanwhile, were more concerned with the moral and spiritual risks, blaming corsetry for exciting impure desires and imploring men to take their women in hand before it was too late.

There were even rumours of a young lady who had perished as a result of her refusal to take off her new corset. A doctor had apparently tried to remove it for her—surgically. The bizarre case was reported in the papers but the details were vague and so wholly outlandish that no one lent the story any credence.

Naturally, the dancers were delighted to be at the centre of a city-wide fashion revolution and its ensuing controversy, but it did rob their act of some of its mystique. With almost every woman in London now benefitting from the magnificent corsets, they needed to find a new angle to exploit. It was time to revamp the show.

"Aerial acrobatics?" Claire suggested.

The others shook their heads. The public had seen it all before in countless other shows, along with everything else from magicians to lion tamers.

They brooded in silence and after a while Nettie murmured, "Water."

"What about it?" Vesta asked.

Nettie blinked as though unaware she had spoken. "Oh, it's just...I had rather a peculiar experience last weekend. The Baron flew me to the seaside in his airship and—"

"You lucky thing!" Daisy cried. "I wish I could find a man that rich! My Mr Chapman still insists on using his rickety old tandem pedal balloon when we travel. It always leaves my hair in disarray and absolutely everything in the sky races past us!"

Daisy had always been the quiet one but their success had made her positively garrulous. It had had the opposite effect on Nettie, whose former nervous energy was nowhere to be seen. Now she always seemed calm and serene.

"Go on, Nettie," said Vesta, ignoring the interruption.

"Well," she continued, "they had a sort of aquatic zoo there and I saw the queerest creature. The keeper said it was a new species. He called it a lightning squid."

"A what?"

"Lightning squid. Apparently it imparts an electric shock through its tentacles to stun its prey. It's quite extraordinary."

Lotte shuddered. "Ugh! It sounds horrible!"

But Nettie shook her head, a haunted look in her eyes. "No, it was beautiful. I watched it for hours. What struck me most was the way the creature moved. Its legs rippled like waves. So graceful, so slender, so—liquid." She hesitated. "Like us."

The other girls considered this, nodding thoughtfully.

Lucy felt a sense of *déjà vu*. Water. A strange creature.

"Yes," she said darkly. "Liquid. That's exactly how I've felt since wearing the corset. Since the very first moment I put it on. Didn't one of our notices say we moved like fish through the air?"

"Bah," said Vesta, "they're just trying to compare us to an animal act."

"I thought it was a compliment," Lotte said, blinking her wide innocent eyes.

"It *was* a compliment," Nettie asserted. "And to be completely honest, I haven't really felt at home on the ground since."

Lucy found she was absently stroking her now thirteen-inch waist. She knew exactly what Nettie was talking about because she'd felt it too. As though her body were someone else's and she was just along for the ride. But while it felt alien, it was also intoxicating. When she moved she felt lighter than air. The corset had truly changed her life.

If she entertained the thought of trying to remove it she was immediately suffused with warmth, with a sense of blissful intoxication that made her leave the laces tied. And if she tried to resist the pleasant feelings ...

"Well, what's so strange about that?" Daisy asked. "It's hardly surprising we feel more graceful in such lovely corsets."

"That's not all," Nettie continued, her voice low, her face pensive. "We went bathing in the sea afterwards and at one point I slipped down beneath the waves. I swam in the water as though I were merely dancing. I had no measure of how long it was but I must have been down there for some considerable time because when I emerged my fingers and toes were puckered as though I'd spent too long in the bath."

Lotte looked horrified. "But you might have drowned!"

"Yes. And by all accounts I *should* have. But I didn't." She lowered her voice. "I felt as though the water was where I belonged."

As this sank in Lucy could see from the other girls' faces that they had all experienced similar feelings. Even Daisy was silent.

"I did that too," Claire said at last. "I was in the bath the other night and I put my head down under the water. I didn't think it was odd at the time. I was only pleased that I hadn't spoilt my corset by getting it wet."

"That's perhaps the strangest thing of all," said Vesta. "We've all been wearing them for weeks and yet look at them." She unbuttoned the front of her dress to reveal her shining yellow corset, its colour as bold as the sun and as immaculate as the first day she had worn it.

A sense of unease came over Lucy. In her mind's eye she saw a book, but she couldn't make any sense of the image. "When I first went to the shop Madame Hadal said it was her special secret. I wonder what that secret is?"

Daisy pressed close to Claire. "Do you suppose they might be … bewitched?"

"Surely not," said Lotte with a nervous laugh. "Besides, even if there were some sort of magic involved, why would we feel so much better? Shouldn't we grow warts and turn into hideous crones or something?"

"There's no such thing as magic," Vesta said gruffly, "but there is most definitely something peculiar about these corsets and I'm going to find out what it is. Lucy, Nettie, will you accompany me?"

Vesta's certainty made Lucy feel even more uncomfortable. She didn't want to discover some unpleasant truth about the corsets but the girls' combined experiences were too queer to deny and she was becoming frightened. "Very well," she said at last, reluctantly. "Come on, Nettie."

They passed several tight-laced ladies as they headed for the shop and Lucy couldn't help but be struck by their unusual poise and beauty. She knew without needing to ask whose corsets they wore. It was in their beatific expressions, their knowing smiles as they met the eyes of the three dancers and nodded like accomplices in some loathsome plot.

"Something's wrong," Lucy said, peering across the river at the shop. The glare of reflected sunlight on the water made it difficult to see.

She turned the crank that jutted from the small platform at the river's edge and a narrow rail rose dripping and clanking from beneath the surface. The water trolley rose with it and slid along the rail until it reached the bank. They waited for the trolley to drain before stepping into it and distributing their weight evenly along its slim length. Then Vesta slipped a penny into the slot and pressed the button to send the craft across the water.

"Good heavens," Nettie said as they drew near. "The shop's completely flooded!"

They clambered out and looked in horror at the water lapping up around the walls of the little building. It was almost half-submerged.

"But how?" Lucy asked. "It hasn't rained for days."

Vesta shook her head. "I don't know. Come on, let's go inside."

The front of the shop was untouched by the water. A new corset was on display in the window, with the same clockwork device showing off its tight-lacing ability. Business had clearly been booming, for a glittering new sign advertised in huge gold letters the "Sensational Creations by Madame Hadal, Queen of Corsets".

The girls pushed inside and the bell tinkled merrily, as though nothing were amiss. A short expanse of dry floor sloped sharply down towards the flooded back end of the shop and they stood staring in horror at the encroaching water. Then the smell hit them.

Nettie cried out. "Ugh! What on earth—?"

Alarm bells jangled in Lucy's mind and she looked around for the lectern she had seen on her first visit to the shop. "Do either of you remember seeing a book?" she asked.

Vesta frowned. "What kind of book?"

"It was big, like a family Bible. Full of some kind of weird writing and pictures. Just there."

But where she pointed there was only a mannequin sporting a half-finished corset.

"I know I didn't imagine it. And the shop smelled just like this too. Horrible. I remember now."

Vesta looked alarmed.

"Where's Madame Hadal?" Nettie asked. Then she added in a timid whisper, "Do you suppose she drowned?"

Suddenly there was a loud splash and a figure came swimming towards them from the back room. Madame Hadal's head peeked up from the water and her face creased in a wet and wrinkled smile as she recognised three of her customers.

"Ah! Welcome back, my dears!"

They gaped at her, astonished.

"Madame!" Lucy gasped. "What's happened to your shop?"

She looked puzzled and shook her head. "I do not understand."

"The water. Everything's flooded."

"Oh, that!" She laughed, an ugly, discordant sound. "My waterflowers—they like it better this way. Come. It is almost their time. I will show you."

"Almost their time?" Lucy echoed.

The girls exchanged a look as Madame slipped back down beneath the water and vanished from sight.

"That's exactly what I did," Nettie said excitedly, her eyes wild. In a flash she had stripped off her dress and flung it aside. "Come on!"

Before they could stop her she dived in after Madame Hadal. Vesta and Lucy hesitated only a moment before struggling out of their dresses too. They each sucked in a deep breath and followed their friend into the chilly water.

As the waves closed over her head Lucy knew immediately what Nettie had meant when she said she'd felt entirely at ease. Lucy had never been swimming in her life but as she moved deeper into the watery depths of the shop she felt as though she was coming home. The sensation was at once exhilarating and completely natural.

She saw the others up ahead and swam to meet them. They were drifting against the submerged back wall of the shop, which looked as though it had been blasted apart. It now opened directly into the river. Some trick of the sunlight streaming down from above made the shadows flicker all around them like enormous butterflies. But as Lucy swam further in she saw that they weren't shadows at all. They were living creatures. Squid, to be exact. Just as Nettie had described. Just as Lucy had seen pictured in that awful book.

She gazed at them, transfixed. Each was about the size of a cat, with tentacles extending out about two or three feet. A single fathomless black eye peered from each soft bulbous head and a rainbow of unfamiliar colours flickered across each sleek body. When the creatures moved they seemed to take hold of the water, clasping it like a many-fingered hand and using the pressure to propel themselves forward. The languid tentacles writhed and rippled with balletic grace. It was hypnotic.

"My waterflowers."

It took Lucy a moment to realise that she had heard Madame speak plainly through the water. Nettie's voice came next.

"So beautiful!"

She glanced to her left to see Nettie reaching out to one of the creatures. It floated about her, slipping through her billowing hair and caressing her face with its slender legs, stroking her like a lover. But surely it was only her imagination that made Nettie's corset seem to fluctuate in tandem with the creature's movements.

Vesta was beside her, gazing in wonderment as several of the squid swam up to her, darting close and then swimming away, teasing and inviting her to play. Lucy's eyes travelled down the length of her friend's floating body and sure enough, she witnessed the same impossible movement. It looked as though a pair of unseen hands stroked and moulded Vesta's flesh beneath the corset.

If Lucy gasped in fright, the sudden intake of water did her no harm. She had been submerged long enough to drown, yet she was undeniably alive. More alive than she had ever felt. Euphoria flowed through her and her vision grew blurry with ecstatic tears. She had never seen anything as lovely as the creatures that surrounded her, tickling her with their many delicate legs as though dancing with her. And yet, she had the eerie sense that she was not seeing them as they actually were, that they were somehow concealing their true selves.

She recalled the pain when she had tried to remove her corset, the electric jolt that had spiked through her ribs. As if in answer to her confusion, the corset began to ripple against her body. Beneath her skin her ribs waved like fingers and all at once Lucy understood the secret. For had she not sensed the seductive burrowing already? The alien harmony of movement as the tentacles within the corset fused with her bones? The exquisite symbiosis as hundreds of tiny sucker mouths caressed her organs, sipping her blood and humours like nectar?

She opened her mouth to scream, but what emerged instead was a sigh of pleasure. Her limbs moved independently of her will, her arms and legs as boneless as the legs of the creatures which, even now, were narrowing their cyclopean eyes at her. The seduction was over; she was theirs.

The girls swam helplessly among the creatures like living cogs in a fantastic machine whose function they could not begin to guess. Their eyes met Madame Hadal's across the underwater garden of nauseating colour and they shared a hideous smile as the earth began to tremble and crack beneath them.

TENTACULAR SPECTACULAR! A Dazzling Liquid Electric Extravaganza! One Night Only!

The new fork of the Piccadilly River flowed straight through the centre of Leicester Square. It had swallowed the famous Alhambra, along with two other music halls. The former Arabesque Theatre now lay half submerged and whilst passing gentlemen muttered that it would never recover, their wives and daughters exchanged knowing glances.

Many fine houses and buildings had either been demolished or sunk. The spires of the Houses of Parliament rose like stone trees from what was now Westminster Lake. Big Ben still chimed from its depths, giving rise to rumours that it was haunted. As the land had warped and buckled, the great western railway terminus had risen and it now sat perched atop the newly formed Paddington Hill. At its feet lay the broken railway tracks, scattered like so many matchsticks.

The streets were strewn with rubble but nothing would prevent the grand opening of the Aquadrome. The lavish red A was all that remained of the original Arabesque marquee and the theatre was an unusual sight, resting as it was now half-in and half-out of the river.

"Water ballet?" scoffed a gentleman as he snatched the flyer from his daughter's hands. "Utter nonsense! Why, they'd all drown!"

Such was the scene across what remained of the city.

"Charles dear, it's only for one night!"

"Come on, Peter. I hear the dancing girls are the most beautiful ever seen on stage!"

"Oh, Father, don't be silly. Of course, if you'd rather I went alone, unchaperoned..."

Many of the wealthiest families had fled following the most recent quake but plenty of ladies were able to persuade their husbands not to desert the city. The men harrumphed and grumbled and dusted down their frock coats as they reluctantly agreed to stay.

But it was the upcoming show that was the real talk of the town, screaming from the headlines of the *Times* and from posters all across the transformed city.

By the time the doors finally opened the riverbank was lined with people clamouring to get in. There wasn't room to seat them all but no one complained about having to stand. The auditorium was packed to capacity in no time and when the tickets ran out Albert told the doorman to keep letting them in anyway. After all, there couldn't possibly be a fire. Not with the place soaked through.

The wet floorboards shuddered like the threat of another quake as hundreds of pairs of feet stampeded across them. The crowd pushed and shoved as each person tried to get as close as possible to the stage, where the damp red velvet curtains hid whatever preparations were going on behind it.

"It don't 'alf smell!" someone cried.

But no one cared. The awful stench was a small price to pay for what they were sure would be an unforgettable performance.

At last the moment came and Albert marched out in front of the footlights. A reverential hush fell over the audience and he heightened the suspense with a dramatic pause before finally announcing the show.

"Ladies and gentlemen, I give you—Tentacular Spectacular!"

A deafening cheer went up from the crowd and the curtains hissed apart to reveal an enormous glass partition. Behind it was simply the stage. Empty, undressed, bare. Until the watchers realised that the stage was entirely under water. As one they uttered a collective gasp.

There was no music. There was nothing but the vast aquarium and the palpable anticipation as everyone waited to see what would happen.

At last a girl appeared. She swam like a mermaid up to the glass where she hovered, her long legs kicking, her hair flowing like seaweed, her body bare except for a glittering green corset that shone like emeralds in the light and pinched her waist to almost nothing. She performed a few graceful manoeuvres before being joined by a girl in yellow, then another in red. Soon there were six girls, each one corseted in a different vibrant colour, each one a vision of ethereal beauty.

By the time the first person realised that none of them had come up for air yet the dancers had linked arms to form a circle, facing outwards. They spun round and round in the water, drawing closer as they did until they were shoulder to shoulder. They hung still for a moment and began to sink. Then, just before they reached the floor of the stage, they kicked in unison, drawing their feet up, out and then down through the water. Six pairs of long shapely legs undulated like tentacles, propelling the girls upward. Their choreography was so precise they might have been a single creature, with a single mind. The astonishing colours flickered across their bodies as they turned and swam through the tank like a luminous and colourful invertebrate.

"Mama, what's that?" came a child's voice.

Someone cried out as several smaller objects appeared onstage, swimming fluidly alongside the dancers. The waterflowers, as the girls had come to know them, swooped and dived in and among their human partners, their fantastic tentacles waving hypnotically as they released bold flashes of lightning that arced through the water, illuminating the dancers but miraculously not harming them.

For a moment it looked as though the girls really were a single entity, that their bright colours were beginning to blend, that their bodies were starting to merge into one. It was as though the jagged threads of lightning were stitching them together, transforming them. But surely that was just part of the act.

When the girls still did not break apart a few people began whispering uneasily. Skirts rustled and feet shifted and a worried murmur began to make its way through the crowd. The creatures flashed through the water faster and faster, circling the dancers. Then they swam away in a flurry to the darkened rear of the stage. They remained out of sight for only a moment before rushing straight towards the partition.

There wasn't time to react before the army of squid struck the glass, shattering it. The entire crushing weight of the river surged over the audience, devouring it and plunging everything into darkness.

The Aquadrome was a black vortex of chaos and terror. People splashed desperately and shouted for help as they searched in vain for a way out. Below them in the cold inky water they could see flashes of electricity as the mass of writhing creatures paralysed one victim after another. Corpses surfaced in droves, floating and bumping into their still-living counterparts. A smell like that of a flooded graveyard permeated the theatre and from somewhere beneath the human screams came a hideous hydrophonic chorus, like the victory cry of a loathsome and terrible race. A race older than the ground which was now opening beneath the Aquadrome, splitting the earth apart and releasing thousands more of the accursed creatures in a liquid swarm.

The walls of the theatre crumbled as the monsters boiled up from the deep. The newcomers were considerably larger and far more ancient. And hungry. As the feeding frenzy began, the ocean of rippling alien colours was awful to behold. Minds broke like twigs as thousands of baleful glaring eyes fixed on their prey. Lightning leapt from swaying tentacles as the creatures slid slowly and deliberately through the sea of thrashing bodies, killing some, preserving others.

Those women who were under the spell of the creatures that had enslaved them fared rather better than their husbands. They remained oblivious to the horror right up until the moment when their corsets sprang open, bursting their chests apart and releasing the parasitic occupants.

The great pillars of the theatre were reduced to rubble as the water rose ever higher, pushing unstoppably through the city streets, levelling everything in its path.

From the centre of the maelstrom far below a new creature watched, waiting. Its bloated form pulsated with a sickly greenish glow as it drifted up through the untold depths. Vast arms uncoiled from its grotesque body, innumerable sucker mouths tasting the death and fear in the water as it made its horrible ascent. The bulging black eye fastened at last on what it sought and the putrescent creature reached out to claim its prize.

The girls experienced a final moment of awareness before the writhing tentacles closed around their mingled and mutated form. Their faces had melded together, cheek to cheek and each mouth had been stretched wide to form a single contiguous grimace. They could only shudder in horror as the hideous tentacles opened to reveal the gaping liquescent orifice towards which they were being pulled.

FIRST AND LAST AND ALWAYS

TAMSIN PLACED HER HANDS ON EITHER SIDE OF HER phone and gazed intently at the picture of Nicky she'd taken the day before. Her heart soared as she said his name aloud.

"Nicky."

The flickering candlelight gave him the illusion of movement and Tamsin could almost believe she was watching him through a portal, seeing him as he was right at this moment. After a few seconds the picture faded and the screen went dark. She peered into the smooth black surface, focusing on the afterimage—Nicky in negative, overlaid by the reflection of her eyes and the ghostly glow of the flame.

"Nicky."

When the image behind her eyes finally faded too she tried to see beyond the scrying glass of the phone's screen, into whatever dimension the emptiness might reveal. Past, present, future—she didn't care as long as she saw *him*.

When nothing happened after several minutes she tapped the screen to wake it up, to reveal the photo again and repeat the entire process.

It was just a quick candid shot but she'd captured the vibrancy of the setting sun. Nicky had been on his way to rehearse with his band, Valhalla, and he was smiling at someone out of frame. His head was turned slightly to one side. She'd shot straight into the sun, creating a dramatic lens flare that partially obscured one hazel eye. A lock of black hair fell over his other eye, just reaching his cheekbone.

Tamsin tried to visualise herself in the picture with him, her long blonde tresses transformed by the evening light into burnished gold. That was how she liked to imagine she looked to him, anyway. Her hair was her best feature. It fell in lustrous waves halfway down her back and it made her average face a little prettier, gave her the wild, windblown look of a gothic heroine. Nicky had complimented her on it one day when she'd had it down and she'd worn it that way ever since.

"Hey there, Tamsin," he'd said, hearing the click of her camera phone.

His low sleepy voice turned her knees to water. And his smile . . .

"You coming to our show tomorrow night?"

It was only a half-hour spot at a local student hangout but to Tamsin it may as well have been a major concert.

"Of course," she'd said, thrilling to the sound of his voice. It rang in her ears as she cast about for something else to say. Anything to keep him there for another minute. "Oh—I saw the video you guys posted on YouTube."

He'd blushed then, shyly lowering his head as though he had anything to be shy about. She'd played the clip endlessly, imagining that every time he looked into the camera, he was looking right at her.

"Oh, it's just a demo," he said offhandedly. "Rob said we should build up a presence online before we send anything to the record companies."

"Just a demo? It looked completely professional to me!"

"Thanks."

Nicky smiled again and they shared an awkward silence before he glanced at his watch. "Well, guess I'd better go."

"Yeah," she'd said, dying but not daring to take another picture of him. She'd already copied all the ones on his Facebook profile and even printed some of them out. Her favourite one sat in a little gold frame on the nightstand by her bed. His beautiful pale face in close-up, his eyes meeting hers every night and every morning.

"OK, see you tomorrow, then."

"Yeah," she breathed. "See you . . ."

The memory of the conversation echoed in her mind as she woke her phone up again and said his name, willing him to hear her in his mind, to acknowledge his true feelings for her. She was dressed and ready for the concert, determined that tonight would be the night. Tonight he would love her back.

But it was not to be.

Valhalla played five songs and Nicky was brilliant, as always. The pub was full of students who cheered as though they were at the Glastonbury Festival. Tamsin stood as close to the stage as she could but Nicky didn't look her way once. He seemed completely lost in the performance, singing with his eyes closed, oblivious to everything but the music. Someday he would be a big star. Tamsin had no doubt about it. But she had to make sure he was hers before that happened. Once he was famous he would be hounded by groupies. Girls with tramp stamps and black lipstick. Tamsin was what he needed, what he really wanted. He just didn't know it yet.

After the show he was surrounded by his friends and Tamsin's stomach clenched with jealousy at the sight of all the other girls flocking around him. There was no way she could push her way through the crush of bodies. It was torture to be so close to him, yet unable to reach him. Torture to watch him with all those other girls, none of whom understood him the way Tamsin did.

Tears blurred her vision and she wiped her eyes with the back of her hand, smearing her mascara. She couldn't let him see her like that so she made herself turn away. As she opened the door of the pub she glanced back one last time, hoping he would sense her anguish and signal to her to stay. But wishing only made the reality worse. He hadn't noticed her at all.

That night she sat cross-legged on her bed, staring forlornly at an uninspired Tarot spread. It was her third attempt. Each time she had managed to draw cards that told her nothing meaningful or even relevant. The Knight of Cups hadn't appeared in any of the three spreads. Cups represented the world of feelings and the Knight was the most romantic card of all. But he was nowhere to be seen tonight. Nicky's symbolic absence felt like a sickness, something that would grow and spread until it consumed her and spat out her indigestible heart.

She swept the cards away in disgust. Her chest felt tight, as though her insides were trying to shrink away from the pain. If she closed her eyes she saw his face. Her skin burned for the touch of his hands.

Her flatmates had teased her about him, calling him "goth boy" and other dismissive names. Beth had drawn a cartoon of him as Dracula and Chrissie had once left a pair of comedy fangs in the bathroom for her to find. Tamsin was sure they didn't mean to be cruel; they just didn't understand. After all, neither of them had a boyfriend either.

At least they didn't mock her religion. Beth had got Tamsin a book on witchcraft for her birthday and she had tried both the love spells in it. They were of the "bad poetry and herbs" variety, probably inspired more by Harry Potter than by any real magic. But she'd tried them anyway, feeling silly for doing it and then feeling even sillier when they didn't work. What had she expected?

She'd been so sure he would notice her tonight. Her feelings were too intense to be only one-sided. In desperation, she powered up her computer and began searching online for proper love spells. She quickly found a naff website hawking "love spells that totally work", along with "amazingly accurate" astrological charts and other rubbish that was probably just designed by spammers to harvest your email address if you were gormless enough to provide it for a "personalised" reading. But there must be other witches online, real witches who knew what they were doing.

It was on a forum called eBook Of Shadows that Tamsin finally found what she was looking for.

In order to truly love something, you have to make it part of you.

The post was by someone called Osprey and she was relating a story her gran had told her.

There was a young girl who lived with her family on a farm. Times were hard and one year there was a drought, the next year a flood. The crops were destroyed and the family was facing ruin. But the girl was in love with a boy from the neighbouring village and she was terrified that her parents would decide to move. If they did she knew she would never see her true love again.

So she cast a spell to bind them to the land. She took a spoon and circled the farmhouse, collecting one scoop of soil for each member of the family. That night she sprinkled it into the stew her mother made and mixed it well. She said a few words over it and wished very hard for it to work. Her family complained that the food tasted strange but they ate it all the same.

A year passed and love continued to blossom between the girl and the boy even as the crops failed yet again. Her family was forced to sell all the animals but they insisted on staying with the farm. Friends and neighbours urged them to sell up and move somewhere else, suggesting that the land was cursed. No one could understand their stubborn refusal to stay. No one but the girl, who lamented their poverty but was comforted by the knowledge that now she could never be parted from her soulmate.

Tamsin had no idea if the story was true or not, but she liked to think it was. At least the happy part. She knew she was supposed to be too old to believe in fairy tales, but she couldn't help it; she was a romantic. She wanted to believe that wishes came true, that love conquered all. Most of all she wanted to believe that there were magic spells that worked.

She lay awake in bed for several hours that night, her mind racing.

In order to truly love something, you have to make it part of you.

How could she make Nicky a part of her? The girl in the story had bound her family to the land by physically feeding it to them, although perhaps she should have tried binding herself to the boy instead. Tamsin had tried so many different love spells over the months but nothing had worked. Was it because none of the spells had any physical link between her and Nicky? Gazing at his picture and saying his name wasn't getting her anywhere. She might as well be clapping to keep Tinkerbell alive.

She was always hearing about girls who had date-rape drugs slipped into their drinks. How hard could it be to turn the tables? But the very thought made her feel like a stalker. She didn't want to rape him; all she wanted to do was make him recognise what was already inside him. Surely there was no harm in that. But even as she brainstormed different scenarios, she knew she couldn't spike his drink in a public bar. If he saw her—or worse, if someone *else* saw her—that would be the end of everything.

No, whatever she did had to be done in private. And the only way to do that was to screw up her courage and invite him over for dinner. But what could she feed him? It had to be something she could sneak into the food undetected but most importantly, it had to be something uniquely hers. Uniquely *her*.

The question obsessed her over the following days. Then one night while she was revising for a poetry exam, the answer jumped out at her. It was a line by Thomas Carew.

Those curious locks so aptly twin'd
Whose every curl a soul doth bind.

Her hair. The thing she prized most about herself. The thing even Nicky had noticed. How could she have overlooked something so obvious?

She sat before the mirror, her heart pounding. In the joy of her discovery she looked radiant and she brushed her hair slowly, sensuously, as she focused her mind on crafting the perfect spell. She pulled several loose hairs from her brush, wondering how many she would need. But as she looked at them, curled in her palm like a tiny nest, she knew it wasn't right. Those hairs were already dead. She dropped them in the bin and met her eyes in the mirror.

Then she carefully selected a strand of hair from the top of her head. She smoothed away the other hairs around it and tugged. It did not come free at once. She had to pull it several times before she yanked it out at the root. The pain was astonishing. It was only a single hair but it felt like someone had jabbed her scalp with a needle. She cried out as it came free and wasn't surprised to see a tiny drop of blood on the end.

Her voice trembled as she whispered, "First."

With her fingers she combed through her hair on the left until she isolated another strand. It also proved reluctant to come out and when it did it brought with it another drop of blood.

"And last."

She moved to the right for the final strand, taking hold of it firmly and holding her breath. She yanked, hoping it would pull out more easily than the others. But it was the most difficult of all. Only after many painful jerks of her hand did it finally come out. She yelped and had to resist the urge to scratch her scalp, to rub away the burning sensation where the hairs had been plucked.

She took a deep breath and laid the three strands side by side on her dressing table. "And always," she said. "Mine."

The blood held them together at one end and Tamsin weighted them down with her phone while she set about plaiting them together. She found herself humming as she did, barely aware of the warm trickle from her scalp until the blood dripped into her eyes. She paid it no mind. Her hands completed the task as though guided by external forces.

When at last she had a long thin braid she wiped the blood from her face and knotted the ends together to form a circle. It would remain unbroken until the right moment.

She tucked the charm beneath her pillow to keep it close to her while she slept. She knew it would bring her dreams of Nicky, dreams that were about to come true. In the morning her pillow was stained with blood.

She saw him the next day, chatting with his friend Rob, and she didn't hesitate. She had dressed up for the occasion. Her athletic frame was show-cased in her tightest jeans and a lacy purple top. She'd worn a push-up bra and gothed up her makeup. Smudged black eyeliner and blood-red lips. Just enough to get his attention.

It worked. His face broke into an easy smile as she walked boldly up to him before she could lose her nerve. Rob was eyeing her cleavage.

"I saw your show the other night," she said breezily. "It was awesome!"

Nicky's smile broadened. "Hey, thanks! I wasn't sure about that Sisters of Mercy cover. Was it really OK?"

Rob jumped in before she could answer. "Of course it was. I *told* you." He rolled his eyes at Tamsin as though compelling her to agree with him.

But Nicky was still watching her expectantly, waiting to hear what she thought. She hid her exhilaration and nodded as though she had any business telling him whether something was good or not.

"I thought it was brilliant. Better than the original."

His eyes shone with genuine delight and her heart twisted a little at the thought of him doubting his talent. And before the opportunity could slip away she said "Do you want to come to mine for dinner tonight?"

He blinked in surprise but his smile didn't falter. Out of the corner of her eye she saw Rob's face fall a little.

Nicky glanced at his friend and then back at Tamsin. "Sure," he said.

"Great! I'm making a curry. Hope you like it spicy." She knew full well he did, just as she knew loads of other little things about him that he'd never told her. Just to leave him in no doubt about what was on offer she added, "My flatmates are away for the weekend."

He actually blushed. "Brilliant," he said.

Her heart leapt and it was all she could do to maintain the casual act. "Cool. It's a date. I'll text you my address. What's your number?"

It was almost too easy. Just like that, the deal was sealed.

"Well, I've gotta get to class," she said. "See you tonight!"

Nicky waved as she trotted away, pretending to be in a hurry. She felt lighter than air.

Mine, she thought.

She skipped the class she'd pretended to be late for and went to Waitrose to buy the poshest ingredients she could find. Then she spent the whole afternoon making the curry. Soon the aroma of coconut milk and chillies permeated the flat and Tamsin left it to simmer while she tidied away the few things Beth and Chrissie had left lying around. She closed the doors to their rooms and opened her own like an invitation.

She placed two red candles on the small dining table and set it as though she were entertaining royalty. A bottle of chardonnay was chilling in the fridge although she suspected Nicky would prefer beer. Too bad. This was her big night and it was going to be classy.

Choosing what to wear took even more time. Jeans were too casual but a party dress would look like she was trying too hard. She eventually settled on a flirty red skirt and a black velvet top. She admired herself in the mirror and looked at her watch for the hundredth time. She'd told him to come at six and there was still nearly an hour to go. She spent it pacing, checking the curry, making minute adjustments to the place settings, straightening the pictures on the wall and making the bed. With a gasp she suddenly spotted the framed photo of Nicky by the bedside and she hurriedly shoved it to the bottom of her underwear drawer.

That done, she returned to the curry. She would have to wait until the very last minute to add her secret ingredient. The kitchen smelled heavenly and she was sure the lethally spicy brew would disguise any odd flavour. But she threw in an extra chilli and another splash of ginger wine just to be safe.

At ten to six she put on some music and tried to slow her galloping heart as she waited for Nicky to arrive.

He was almost ten minutes late. Tamsin had been just about to text him when she heard the entryphone ring. She took a deep breath and picked it up.

"Hello?"

"Tamsin? It's me, Nicky."

Warmth flooded her face and throat at the sound of his voice. "Hang on, I'll buzz you in."

She hung up the phone and pressed the button to unlock the downstairs door. Then she ran to the bathroom for a last look at herself in the mirror before racing back. She could hear his boots thumping up the stairs and she held her breath until he reached the door, opening it before he could knock.

To her delight, he had worn her favourite shirt. It was deep silky black with vivid green pinstripes. He always wore black but the green brought out the colour of his eyes. She stilled her trembling hand against the door as she closed it behind him.

"Smells good," he said.

Tamsin smiled. And when he told her she looked nice she thought she would faint. "Want some wine?" she just managed to ask.

"That'd be great, thanks."

They sat side by side on the couch for a while, drinking from the chipped goblets Tamsin had found in a pagan shop. Every time he met her eyes she felt her stomach swoop as though she were falling from a great height. They talked about music, university, films, games, poetry, life. To Tamsin it seemed they talked for hours. She wanted to drown in his voice.

Eventually the talk turned back to Valhalla and Tamsin told him again how awesome she thought his songs were. What he said next made her want to pinch herself.

"I wrote a new song last night. No one's heard it yet. It's just me with no music and it's really rough but . . ."

"Yes," she said before he'd finished. "I'd love to hear it!"

He smiled shyly and lowered his head as he fished his iPod out of his pocket. Tamsin took it from him as though it were a priceless artefact and swapped it for hers in the docking station. She navigated to the track he directed her to and she sank back on the couch to listen.

It was all Nicky. Nothing but his voice. It sounded slightly husky and out of tune but none of that mattered. The song was called "Blood Mirror". And he was singing it just for her.

His hesitant voice sang about what lay beyond the mirror, what could be seen and what couldn't. Black mirror, velvet mirror. A reflection of dreams, of screams. Then nothing at all.

Tamsin felt the words circling her, seeking to enter her and redefine themselves according to her needs. A mirror revealed things. Sometimes hidden things. Like feelings. But try as she might, she couldn't make the lyrics fit. The song ended on a line about fangs and a reflection in blood and she realised that it wasn't about her at all. It was only a song about a vampire.

After a lengthy silence Tamsin opened her eyes.

"You don't like it." He said it with such dismay that she immediately felt guilty.

"Oh no," she assured him, "I loved it! I was just . . . imagining how the video would look."

She smiled then, picturing Nicky in period clothes, white lace pouring from his cuffs and collar, his razor-sharp cheekbones enhanced by the shadows of the gothic castle he would be prowling as he sang. He would carry a candelabrum, dripping red wax as he leant down over a sleeping maiden (Tamsin, of course), her pale throat exposed and vulnerable.

"Cool," Nicky said, relaxing. "I'm glad you liked it. I just wasn't ready to play it for the guys yet."

"I'm honoured to be the first," Tamsin said and she genuinely meant it. She had recovered from her initial disappointment. It didn't matter anyway. After tonight *all* his songs would be about her. "Are you hungry?"

"Starving."

"Good. Put on some music if you want and I'll get the food."

She left him on his own while she went to the kitchen and divided the curry into two bowls. Her hands shook as she removed the plaited coil of hair from where she'd tucked it inside her bra. She'd wanted to keep it close to her skin until the very last moment. With a pair of scissors she cut through it once to break the circle and then began snipping carefully along its length, cutting as finely as she could and sprinkling the tiny bits into Nicky's bowl. The pieces vanished into the liquid where she hoped they would be undetectable.

She put the bowls on a serving tray with a dish of jasmine rice and carried it in to him. Her hands were shaking but she managed not to spill anything. It seemed like a good omen.

"Here we go," she said. "I hope you like it."

And she could see that he did. He closed his eyes in bliss at the first bite and made appreciative noises throughout the meal.

She first sensed the spell was working when she caught him watching her as she refilled their wine glasses. When she looked up at him he averted his eyes and she heard his spoon scrape the bottom of his bowl. As a test she gathered her hair in her hands and piled it up on top of her head as though it were suddenly too hot to wear it down.

Instantly Nicky's eyes flicked back up to her and he stared openly as she twisted her hair into a loose knot, only to let it fall again. It spilled over her shoulders like molten gold. Nicky didn't blink.

"Still hungry?" Tamsin asked, nodding towards his empty bowl.

He rose slowly to his feet, shaking his head. He didn't take his eyes off her.

She woke several hours later in a tangle of limbs, her hair spilling coolly over her naked skin. Late afternoon light was painting the room orange and she opened her eyes to look at Nicky. He was still deeply asleep. In his bliss he looked like a dark angel.

She tried to turn her head but found she couldn't. Locks of her hair were wound tightly around both his hands, as though she were his lifeline. Tamsin usually plaited her hair before bed but last night she had left it loose and wild for him. Tears welled in her eyes as she replayed the night's countless pleasures. Kisses and caresses, skin on skin, a blur of passion. Her dream come true.

She didn't want to leave him but nature was calling and it took some manoeuvring to finally slip out of his grasp. She took the opportunity to clean her face and brush her teeth, not wanting him to wake up and see her with panda eyes.

How he had loved her hair! She could still see the otherworldly shine in his eyes as he gazed at it in the firelight. His fingers had stroked it reverently, combing through the glorious waves and clutching handfuls of it as he made love to her.

"Beautiful," he'd said, over and over. Like someone in love.

She sighed as she gazed at the girl in the mirror. Her skin was flushed, her eyes dreamy. A girl fulfilled. Her scalp tingled pleasantly as she ran a brush through her tangled curls, each stroke hissing and popping with static. She dropped the loose hairs into the bin and stared down at them, remembering the spell she had cast. It had worked. She was a part of him now, forever.

"Tamsin?"

The sound of his voice made her jump and she shook herself out of her reverie. When she emerged from the bathroom she saw him standing before the window, his body silhouetted against the autumn light.

"I'm here," she said, curling into his embrace.

He kissed her head and then held her face between his palms, staring at her as though unable to believe she was real. "Last night was incredible."

Tamsin sighed as she let the words wash over her. There couldn't possibly be another person anywhere in the world as happy as she was at this moment.

"I have to see you again."

"I'm yours," she said, her voice catching.

"Mine," he whispered, sounding bewildered. He repeated it with more conviction. "Mine." Then he clutched her tightly and pressed his lips to hers so hard it hurt.

He hadn't wanted to leave and she hadn't wanted to let him go. But they both had classes that evening and, frankly, Tamsin needed some time to recover from his attentions. She hadn't counted on him being such a violently passionate lover. Her insides burned with a deep dull ache and she wasn't at all surprised to find bruises on her inner thighs. Even her face felt bruised from his kisses. At times it had felt as though he were trying to force his entire body inside her, to devour her.

When she'd finally persuaded him to get dressed and follow her to the door, his eyes had shone with such fervour as he said goodbye that it became uncomfortable. She'd had to look away as she promised she'd see him again later that night.

Tamsin found it difficult to concentrate. Not even her favourite professor could distract her from the strange disquiet. She was thrilled that the spell had worked and the night had been truly magical. But Nicky's intensity was a little unnerving. There was something alien in the way he had looked at her as she'd shut the door that morning. After he left she'd gone to the window and was further unsettled to see him standing across the street, staring intently up at the building, his face a blank, pale oval. Not seeing her, but *searching*.

But then she shook off her misgivings. Of course he was bound to be acting a little weird; she'd *bewitched* him! She hoped he wasn't wondering too much at his newfound feelings. It should have felt like coming home. But perhaps it would take a little time for it all to sink in. Until then she would have to be patient.

She glanced down at her notebook and saw that she hadn't written a single word. Professor Canning was talking animatedly about Walt Whitman but Tamsin hadn't taken in a thing. With a sigh she closed her book, gathered her things and slipped out at the first opportunity.

Her legs ached as though she'd overexerted herself at the gym and she grimaced as she made her way down the corridor. She pushed open the front door of the building and was dazzled for a moment by the glare of the streetlights. The nights were getting longer and the darkness only reminded her how tired she was. She'd barely had any sleep the night before; Nicky had seemed inexhaustible.

Despite her pain and weariness Tamsin felt a smile tugging the corners of her mouth as she recalled the past few hours. She knew that Valhalla had another gig at the end of the month and she dreamily imagined Nicky coiled round the microphone, his silky voice singing words he'd written for her, *about* her. She knew Rob didn't like her and the others would probably side with him in thinking she was breaking up the band. But Nicky was better than all of them put together. He could make it on his own if he had to, with Tamsin as his partner and muse.

As she made her way home she became aware of a soft crunching behind her, the sound of someone treading through dry leaves. A chill slithered up her back as she realised she was being followed. She braced herself for a confrontation and then whirled round.

"Hey, creep—"

But it was only Nicky. Her surprise gave way to delight, but her smile melted as soon as she saw his face. His eyes blazed, red and bloodshot.

"Nicky, are you OK?"

"I love you," he said immediately.

His wild expression dampened the joy she should have felt. "But why didn't you say anything before? Why were you following me?"

He frowned. "I love you," he repeated, as if that explained it all.

"I love you too." The words came naturally to her. She'd said them hundreds of times on her own. But she said them now out of obligation and a sense of—yes, fear. There was something dangerous in his eyes, something akin to religious mania.

He took a step towards her and she flinched at his outstretched hand. But then a look of puzzlement crossed his features and she softened. She took his hand and kissed it, trying to remind herself that this was Nicky Renwick, the boy she had loved from afar ever since starting university. The boy she had now charmed into loving her back.

He shuddered as her lips touched his hand and he moved closer, winding his arms around her. He pressed his face into her hair and moaned softly.

"Nicky, no," she said, trying to disentangle herself from him. "I was just going home to try and get some sleep."

"We could sleep together," he offered immediately, still stroking her hair.

She forced a laugh. "I'm not sure we'd get much sleep." She cast about for more excuses. "Look, I need to do some major revision anyway. Why don't you come over tomorrow?"

He blinked at her slowly. "Tomorrow?"

"Yes. I'm really sorry but I'm totally knackered after last night. Hey, why don't you try to write a new song? Then you can play it for me tomorrow night."

Her words seemed to be causing him physical pain. His eyes glistened with tears at the rejection, although they widened slightly at the suggestion of a song.

"Tamsin," he murmured, as though tasting her name. "Yes. I'll write another song about you."

She heard the words in spite of her desire to get away from him. Her heart flickered with excitement even as she found the idea unsettling. *Another* song about her. When had he had time to write a first one?

"This afternoon," he said, answering her unspoken question. "While you were in your lecture. I watched you through the window."

The skin on the back of her neck prickled. He'd sat outside watching her, composing a song about her. And then he'd followed her. How long would he have kept it up if she hadn't heard him and turned around?

She forced another smile. "Nicky, that's really sweet. And I can't wait to hear it. But let's wait until tomorrow, okay? I really have to do some work."

For a moment he looked as though he wasn't going to accept her request. But then he nodded slowly and took a step back. "Okay" was all he said.

The silence stretched between them for an awkward minute before Tamsin finally said, "Right, then. I'll see you tomorrow." She waited for him to say something and when he didn't she turned and walked away. She could feel his eyes on her the whole time, burning through her. It was all she could do not to glance back. But she didn't need to. She knew he was still watching her.

Relief flooded through her when she finally reached the flat. She closed the door behind her and flopped into a chair, exhausted by the strange encounter. Clearly the spell had been too strong, but was there any way to moderate it? She hadn't imagined it would be like this. Still, she was hopeful that it would mellow.

She was too wound up to sleep so she dropped her books on the dining table with the honest intention of trying to do some work. But it was useless. She couldn't concentrate. The dishes from last night seemed to mock her and the candles had dripped onto the tablecloth to form a waxy bloodstain that reminded her of the hairs she had plucked. Suddenly the flat felt close and stuffy and she pushed her chair away and went to the window. She jerked the curtains open and was about to open the sash when she noticed the figure standing by the streetlight. Nicky.

He was staring up at the building the way he had been earlier. Only this time he saw her. He raised one hand and waved faintly but Tamsin couldn't bring herself to return it. She was starting to get seriously creeped out.

She closed the curtains and edged away from the window. Maybe she should go back to the forum and see if anyone there had any ideas. She had just booted up her computer when she heard the thumping. As she made her way past the kitchen she realised with a sense of dread that she'd heard the sound before. It was the sound Nicky's boots had made on the stairs last night. As he came up.

Either she hadn't closed the outer door properly or someone else had left it open. She braced herself, expecting him to knock, but all she heard was a soft scratching.

The sound unnerved her more than any dramatic pounding could have done. Tears filled her eyes at the thought of him standing out there, too hooked on her to be able to leave her alone, reduced to scratching plaintively at her door like an abandoned puppy.

"Nicky?" she called, trying to keep her voice steady. "Go home, OK? Please? I've got a lot of work to do. Why don't you come back in the morning?"

He was silent for a moment and then she heard a ragged sob. "Tamsin," he said, his voice choked with tears.

Her heart burned with shame and pity and she couldn't bear the thought of the pain she was causing him by leaving him out there. It was her fault he was lovesick and desperate. What was that old saying about being responsible forever for someone whose life you'd saved? Surely the same applied to someone you'd bewitched. He was her responsibility now.

With a heavy heart she turned the lock and opened the door.

He flew into her arms, burrowing his hands into her hair as he whispered fervently that he loved her, he loved her, he loved her.

"I love you too," she said helplessly, all the time wondering what the hell she was going to do.

He pulled away to gaze at her face. "You're so beautiful."

Last night it had thrilled her; now it made her skin crawl.

She pushed him away gently. "I have to use the loo," she said.

His blank expression betrayed no understanding but at least he didn't try to force his way in after her.

She splashed water on her face and stared at her haggard reflection. She suddenly looked ten years older. Maybe Beth or Chrissie had some sleeping tablets. She could knock him out while she figured out what to do. But a search of the medicine cabinet revealed nothing but an empty packet of birth control pills.

With a sigh she dropped the box into the bin below the sink. Then she glanced down at it. Something wasn't right. It took her a minute to realise what was missing. The loose hair she'd dropped into it that morning was gone. With a sinking feeling in her gut she suddenly understood what had gone wrong.

But she didn't have time to berate herself for her foolishness before the door crashed open and she cried out as she saw the look in Nicky's eyes. It was the stare of a starving animal, crazed with hunger.

"I love you," he said softly, his eyes fixed on her hair. He took a step forwards, closing the space between them. Tamsin immediately backed away. Confusion flickered in his eyes for a second and then he moved forwards again and reached out for her before she could move.

She shuddered as his hand settled on her hair and then he was winding it around his hand, pulling it hard.

"Stop it!" she yelped, flailing at his hand. "Let me go!"

He didn't seem to hear her. He continued to wind her hair around his fist, pushing her down onto the cold tiles as he did so.

She screamed when the hair at last tore free from her scalp. Blood poured hot and wet over her face and into her eyes, blinding her. All at once she couldn't breathe. She struggled frantically, her hands flailing against the side of the bathtub, feeling for anything she might use as a weapon. From somewhere behind her came a terrible sound. A wet munching. Sickness rose in her throat and she crawled away, slipping in the pool of blood as she felt for the open doorway.

She only got a few feet before she felt his hands in her hair again. The world went black with pain as he wrenched another fistful from her head.

The last thing she ever heard was his voice. Between hungry mouthfuls he whispered, "Beautiful."

No History of Violence

I T WAS TIME TO GO. SARA ZIPPED UP HER COAT AND TURNED towards her husband. Robin was looking out the window, his eyes empty.

"Are you ready?" she asked softly.

He didn't answer. She hadn't really expected him to. He stood like a statue, gazing at nothing for several seconds. Silent, but not at peace. After a while he swiped at his face. "Eating, eating," he whispered. "Inside me."

"I know, sweetie," she said. "They'll be gone soon, I promise."

He stared at her, his face a mask of misery and pain. "They're all I am now."

Sara's eyes filled with tears. Sometimes she was convinced she could see the bugs herself, hear their hellish chewing.

Then, as quickly as it had come, Robin's lucidity faded and he was gone again. He gazed blankly out the window, seeing nothing of the world outside.

Most people took their sanity for granted, never knowing how awful it could be to have to fight for it, gaining ground inch by torturous inch. Now it seemed like a wish denied. Had she dreamt it all? Robin was the one with the hallucinations but Sara suffered alongside him. It was no picnic being "normal" when your partner lived in a world you couldn't even see.

The bugs had been there since childhood, he'd told her. Kids in school had made fun of him, teasing him relentlessly about the voices he was so obviously hearing. Robin had been confused, never realising that he was the only one who saw and heard certain things, who talked of parasites devouring him from within. Finally, a teacher realised what was happening and Robin was referred to a psychiatrist. Now, more than thirty years later, he had finally reached something like stability. For the past ten years they had lived like other people did, like *normal* people did.

Robin had been free of the nightmare for so long Sara had almost forgotten how terrible things had once been. She'd done her best to forget the bad times, the times when her husband had seemed like another person entirely. One moment he would be perfectly fine and then the next his expression would turn flat and empty, his eyes looking through her, *beyond* her. Sometimes he would mumble words that sounded like another language. More than once she'd heard the word "kill".

And then there were the truly black days. Those were the times when Robin seemed to disappear completely. He would sit staring into the middle distance, focused intently on nothing. Calling his name or shaking him had no effect. He was simply *not there*. Except for the slow rise and fall of his chest she could almost believe he was dead.

Sara wasn't immune. Like an infection, Robin's darkness spread to her, poisoned her optimism and destroyed her sense of hope. At times like that she could see nothing but shadows and storm clouds. She could feel nothing but despair. Fantasies of death began to intrude into her thoughts and she found it harder and harder to push them away. Her own voices began to whisper insidious thoughts.

Wouldn't it be easier if . . .

Wouldn't it be kinder if . . .

Every time it happened she tapped a hidden well of strength and pulled herself out of the pit. It was like climbing up out of a deep well where they had both been left to drown. Getting herself out was hard enough; once out, she then had to pull Robin up after her. It got harder every time.

And then those terrible days became a thing of the past. At last, all the delicate juggling of pills and counsellors and psychotherapy paid off and Robin began to come back to her. He stopped hearing voices. He stopped obsessing about parasites. He stopped getting lost inside his mind. Finally, he began to recognise reality. Like a miracle, Robin was whole again. And they had been so happy.

Oh, but now. The bugs. The blackness. Sara felt it pressing on her like a weight. There was the terrible sense of sliding back through time, as though down the slimy walls of the bottomless well they had spent so many years climbing out of.

Sara licked the envelope, sealed it and laid it on the kitchen table where it could easily be found. Robin watched her without really seeing. He was scratching at his face and she could see he had already drawn blood.

"Cut me open," he moaned, "they'll spill out."

Sara's heart twisted. She couldn't even imagine what he was going through but she was determined to stop it.

"Just hold on a little longer," she said. Even though at times Robin seemed far away she always treated him as though he were right there with her. Maybe deep down inside, in some lost little place, he could hear her. "We'll make them go."

When the local hospital began to shrink under the budget cuts, one of the first things to go had been the mental health treatment programme. Naturally, the support group for partners went along with it. Sara had the luxury of finding her own support group online but of course Robin needed so much more than that. They'd both searched for alternative solutions but they were told the resources simply weren't there.

"It's a death sentence," Sara had said to more than one administrator, but her words fell on deaf ears. Each person had spread his hands and made sympathetic noises but to them Robin was just another casualty of a failing system. One of many. There was the implication that they shouldn't think they were special.

It was like being at the mercy of a killer. The police couldn't do anything until a crime had been committed and by then it would be too late. With no more access to the treatment that kept Robin in touch with the real world, their only option was to wait until he lost it completely.

"Then, of course," said a nurse who was probably ten years younger than she looked, "you would have the option of coercive care."

Sara felt her skin crawl. "Is that the PC term for 'sectioned'?"

"Well, yes." At Sara's look of horror she added, "Only if he turns violent."

"My husband has never been violent in his life."

The nurse shrugged helplessly. She had the bloodshot eyes of someone who never got enough sleep and Sara could practically read the girl's mind. She was a victim of the whole mess too. Overworked, underpaid, terrified of being cut loose herself, however thankless and gruelling her job was. Like a volunteer at an animal shelter, she simply couldn't afford to get attached to every sad stray that was brought in. All she could do was offer hollow reassurances and move on to the next distraught family member, the next hopeless case.

Robin had only been hospitalised once before. When he was a teenager his parents had him committed and the experience had traumatised him. The bullying he'd suffered at school was nothing compared to the bullying he suffered from his fellow inmates. There weren't enough staff to keep an eye on everyone and Robin had been too weak, frightened and sedated to fight back. His supposed "carers" were no help either. They told him he'd imagined it.

Robin had made Sara promise never to lock him up again. He'd told her he'd rather die.

Sara had promised without hesitation.

Now they had run out of options. Medication alone wasn't enough to keep Robin from the creeping madness that overwhelmed him and he was slowly slipping away from her. Bewilderingly, Robin had been passed fit for work by the "expert" who'd glanced at him for five minutes and signed him off.

So Robin had stayed in his job, working alongside Sara. It wasn't terribly demanding. Just general catering duties, although he wasn't allowed to prepare food without supervision. Presumably someone had the sense to realise that thwarted benefits scroungers like her husband might have access to poison. Or that their wives might.

"Kill them," Robin said, a note of desperation in his voice now. He looked confused and frightened as he clawed at his skin. "Please."

"We will," Sara said, wrapping her arms around him. He shuddered, swatting at the air around them both as he mumbled other random words and sounds that meant nothing.

Even in his worst hallucinatory states, Robin had never been dangerous. Not intentionally. He hadn't meant to hurt her that time. He'd been lashing out at what he thought was a bug. He hadn't even known Sara was there. Afterwards he had no memory of it and of course he believed her story about tripping over the cat. She wasn't sure anyone else bought it and she deeply resented the stares of her co-workers over the next week as the bruise on her cheek turned blue, then yellow, then finally faded. She just as deeply resented the fact that, suspecting domestic abuse, no one had expressed the slightest concern.

No one cared.

And that was what it all boiled down to, wasn't it? No one cared. In a society full of victims, empathy was yet another luxury beyond their means.

"Quality of life" was a phrase that kept ringing in Sara's mind. What kind of quality was this? The slow downward spiral to inevitable hospitalisation, out of Sara's control. Robin would be too doped up to know who she was when she tried to explain. Too doped up to fight back if he were mistreated as he had been before.

In his fractured mind, would he hate her for the betrayal? She knew the answer to that and it chilled her. Yes. He would. That strange, alien part of Robin would hate her. The stranger who talked about parasites wasn't the Robin she had met and married all those years ago but he was the one increasingly in control now. He was a person she didn't know at all. A person she feared.

But it wasn't his fault. The *state* had made him into something to fear. And now it was time for them to pay.

Sara swallowed her tears as she tucked the gun into her bag. "Come on, we have to go to work."

He stared at the bag for almost a minute. Maybe the sight of the weapon had shocked him back into himself, had momentarily returned him to her, however briefly. He stopped clawing at his eyes and looked at her, as though he understood what she was about to do. As though he were almost there with her.

"Work?"

"Yes, sweetie. For the last time."

He was calmer as he followed her out to the car, as though he had managed to fight his way through the fog to be with her. He didn't ask where they were going and Sara sensed that he knew.

They'd picketed outside Parliament once, with other casualties of the system. They were the helpless prey of the men and women inside who had sworn to protect their constituents. The ones who had then voted to cut that very protection while aligning themselves with the powerful companies who had quite literally ruined the lives of thousands of people.

Tonight some of those men and women would be dining in luxury at the five-star hotel that Sara's company was catering for. The dinner would be lavish and extravagant, just the sort that men who made life and death decisions for others felt they deserved. It was probably a good way to escape the horror of their consciences, the reminder of all those broken promises. They could numb themselves with exquisite food and drink and tune out the shouting from the streets below.

Robin hesitated when they reached the service door. He turned to Sara, a look of confusion crossing his features as he scratched absently at his scalp. "I can still feel them," he said. "What if I . . . ?"

"You won't," Sara said. She withdrew the gun and checked that it was ready for action. "*I* will."

For a split second Robin looked frightened. Then his expression softened into one of complete understanding. And gratitude. He pulled her towards him and kissed her, hard, one final time.

"I love you so much," he said. "Even though I'm crazy, I've never lost sight of that."

Sara clung to him, savouring the moment for as long as she dared.

"You're not crazy," she said fiercely. "The parasites are real. They always have been."

LITTLE DEVILS

"**Y**OU'RE NOT SUPPOSED TO GO IN THERE!**"
The kids stopped at the torn chain link fence and Arabella shot her sister a scathing look. "You squeal, you little horror, and you'll be sorry."

Pippa drew back, aghast. Clearly she'd thought she could influence the older kids, though whatever delusion had made her think that, Arabella couldn't begin to guess.

They all stared at her, Freddie with his eyebrows raised comically, Scarlett with her arms crossed, looking bored. William slung his school blazer over his shoulder and crouched down to look Pippa in the eye.

"Look here, Pips," he said, using the nickname they all knew she despised, "there's six of us and only one of you. Do you really think we'd let you get away with telling tales on us?"

"Yeah," Rupert put in. He gestured theatrically towards the building site. "There's a lot of wet cement around here. A little girl like you could fall in so easily."

"Just like someone in a gangster picture," Freddie added, rubbing his hands together.

Arabella grinned smugly at the terror on her sister's face at that but Georgie looked worried.

"You oughtn't tease her so," she said with a frown. "She's only little."

But Pippa didn't seem to appreciate the older girl coming to her defence. She glared at them. "You lot are only twelve!" she blurted out with surprising boldness.

William gave her a tight smile, then took hold of her school tie and pulled her in close until they were nose to nose. "And if you want to live to be twelve yourself," he growled, "you'll shut your mouth and be grateful we let you tag along at all."

That got to her. Pippa's eyes filled with tears and her lower lip quivered. For one moment Arabella almost felt sorry for the little brat.

Scarlett heaved a dramatic sigh. "Such a bore. Now she'll start bawling."

"No she won't," said William, still smiling coldly at Pippa. "Will you, Pips?"

The six-year-old shook her head, blonde plaits swinging. She swallowed loudly and got control of herself, glancing fearfully up at her big sister as if seeking confirmation that William meant business.

Arabella merely gave her a withering look. "Honestly," she snorted, "you're such a baby." Then she turned on her heel and followed Freddie and Rupert through the opening in the fence.

Scarlett went next, after only a moment's hesitation. "The place is probably crawling with rats and spiders," she said with a shudder, pressing closer to Rupert.

The boys looked excited by the prospect but Arabella wished she hadn't said it. It was only likely to terrify Pippa more and if she ran off and told their parents where they'd been they'd all be for it. Then Pippa would really suffer. Oh, yes.

Georgie hung back, eyeing the fence uneasily. "I'm not sure this is such a good idea," she said. "Daddy says you can catch diseases from builders."

Scarlett shrugged. "Please yourself." She looked only too happy for their little group to lose one of its female members.

"Aww, come on, Georgie," Freddie said. "We'll protect you." He snatched up a length of metal pipe from the ground and brandished it like a sword.

Georgie smiled but shook her head. "No, I think I'll leave you to it. I've got my riding lesson this afternoon anyway. See you."

Freddie tried one last time to persuade her but she clearly wasn't keen. Georgie waved goodbye as she turned and walked away down the street. Pippa watched her go, looking as though she regretted snapping at her. Now her only advocate was gone.

That'll teach you, Arabella thought.

William brought up the rear, grabbing Pippa by the wrist and hauling her through the gap. Arabella flushed a little at the thought of William taking *her* arm like that and then brushed the image aside, embarrassed. Once Pippa was inside the fence she ran to her sister and Arabella reluctantly allowed her to clutch her hand. Now that they were stuck with her they couldn't afford to let her run off.

The others had already disappeared into the half-finished building. It looked like the skeleton of a house, with sheets of torn milky plastic flapping against the sides like loose skin. A rude picture was spray-painted on one wall of a nearby Portakabin, along with a girl's name and a phone number. Underneath this were other scribbles and weird symbols. Possibly it was some language used by the gypsies who passed through the area in their battered caravans, only to be turfed out again.

They'd often seen scruffy kids from the comprehensive school playing on the site and once or twice they'd seen the police there. It was a place their parents and teachers had warned them to stay away from, a place nice people didn't go.

She heard a dramatic shriek followed by laughter as Scarlett no doubt clung to Rupert for protection from the creepy-crawlies inside. It had been Rupert's idea to go exploring and Arabella suspected that Scarlett had gone along merely so she could sneak off into a dark corner with him. As for herself, she'd gone because of William. Then bloody Pippa had tagged along and spoilt it all. It would serve her right if she stepped on a rusty nail.

Pippa's grip tightened on her hand as Arabella picked her way carefully across the rubbish-strewn site, following the laughing voices of her friends. There was the rattle and clank of empty beer bottles as the lads kicked them around and then laughter as one smashed against something. Arabella could imagine Pippa totting up the damage in her little head, like some horrid school monitor.

When they reached the house she made Pippa let go. Her own hand was clammy now and she wiped it on her pleated skirt as she frowned at her sister. The builders had left a mess behind. It looked like they'd had some kind of party. In addition to the beer bottles there was a scorched area on the floor where there had obviously been a fire.

"Ugh, squatters," Scarlett said, nudging the charred wood with the toe of one polished shoe.

"Looks like they had a barbecue," Rupert said. "Probably nicked a lamb from Harlow Farm and cooked it."

William peered closely at the remains of the fire. "A cow more like." He pulled out a long scorched bone and held it up for everyone to see. Strings of blackened meat still adhered to the bulbous joint.

Freddie turned to Pippa with a look of cruel glee. "Or maybe it's the bones of a little girl who wandered in here one night."

Pippa whimpered and clutched at her sister's skirt but Arabella kneed her away roughly. She fell to the floor with a cry and immediately scrambled to her feet. Her right hand was bloody, pierced by a shard of broken glass. She stared at the sight in horror and Arabella knew that once she got over the shock she'd start to cry.

"Look what you did," she snarled, digging in her blazer pocket for a tissue and thrusting it at her sister.

"I'm bleeding," Pippa whimpered.

"Oh, for God's sake!" Arabella wasn't gentle as she plucked the glass out of Pippa's palm and threw it to the floor. "Now tidy yourself up and don't start crying or we'll lock you in that filthy toilet outside."

Pippa's lip quivered as she mopped up the blood but she managed to hold in her babyish sobs. The others were getting just as tired of her drama.

"I'm going upstairs," Rupert said. Scarlett immediately trailed after him.

There was a dead rat on the landing. It was lying in a dark brown stain and its head had been crushed. Freddie peeled it up from the floor by its tail and dangled it in front of Scarlett, who shrieked and ran to hide behind Rupert. The three boys laughed and Arabella felt Pippa shrinking back lest Freddie throw the thing at her. But he dropped it with his own cry of disgust when he saw the little white maggots wriggling in its mangy fur. He smeared his hands up and down the wall, leaving behind a foul-smelling greenish smear.

"Revolting," Scarlett said with a shudder. She took Rupert's arm and hurried up the second flight of stairs.

Arabella eyed the rat warily as she edged past. Something about it was wrong. The maggots must have been burrowing underneath the rat's body and Freddie had dropped it so that the maggots were on top now. They writhed in the rat's flesh with renewed vigor and several of them, dislodged in the fall, were bending and twisting on the dusty floor like tiny worms, blindly searching for the putrefying feast they'd been evicted from.

"Come on," Pippa whispered, tugging at the sleeve of her blazer.

"All right, all right!"

They came to the top of the stairs and had a choice of directions. Some-day there would be doors here. The hall would be carpeted and the walls painted. Someone would live here. She could scarcely imagine how it would look when it was finished. Right now it looked less like a future home than a project that had been abandoned and left to rot for years. But they'd seen builders on the site that morning on the way to school. She recalled think-ing how easy it would be to fall from the top floor onto the unforgiving concrete foundation below. What would it look like? How would it sound?

When she became aware of the strange silence she looked up. Everyone was watching her.

"What? What are you staring at?"

Scarlett looked uneasy. She chewed her lip and glanced at Rupert before speaking. "What was that you said?"

Arabella blinked in confusion. "Huh? All I said was: What are you staring at?"

"No, no, before that."

Puzzled, she glanced down at Pippa. "Did I say something?"

The look on Pippa's face told her she had and that, whatever it was, it hadn't been nice.

"It sounded like Latin," said William. The other two boys confirmed this with a nod.

Arabella laughed. "I don't know any Latin," she said. "And I didn't say anything anyway. You lot are hearing things."

But Scarlett wasn't prepared to let it go. "Arabella, you absolutely said something. And it sounded *evil*."

Bewildered, she turned again to Pippa. Her little sister had inched away, her expression corroborating the claim that she had said something weird. It sent a chill through her spine.

"I may have muttered something about the rat but that's all. I certainly didn't say anything evil. In Latin or French or even English. Now can we please move on?"

The others eyed her warily for a few seconds before relaxing. One by one they turned away and headed off into the various rooms of the skeletal house. Pippa seemed torn between her sister and the others but after a moment's indecision she stuck with Arabella.

"I don't like this place," she confided in a whisper, her voice full of hope that Arabella felt the same. "It smells."

That was certainly something Arabella could agree with. "Yeah, it does."

What were they doing here anyway? Of course the boys wanted to explore the building site; boys were like that. And girls didn't have to sit at home and play with dolls and bake pretend cakes; that's why they were there with them. But really—what was the point of exposing themselves to this filthy old place with its charred bones and dead rats? Just because their parents told them not to go there? What if it really was dangerous? The rebellion hardly seemed worth the risk. Maybe Georgie had had the right idea.

She was just opening her mouth to suggest that they'd seen enough and they could go now when she heard the sound. She frowned and listened. From somewhere down the hall came the low murmur of voices. It sounded as though they were chanting.

Pippa's hand was immediately around hers like a vise and Arabella gasped at the pain as her knuckles were crushed. "Oww!" She hissed at Pippa to let go.

"I really *really* don't like it here," Pippa whimpered. "I want to go home."

Pippa's fear gave Arabella courage and she made a face. "Don't be such a baby," she snapped. "It's only the others trying to scare you." She'd been on the verge of saying "us" but she didn't like the thought of being left out of whatever game her friends were playing.

"Come on, Pippa."

She dragged her little sister along the corridor and turned a corner. A thick plastic curtain hung down in an archway at the end, where a door would one day be. It was streaked with mud and Arabella gave a shudder as she wedged her hands into the split and pushed the plastic to either side.

The voices were louder and as she drew nearer she thought it sounded like Latin. She didn't know any herself but she'd heard it spoken at church and in films. It must be what the others had heard and thought was her.

This room was warmer than the others and she realised why at once. Something was burning. It wasn't entirely unpleasant and it made her think of Bonfire Night. In fact, the strange figure slumped smouldering in the centre of the room might be a small ragged Guy. It looked like a scarecrow that had fallen from its crossbeam. Its clothes had been stuffed with leaves and mulch, the charred remnants of which spilled out from the sleeves of its splayed arms. Wisps of smoke curled up from the scorched clothes like steam.

But November was a long way off and she couldn't imagine what other reason someone would have for burning a Guy. It certainly hadn't been any of her friends' doing; she'd have noticed one of them carrying something that size.

She lifted her head to call out to William and her voice froze in her throat when she saw what was on the walls. All around her were weird symbols, like the foreign writing she'd seen scribbled on the Portakabin outside. The dark red smears and splashes looked like the finger-painting of a mad child. Some of the symbols she recognised: they were the signs of the zodiac. She saw her own—Pisces—and felt a twinge of apprehension without knowing why.

Her symbol was surrounded by other crazy scrawls and a large picture dominated the far wall. It was sketched in black and the light from the fire made it gleam like metal. It looked like the figure of a person with a deer's head. Or maybe it was a goat. But it was all wrong. The thing had wings and Arabella couldn't tell if it was meant to be a man or a woman. It looked male but it also appeared to have breasts. One arm was up and one was down, with the first two fingers of each hand pressed together and extended as though pointing.

The voices were coming from the next room. Pippa hung back, staying close to the plastic curtain and shaking her head as she stared wide-eyed at the burnt effigy.

Arabella took a deep breath and moved further into the room, where she found the source of another smell. Scattered around the base of the painted goat-thing were the mutilated bodies of rats.

She covered her mouth to stifle her cry of horror. They were in piles. Dozens of them. It was only once she saw them that she heard the drone of flies buzzing lazily around the corpses and realised what had bothered her so much about the other rat on the stairs.

She didn't know how long it took for maggots to devour something like a rat but she remembered vividly when their pet rabbit Hoppy had died last winter. It was Arabella's week to feed him and she had forgotten three days in a row. She didn't want to be blamed so she didn't tell Pippa or her parents that she'd found him dead. She'd left him lying cold and stiff in his hutch outside for the rest of the week so her sister could find him. When it was Pippa's turn to feed him Arabella followed, her stomach fluttering with morbid anticipation. The sight was even worse than she'd imagined. So was Pippa's reaction. She looked like something possessed as she screamed and sobbed hysterically and finally fled into the house.

Arabella felt a strange mingling of guilt and excitement. Finding Hoppy dead had been a nasty shock for her but how much worse must it have been for Pippa? She crept up to the hutch and peered inside, curious to see what the passage of time had done to their dead pet. What she saw made her stomach clench. Hoppy's body looked like it was melting, collapsing in on itself. And just underneath the fur was the ripple of living things eating their way out. One pale eye stared at her with silent reproach and she backed away from the hutch, whispering apologies as tears shimmered in her eyes.

The rat on the stairs had looked just the same. But how could it have been lying there dead for days when there had been workers here only a few hours ago? Wouldn't they have seen it? Got rid of it? And how could a fire be smouldering up here when she and her friends were the only ones on the site? All at once she felt watched. They were not alone. Someone else was here.

She turned slowly towards Pippa but the little girl was crouched on the floor, hugging her knees to her chest, her eyes glued to the image of the goat-man.

From the other room the chanting rose in volume, a chorus that seemed to contain more than just the voices of her four friends. She didn't want to go in there. But, just as with Hoppy, she had to see. The urge was powerful and she felt as though invisible hands were gently urging her through the open doorway.

The room flickered with the orange light from the candles spread across the floor. The billowing plastic walls made it seem like the room was breathing.

William, Freddie, Rupert and Scarlett stood in a circle, their hands upraised, their faces blank. Their mouths moved but the voices were not those of children. On the floor at their feet, in a circle of candles, was the largest book Arabella had ever seen. Larger even than the antique dictionary her father kept on a stand in the library at home. Her eyes were drawn immediately to the open pages and she gasped at the sight. The pages were crawling with maggots, as though the book itself had once been alive. Around the squirming bodies were the scratches, loops and swirls of some strange writing. And as she looked, the text began to move too.

Like tiny snakes the black lines of unfamiliar letters coiled and slithered over the pages, forming pictures that then melted into other images. She saw the goat-man again, crackling flames, a knife, a screaming mouth.

In the corner of the room a mass of shadows swarmed. At first Arabella took it for a pile of blankets. Then she saw the pale slender arm lying alongside it and her mind began piecing the image together. It was a woman, naked and dead. Arabella didn't need to look closer to know that the shadows were a cloud of flies, that the woman's body was also home to the writhing, hungry worms.

But that wasn't all. The plastic gave a violent rattle in the wind and the flies buzzed angrily, rising to reveal other lumpen shapes scattered around the dead woman. Boots and hardhats swam into focus and Arabella felt a scream gathering at the back of her throat as she tried to understand what she was seeing, what must have happened here.

The builders were dead too, mutilated just like the rats. Strange writing adorned the plastic above them, smeared in what could only be their blood. In the afternoon half-light it looked like jam.

She wanted to run. She wanted to go home and forget they'd ever come here. Whoever—or whatever—had done this was still here. But her legs didn't seem to want to move. She felt dizzy and weak, like she was going to be sick. Gradually she became aware again of the chanting behind her and she turned to see that the others had joined hands.

Slowly her legs began to move, but instead of carrying her away they took her towards the others. The pages of the book shivered as she approached and she became aware of a strange humming sound in her ears. She felt her mouth moving along with the rhythm of the chanting and she realised that the humming was her own voice. She had joined in, speaking the alien words.

William and Freddie turned to her, their eyes like those of blind men, milky white and unseeing. They broke the circle and reached for her. Arabella moved towards William as if in a dream. She understood that she was wanted here, needed. There was something she was meant to do. Something important. She let them take her hands and guide her into the circle, closing it once more. She was part of the ritual now, for that was what it was—a ritual. Just like in church.

She was only vaguely aware of her fear. A wall of numbness separated it from her in her mind. If she could break through and touch it she would be terrified. She would scream. She'd be able to run away. But she was cut off from her emotions as effectively as from pain at the dentist's. It was there and she was aware of it; it just couldn't reach her.

From far in the back of her mind came an image of Pippa, cowering on the floor in the other room and staring at the painting of the goat-man. Arabella could see him moving, stepping down from the smeared plastic and onto the bloodstained floor. His hooves clacked on the floorboards as he approached the little girl.

Part of her wanted to call out to Pippa to run but her body was as numb as her fear. Untouchable. Unreachable. She stayed where she was, part of the circle, chanting the unfamiliar words that felt as natural to her as breathing.

The goat-man crossed the floor, his wings flexing, stirring the dust. Pippa gazed up at him, wide-eyed and curious. Why wasn't she afraid? Why didn't she run?

She could see everything as clearly as if she were right there. The goat-man leaned down to Pippa and reached out his hand. Pippa gazed at it wonderingly for a moment before getting to her feet. She held out the hand she had injured and Arabella could smell the blood pooling in her tiny palm. It was bleeding a lot for such a tiny injury. Pippa cupped both hands and raised them up to the goat-man. He lowered his head and dipped his snout into the blood and Arabella heard the slurps and snorts as he lapped up the offering greedily.

When he had drunk his fill he raised his head and a deep cold look passed between him and Pippa. Arabella's eyes began to tingle, as though the vision was damaging her sight, blinding her. The room grew hazy but they continued to murmur the strange words, clutching one another's damp hands in their little circle. Beneath them the pages of the book fluttered and the text writhed, forming images that melted into other images.

Arabella saw the goat-man turn slowly towards the room they were in. Fear leapt in her chest but she could do nothing about it. As he made his way towards them Pippa followed.

Now the creature stood behind them. Arabella could see him in the pages of the book as though in a mirror. He regarded each of them one by one, then closed his eyes and tilted his head back, listening to their voices. Suddenly Arabella knew they were speaking his name, calling him, giving him strength. She tried to close her mouth, tried to silence the many ugly syllables that defined him, but she was completely cut off from herself.

From behind her came a laugh and a glance at the book showed her Pippa, an expression of savage delight in her eyes. She put her bloodied hands up to her face and smeared them over her cheeks, her neck, her white shirt and striped school tie. She smiled. Then she pointed towards the circle, at William specifically. The goat-man nodded.

Arabella felt William's hand tighten on hers for a second. Then he was ripped from her grasp, torn from the circle as violently as if a bomb had gone off in his face. He didn't make a sound as his body struck the plastic, splitting it open. He fell silently, hitting the ground outside with a wet thud.

Pippa ran to the corner of the room to see, grinning madly at the sight that greeted her down below. Then she scampered back to the goat-man's side and this time Scarlett was her choice. Arabella sought refuge in the encroaching blindness as one by one her friends were snatched from the circle and sent flying to their deaths.

When only Arabella remained her voice grew silent at last. Pippa stood before her, her face a crimson mask.

"He needed blood," she said simply. "The blood of someone innocent." Her voice sounded like the rasp of an old woman.

Arabella tried to speak but now no sound would come out.

"She wasn't innocent," Pippa said, jerking her chin towards the dead woman in the corner. "She said she was but she lied. And they—" she indicated the builders "—interfered."

Arabella stared at the pile of bodies, the unsatisfactory sacrifice and the slaughtered workers. The ones who had simply got in the way. Had they interrupted the original ritual, perhaps tried to rescue the woman? Who had killed *them*?

A soft laugh came from the shadows. Arabella could just make out a figure there, clothed all in black, his gaunt face gleaming like bone. He moved away from the wall and Pippa went to him, smiling, and took his hand. Then she turned to Arabella and her expression grew cold and pitiless.

"Everyone wants power and knowledge," Pippa said, still speaking in that strange other voice, "and everyone assumes they deserve to have it." She glanced over at the dead woman. "Unworthy whore. Ah, but then you came. You and your little friends. But only one of you was worthy. We asked. She accepted."

Listening to Pippa speak about herself like this was terrifying, as though she'd gone mad. Somehow she knew it was the cowled figure speaking through her. The goat-man stood beside her, a towering figure of evil, a monster of the kind she'd used to tell Pippa about to scare her. But this was no made-up bogeyman; this was real.

It took all her strength but at last Arabella managed to move. She took a step towards Pippa. For a second the little girl gasped in surprise, but then she got control of herself again. Her eyes gleamed unpleasantly bright in her gore-streaked face.

"Not bad," she said. "You could have been useful to us. Stubborn. Strong. But this one is stronger. Stronger than any of you. Oh, how the seeds of bitterness and resentment grow. How they fester. They ripen into such poisonous fruit."

Arabella tried to move again but she was frozen to the spot. She could only stare in horror at her little sister—what *used* to be her little sister—and the hideous goat-man she had revived and nourished with her blood. He held out his arms and Pippa stepped into his embrace. She reached up to stroke the goat head, running her bloodied hand down its filthy muzzle as though it were a pet.

The wind lifted the plastic and the candles flickered. Pippa had vanished, along with the goat-man and the cowled figure. Arabella looked wildly around the room but she couldn't see her sister anywhere. Then something drew her eye down to the book on the floor. There was a new image crawling across the pages. Another goat-like creature stood pawing at something on the ground with its cloven hooves. A girl lay in a pool of blood, her body a mass of injuries. The goat-thing was eating her flesh. It lifted its head from the book, casting frightful shadows with its horns on the makeshift walls. Their tips were covered in blood.

"Pippa," Arabella whispered.

The goat-thing smiled as the candles guttered and went out.

BAD FAITH

(with Joel Lane)

THE FOX STARED AT DEREK WITH COLD, CLOUDY EYES, its body in pieces. Tufts of rust-coloured fur drifted in the steaming air like feathers. From the shadows, something growled at him. A dog. A big one by the sound of it. Derek edged away from the kill, watching until he reached the corner, but the dog didn't appear.

The pub wasn't crowded. A scattering of old men sat nursing ales at separate tables, weighed down by the heat and their solitude. A portable fan propped on the bar stirred the dense air without cooling it.

Derek ordered a pint from Paul and stood at the end of the bar, too listless to move. He watched the quick, repetitive movements of Paul's hands as he worked, doling out drinks and gathering up empty glasses. He moved like an automaton, the sweat stains beneath his arms the only evidence that he was flesh and blood.

He pulled on the handle to fill a glass with something dark and frothy for a man in a high-vis jacket. The neon yellow seared into Derek's eyes like a contagion of the sun and he turned away. He scarcely noticed that Paul had returned to his end of the bar.

"Did you hear about that burglar?"

Derek pressed his pint glass to his forehead, but the beer was too warm to cool him. "What burglar?"

Paul grunted. "The one you didn't hear about."

"Sorry, no. What about him?"

"Busted into the wrong house, he did. Dog fucking tore him to pieces. Police had to take him out in buckets."

Derek swallowed. The beer felt like wet cement in his throat. "Jesus."

"I heard about that," the yellow-jacketed man said a few moments later, as though the news had taken time to penetrate the sweltering air and reach him further down the bar. "Serves the bastard right. Wish I could have seen it."

Derek winced. "Surely no one deserves *that*."

But the man nodded, his expression cold and serious. "Fucker broke the law, didn't he? Got what was coming to him."

Paul was keeping quiet. Bartenders wisely never let themselves get drawn into discussions like this. He moved some glasses around as he pretended to be busy, a silent robot again.

Derek couldn't stop thinking about the dismembered fox. Had it been the same dog? Had the fox been alive when it was torn apart?

"Just seems like a bad death," he said. Burglar or not, he couldn't help feeling it was an awful way to go.

But even his noncommittal response seemed to aggravate the man. He moved closer, the blazing yellow of his jacket like the spreading of flames in a house fire. Derek flinched at his nearness. The man armed sweat off his forehead as he set his empty glass down on the bar with a thud. "You know why people break the law? Because they're fucking criminals."

Derek took another swallow of his beer. It tasted like canal water. "That's like saying people die because they're corpses."

The yellow man didn't know what to say to that. He frowned as he thought about it, then turned away in disgust, muttering something under his breath.

"What happened to the dog?"

Paul blinked at Derek. "Huh?"

"The dog. What happened to it?"

"Put down, I guess," Paul said with a shrug. "Vicious thing like that."

The yellow man laughed, a sharp, nasty sound. "You looking for a pet, boy?"

Derek ignored him and finished his drink in one long swallow. It did nothing to quench his thirst. He'd heard about dogs that were trained to fight. Their owners made them vicious. Beat them and fed them steroids and amphetamines. Probably this poor dog was one of those. Once he'd even seen a dog with a swastika tattooed on its chest. There were good people in the world, he knew, but sometimes it was hard not to lose faith in that.

"Well, see you," he mumbled, giving Paul a desultory wave as he left.

Outside the sky seemed to be melting. Sweat trickled across his scalp and ran into his eyes. He scrubbed it away as he made his way down the street. It looked different in the heat. Forsaken.

Even the flat looked different, as though someone had been inside and changed things. Andrew wouldn't have done it, and anyway, he was still at work. Derek thought of the burglar and did a quick walk-through, but nothing appeared to have been taken. There wasn't much to steal in any case.

He clambered into the shower, but even the water from the cold tap was like soup, warm and cloying. He was dozing on the couch afterwards when he heard the barking. It was a low, muddy sound, as though reaching him through dense fog. He pushed the curtains aside and saw motion outside in the darkening streets. Dogs. They were everywhere.

The pack was running, driving a group of people before them. Long pink tongues lolled between the razors of their teeth.

Derek drew back, startled. The dogs must have sensed his motion because they stopped at once, like a flock of birds shifting mid-flight. They stood perfectly still and only their heads turned to regard him. The movement was unnatural. *Alien.* They stared at him, eyes gleaming red, breath steaming in the heavy air.

The people they had been chasing stopped too. But they didn't run or try to get away. They stood where they were, staring down at the ground like toys that had wound down. Derek could see that some of them had been bitten, chewed. The wounds looked black. Flesh hung from them in scarlet tatters. Still, none of them moved.

He turned away and closed his eyes, shutting out the scene. The barking resumed and he heard the scraping of claws on the pavement as the pack began to run again. The sound was drawing nearer. His eyes flew open at the sound of the front door opening and he blinked in wild confusion to find himself back on the couch. The dream had fractured. Before he could feel relief, however, he heard the fading echo of a howl.

He sat up, watching helplessly as a tall, thin figure advanced towards him. It was only a silhouette in the darkness. Its body was human, but he recognised the shape of the head as something else. The pointed ears, the long snout. It reached a long arm for him and he screamed, batting the hand away.

"Hey, it's just me! Calm down."

The light came on and Derek saw that it was only Andrew. He looked terrified.

"Are you hurt?" he asked, grabbing his partner's hands and turning them so he could see the arms. "Did they attack you?"

But Andrew only looked baffled, shaking his head, his eyes wide. "I don't know what you're talking about. Did *who* attack me?"

Derek scrambled to his feet and flung the curtains aside. The streets were empty.

The next evening he eyed his surroundings warily as he made his way home. He stopped by the place where he had seen the dead fox the day before, but there was no trace of it left.

He peered down alleyways and side streets, expecting to see dogs lurking there, waiting for him. He couldn't shake the image of those terrible red eyes, that icy breath pluming from snarling mouths.

Andrew wouldn't be home for hours yet and Derek didn't want to be there by himself. He hesitated outside the pub, not really wanting company but not wanting to be alone either. The yellow man was standing by the bar as though he'd never left, his lips writhing in conversation with Paul.

A man and a woman sat near the open window, eating something Derek couldn't identify. It looked as though it had been scraped off the road. He watched in horror as the woman plucked a long white hair from her mouth. She showed no disgust. She just resumed eating, her eyes as dead as what was on her plate.

Derek's stomach gave a lurch and he walked on.

The streets were deserted and the hot air pressed down on him like the weight of the ocean. Cloying, stifling.

From somewhere in the night came the barking of a dog. Derek froze in his tracks, listening. Soon it was joined by another, then another. Like a wolf pack joining the howl one by one, more dogs added their voices to the chorus.

Derek moved quickly, turning down the street that led home. He felt stalked, pursued. He peered into the swarming shadows of car parks, the coiling nothingness that lurked in the passages between houses. The barking echoed as if from the sky, coming from everywhere all at once. He strained to hear beyond it, listening for the sound of running feet, of untrimmed claws clicking on the pavement, and the snuffling of animals on the hunt.

As he passed houses he chanced to look inside one. The curtains were splayed, the window open wide. At first he couldn't believe what he thought he'd seen. The sight he'd glimpsed was wrong. So wrong that he was compelled to backtrack, just to check that his mind had indeed played a horrible trick on him.

But it hadn't.

Inside the house, an elderly couple sat staring blank-eyed at a wall, completely still. For a moment he thought they were dead. But there was a stiffness to their posture that suggested they were deliberately holding the pose. Or *being* held. Like puppets awaiting manipulation. But what disturbed Derek most were the dogs. The room was packed with them. All breeds, all shapes and sizes. They too were perfectly still. They stood staring at the couple, as though waiting for something. A sign.

Derek felt his stomach lurch as he noticed the wounds. Both people had been bitten and their bare arms sported hideous open wounds, black and raw like the lips of the dogs who had chewed them. There was blood on the muzzle of the nearest dog.

A strangled little cry escaped Derek and then there was movement in the house. The people turned their heads, a synchronised, mechanical act. They looked right at Derek without seeming to see him. But the dogs did.

Before they could respond, he ran.

Behind him he heard the noises he'd been afraid of hearing, the sound of their pursuit. Growling, snarling, panting, they chased after him as he pelted along the street.

He saw similar tableaux in other houses as he ran, people frozen like statues in houses full of dogs. How many were there? How many could there possibly be?

When he reached the end of the road he hesitated, not knowing where to go. He didn't recognise his surroundings. The streets were a maze to him. Choosing a direction at random, he found himself in a cul-de-sac. All around him the barking continued, but it was only a single dog that ultimately confronted him, its fur glossy and black, its eyes gleaming like rubies. He couldn't look away and he couldn't move as the dog approached him, walking calmly up to him. There was no sign of emotion behind its eyes, only cold instinct. He found himself holding out his arm, offering it to the creature.

The dog sniffed him once before placing its mouth on Derek's arm, sinking its teeth in, slowly and deliberately. When the fangs scraped the bones within, Derek screamed. The pain broke the spell and he fought back, yanking at his arm. Blood fountained over them both as he pulled away. The dog stared at him for several moments. Then it licked the blood from its lips.

Derek fled, running past the dog and back into the night.

The bite throbbed and burned, and one glance showed him an ugly wound, the flesh savaged. Dark blood pumped from it in sharp jets and he clamped his hand over it with a cry of pain. The unseen pack fell silent for a moment, and then began to howl. Had they tasted him through the bite? The thought made him lightheaded and he stumbled as he continued in his flight. A left turn took him along a curving lane of darkened shopfronts and he saw a sign for the train station. How had he come so far? He felt as if he'd been running for hours.

There was no sign of the pack, only the humid night echoing with their barking. He couldn't remember the way home. But did he want to lead the dogs there anyway? What if Andrew had already let them in? Could he taste Derek's blood also? Lost and confused, Derek ran for the station, desperate to find other people, anyone who might help him.

As he plunged into the station, the din behind him began to fade. The concourse was crowded with people and he let go of his arm as he waved frantically at them.

"Help," he gasped. "Please help me."

His arm was caked in blood and more was pooling on the floor at his feet. He was beginning to feel faint. The crowd swam in his blurring vision and he sank to his knees.

"Hospital . . . "

He shook his head, fighting the dizziness. The people were eerily silent. When he looked up he saw that their heads were the heads of dogs. Steam misted from their snouts as they turned, as one, to regard him. They looked hungrily at his arm, at the ragged black wound. The torn edges of the flesh moved like a mouth, opening and closing. Sounds came from there, a kind of dull whimpering.

One by one the people began to drop to their knees. They placed their hands on the floor in front of them and crept towards Derek. There was nothing behind their eyes. No reason, only cunning. Nothing like life. His heart lurched with horror, but he couldn't move. The pressure on his injured arm sent a river of blood across the floor, and as it reached them, the dog-people lowered their heads and began to lap at it.

His arm was twitching, shuddering. The mewling inside it was gaining in strength. Now he could feel the fur at the edges of the wound. The dog in his arm was trying to get out.

Derek tried to scream, but his mouth seemed too large to form words. His tongue felt thick and heavy. He lowered his head and saw himself reflected in the blood.

Behind him, the doors swished open and he heard the padding of stealthy feet as the pack began to circle him. His last thought was of Andrew. Through his fading consciousness he could see him sitting in the front room, staring in frozen horror at the dogs that surrounded him, the dogs draining him of the rest of his life.

Maybe it was true after all, that people died because they were corpses.

MADE IN HONG KONG

CAITLIN KNEW SHE WAS DREAMING. EVEN SO, SHE couldn't understand why her mobile phone didn't work. It was ringing but she couldn't seem to answer it. She tapped the buttons on the screen repeatedly, calling "Hello!" and trying to pick up the call. Nothing worked.

After what felt like ages of helpless fumbling, she finally opened her eyes. Her phone was still ringing beside her on the nightstand, its screen infusing the dark room with a spooky bluish glow. She snatched it up, almost dropping it.

"Hello?"

The line was dead.

She scowled at the phone. The display said it was 3.13. Who the hell would be calling that late? In the list of missed calls there was only an entry for "unknown". She fell back into bed with a groan. A wrong number, then.

She returned the phone to the nightstand and pulled the duvet over her head. Sleep reclaimed her almost immediately but it wasn't long before the phone began to bleat again, this time with a message alert.

"For fuck's sake," Caitlin grumbled, squeezing her eyes shut tightly against the intrusion. The text could wait another two hours for her alarm to go off.

But it was no use. She'd been ripped from a deep sleep twice now. Maybe she should just turn the phone off. Or at least silence it. Who called anyone at three in the morning? And then sent a text when no one answered?

Her mind kept circling around the issue until she realised there was no hope of going back to sleep. She picked up the phone again to see the text.

they r alive hear them at nite coming 4 me hav to destroy sry 4give me

She stared at the message and her skin began to crawl as a growing sense of unease settled over her. There was nothing familiar at all in the madness of the text and yet some filament of connection hung in the air. It was as though a part of her knew the truth but refused to acknowledge it.

Her denial didn't last long. A searing pain flared behind her eyes and she clutched her chest, suddenly unable to breathe. It felt like someone had struck her from behind, knocking the wind out of her. The sensation was followed by a flash of intense heat and the prickling of tiny needles all over her skin.

The moment passed quickly and she lay gasping and panting in bed. Was she still dreaming? Had she had some kind of attack? Bewildered and frightened, she grabbed for the phone again to see the time. The screen had gone dark and when she woke it up she was surprised to see that it was nearly 4 a.m.

The doorbell rang some time later and she knew with a sinking horror what had happened.

"I should have answered the phone," Caitlin said, wiping her eyes with a sodden tissue. It was all she could think of to say.

The policeman offered her another tissue and she took it, wadding it into a ball, hardly aware of his presence.

She felt disconnected from the moment. She wanted to ask if they were sure it was him, almost felt like she was betraying Sean by *not* asking. But she knew the truth on a deeper level than the eyewitnesses or camera phone footage could show. Her brother had parked his van on the railroad tracks and waited for the train to come. She had felt the impact as though she'd been there with him, had felt the explosion and the heat of the devouring flames, but she didn't want to tell the police that. They'd think she was as crazy as Sean.

"You couldn't have stopped him," the policeman said kindly, stroking her hand.

She'd shown them the text, which they were able to confirm he had sent only moments before the collision. He must have made the call just before driving onto the tracks. If she'd only answered...

"You can't do this to yourself," said the officer, as though reading her thoughts. "It isn't your fault."

But it was. And he could have no idea how much. Caitlin hadn't spoken to Sean in months. Not since her one visit to their parents' old house shortly after he'd moved back in. She hadn't wanted to go back there at all, hadn't wanted to be surrounded by memories and reminders of the past, whether good or bad. But the state of the house had horrified her enough to eclipse all other painful memories and she'd left feeling sick and in desperate need of a shower.

After that she'd let their email correspondence lapse and there was always some ready excuse she could offer as to why she couldn't meet up for lunch. It was easy to let people slip away, even family.

"One thing we'd like to ask you about, Miss Ellis—there were quite a lot of toys found at the scene."

The scene.

Caitlin closed her eyes. She could see it as clearly as if she were standing there, picking over the charred and twisted ruins of the van, the train, her brother's mangled body. Perhaps the first person there had come across a Luke Skywalker action figure, his melted face barely recognisable. Then a collection of plastic dinosaurs, their brightly coloured bodies welded to the tracks. Army men, animals, robots, cars, perhaps even a few dolls and model horses. Which ones would Sean have been clutching as the lights of the train bore down on him and he heard the impotent shriek of brakes?

She shook herself out of her morbid reverie. "Yes," she said. "He collected them."

It was the kindest description. The police would see the "collection" for themselves when they went to the house to sift for more clues. And she'd have to go with them. The thought made her shudder. And then a wave of guilt brought fresh tears to her eyes. She'd known her brother was disturbed but she'd had no idea of the extent of the madness. Certainly never imagined he would do anything like this. And if their parents were still alive they'd only make her feel guiltier, remind her that Sean wasn't as clever as she was, that he was "troubled", that he needed looking after.

Bitterness stirred in her guts and a bad taste rose in her mouth. She swallowed some of the tepid coffee that had been sitting untouched in front of her and tried not to gag on the foul taste. She could smell the burnt plastic and blood, the blackened fusion of man and machine. And toys. So many toys.

They weren't able to find very much of her brother. The fire had melted so much plastic around Sean that by the time the firemen arrived he was almost completely encased in it. And as even more unpleasant facts emerged, Caitlin began to tune them out. The van had been loaded with homemade explosives. The phone he'd used was stolen. For a little while she entertained the fantasy that he'd faked his death, that there wasn't even an actual person in the crash. But three teenagers had watched the event from a nearby bridge and one had recorded it on his phone.

"I thought it was just some macho stunt," he'd stammered through tears. "I thought the van would drive off at the last second."

Caitlin didn't want to see the footage but the police needed a positive ID on her brother. They showed her enhanced screen shots of the driver's face just before the crash. It was clearly visible and it was clearly Sean.

At first they grilled her about him: his history, his friends, girlfriends, acquaintances, jobs, political affiliations, religious beliefs. To most of their questions she could only shake her head in distraught confusion.

"I don't know. I just don't know. I have absolutely no idea."

After a while she became grateful for the mad text. Surely if you were a suicide bomber out to destroy some political target, you wouldn't park on the tracks and greet the early morning high-speed train. And how many terrorists loaded their vehicles with plastic toys? Nail bombs, sure, but Matchbox cars?

No, the only explanation was that her brother had lost his mind. The text was obviously a suicide note. There was no evidence that he intended to take out a school or a shopping mall with him.

And the toys?

"He just—collected them," Caitlin said wearily, for what felt like the thousandth time. She picked up a half-melted stegosaurus from the scattering of toys they'd brought to the station and turned it over in her hands. It had always been her favourite dinosaur. "We used to play with them when we were kids."

She didn't want to go to the house with them but Detective Sanchez had asked very gently. Besides, she didn't like the idea of the police picking over Sean's things without her there. His partner, Detective Richards, drove through the streets of Houston while Caitlin huddled in the back of the police car. Along the way the cops kept up a barrage of friendly, well-meaning chatter to put her at ease but she couldn't help feeling like a criminal. She slid down in the seat so no one could see her as they drove past.

It was a bland single-storey brick house like all the others along Howard Street. White paint was flaking off the dented garage door, littering the driveway like dirty snow. Weeds coiled round one another in the front yard like a warning to stay away and Caitlin hesitated at the front door. The mesh of the screen door was torn, with tufts of fabric clinging to the wires. Sanchez gestured at it with a questioning look and Caitlin shook her head to tell him there was nothing to be alarmed about. It had been that way for as long as she could remember. Sean had once told her that the door ate clothes.

The hinges squealed as she opened the screen door and confronted the peeling brown paint of the wooden front door. At knee height she could still see the scratches she'd left the time she'd locked herself out when she was six. She'd kicked and pounded, sobbing hysterically, convinced that she would never be able to get back inside, certain that she was trapped forever out in the wide world. What was probably only a few minutes had felt like hours.

Her hand trembled as she positioned the key in the lock and she hesitated before turning it.

Sanchez put a gentle hand on her shoulder. "I know this is difficult for you, Miss Ellis."

She took a deep breath and turned the key. Then she opened the door and let them into the tiny kitchen.

The first thing that hit them was the smell. Burnt plastic. Mould. Dust. Along with some putrid chemical stench. At first she thought the worst: murder victims. Her brother had killed people and stacked their decaying bodies in the cramped and cluttered rooms.

But it was only the bubbling cauldron on the stove. The huge cast iron pot had almost boiled dry and the heap of model cars inside had melted and stuck to the sides. The smoke alarm hung from the ceiling, bare wires dangling like severed arteries. Empty bottles of bleach and other caustic liquids lay discarded on the floor. Sanchez turned the stove off and moved the pot off the hot burner.

With the immediate problem sorted they could at last take in the rest of the kitchen. The countertop swarmed with tiny soldiers and animals. Except they weren't right. They were misshapen and grotesque. Bodies were elongated, heads were twisted and faces unrecognisable. Caitlin saw a collection of animals with legs that were more like tentacles and there was a row of action figures whose heads looked like they'd been flattened by a miniature steam roller. Several pairs of pliers sat on the edge of the counter, laid out like surgical instruments. The room looked like a torture chamber for toys.

Caitlin shuddered and looked away. Immediately she spotted one of her own toys that appeared to have been spared. A horse with synthetic hair for its mane and tail. She'd used to brush it and plait it as a little girl. It was still woven with dried flowers that must be at least twenty years old. She reached out a trembling hand to touch it while one of the detectives opened a window to let the smell out.

The floor was littered with more toys, more than they had ever owned as children. As he got older Sean had become obsessed with them, collecting and then hoarding all he could find. He scoured garage sales, thrift shops and websites for them. At one time he'd displayed them on shelves but as fascination evolved into obsession, he'd abandoned any attempt at order. And as Caitlin and the detectives made their way into the den they saw the full extent of Sean's madness.

Toys covered every inch of the floor, piled knee-deep in places and heaped against the walls. There was just room on the couch for one person to sit and the cops had to slide their feet through drifts of plastic to get through the room.

"Jesus," Sanchez said softly.

Caitlin stared in horror at the mess. "I had no idea it had gotten this bad." The last time she had been here, the shelves had been crowded with toys and figurines and there had certainly been plenty scattered across the floor. But nothing like this.

As they made their way along the hallway to Sean's bedroom Caitlin held her breath, bracing herself. His bedroom was even worse than the den. The bed was almost completely buried in plastic toys and Caitlin shuddered at the thought of her brother sleeping on it, like an ascetic on a bed of nails.

On one side of the bed was another faithful old friend: a large articulated monster with six legs. Nostalgia overtook her as she recalled playing with it with Sean. The battery-powered creature resembled a dinosaur but it moved like an insect, inching slowly towards Sean's army camp, its red eyes gleaming, until one of the soldiers stopped it in its tracks with a laser gun. It was one of their most beloved toys.

One night when their parents were out they had closed all the doors, turned off the lights and set the monster loose in the pitch-dark hallway. The noise of its mechanical movements and occasional roar made them scream with fright and they aimed a flashlight at the sensor in its throat to stop it before letting it resume its relentless search for them in the dark.

Caitlin's eyes blurred with tears and she hugged the creature to her chest as though it were a lost pet.

"I'm very sorry," Sanchez said, startling her out of her reverie. The pity in his face told her all she needed to know. They both knew Sean wasn't any kind of political or religious extremist. No, he was simply mad.

Caitlin peered around the room at the mess. It looked like a place where toys went to die.

Sanchez followed her gaze and picked up the large model elephant she was staring at. Its body was hard plastic but the trunk was soft and pliable and Caitlin was hit by another flood of memories as she remembered all the things that elephant had held in its trunk over the years. They'd left it on the dining room table with flowers for their mother and once with a can of beer for their father.

Sanchez handed the elephant to Caitlin and she turned it over to see the embossed words on its belly. "Made in Hong Kong," she read aloud.

"Yeah, they all were, weren't they?" he said with a smile.

She nodded. "When we were kids we thought Hong Kong must be this magical place, like the world's biggest toy factory. We thought it was where all the toys in the world came from. If we went there the streets would be crowded with soldiers and plastic dinosaurs. The buildings and houses and streets would all be made of Legos."

She laid the elephant down on the scattering of toys on the bed and ran her hand over the upraised limbs and tails and wheels until her fingers came to rest on a small electric train. She turned away with a sob.

With their parents gone there was no one but Caitlin to clean up the mess Sean had left behind. The first few days had been awful, with callous reporters ambushing her at her apartment and demanding answers to their lurid speculation. The police had assigned a couple of officers to chase them off like pit bulls. Soon enough the tragedy was yesterday's news and the press found fresher, more accessible blood than Caitlin's.

Sean hadn't left a will but there was no question that his body—what little of it could be salvaged—would be cremated. Caitlin paid a local funeral parlour to handle everything. She didn't want to keep the ashes; she couldn't help the image of someone picking through his remains to find only lumps of melted plastic.

The house was hers, obviously, along with its mountains of toys and junk. Clearing it out and selling it was a chore she dreaded but she couldn't put it off any longer. She'd taken a few toys home with her that first day and they sat on the kitchen table like fragments of her childhood. A horse, a dinosaur, a doll. Things she just couldn't bring herself to throw away.

She returned to the house on Howard Street a week later and let herself in. Without the policemen for company she felt like an intruder. She'd brought along a few large cardboard boxes, reassuring herself that it wouldn't be that big a job. Surely it had only been the trauma of the event that had made her think there were that many toys in the house. Surely it was just a bit of clutter she could clear away in a handful of trips back and forth to the dump. But no, the chaos was every bit as bad as she remembered.

With a sigh she set to work, gathering armfuls of toys and filling the boxes, then carrying them out to the car. Back and forth, back and forth. When she ran out of boxes she used bags. A chill crept down her spine at the thought that Sean had done this too. Only he'd filled a *van*. How many more toys must there have been to do that?

She pushed the haunting thought away and tried to empty her mind, focusing only on the job. Her hands and arms were a mosaic of scratches and scrapes from all the plastic hooves, claws and other sharp edges. She cursed as the occasional soldier jabbed her with his gun and she hurled a tiger figurine across the room after cutting herself on its bared fangs.

Toys were probably a lot safer these days but she remembered plenty of minor injuries as a child. Sometimes models came out of the press with bits of untrimmed plastic sticking out from the seams. One set of multicoloured monkeys in particular had needed extensive trimming with their mother's manicure scissors to stop them looking silly. Caitlin wondered where those particular monkeys were now. Perhaps they were some of the chosen ones Sean had taken with him.

She shuddered at the thought. Chosen ones.

Soon the car was filled and ready for its first trip to the dump. Fallen toys littered the path from the house to the drive like escapees from Santa's workshop. Caitlin left them. There would be plenty more on the path before she was done; she could clear them all away at the end. She drove up to the metal skip marked GENERAL WASTE and tipped the first box inside. They tumbled in, a riot of colour, bouncing and clattering as they hit the bottom. She emptied the next box, then the next. The car had been full to bursting and yet the toys made no impression on the enormous skip. She wondered how much fuller it would be by the time she was done.

After another two trips she took a break. She sat at the table in the now-empty dining room and picked over the objects she'd been accumulating there. The motorised blue dolphin that swam in the bathtub, bumping blindly into limbs and the sides of the tub. A set of exquisitely crafted racehorses, some with broken or missing legs. And her favourite doll,

Natalie, looking a little ragged and forlorn. Her once-beautiful velvet gown was stained and moth-eaten and her porcelain face was cracked. But she had triggered such a flood of nostalgia in Caitlin that the thought of pitching her into that skip had physically pained her.

As Caitlin cleared more of the house she came across others she couldn't part with. She imagined that this was how Sean's obsessive hoarding had begun. But unlike Sean, Caitlin was actually throwing most of the stuff away, keeping back only the treasured few.

There was the Pegasus statue from *Clash of the Titans*, its moveable rubber wings a delight among countless other horse figurines that were frozen in one position. And there was the original model of the starship Enterprise, battleworn and falling to pieces but full of so many memories it was indispensable. By the time the sun had begun to set Caitlin had swapped the box for a larger one and added a few more animals, a few more dolls.

The house was still piled high with toys, but Caitlin was exhausted. Six trips to the dump had still barely made an impression on the skip. As she emptied the contents of a final box into it she was sure for a moment that she'd heard a tiny shriek of outrage. She froze and listened, straining to hear, but there was only the soft rattle of smaller toys falling down to the bottom of the skip.

The shadows had lengthened, stretching arms and legs into tentacles and creating the illusion of movement. Caitlin squeezed her eyes shut. No doubt her senses were just overloaded by the endless parade of toys. Soon they would start to talk to her.

She shook her head before that thought could take shape and headed home.

The dolphin's plastic tail flicked up and down as it powered its way around the tub, disappearing into clouds of bubbles to reemerge, smiling. Caitlin was soothed by the noise as she lay back and closed her eyes, soaking away her exhaustion. She steered the dolphin away whenever it got trapped by her body, sending it back into the small soapy ocean of the tub. The novelty wore off soon and when she had tired of it she plucked the dolphin out and set it on the bath mat. Then she dozed, letting her mind wander away from the horror of the past few days.

She was almost asleep when she first heard the rustling in the other room. Just a papery fluttering at first, like a moth trapped in a box. But the sound grew louder as whatever it was doubled its efforts.

A rat, she thought with disgust. She was sure now she could hear the scrabbling of tiny claws, the soft clatter as something was knocked to the floor. So much for the long relaxing bath.

Caitlin pulled the plug and the water began to gurgle noisily as it was sucked down the throat of the tub. She stepped out, reaching for her towel, and her foot came down on something sharp that gave way with a brittle crack. She cried out as she stumbled, falling to her knees on the floor. The pale yellow bath mat was streaked with blood and her left foot throbbed angrily. The dolphin lay beside her, its thin sharp tail snapped into bits.

"Thanks a lot," she muttered. Even though it was her own stupid fault. How many times had her parents nagged her and Sean when they were kids about leaving their toys lying around? It was almost funny.

Then she cursed as she saw the jagged shard of plastic protruding from the tender arch of her foot. It was only a tiny piece but it hurt like hell. Wincing, she pulled it out and blood flowed freely, pooling on the bath mat. She struggled up on her good foot and limped across the room to the medicine cabinet for a Band-Aid. Her wound patched, she glowered at the dolphin. She snatched it up and flung it into the wastebasket where it lay nestled among the tissues and empty toilet paper rolls, smiling up at her.

She had already forgotten what had drawn her attention from the bath in the first place but as she got ready for bed she heard another sound. And this time she was sure she also heard a voice.

Her stomach swooped as panic began to uncoil inside her. Someone was in the apartment. In the *next room*. Feeling horribly vulnerable in her nightgown and slippers, Caitlin tiptoed towards the phone by the bed, the pain in her foot forgotten. She snatched up the cordless handset and called 911, silently making her way towards the closet all the while. A clatter came from the kitchen and she bit back a little scream as she slipped inside the closet and huddled into the farthest corner.

The operator was on the line, asking what her emergency was.

"Police," Caitlin whispered, and gave her address. "There's someone in my apartment."

The operator lowered her own voice to a whisper too and reassured Caitlin that the police would be there very soon.

"Just be quiet and remain calm," the operator said. "I'll stay on the line with you."

Caitlin nodded absently, barely hearing. She was too focused on the sounds coming through the wall. Sounds like an army of rats might make as they ransacked a kitchen. Again she thought she heard a voice but it was so faint it might have come from outside. Was she just hearing her neighbours?

Before long the wail of a siren reached her and grew, drowning out the clattering sounds. The intruders would hear it too and probably run and Caitlin hoped the police would be in time to catch them.

There was the slam of a car door and then someone was knocking on the front door.

"Miss Ellis!"

Come in, she thought. *Why don't they just come in? Surely the door's open.*

"Miss Ellis, it's Detective Sanchez! Can you come to the door, please?"

She had been expecting angry shouts, the sounds of a struggle, possibly even gunfire. Had the intruders escaped?

"I'm coming," she called as she came out of hiding and limped towards the door. Her hands were shaking so violently she could barely work the lock as she let the police in. She hardly noticed the overturned box of toys. Animals and dolls were scattered across the floor.

Detective Richards immediately swept the apartment, going from room to room while Sanchez stayed with Caitlin. The search didn't take long; there were only three rooms and a hallway. Four rooms if you counted the bathroom, which didn't even have a window.

"There's no evidence of a break-in, Miss Ellis," Richards said with a dubious expression. He shot a meaningful look at Sanchez.

Caitlin nodded vacantly, her eyes straying towards the front door. No, of course not. She'd had to unlock the door to let them in.

"I'm sorry," she murmured, feeling embarrassed. She suddenly felt like a child again, told by adults who knew better that there weren't any monsters under the bed. Only silly little girls believed in such things and she was much too old to be jumping at shadows.

The officers shared a sympathetic glance as Caitlin told them what she'd heard from the bathroom, backtracking through the tiring day of clearing out the house and then backtracking further, to the events of the past week. But even as she went over the horrible events she knew how it sounded. She also knew exactly what the cops would say.

"Your mind can play some funny tricks on you when you're tired or stressed," Sanchez told her gently as he helped Caitlin pile the scattered toys back into the box.

"I'm sorry," she repeated, not knowing what else to say. "I didn't mean to waste your time. I really thought I heard someone in the apartment."

Sanchez knelt to retrieve a battered plastic frog from the floor. He set it on the table without winding it and it hopped a few inches and stopped, as though making a point.

Caitlin blushed and looked down at her feet. Just the toys. Just a box full of plastic creatures, some of which must have a final couple of moves left in them since the last time they were played with. One of them must have started up, upsetting the balance and toppling the box. There was no other explanation.

The policemen offered their sympathies and bade her good night with the reassurance that she shouldn't feel bad at all, that it was always better to call if she wasn't sure, that it was their job. They were there to make her feel safe.

Caitlin smiled gratefully and tried not to feel patronised. She shut the door behind them and locked it. She checked the front window too. Locked. Everything was locked. She was safe.

She dreamt of toys all night, of the plastic Wonderland she and Sean had imagined Hong Kong to be. Doll-sized, Caitlin lived in a white Lego castle with a drawbridge over a fish pond while Sean stood on the deck of a model pirate ship with a fluttering skull-and-crossbones pennant. The ground rumbled beneath the stomping feet of dinosaurs and the rhythmic marching of tiny soldiers. Horses pranced across the synthetic turf and a steam train wound in and out among the trees and hills and over a stream filled with schools of rainbow-coloured fish.

But the idyllic scene didn't last for long. Playful creatures turned menacing and the thrill of being toy-sized quickly became terror. Caitlin's tiny legs moved far too slowly as she ran ahead of a stampede of misshapen horses, their hideous legs elongating and tapering to jagged points as they reached for her. She tried to leap onto the train but it was always just a few feet ahead of her. The horses snorted and neighed with monstrous fury as they gained on her, running her down, pounding her into the razor-sharp blades of grass, gouging her skin, her face, her eyes, filling her mouth with the synthetic taste of plastic.

She woke with a cry, panting and sweating and terrified, only to drift off to sleep again and find herself back in the same nightmare.

When morning came she could only remember vague snatches of the horror. It felt like a dream she'd had years ago, like something that had stained her memory. She shook off the obscure sense of unease and downed two cups of coffee to wake herself up. She followed it with a glass of orange juice in lieu of breakfast. Something made a small grinding sound behind her and she turned to see the little plastic frog hop twice across the kitchen table.

"Oh, no you don't," she said, scooping it up and depositing it back in the box.

It fell down between a sad-faced doll and a growling tiger. She frowned. Funny, she didn't remember bringing the tiger back with her. In fact, hadn't she thrown it across the room for biting her?

She plucked it from the box and scrutinised its gleaming eyes and snarling mouth, its rippling muscles and fearsome claws. All four legs were on the ground but tensed as though it were ready to spring at its prey. It had been pressed from a mould like so many millions of other plastic toys but it was no less realistic for that. It looked sculpted from life, from a real tiger prowling through the grass.

Caitlin shrugged. She'd seen so many toys in the past few days it was a wonder she could tell a Rubik's Cube from a NERF ball any more. She set the tiger on the table beside the box and left it there like a sentry as she got dressed and headed off again for Howard Street.

The piles of toys seemed even more daunting than they had the day before, as though she'd made no progress at all in clearing them away. Perhaps they multiplied like coat hangers. With a weary sigh she set to work again.

She worked all day, taking a break only to eat one of Sean's frozen pizzas and drink the last of the soft drinks he'd left in the fridge. She'd transferred all the perishable food into the freezer, to be dealt with later. For now she had her hands full with just the toys.

She went home feeling even more exhausted than she had the day before. While cleaning she'd found more childhood memories she couldn't leave behind and she set the new box on the table beside the first one. Then she froze when she saw the tiger. It was staring straight at her, fangs bared, one deadly paw raised as if to slash at her. This morning she was sure it had had all four feet on the ground.

But last night she'd been sure she'd heard voices in the next room too. She'd dreamt of toys chasing her all night and she'd almost spooned sugar into her orange juice that morning. She'd also spent nearly an hour at the old house filling a Tonka dump truck with Transformers and then sending it hurtling down the hallway to crash into a closed door again and again, collapsing with hysterical laughter each time.

Caitlin yawned and dropped the tiger back into the first box. The second box contained even more toys than the first and for a moment she felt the urge to throw everything out. Then the feeling passed and she patted the head of a velvety panda before turning out the light and falling into bed, dusty, unwashed and wiped out.

The voices woke her a few hours later.

She crept out of bed and down the hall to peer around the door frame into the front room. Things were moving around in there. There was the soft clatter of plastic on the floor and the scurrying noises she'd heard the night before. A tiny voice whispered and Caitlin was sure she heard an answering giggle.

She flicked the light switch on. Then her hand fluttered to her mouth to stifle a scream. The toys were littered across the floor in attitudes of play. The light-controlled monster was advancing on a herd of plastic animals that streamed away in all directions. A model airplane appeared to have crashed nearby and the large elephant was nudging it with his trunk. Several dolls stood in a neat row along the windowsill like spectators. Two were holding hands. Their heads turned sharply and they watched Caitlin with bright cold eyes. From somewhere else came the sound of breaking glass.

Caitlin felt dizzy as she took in the scene. Her legs crumpled and she fell to the floor, vaguely aware of the throbbing pain in her left foot. It seemed to draw her eye away, to the centre of the room, where the dolphin sat smiling at her. She only had a moment to wonder whether it had escaped from the wastebasket by itself or if it had been helped. Then she noticed the tiger.

It seemed a lot bigger than she remembered and it had changed position again. Now it was rearing on its hind legs in mid-pounce. She didn't have time to scream.

Morrow and Tranh stood staring in disbelief at the chaos in the house. Sanchez couldn't blame them for thinking he'd been exaggerating; his description couldn't have prepared anyone for the reality.

"Holy shit," Morrow said. "Makes you wonder how much worse it was before Ellis loaded up the van and met the train."

Sanchez nodded. He'd seen the same look of horror on Caitlin's face as she got her first glimpse of how her brother had been living. But when he and Richards had responded to her false alarm the next night she'd told them she'd been clearing out the house. And the next-door neighbour on Howard Street confirmed it. She'd seen Miss Ellis carrying box after box out to her car before driving off and returning to repeat the process. The toys littering the grass and front porch were evidence of that, although it looked like she'd dropped more than she'd managed to get into the car.

A shudder went through Sanchez's body as he pondered all the possibilities. Caitlin Ellis had been missing for several days. They'd gone to her apartment first. The manager let them in, cursing when he saw the broken window. A tree just outside had shielded it from view or someone might have noticed sooner.

There was no sign of Caitlin. The stuff in the fridge had gone off some time ago, as though she'd left suddenly. The bath mat was stained with blood and two empty cardboard boxes lay on the floor of the front room, surrounded by shards of glass. Dried blood was smeared on the broken window frame. A break-in, then? Possibly Caitlin had found something valuable in her brother's house and been followed by someone who later broke in to steal it. Had he also killed Caitlin?

There were no clues to her whereabouts among the profusion of toys, no evidence that whoever had taken her had come back to loot the house of further valuables. The neighbours hadn't seen or heard anything suspicious. They'd known Sean wasn't quite right in the head but they never imagined he would do what he did.

Sanchez picked his way through the mountains of junk, pausing occasionally to examine things that caught his eye. It was overwhelming, as though a toy shop had exploded. He opened a closet and jumped as a red plastic pedal car rolled out. It too was filled with toys, an eerie echo of Sean Ellis' fate. He hadn't noticed the larger pieces before. In one corner was a child's wooden clubhouse, tipped on its side. And partially hidden behind the living room curtains was a large metal slide, the kind you'd find in a playground. He wondered how he could have missed that.

He could picture Caitlin here, confronting the task of sorting out the clutter. He could see her picking desultorily through the mess for things with sentimental value, dumping armfuls of manageable pieces into boxes before feeling overwhelmed by the sheer scope of the job.

"There's no sign of her anywhere, sir," said Tranh, appearing in the doorway. He grimaced at the junk heap of the room. "Maybe she just couldn't face it and took off?"

Sanchez thought of the blood in her apartment. The broken windows and empty boxes. The toys set out on the kitchen table when he'd responded to her call that night. Something didn't fit.

Tranh was picking through piles of action figures. "Incredible," he said. He handed an articulated alien to Morrow, who smiled.

"I bet some of these are worth a fortune," Morrow said as he made the creature's arms and legs move in the air.

As Sanchez opened his mouth to comment a tinny voice reached him from somewhere. He and Tranh froze, listening for a moment before fixing on the direction. Sanchez heaved aside a model train set to uncover a large misshapen lump of plastic. Rubbery appendages protruded from its greyish-yellow body in places. It reminded him of the toys Ellis had been melting on the stove and mutilating with pliers when they'd first explored the house. Perhaps he'd melted a hundred Barbie dolls into one giant mass. Sanchez winced at the unpleasant image and took a step back.

"Obviously the guy just lost his mind," Morrow said, interrupting his thoughts. "Didn't that text he sent say something about the toys moving at night?"

Sanchez nodded. It had been so similar to Caitlin's report the night she'd called. It was hardly surprising the things could seem to have a life of their own, especially in such profusion.

"Well, I think we're done," Sanchez said sadly. "She's not here."

"What's going to happen to all this stuff?" Tranh asked.

Sanchez shrugged. "Someone will have to come and clear it all away, I guess. Take it to the dump. Melt it down. Who knows?"

"Is it okay if I take this, then?" Tranh held up a gleaming black Matchbox race car.

"Sure, why not? No one'll miss it."

"Cool. I had the whole set when I was a kid but my dad threw them out. Talk about a blast from the past."

Sanchez managed a faint smile. "Come on, guys. Let's get out of here."

The strange tinny voice came again and for a moment Sanchez almost thought he could make out words. He paused, listening. He was about to call Caitlin's name when a wind-up robot began to move down by his feet, its levers and gears turning as it tried to walk. Sanchez bent down to set it upright and the robot inched its way through the clutter on the floor until it bumped up against the lump of molten plastic.

There it marched in place, unable to move past the obstacle. Its gears turned slower and slower until it wound down and was still. Sanchez blinked. His eyes must be playing tricks on him. For a moment he was sure he'd seen the mass of plastic jerk as the robot pressed against it. It almost looked like skin.

WASPS

"**M**URDERER*!*"

The voice of pure rage is scary enough from grown-ups. From another kid it's bone-chilling. The little girl's voice was shrill and choked with anguish and I almost fell off my bike when I first heard it. Over and over she screamed it at the top of her lungs.

"Murderer!"

I tried to ignore it and ride on, but her voice was in my head and it refused to go away, even when she paused for breath. I kept thinking any minute she'd stop, but the pain in her voice told me she would go on as long as it took. And besides, I was curious.

It wasn't hard to find her and by the time I did, a hoarse old man's voice yelled for her to shut up. It only made her scream louder.

I climbed over the chain link fence into an empty lot. The foundation of a demolished house sprawled over the weed-infested ground like the chalk outline of a murder victim. A girl my age was standing at its edge, clutching the limp body of a huge orange cat. She wore a torn black T-shirt thin as tissue and shorts that were way too big. I instantly pegged both as hand-me-downs from some older sibling. She was barefoot, her feet and legs streaked with mud. Definitely what my parents would call "poor white trash".

Something about her both frightened and fascinated me and I approach-ed her as I might a wild animal. "Hey," I said softly.

She whirled with the cat in her arms, a frenzied look in her eyes.

I took a step back, startled. "It's okay," I whispered. "What happened?"

She eyed me for a moment as though sizing me up. Then she nodded towards the back of the house adjacent to the empty lot. "That old man," she said. "Fucking psycho!" She spat in his direction.

I had never heard anyone my age use the F word before and I felt a surge of awe. I would never have had the guts to scream and curse at anyone, especially not some crazy old man I thought had killed my cat.

"His name is Ivan," she said quietly, tears spilling from her eyes. She scrubbed them away with a grimy fist, transferring the heavy cat to one arm. His head lolled and fixed me with a dull, glassy stare that made me shudder. She tried to scream once more, but her voice caught in her throat and she surrendered to her tears.

I could never stand to see anyone or anything in pain and my heart ached for her. I wanted to reassure her, to tell her it would be okay. But I was afraid to get too close to her. I was afraid of the cat she clung to with no aversion to its death.

"What did he do?" I asked at last.

"He said he was going to make me get rid of Ivan because he kept climbing in his attic." As she spoke she caressed the lifeless fur of the cat, making its head sway like a stone in a sock. "So he killed him."

I winced, not wanting to know the details. Earlier that year, my own beloved cat, Domino, had run away. I put up fliers with his picture, desperately hoping he would turn up on the doorstep. A few days later a neighbour came by and said he thought he'd found my cat. My heart sank at the sympathetic tone in his voice. It told me everything. It was a long walk down the street to his house. Black and white tufts of fur led the way into his garden like nine discarded lives. Domino's open-mouthed, vacant face haunted me for weeks, and I woke from nightmares of yowling, hissing cats in my head.

Domino was the first dead thing I ever saw. Ivan was the second.

"Let's bury him," I said.

The girl locked steady eyes on mine and stared at me for a long time. Then she nodded. I had the weird sense that I had passed some kind of test.

The sky was dark, threatening to drench us with rain as we scouted broken bottles to use as spades. We didn't talk much while we dug but she told me her name was Mitzie. It was a strange, scratchy sort of name but it seemed to fit her.

We couldn't make the hole very deep but we did our best. When we were done Mitzie lifted her arms like a priestess and bowed her head over the grave to say a few words. There was something of a rehearsed quality to it all and I began to suspect it wasn't the first funeral she'd presided over.

When the rain began to fall, Mitzie didn't move, so I didn't either. I was mesmerised by her. She was a force, this girl. She felt things so intensely and it seemed a kind of honour to be allowed to share in her grief.

I stood there with her in the cold rain, perversely enjoying the misery of it as I waited for her to finish speaking. Then I asked her meekly if I could be her friend.

The first night we spent together, Mitzie wanted us to prick our fingers and share our blood like she'd seen in a movie, but I was too afraid of the pain. Mitzie looked stunned, as though I'd said something in another language.

"What do you mean you're afraid?" she asked, staring at the sewing needle she was going to use.

I shrank back as she poised it over her hand, and then pressed it into the tip of her little finger. She didn't even do it fast. She took her time and pushed it in slowly, like she was enjoying it. Blood welled from the puncture and she held the dripping needle out to me.

"Your turn."

"No way! I can't do that!"

"Then how are we gonna be blood-sisters? You have to make a sacrifice."

I tried to think of alternatives but Mitzie's suggestions (knife, razor) were even scarier than the needle. In desperation I tried scraping my hands against the icicles in her parents' empty freezer. I'd once cut myself like that by accident, but it wouldn't work when I tried to do it deliberately.

Impatient with my squeamishness, Mitzie finally grabbed my hand and jabbed the needle into my finger.

"Oww!"

"Don't be such a baby!" she laughed, pressing my bloody finger to hers. She smiled. "Now you're a part of me." When it was done she licked both our fingers. My stomach fluttered with unease.

I was too naïve to understand the dark side to a fascination with blood. Instead, I simply admired her bravery. And even though I was always a little afraid of her, she made me feel special. I was someone she wanted with her forever.

"Come on, let's go play in the funhouse!"

Mitzie raced off then, leaving me on my own. It was part of the game for me to have to follow her in so she could jump out and scare me. Just another part of my mysterious role in her life.

The funhouse was what she called the shack in the weed-choked field behind her house. It was a pile of rotting timber that any parents but hers would have torn down years ago. She didn't know who had built it but her grandfather had lived and died in it. Mitzie adored the place and she cherished the memory of a man she had barely known, though I had to wonder what kind of man would be banished to a shack behind the real house.

She loved to wait behind the door and pounce on me when I came in, covering my eyes with her hands and leading me blindly around the room. I had to trust her to steer me around the holes in the floor and the drips from above. One time she made me close my eyes while she put something in my hand. I thought it was a rock but when she finally let me look I realised it was the skull of a bird. I dropped it in fright and brushed my hand on my jeans. Mitzie just laughed, her eyes gleaming.

It was one of the hottest summers on record. Even so, we spent most of our time outside. My parents didn't want "that trashy girl" in their house, but we didn't mind our exile. Her field contained just enough trees to count as a forest, and we created our own little world out there. We pretended to be witches, making potions and casting spells we were sure would come true if we only wished hard enough. Instead of animals we sacrificed locks of hair or fingernails. Occasionally a bug if Mitzie insisted on something living.

Before I met her I would never have dreamed of sneaking out of my house at night. Now I thought nothing of slipping out through my window with only the light of the moon to guide me. The spirits of the forest were there, Mitzie said, watching over us. They would protect us.

But nature isn't always kind, as I soon found out.

I was so excited that day. I had finally climbed my parents' huge magnolia tree all the way to the top, a feat I never thought I would manage. I cheered and shouted down at Mitzie, exuberant in my triumph. I felt like I'd scaled a mountain.

And then I heard it.

There was no mistaking the sound—the telltale buzzing that surrounded me like a cloud. I wasn't alone up there. As the sickening realisation set in, I stared into the swirling black and yellow vortex for several slow-motion moments. Then the wasps began to attack.

I screamed, waving my arms at them and almost losing my balance. The hard ground and a broken leg seemed a small price to pay for escaping, but some rational part of me refused to let me jump. I was too high up and, even in my hysteria, I knew that the fall could kill me. So I started climbing down. And they started stinging.

I looked down as I climbed, searching frantically for Mitzie, hoping she would save me somehow. Instead I saw her running away. My heart twisted but the wrenching pain was nothing compared to the nightmare of the wasps.

They were everywhere, filling the sky like smoke. I could barely see. I flailed at them, their hard little bodies knocking against my hands and veering dizzily away, only to circle back with renewed fury once they'd regained their balance. Others clung to me—my skin, my clothes, my hair. One flew right into my face and my senses were so heightened that I actually felt its wing brush my eye as it tried to blind me with its evil stinger. I heard my voice as though from miles away or under water. Screaming, screaming, screaming.

I slipped on the branches as I scrambled to get down, trying desperately not to lose my grip completely and fall. My palms were slick with blood, but the only pain I felt was the terrible stinging. I thought of witches burned at the stake, flames licking all around them, charring their flesh. Excruciating. Inescapable. I was drowning in fire. Through the terror and the pain came a final coherent thought: I was going to die.

And then suddenly the world was full of water. I cried out at the shock of it, bewildered by the cold wet blast. It was raining! No, that was impossible. But some of the wasps had been washed away and I could see again. I was soaked to the skin before I realised that the icy spray was coming from below me, from the base of the tree. Mitzie hadn't abandoned me after all.

The swarm broke apart like confetti thrown to the wind, powerless against the onslaught of water. I was able to climb faster now and when I made it down to the first fork in the trunk I jumped, landing hard in the wet grass.

Mitzie ran to me, still spraying me with the garden hose. I couldn't do anything but cower on the ground, trembling, sobbing, swiping at the endless sites of pain. Mitzie peeled away a few wasps that were still tangled in my hair and I howled as another one stung my lower back. It had crawled inside my shirt. With renewed panic I started tearing out of my clothes.

"You're okay, you're okay," Mitzie said firmly, holding me still and patting me down as though searching for weapons. "They're gone."

It took me a long time to believe that. Even once I was safe inside the house, I could still feel their jagged little legs crawling on my arms, my face, the back of my neck. Violent shudders racked my body and I kept running my hands through my hair, convinced that some were still hiding in there. And the buzzing. I didn't think I would ever stop hearing it. If Mitzie hadn't been there . . .

More than a dozen of the evil things had stung me. The worst one was just below my left eyebrow and it swelled into what looked like a black eye. Mitzie thought that was cool. But then, she would.

"I've never seen anyone look so scared," she said. She was breathless with exhilaration.

My parents were horrified when they saw what had happened and, I suspect, not a little disappointed that they couldn't somehow blame Mitzie for it. I told them again and again that she had saved my life and they grudgingly thanked her and said she could play inside with me until I recovered.

It only took a few days for the swelling to go down enough for me to feel halfway normal again, but even though Mitzie was welcome inside now, it wasn't the same. We couldn't lose ourselves there the way we could in the forest or the funhouse. Mixing potions from household ingredients felt like a cheat after seeking out exotic roots and mushrooms in the field and we missed the flowers, the birds and the squirrels. We were like wild animals in a zoo, caged when we should be running free.

But even though I felt trapped, I was terrified of venturing back outside. My dad promised he'd hired an exterminator to kill the wasps and destroy the nest and Mitzie confirmed that she'd seen it. They were all dead, she assured me. Hundreds of them. The nest was the size of a basketball.

It didn't matter. In my mind they were still there, buzzing, stinging, circling and coming back. They weren't like bees, which could only sting once. A bee sting was a suicide mission. Wasps could hurt you forever.

Mitzie was patient with me but after the first two weeks she couldn't hide her frustration any longer. I felt awful, like I was letting her down. She'd saved my life and in return I was depriving her of our magic world. My parents were civil to her but she knew she wasn't wanted. The forest was the only place she could escape to, and only with me.

"You'll be safe in the funhouse," she promised. "Nothing can get in there."

But the old shack was full of holes and open to the elements. There were always ladybirds and moths inside so why couldn't there be wasps too?

I *wanted* to go outside. I missed our games as much as she did, even the ones where she scared me. But every time I tried to set foot outside the house, my heart would start hammering and I would gasp for breath like a drowning person. Days and then weeks passed like that and gradually the precious summer melted away.

Eventually Mitzie stopped coming over to see me. I looked for her through the window and I even opened the front door sometimes, hoping to see her outside. But she just wasn't there.

The day before, she'd told me a weird bit of news. The old man who'd had it in for Ivan was dead. Some kind of allergic reaction. He never left the hospital. Something about that felt wrong but I didn't really give it much thought. I was too upset about having wasted the end of our summer. And then Mitzie was gone and I couldn't think of anything but how I had lost my best friend.

I cried myself to sleep every night after that. I felt the way I had when Domino had run away—bereft and helpless. This time she really had left me behind. My parents tried to hide their relief and it only made me feel more heartbroken. The wasps had taken her from me.

When school started in the fall I had no choice but to leave the house. And by then it wasn't so bad. The terror had faded to a manageable level in my head and I found myself thinking about the attack less and less. I looked for Mitzie at school but she wasn't there. I guessed she might have gone to a different school, but then I had to wonder if perhaps she didn't go to school at all.

A couple of times I went by her house but I didn't have the courage to knock. It didn't look like anyone was living there. Maybe her family had moved away. The thought didn't fill me with the grief it once would have.

Time passed and I made new friends, as kids do. The emotional scars never went away entirely but they did fade. Christmas came and went, then Easter. At last it was June. The final bell rang at school and I was free again for another whole summer. I raced home and let myself in, not knowing how I would spend the rest of the glorious day, but thrilled beyond all reason just to be free. School was out! I opened the door to my room and froze. There was a note taped outside my bedroom window.

I have a surprise for you, it said. *But you have to come see it.* It was signed simply, "M."

And just like that I was back in time, back in last year's summer. Back with Mitzie.

I knew exactly where she wanted me to go. I also knew that there was no question that I *would* go.

My hands shook with nervous anticipation as I pushed open the creaky door of the funhouse and it was as though the intervening year had never happened. Mitzie stepped out from behind the door and put her hands over my eyes, just as she had done so many times before. And even though I'd been expecting it, I jumped and gave a little cry. Her skin was cool but her touch felt strange. I couldn't help but wonder how much she had changed, and what the time apart had done to her.

Without a word she led me inside. The funhouse felt charged with unnatural energy, as though all the warped and mouldy boards were humming with electricity. After a few steps, she stopped and guided me to the floor, where I sat cross-legged. She didn't have to tell me to keep my eyes closed. I listened to her footsteps as she moved around to stand in front of me. At last she said I could look.

I blinked my eyes open and saw Mitzie for the first time in a year. Her hair was a little longer, a little stringier, but it was the same girl. Her hands were clasped in eager anticipation as she smiled down at whatever her "surprise" was. There was something odd about her but I couldn't pinpoint exactly what it was. And once I dropped my gaze to the floor and saw what was in front of me, I forgot all about Mitzie.

Panic mushroomed from my heart and I scrambled backwards like a cartoon character on a wet ramp, my rear hitting the wooden floor more than once before I found my feet.

Confusion and amusement danced in Mitzie's eyes and then she reached for me. "Hey, it's okay—"

"It's a wasp!" I gasped, my old wounds awakening like fireworks in response to the angry thing buzzing less than two feet from me. I felt consumed by flames.

"No, wait!" She grabbed my arm and I resisted, struggling against her, lost in the blossoming memory of that awful day in the tree.

"Look at it!"

At last came the gentle touch of reason as I saw what she wanted me to see. The wasp couldn't hurt me. It was quite helpless. Slowly, I turned to look at Mitzie.

"See?" she said. "I told you. You're safe." Then, at my confusion: "I did it for you."

Slowly, very slowly, the panic faded to fear, then revulsion, and finally horror as I saw what she had done. The hideous buzzing thing was missing a wing, the other vibrating like a tiny propeller. Its long alien legs were walking in a meandering, out-of-step cadence in the air and its gleaming black and yellow body was turning, rotating, unable to move. Mitzie had pinned it to the floor.

She bounced over to it, grinning, clearly pleased and proud of what she had done. I couldn't speak. I was transfixed by the sight.

After a while Mitzie looked back up at me, her eyes narrowing. "I did it for you," she said again, and this time her voice contained a note of resentment at my ingratitude.

"Thank you" was all I could manage, and that in a dry heave of a whisper.

"I told you." Now she was speaking to her captive. "No one hurts my friends and lives." I hadn't seen her face so grim since Ivan's funeral, and now it was blended with unashamed sadism.

She reached out and took the wasp's remaining wing between expert fingers. Her eyes gleamed at me and then at her victim as she pulled the wing from its socket. It was so deliberate I could almost hear the miniature fleshy rip as it came loose. The wasp buzzed in fury, its body vibrating faster and more frantically. And although there was no creature in the world that could have terrified me more, the suffering of Mitzie's prisoner tore something in my mind.

I had poured salt on a slug once to see what would happen and I watched with mounting nausea as it writhed in slow motion, its moist form disintegrating under the salt. I didn't understand how something so repugnant could communicate pain or inspire such pity, but I was sick with guilt and I poured even more salt over it, trying to speed its merciful death. But that only seemed to make it suffer all the more.

Mitzie was oblivious to my distress as she reached for something else to pluck. This time she took hold of one of its legs. It was as though I were watching the scene through a high-powered lens, every hideous detail of the wasp's mutilated body vivid and crystal clear. The creature jumped and twitched, trying desperately to turn its body, to aim the vicious barb of its stinger at her.

Mitzie laughed and used her other hand to hold it steady and I realised what had been so odd about her touch. The little finger of her left hand was missing.

"Oh my God," I breathed, "Mitzie, what happened to your hand?"

"Hmm?" She looked at me, then down at her hand. She wiggled the remaining fingers and smiled. It was a terrible smile, full of madness and cruelty. And as I watched she pressed her fingertips down hard on the wasp, smearing it into a pale yellow paste against the floor.

My stomach lurched and I clawed for the door behind me. I managed to stumble into the grass but I crumpled to my knees before I had gone ten steps and I was sick in a pile of weeds. When I finally looked back through the open doorway, Mitzie was licking her fingers.

I didn't remember running home but I must have because I found myself back in my bedroom, drenched in sweat, my sides aching from exertion. I was convinced I could hear something buzzing and I did the deep breathing exercises my dad had taught me the year before. Inhale slowly. Hold. Count to five. Exhale slowly. Again. It calmed my racing heart but it didn't erase the images from my mind. If I closed my eyes I saw Mitzie's mad grin, her ruined hand, her mutilated victim.

I lay awake for hours that night, unable to purge the memory of Mitzie's "surprise". That she thought it was some kind of gift for me was the worst part. Had she honestly believed I'd be happy about what she'd done? Maybe she'd even expected me to join in.

My thoughts led me into all sorts of unpleasant places. I thought of the day I had first met her, the way she had clung to her dead cat and cursed the old man. I thought of our days in the forest. Mostly I thought of the funhouse and the dark games Mitzie had always liked to play. Something was nudging at the edges of my mind, some glimmer of understanding I couldn't quite grasp.

When I finally slept, my dreams were haunted by wasps. I felt them crawling over me, creeping inside my pyjamas, exploring my skin. They crawled inside my mouth, my ears, my eyes. Several times I jolted awake, brushing frantically at myself. But there was nothing there. I stared at my trembling hands and my eyes were drawn to the left little finger.

What had she done? I knew in my heart that, whatever it was, it hadn't been an accident. She had cut it off herself. Had she been as unfamiliar with pain as she was with fear? Was it some twisted experiment to see if she could feel? Or was it something even more sinister?

Suddenly I remembered the story she'd told me about the old man. It hadn't really sunk in at the time. An allergic reaction, Mitzie had said. Now it occurred to me to wonder what kind of allergic reaction. To what exactly? And why had Mitzie seemed so smug about it?

My mind strayed back to the night she made us blood-sisters. My *sacrifice*. "Now you're a part of me," she'd said.

My skin crawled and again I brushed away imaginary wasps, recalling the unnatural shine in her eyes after the attack.

I've never seen anyone look so scared.

I didn't want to go back there but I knew I would never rest until I faced the truth. The moon hung high and bright overhead as I made my way down the street and across to her side of town. The funhouse loomed in silhouette, its splintered boards like claws raking at the summer night sky.

The door was open and I stepped inside, half-expecting Mitzie to jump out at me. But there was no need for that now. I had no fear left to give her.

When I heard the buzzing again I didn't scream. I'd known it would be there. The noise surrounded me like mist and I closed my eyes, holding very still.

"Hello, Mitzie," I said.

The buzzing intensified for a moment, then subsided to a murmur.

Her voice was soft when it came. "Open your eyes."

I did. Moonlight streamed through the empty windows, illuminating the funhouse. There were no wasps. Only Mitzie.

For a moment she looked like a normal little girl again. And maybe she'd truly been that once. But now that little girl was gone and in her place was something else.

"Tell me what you did," I said.

She gazed at me, her eyes glinting in the pale light like an animal's. "You were always so fearful, so easy to scare," she began. "But that day in the tree . . . I'd never seen anything like that before. All I could think was that I wanted it."

"Wanted what?"

"Their power. You were terrified. You thought you were going to die. You even thought of jumping out of the tree. You knew it would kill you but you thought it anyway. I saw it all in your mind."

The pieces were coming together at last.

"The old man," I said.

She nodded. "He was scared too. But that was just a jarful released into his house. It was nothing like what happened to you. He got off easy."

All around me I could hear the rustling of wings, the scratching of tiny legs crawling over the rotting walls of the shack. Mitzie didn't seem to hear it. I looked down at the floor. The yellow smear was still there, luminous in the moonlight.

She smiled and held up her hand for me to see. The skin over the stump was stretched thin and tight, glistening with an unnatural sheen. "My sacrifice," she said. "Your gift. For the power."

She was insane. That much was clear. But there was far more at work here than just one little girl's madness.

"It doesn't work like that, Mitzie."

She shook her head and frowned. "What do you mean?"

My skin tingled with the memory of tiny legs clambering over it all night, climbing in and out of me. I couldn't answer her. I didn't know how to tell her she'd got it terribly wrong.

Mitzie looked disappointed, as though I'd failed to grasp some simple concept. "Don't you see?" She showed me the mangled finger stump again. "I released you."

I instinctively curled my own fingers, remembering the pain when she had pricked me with the needle, the way she had licked away my blood. The promise I had made was now just a smudge on the floor at my feet. Mitzie had made a different promise, to something else entirely.

"Don't *you* see? You killed one of them. Tortured it."

"It was an offering. We suffered together."

She still didn't realise what she'd done. All that fear. She'd tended it like flowers in a garden. It was here with us now, massing in the forest and in the rotting boards of the funhouse. My own fear was part of it, had helped create it. Mitzie had always believed she was the one in control, but she was wrong.

The air around her began to shimmer and the room grew suddenly cold. As I watched, her skin took on a sickly glow. Her eyes widened and I saw her afraid for the very first time. The *only* time. She opened her mouth to scream but the sound died in her throat. Shadows passed over her body in long, wavering stripes. Then the skin itself began to ripple and contort, as though thousands of living things were inside it, struggling to hatch.

And then they did hatch. The flesh at her throat split first, spilling forth a crawling swarm of wasps. They scuttled over one another in a buzzing frenzy, their wings vibrating, their antennae quivering. I saw their tiny jaws working furiously, devouring the shell from which they had emerged, leaving no trace of it behind.

Then, in a burst of wild humming, they formed into a cloud, billowing around me. My heart was pounding but there was nothing for me to fear any more. They moved with the eerie precision of a flock of birds and I saw how beautiful they could be. I reached a hand up into their swirling masses and they flowed over me like rain.

Behind the Wall

JULIE CLOSED THE DOOR OF THE HOUSE, SHUTTING OUT THE world. The removal men would be here soon enough, filling the rooms with all her possessions, but for now she savoured the emptiness. She felt hidden and safe.

After a while she spoke, her voice echoing in the bare room. "Well, what do you think, Sam? Did I do okay?'

Her husband didn't answer, so she answered for him in her head.

It's perfect. We could have been so happy here together.

Tears burned her eyes, blurring the room. The rest of her life stretched out before her like a long and desolate road now that Sam was dead. She couldn't stay in the home they'd made together, couldn't face each day in a place where memories assaulted her everywhere she turned. She needed a fresh start, one without constant reminders of her partner of almost twenty years. Finding her own place to live had been a surreal experience. At times it had felt oddly transgressive. Weird and wrong. Sam should be here with her. She shouldn't be alone.

She'd grieved for weeks and weeks, eventually alienating casual friends with her bottomless depression and morbid preoccupations. The ones who truly cared did their best but at last she succeeded in shutting them out too, pleading with them to understand. She didn't want to be around anyone who'd known them as a couple; the reminders were just too painful. It was all she could do to get up each morning and remember to breathe, to live. Alone.

And now she was here.

Strethkellis was a strange-sounding place, with something ancient and esoteric about it. It was a village where Sam had stayed occasionally when he was on the road in Cornwall for business. He hadn't liked to stay in nearby Truro so he'd found a secluded little village to use as a base instead. He loved it for its peace and quiet, its isolation.

Julie had never been there herself. But when she finally began to pull herself together and realised she needed to start again, it was the name that kept coming up in her mind. She had to get away and it was a place with a connection to Sam. So she went there.

The village was as strange as its name. A narrow, winding road led into a hilly wood crowded with enormous trees. They closed over the road like a tunnel, hiding the sun until they opened out again at the picturesque glade where the village sprawled. A rustic stone marker was almost entirely obscured by thorny bushes but the name was there in chipped black letters: STRETHKELLIS.

It was larger than she'd imagined, with a scattering of cottages and several larger houses arranged around a village green with a pub called the Bird in Hand at one end. It looked like an old coaching inn, with a central cobbled courtyard decorated with potted plants. She gazed up at the windows above the pub, remembering the first night Sam had rung her from here and wondering which room he had stayed in. The view he'd described from the window was every bit as idyllic as he'd claimed. And he was right: it was quiet. The only sounds Julie heard were songbirds twittering in the trees and ducks splashing in the pond.

Naturally, she had expected the locals to be unwelcoming to an outsider but they were nothing at all like the surly peasants she'd anticipated. They treated her like a long-lost relative returning to her ancestral home. She had fallen in love with the place at once, just as Sam must have. And the fact that the charming Little Owl Cottage had just gone on the market only further convinced her that this was where she was meant to be. Perhaps it was Sam's last gift to her.

The cottage was peculiar, small enough to be cosy but with an absurd number of rooms, many of them no larger than a closet. But its quirkiness was part of its charm. The rooms were like spaces on a shelf that needed filling, or a jigsaw puzzle that needed someone to put it back together.

"I miss you, Sam," she said, stroking the pale blue wallpaper.

I'll always be here, she thought she heard him say.

"How are you settling in, dear?"

Julie jumped at the voice, startled out of her unpacking. It was like coming out of a trance. Her elderly neighbour was standing there, holding an old-fashioned picnic basket with a tea towel draped over it.

"Oh, Mrs Trevenan, it's you."

"Yes, yes," the older woman laughed, "only little old me! My, but you've been busy, haven't you?"

Julie looked around her at the chaos. Books, pots and pans, books, bathroom stuff, books, clothes and more books. She'd been at it for hours, relishing the simple but laborious task of taking things out of boxes, finding homes for them and then flattening the boxes. It was the best distraction in the world and she'd made a considerable start in just a few hours.

"I thought you might like a cup of tea," said Mrs Trevenan, brandishing a teapot under a flowery pink cosy. "Your front door was open."

Julie couldn't believe that was true but if the woman had knocked and got no answer she might have assumed it was OK just to wander in. It seemed like that kind of village. Back in Taunton Julie might have bristled at the intrusion but the lure of tea was too cosy to refuse.

"That would be lovely," she said, relenting. "There's a table and some chairs around here somewhere."

"Right by the window," Mrs Trevenan said, nodding with approval at the arrangement in the breakfast nook. "Charlene—she lived here before you—had bird feeders in the apple tree. We used to sit here for hours watching them."

The image was so serene Julie made a mental note to get a bird feeder for herself.

"I've also brought some gingerbread. I just took it out of the oven."

She held up a small plate and Julie inhaled deeply. Was there anything in the world more heavenly than the smell of freshly baked gingerbread? It was a nostalgic breeze all the way from her childhood. Her eyes threatened to water and she chided herself for her mawkish sentimentality. The last thing she needed in her life right now was a surrogate mother. But perhaps she could do with a bit of companionship.

Julie smiled. "Mmmm, you said the magic word. And it just so happens I found all the kitchen stuff a little while ago." Although she didn't doubt that Mrs Trevenan could have pulled an entire dining set from her picnic basket.

She had to open several cabinet doors to find where she'd stashed the coffee mugs but eventually she found them and she sat down for the first time that afternoon. The tea was unexpectedly strong and the gingerbread was every bit as delicious as it smelled.

"Have another piece," the old woman said, pushing the platter across the table.

"Are you trying to fatten me up?" Julie laughed.

Mrs Trevenan frowned slightly. "It won't do you any harm, pet. You're thin as a rail."

"Yes, well . . ."

Over the past few months Julie had wondered whether her appetite would ever return. Without Sam nothing felt or tasted right. There was a hard little knot in her stomach, as though her intestines had been tied together. The pain came in waves, overwhelming her and then subsiding only to return again even stronger. Then, after a while, her emotions seemed to desert her entirely. It was if she'd finally run out of tears. Even music lost its ability to move her. She had drifted through endless days, feeling nothing, seeing nothing.

"Julie?"

She came out of the fog, blinking. Mrs Trevenan was staring at her.

"Oh, I'm sorry," Julie said. "It's just . . . Sam. My husband. He—he died last year and I'm still not . . . Well, I don't know if I'll ever be . . . "

"It's all right, dear. I understand completely. It was just the same with me when my Harold went." The old woman sighed and sipped her tea.

Julie didn't say anything. She was grateful not to hear the same old platitudes again. (*I'm sorry for your loss. He's at peace now. You're in my prayers*.) She certainly would never say them herself. She gave a slight smile of understanding and swirled the dregs of her tea.

"Which room are you going to wall up?"

For a moment she wasn't sure she'd heard the old woman right. In her mug flecks of tea leaf circled like a school of tiny fish, coming together and then spinning out to the sides of the mug before settling again at the bottom. She looked up, confused.

Mrs Trevenan smiled. "Most people choose one of their smaller rooms but I picked our bedroom. I even left the door in place. Sometimes I knock on it when I walk past." She gazed out the window in dreamy reminiscence. "Oh, look! There's a goldfinch. You almost never see them this time of year."

Julie shook her head, confused. "Pardon me, but what did you say?"

"The goldfinch. You almost—"

"No, no, before that. About a wall?"

Now it was the old lady's turn to look puzzled. "Well, I asked you which room you were going to wall up." At Julie's baffled look, realisation dawned in her face. "Oh, I see. I assumed that was why you'd moved here."

"No, I came because Sam had been here before and said it was lovely. He was right. But he never said anything about walling up rooms."

"Of course not, dear. He hadn't lost anyone, had he?"

"I'm afraid *I'm* the one who's lost, Mrs Trevenan."

The old lady patted her hand with a grandmotherly smile. "Strethkellis is a very ancient place," she said, "with very ancient customs. And here, when someone dear passes, we wall off a room for them to stay in. Then they're always with us."

Something fluttered uneasily in Julie's stomach. She thought of the many tiny rooms scattered throughout Little Owl Cottage. Were all the homes here like that? Built with extra rooms to house the dead? Her skin suddenly felt cold.

"But Sam...He's...Well, he's already buried. Back in Taunton."

Mrs Trevenan stared at her for a few seconds, then broke into laughter. "Good heavens, no! I didn't mean we preserve our loved ones' remains."

"Then what *did* you mean?"

"Our custom is simply to wall off a room. We only leave the *spirit* of the dear one inside it and it becomes *their* room. That way we know they're still here."

Julie didn't think that sounded any less morbid. "You mean like a shrine?"

"Not at all. You see, you can't go in the room once you've closed it off. Some people leave a door, like I did, but it's sealed shut. I know my Harold is there, behind it, with me forever. And when it's my turn someone will break down the wall and I'll join him there." She smiled as she nibbled a slice of gingerbread.

The kitchen suddenly felt very cold. Julie wondered if every house in the village had a walled room.

As though reading her mind Mrs Trevenan said "The Hollisters sealed off the entire garage when they lost their boy because that's where he used to play his drums. And Martin Evans at the Bird in Hand—he gave the best room in the pub to his wife Sylvia when she passed. That was almost twenty years ago. Do you know, people have stayed in the room next door to it and claimed the place is haunted." She laughed brightly. "Can you imagine?"

Julie could, all too well. She thought of the old custom of covering the mirrors in a house of the dead so the spirit of the departed one wouldn't be trapped in the house. This seemed like the very opposite. There was something slightly delusional about it. Everyone wanted to believe their loved ones were still with them in spirit, but who wanted to imagine they were trapped in a secret room?

"Are you all right, pet? You look a bit pale all of a sudden."

"No, I'm fine, Mrs Trevenan. Just tired from unpacking." She forced a smile and finished her tea in one long swallow. It had gone cold and the dregs felt like dust in her throat.

But the old woman saw right through her. She took Julie's hand in both of hers, peering intently at her. "It's not a morbid fantasy, you know. It's simply a tradition in this part of the country. I think you'll find it as comforting as we do."

Julie nodded absently. She didn't like the presumption that she would naturally do it because it was the custom of the village. "I think I'd better get back to work," she said. "Thank you so much for the tea and ginger-bread."

Mrs Trevenan smiled as she rose and collected her things. "You're more than welcome, my dear. If you ever need anything, you know where I am. Pop round any time. The door's always open."

"Thanks," Julie mumbled. She didn't doubt the woman kept her door unlocked in the hope that someone would wander in for a chat. She didn't doubt that that was yet another custom of this strange village. She couldn't help but wonder how many others there were.

Julie kept to herself for the next few days, unpacking and setting up the cottage. She made sure the doors were locked although three different people had pushed notes through the letterbox welcoming her to the village and inviting her round and one lady had left her a basket of fruit from her garden. They were so aggressively friendly and welcoming that Julie began to feel guilty about her reclusive behaviour. She'd driven thirty miles to the nearest supermarket for groceries rather than buy her food in the small village shop but she knew she wouldn't be able to keep that up. Besides, wasn't that the whole point of coming here? To get away from her previous life and start a new one? She resolved to accept the next invitation she got, however it came.

As it turned out, she was meandering along a little path at the end of the village, enjoying the birdsong, when a black labrador came bounding out of the woods. The dog wagged his tail frantically and ran right up to her as though delighted that she had come here just to see him.

"Well, aren't you a handsome boy?" Julie said, reaching down to pet him. He stood still for a few seconds while she stroked his sleek head, then danced around in a little circle before tearing off again into the trees. She smiled after him and he soon returned, this time with his owner, a man in hiking clothes. He looked to be about her age.

"Hi there," he said. "I hope Pepper didn't scare you."

"Not at all. He's lovely."

Realising he was being talked about, Pepper barked and looked up at each of them in turn, pink tongue lolling in a huge doggy grin.

"Yeah," the man said, "he loves everyone. Haven't seen you around before."

"I'm new here. My name's Julie Young."

Recognition dawned on his face. "Ah! You must be the lady who bought Little Owl Cottage."

"That's me."

"From the big city, they said down the pub. Must be quite a change. How are you settling into village life?"

Julie had to laugh. One could hardly call Taunton "the big city" but it must seem that way to someone from a secluded little village like Strethkellis. "I love it here. It's so peaceful. And everyone is very friendly."

"That's good. My name's Jim, by the way. Jim Evans."

The name rang a bell. "Evans? From the Bird in Hand?"

"Yeah, that's my dad. He owns it. I think you stayed there before you bought the cottage, right?"

"I did. Two nights. That's how long it took me to decide I wanted to stay."

Jim smiled. "It's an easy place to fall in love with."

Julie recalled what Mrs Trevenan had said about the pub owner giving his dead wife the best room in the inn and she couldn't help but wonder what that must be like. Did Jim think it was weird to pretend that his mum was in there forever, behind a sealed door? Then again, maybe it was no weirder than the tombs and mausoleums people built in memory of their lost loved ones. Gardens of dust and remembrance.

"When you're feeling up to it," Jim said, "perhaps you'd come along to the Bird one night? We'd all like to welcome you properly."

It might have sounded ominous from someone else but from Jim it seemed like a sincere, neighbourly invitation. Moving here had definitely been the right thing to do to start the healing process. The aching pain of widowhood would never go away, she knew, but it grew a little less agonising with each day of her new life. She relented.

"Sure. That would be nice."

"Great!" Jim said. Then he looked down at the ground, his expression turning serious. "I know what it's like to lose someone," he said softly. "It feels like it will never end. The pain I mean."

Julie could only nod. If she spoke Sam's name she felt she'd burst into tears. She watched Pepper pounce on something at the edge of the trees and then he lay down to gnaw a stick.

"The wall will help," Jim said.

The wall. Julie nodded again, absently. For a moment she allowed herself to imagine what it would be like, devoting a hidden space to Sam. The cottage was a honeycomb of tiny rooms. She needed a bedroom and an office but that was really all. Maybe a guest room down the road when she was up to having friends come and visit—assuming she hadn't scared them all off for good. But the rest were just empty spaces she couldn't hope to fill.

What if she did give one to Sam? Could she pass by it every day and wonder what he was doing in there? The ancient Egyptians used to bury people with all their possessions, to take with them into the next world. What if she put a few things in there from their life together? Photos, books, mementos?

All at once the idea didn't seem mad at all. It felt rather sweet.

"The wall," she murmured, barely aware that she was speaking aloud.

The Bird in Hand wasn't a very large pub and it was full of people by the time Julie got there. Everyone greeted her warmly and introduced themselves but after the first few names she lost track. She couldn't believe things like this happened, that an entire village would throw a welcoming party for a new arrival. It was like she'd gone back in time to a friendlier age. It felt nice. She was soon lost in a mélange of pleasant conversation.

"—and that's Simon who runs the bakery and his wife Carla and their daughter Jeanette—"

"—must see the waterfall over in the glen—"

"—another glass of wine—"

"—our David can mend anything at all for you—"

"—and sometimes the deer come right into my garden—"

Julie was amazed to find herself laughing along with several anecdotes and enjoying the gathering. She'd only intended to put in an appearance and then leave, but she found she was actually having a good time.

Pepper worked the room, charming his way through the crowd to her. She slipped him a cocktail sausage from her plate and he wolfed it down. He pleaded with his eyes for more and when she held up her empty hand to show that was all he was getting, he slipped away to find someone else to mooch off. Julie smiled. It was the first time she'd felt the knot in her stomach begin to loosen properly. She felt like part of the village, as though she belonged.

She spotted Allan Curtis, who had built the wall for her. She hadn't liked the idea of keeping the door; she preferred to imagine that Sam was at the heart of the house, a secret no one else could see. Allan had kindly taken the door away when he was done and now there was no evidence that there had ever been a room there. Unless, of course, you did a circuit of the house and realised that the measurements didn't add up.

She often stroked the wall and whispered through it to Sam, as though he truly were just beyond it. And lately she'd begun to think she could hear him. She imagined him listening to the CDs she'd left in there for him, reading the books. Was he lonely in there? Or was he content to be absorbed into her new life? That very morning she'd been sure she could hear footsteps, the soft *shoosh* of slippers on the carpeted floor. It had instantly evoked memories of his clumsy morning gait, his sleepy stumble out of bed and into the bathroom before getting dressed for work.

"Go back to sleep, my love," she'd whispered through the wall. "You can sleep as late as you want to now."

Instead of piercing her heart as such a thought would once have done, it brought her comfort. He seemed more present in the secret room than he ever had at his gravesite. In the beginning she'd gone to the churchyard several times a week, sobbing into the ground and crushing the flowers she brought for him. Now she wondered if the pain she'd felt there had been due to his profound absence. She had felt nothing of Sam in that patch of ground, that cold marker. The wall was different. Sometimes she could almost see him standing behind it, mirroring her position, pressing his hands against hers.

She had already thanked Allan profusely for building the wall and she thanked him again now.

"It's nothing," he insisted. "Just our little tradition."

"I hung our wedding portrait on it," she confided to him. "It doesn't hurt so much to see it now." It felt good to share, to be so open, as though she'd been keeping Sam trapped inside her heart and at last she had released him. She felt like a whole person for the first time in months.

"That's good to hear," Allan said. "Most folks find it a comfort."

She accepted another glass of wine from Jim, who had insisted that tonight was her night and she was not allowed to pay for anything. As she took it from him she saw a young woman across the room, watching her.

The girl was very pretty, with long dark hair and delicate features. Julie didn't think they'd been introduced yet, but she couldn't be sure; she'd met so many people. In any case she was sure she'd have remembered someone so striking. She smiled over at her, but the girl didn't smile back. Her eyes went wide, as though something had startled her.

Puzzled, Julie excused herself and tried to make her way across the room. But they were packed like sardines in the pub and by the time she got to where the girl had been standing, no one was there.

Julie felt uneasy about the silent encounter without knowing why. Maybe the girl was just shy and she'd scurried off rather than have to chat with someone she didn't know. That seemed inconsistent with the rest of the village, but then, people were individuals. They couldn't *all* be so outgoing and gregarious.

She made her way over to Mrs Trevenan, who was chatting with Martin Evans, the publican.

"There you are, pet! It's quite a gathering, isn't it? I hope you're making lots of new friends."

"Everyone's been lovely," Julie said. "But I saw a girl a little while ago—about thirty, dark hair, really pretty?"

"Oh, that'll be Alice Carew. She's a sweetheart, isn't she?"

"I didn't actually get to meet her. I tried to go over and say hi but she disappeared."

"Disappeared?"

"Yeah, she looked like something scared her off."

Mrs Trevenan gave a sigh and nodded as if she suddenly understood. "The poor thing. She lost her boyfriend last year."

"Oh." Julie's heart twisted. Had everyone in this village lost someone?

But the publican was frowning. "It's still not like Alice," he said. "She was fine just a few weeks ago. And I've never known her to skip out on a party before. She's usually the one talking your ear off about this, that and the other."

Mrs Trevenan didn't seem to know what to say to that but Julie could see that she was puzzled too.

"Well," Julie said, "maybe she wasn't feeling well." But even as she suggested it, she knew it didn't ring true. In fact, now that she thought about it, the girl had looked positively *terrified*. She wondered where Alice's wall was, and what sounds she heard coming from behind it.

"Good morning, Sam," Julie said, stopping by the wedding portrait. She stroked the wall and put her ear against it. There were no sounds this time but she sensed a kind of heaviness, as if someone were standing just on the other side, listening. Her skin prickled. She held herself perfectly still, straining in the silence to catch any sound. A floorboard creaked then and she jumped back with a gasp.

Before she could stop herself she said "Sam? Is that you?"

Of course there was no answer and she immediately felt foolish. She tried to laugh at herself, laugh it off, but she didn't like the sound that came out.

"I'm going to make breakfast, Sam," she forced herself to say in a cheery voice. "I'm sure you'll smell it burning."

She moved away quickly, unable to shake the feeling that she wasn't alone. And then she froze. A dark shape stood beyond the frosted glass of the front door.

Her heart pounded as she stared at the figure for what felt like endless minutes before it raised one arm and rang the bell. The noise jolted her and she gave a little cry.

"Mrs Young? Are you OK?"

The voice was female and Julie relaxed immediately, feeling even more foolish than she had earlier. She was turning into a jumpy old lady at the tender age of forty. Next she'd be filling the house with cats.

She opened the door and was surprised by her visitor. It was Alice.

"Hello," Julie said.

Alice offered her a weak little smile. "Hi."

"Do you want to come in?"

The girl glanced behind her as it to check that she wasn't being followed, then shifted her feet uneasily on the mat. "I probably shouldn't."

Julie pulled her dressing gown a little tighter. "Don't be ridiculous. It's freezing. Please come in."

Alice chewed her lower lip for a few seconds and then relented. She glanced around at her surroundings and Julie suspected she was looking for the wall. The girl's eye fell on the wedding portrait and she instantly looked away.

"Would you like some tea?" Julie asked.

The girl shook her head as though she'd been offered poison. "Listen," she said, "I can't stay. I just . . . Oh God, this is so hard for me." She stared down at her shifting feet in an agony of discomfort.

Julie touched Alice's shoulder. "I understand. They told me last night about your boyfriend. I lost my Sam a few months ago too."

At the mention of Sam's name, the girl winced. For a moment Julie simply believed she'd hit a nerve by bringing up the dead boyfriend. Then Alice raised her head and with slow, dawning horror Julie realised what this was about. The look in the girl's eyes told her everything.

"Oh my God," she whispered.

"I'm sorry," Alice said. "I'm so sorry."

"Not Sam."

"I never meant to hurt anyone. I didn't even know he was married."

Julie's stomach lurched and suddenly she felt dizzy. The floor seemed to be tilting. She reached out a trembling hand to steady herself against a bookcase.

"I saw your picture on his phone once," Alice continued, "and then when I saw you at the party last night and I realised who you were—"

"Just stop," Julie choked out. Her legs felt like they were made of water and she turned away, groping along the corridor towards the wall. The wall with the wedding portrait. She supposed all the signs had been there and she'd just been too stupid to see them. The village Sam had spoken of so glowingly had clearly held one extra spark, one special little added attraction. All those calls home—had he rung her from this girl's bedroom? Had he actually ever stayed at the pub at all?

"Why are you here?" she whimpered.

"You're in danger," Alice said. "You have to get away from here."

Julie laughed, a harsh and ugly sound. "Or what? You'll steal my husband? You lot and your crazy walls!"

"That's just it. The walls."

Julie scrubbed her eyes with the back of her sleeve. "Whose wall? Mine or yours? Because you've got Sam too, haven't you? Did you fill the room with nice little reminders of your stolen moments together?"

Alice looked as if she'd been slapped. "Please believe me, I had no idea. He lied to us both. But you have to listen to me. Yes, I built a wall for Sa— for him. But then so did you."

"Yes I did," Julie said. The shock and helplessness was wearing off and anger was taking its place. In one vicious movement she tore the wedding portrait down and smashed it on the floor. Then she kicked the wall with her bare foot. There was a crunch and she supposed she had hurt herself but she could feel nothing. Only the satisfying *thunk* as she dented the soft plasterboard.

Alice screamed. "No! No, you mustn't!"

But Julie was beyond hearing. Grief was nothing compared to the pain of this betrayal. She pounded on the wall, shouting through it at Sam, as though he could actually hear her.

Something shifted beyond it and she imagined him in there, a guilty ghost. Would he slink out now and offer grovelling apologies? Plead with her to forgive him? She landed another satisfying kick and heard the boards splinter.

"You can't do that!" Alice cried, pulling Julie away from the wall. "Please! It's not him!"

Julie looked at the beautiful young woman her husband had deceived her with. She had wasted a year of her life in misery, grieving for an unworthy man. Her heart felt like it was rotting.

Alice stared in horror at the hole Julie had made just above the skirting board and backed away slowly, tears streaming down her pretty face. "Sam already has a wall," she whimpered, "and I know he's there. So—whatever's behind that one isn't Sam."

The words seemed to reach Julie like a transmission from a fading signal. *Not Sam.* Rationality returned bit by bit as she recalled the uneasy feeling she'd had that morning, the sense that she wasn't alone. The sounds had been wrong. She'd known they were wrong. She'd just been so desperate to buy into the village's mass delusion.

Now, as her foot began to throb with delayed pain, she felt the presence even more strongly. There was an icy malevolence in the air, as though a door had been opened. A door to a place she didn't want to see.

"It's too late," Alice whispered. All the colour had drained from her face. She covered her mouth with both hands.

Julie barely registered what happened next. The hole began to widen by itself, the plaster crumbling to dust. There was a dull cracking sound and Julie wondered if it might be her mind. She closed her eyes and sank to her knees, leaning back against what was left of the wall.

"Sam," she moaned, "tell me it's not true. Tell me you love me."

A hand brushed against her face and then his arms were around her, drawing her close and tight. She sighed as she lay back against him, melting into the crushing embrace she had missed so desperately. It *was* Sam. She would know his touch anywhere. How could she ever have doubted him? Alice had lied—about everything.

He was so much stronger now, though. She had made him stronger, by believing. His face was rough and scratchy as he pressed it to hers, and she heard his voice then, whispering in her ear. He sounded different, but he told her what she wanted to hear, what she *needed* to hear.

Then he slowly let her go. Julie listened to the sound of his heavy tread as he moved away across the room. And she smiled as Alice began to scream.

Vile Earth, to Earth Resign

*T*HE FOLLOWING CORRESPONDENCE WAS FOUND IN THE *wreckage of a New World Pharmaceuticals medical facility located on the Cornish coast in what used to be known as Exmoor National Park. The pages had been carefully wrapped in plastic and placed inside a locked container. It is unknown who put them there.*

It's 3 a.m. and I can't sleep. I keep thinking about this girl. She's the most beautiful thing I've ever seen in my life and I can't get her out of my head. Do you know who I'm talking about? If you do, even if you just THINK you do, send me a message. If you leave a note under your mattress I can get it when they take you to the lab. You know who I am. I'm the guy with his heart pinned to his sleeve. But you can call me Peter.

I hate this place. They took your note away from me before I could even finish reading it. Dr Jernigan told me it's against the rules to have personal

233

contact with "the subjects". As if I didn't know that. I said yeah, OK, I wouldn't do it again and I think he believed me. He's got his own stuff to worry about so I don't think he's that bothered, really.

At least I know your name now. Elaine. And I wish I COULD send you a picture. Or a text. God, I miss my phone. My computer. My car. I miss so many things about the world before. Mostly I just miss living in a world that wasn't us-or-them. What do you miss the most?

I'll say your name until I fall asleep tonight. Elaine. Elaine. Elaine.

Elaine,

I'm glad you could hear me last night. I wasn't sure. You looked so peaceful, like you were dreaming of happier times. And I saw you on the way to the lab this afternoon. They took you through the garden. Is it nice for you to go outside? Or is everything just a reminder that you're here against your will? Do you have memories of your life before?

I can't believe you miss swimming the most! In this country? Are you crazy??? LOL I don't even know how to swim. Hey, maybe if we ever get out of here you can teach me.

To answer YOUR question, no, I'm not here because I want to be. I was just a lowly medical student before all this happened and they gave me a very clear choice: come in or get out. And "out there" was the Death. I mean the Death before—well, before the ones like you.

I don't like what they do in this place and of course I probably don't even know the half of it. But what I do know is enough to make me angry. They call themselves doctors and scientists but they're a bunch of bloody Nazis. I wish I could take you out of here and away from all this. They can see you're not dangerous. I just don't understand why your kind (I refuse to use the Z-word) have to be kept prisoner here. You deserve better.

I want to ask you something. But I don't want to freak you out or stir up bad memories. But this is the only way we can talk so I have no choice. Were you dead before you came here?

Your friend,
Peter

Peter,

I would love to teach you how to swim. And I'd give anything to see the ocean again. To hear the waves. To feel alive. Really alive. Sometimes I think I can hear it. We must be near the sea.

Do I have memories? Oh yes. They're *all* I have. Some are so bad I wish I could erase them. My whole family is dead. My parents. My sister. Even my dog. I wish I could scratch that whole day from my mind. And most of the ones since. But I have happy memories too. I try to think of those the most.

It's nice to have a friend. It's comforting to know someone here cares about me. Thank you for that.

Elaine

My dear Elaine (I love writing your name), I'm so sorry about everything, especially what happened to your family. It's terrible you remember all the bad things. And I understand if you don't want to tell me the details. I mean, you don't know me at all. I have no idea where my own family are, or if they got away when the world went crazy.

Dr Jernigan says things are getting even crazier. I can't remember the last time I saw a news report or read a paper but I gather there's a war going on outside. I'm sure they'd like to keep us all in the dark here but I wonder if you know anything? They say you can sense things.

I'll try to come by your room tonight. Stay awake if you can and maybe this time you'll see me!

Your friend,
Peter

Dear Peter,

I saw you last night at my window. It was wonderful to see someone smile for once. And at me! I recognised you too. You were there the day they first brought me here. Do you remember? You looked very sad that day, like you'd been crying. I certainly had. I'd just been told my whole family was dead, killed by zombies. They said I'd be dead too, very soon. Because I'd been bitten. I tried to tell them it wasn't a bite. But they knew that, really. I guess they thought it would be easier for me (or them) if they could just pretend I'd turned naturally.

They wanted healthy human subjects and there weren't many of us left. They said we'd be doing a great service to mankind. And what they did changed me. I'm no longer human. It's weird to see that in writing. *I'm not human*. I have scars on my body from the things they did to me. Someone else's heart beats inside my chest. Some *thing's* heart. Some *thing's* blood flows in my veins. The dead Other gives me life, so I can't really bring myself to hate it. (Him? Her?) And I'm one of the lucky ones. I've heard stories about other kinds of experiments, things I can't even bear to think about.

But you know all this. And it gives me hope to know that you don't agree with what goes on here. I remember thinking when I first saw you that you had a kind face, that you didn't belong here. The day I arrived— was it your first day too?

I wish I had happier things to tell you but maybe it will help to write the bad ones down. I have no one to talk to and it's so lonely here, especially at night. I like the thought of you watching over me while I sleep.

And I dreamed last night! I haven't dreamed in so long. You were in it. You made me feel human again.

You asked if I could sense things. I probably shouldn't write this since you said they took my first note away but there might not be much time left. They think they're keeping us in the dark too but we have secrets they'll never find. So many secrets.

Yes, there is a war out there. Between humans and zombies. (I don't mind the term. There is no other word for what I am now.) They weren't expecting us to change like we did. In our minds. They thought we'd stay brainless shambling monsters until we rotted away, but that wasn't what happened. Now that they know we can think and reason just like them they're even more afraid. They should be.

I can't read thoughts. It's not like that. I can smell fear. Like an animal, I guess. And I can sense moods. I know who it's safe to trust, which is why I know I can trust *you*. And it's why I want to warn you. A revolution is coming. The others here—the other infected—are going to fight back. They can communicate with the ones outside and they're going to destroy the facility and free us. But I don't want to go with them. I don't want any part of their stupid war, not on either side. I just want to be with you. You're the only person who's seen me for who I am—who I *was* – since the whole nightmare began.

Is it too soon to say I think I love you? Maybe it's not soon enough.

xx Elaine

My dearest Elaine,

I should probably destroy your last note like I did most of the others but I just can't. Not when you said what you did at the end.

Oh Elaine, I think I love you too.

I went by your room again last night. (I know it's a cell but I can't stand to think of it that way.) You were asleep. I tapped on the window but you didn't see me. Did you dream again? I never remember my dreams, not even good ones. I guess I envy you that.

What an ugly place the world has become. Only a few months before I might have been smiling at you in a coffee shop on the high street as we both studied for exams. I might have even got up the courage to ask you out. Now here I am like a character in some old Victorian melodrama, pouring my heart out on the page to you every night. You're the only light in the darkness.

I promise I will keep all your secrets. Dr Jernigan asked me yesterday what was wrong with me. He said I looked distracted. I wonder why! They've got me writing up their notes and doing other menial tasks, probably to keep me out of the way of their Important Work. They know I don't approve but I'm the low man on the totem pole so even if I objected

I'd be no threat to them. So I'm going to keep my head down for now and at the first sign of trouble I'll come find you and we can go away together, find someplace safe. There must be places out there untouched by all this. I have to believe there are anyway.

Love,
Peter

✦ ✦ ✦

Peter,

I had the most wonderful dream last night. I dreamed you came to my room while I was sleeping and held me in your arms all night. I dreamed you talked to me and whispered that you loved me and said you wanted to be with me forever. I dreamed all this and when I woke up I had to remind myself that it wasn't a dream at all. You were really there!

Sometimes I think I must be going crazy, that you're too good to be true. How can a soul as beautiful as yours exist in such a terrible place?

I keep playing last night over and over in my head. Seeing your face in the window. Seeing you smile. Watching the doorknob turn and watching you come inside. You were so warm. I felt like I could just melt into you. I'm sorry I couldn't stop crying. I just couldn't believe you were real. Just hearing your voice, a loving voice, was almost more than I could handle. I'm glad my scars don't bother you. I think they're hideous. But you said they were beautiful because they were part of me. Now I'm crying again.

Like I told you, I have no idea how long I've been here but you are the only person to show me any kindness in all this time. Sometimes it's overwhelming.

I want to get out of here so much. I want to be with you. Please say you'll come again. I don't think I can cope with the rest of my life if you're not in it.

Yours forever,
Elaine

My dearest Elaine,

I can only imagine what it must be like for you but let me reassure you that you are NOT CRAZY. Or if you are, then I am as well and so be it! Yes, your scars are beautiful because YOU are beautiful. Whatever they've done to you, however horrible, it hasn't changed who you are.

You have the bluest eyes I've ever seen. When I stare into them I lose myself. I can see strange and wonderful things reflected there. It's like you're from another world. In a way I guess you are.

We've seen too much horror. We're only young. Our whole lives are ahead of us. We should be out dancing in clubs or going to the cinema. It seems like a million years ago that I used to fight dragons on my computer. Now we might as well be fighting REAL dragons for all the control we have over our fate.

We don't belong in this world. And whatever happens, WE WILL BE TOGETHER. I promise you that.

I love you.
P
(Hopefully I can tell you that in person tonight!)

My love, forgive me. I wasn't able to write again until now. They suspect something, I know it. They killed one of us the other day. You probably know about it. His name was David but to them he was just "ZS 279". They told us he had some dangerous infection and they had to isolate him for treatment but we all heard the scream in his mind when they killed him. He was the strongest of us and I'm sure they just wanted to put down a threat. I cried for hours and I reread all your notes to remind me there is hope.

It won't be long now. The others are furious but we all have to pretend we're unaware. We're going to act as though our brains are slowing. (It wouldn't surprise me if they are with all the drugs they give us!)

I've told the others not to hurt you. I said you're safe and they can trust you. I'm not sure if they all believe me but some of them do at least. I won't be able to send you warning but whatever happens, whenever it happens, just know that I love you.

E xx

My dearest Elaine,

I never thought it would be like this. I had such wild romantic fantasies of rescuing you, of taking you away from everything, taking you somewhere we could live in peace together, away from the rest of the whole rotten world.

The night we spent in the ruins of that old house was the happiest night of my whole life. It was cold and rank and the air still reeked of chemical fires from the facility but because you were finally with me none of it mattered. I saw a picture once of a tiny flower sprouting from the rubble of a bombing, one tiny speck of life in a dead landscape. I think that's how we would have looked if anyone could have seen us. I don't believe in God but I believe in you. In US.

I thought we could get away, head into the countryside and find somewhere to hide. I pictured us living it up in some abandoned manor house or even a castle. I still can't believe the other infected took you away from me. I keep replaying that in my head, that one moment over and over. I didn't want to fight. I thought I could reason with them. Why wouldn't they listen? If not to me, then to you? I keep hearing your voice calling my name as they dragged you away. They must have just knocked me out because I woke up later with a splitting headache. I guess I should be grateful that they didn't kill me but taking you away from me is unforgivable. I wish I HAD fought them—even killed them. I honestly thought they would listen to me. How could I be so naïve?

But I refuse to lose hope. I won't give up. We'll think of a plan and I'll get you out of there. At least I know you're safe for now. I wasn't even sure it was you at first when I saw you through the fence. You looked so thin and pale. So haunted. But then you smiled at me and your face was like an angel's.

I could write pages and pages but I'll keep this short in case someone else finds it before you do. I'm staying with a family not far away. They think I'm a shell-shocked freedom fighter. There are two blokes, Chris and Gareth, and Gareth's wife Alice, plus five kids of various ages from assorted broken homes. They collect them like lost pets and the whole group is like something out of an action movie. They're armed to the teeth and barricaded in their farmhouse waiting for an invasion any minute. I guess it's the same for you in there. How ironic that we're both prisoners of our own kind now.

I do have one funny story I can tell you. We were all sitting downstairs by the fire and one of the little girls, Emma, asked if the Queen was a zombie. We all looked at each other, not sure what to say. Alan, who's "eight and a half" said of course not because kings and queens always got their heads chopped off and everyone knows zombies can't live without their heads.

What about princes and princesses, I asked. Emma told me she was pretty sure Snow White was a zombie because she had black hair (!) and Cinderella was too because there's no way she had that many sisters without someone getting bitten. "My sisters bit everyone," she said gleefully. "They had to shoot my teacher in the head after."

From there she launched into an argument with Rosie (one of the other little girls) about which Disney princesses were zombies and which were not. They were both positive that Ariel was safe because there was no such thing as a zombie mermaid. I had to hide my smile and it was all I could do not to tell them they were wrong.

Well, I said I would keep it short but I just can't. You're all I can think about. I'll try to come to the fence every day at the same time—just before dark. I don't think the guards are all that vigilant because I stood there for almost an hour last night and they didn't even notice me. They must just assume the fence will keep us out. (Me! The Enemy!) So until you can get free at least we can communicate like this.

I miss you so much. I feel like I've known you my whole life. My zombie mermaid, I'd brave the coldest and deepest ocean to be with you.

With all my love,
Peter

Dear Peter,

Oh, your letter made me smile! And I really needed it too. It's so grim in here. I can't understand why the others bothered to escape at all if it was just to come here. I swear it was more fun being a guinea pig in the medical torture lab. At least there I had you.

All they talk about is war and death. Revolution, uprising, death, rebirth. New Society, New Religion, New Era, New People, New World. On and on. I'm so sick of their endless preaching and propaganda. I feel like I'm trapped in some psychotic undead cult.

I tried to tell one of the leaders about you when they first brought me to the compound. I said I didn't want to go with them, that I wanted to stay outside and take my chances. But he said they needed all of us to stick together, to stay strong. I told him surely it was my choice whether or not I stayed and that I didn't want to be part of anyone's war. He just smiled and said we were all "disciples" and that's what really creeped me out. His eyes had that look, that glazed, not-quite-there look of a religious fanatic. He didn't use the word *traitor* but I could see it in his eyes. I kind of even heard it in his mind. So I kept quiet after that. I thought I'd be able to sneak out but they watch us all the time. I guess I missed my chance to pretend I'm not right in the head and therefore no use to them. But who knows? They might have just put me down like a lame horse.

Your new "family" sounds deranged in a happier way. I wish they could meet your zombie mermaid.

Love forever,
Elaine

My beautiful Elaine,

Gareth and Alice told me about the so-called "New Religion". And they know about the compound, of course. They call it the Temple of the New

Era. It sounds awful. Gareth has some kind of homemade radio and he uses it to talk to other people all over the country, which is how they found out about it. Apparently something happened in Wales that changed everything. That's when some of the undead started becoming aware. No one's really sure what happened but somehow that chain of events led to some kind of religious madness.

Whatever you do, don't let them know you're not on their side. Close your mind and don't let them in.

I broke down and confided in Alice. I said there was someone in the Temple I had to rescue. She looked at me like I was crazy, but at least she didn't shoot me in the head! She said she understood how I felt but they couldn't afford to take any chances themselves, that it was hard enough defending the farmhouse against attacks.

The other night we saw a group of the dead on the road. There must have been about twenty or so and they were heading for the Temple. You've probably seen them by now. I think they're being summoned. Your captors are sending word somehow and they're all massing there. I don't know why. If you can find out what they're planning maybe I can convince Chris and Gareth that we need to do something before it gets out of control. They're already talking about moving further north. Right now they're on my side but I'm worried that will change if they think I'm too useful to let go. I didn't dare even tell them I was a medical student in case they decided to promote me to field doctor.

Anyway, something's up. Don't drop your guard for a second. Stay strong and know that you're always in my thoughts, even if you should try to keep me out of yours for now.

Always always yours,
P

It's worse than I ever could have imagined. This place is like something from my worst nightmares. You're right: the others *are* being called here. And I think I know now why they won't let me go. The doctors must have been giving us drugs in the facility to dampen our telepathic abilities because now that I'm no longer being dosed every day my mind is like a receiver for all their thoughts. I'm not the only female here against my will. I know you can guess what that means. I don't know how much time I have before they decide to make use of me.

I have to get out of here.

E

Oh my dearest Elaine, I wish I had good news or at least some words of comfort.

Emma is dead. It's the usual story. Bitten. Shot. Buried. Alice is off her head with grief, like she was her own daughter. She glared at me like it was my fault and said something I won't repeat. I don't belong here. I don't want to be here. I can't stand these people much longer.

I told them all about you. I had to. I was desperate. I told them the danger you were in but they said they couldn't help. They mean they WOULDN'T.

I have one idea. It's crazy but so is the whole world and maybe I am too. If I were to get bitten...

I know, I know. I can guess what you'll say. But it would mean no more being on opposite sides. Your side would HAVE to take me in then. We could be together, even if it's in some stupid end-of-days cult compound.

Don't worry. I won't do anything rash. But I wanted to let you know what I was thinking. Your last note really scared me.

Please write soon. I check our spot by the fence every night and my heart sinks when I don't find a note from you and I start to worry that something's happened.

I miss you so much.

I love you,
P

Peter,

I don't have any good news either, I'm afraid. What they did to me at the medical facility was terrible but I never realised they were also keeping me alive. Now that I'm away from there I feel different. When I was in the facility I felt strange all the time but now I feel ill. *Really* ill. My vision is blurry and my skin is starting to itch. It's coming off in flakes and my nails are turning black. I think I know what it means but I daren't write it down in case that makes it true. I hope it isn't what I think.

Whatever you do, *don't* let yourself get bitten! The doctors made me the way I am. The dead don't all become aware. Some do but there are many more that are nothing but walking corpses. I can't even bear to think about you becoming like that. You have to take care of yourself. And whatever's happening to me, time is running out. I see the way they look at me now. They're wondering if they have enough time. They mumble something like prayers and talk about me as if I can't hear them. Or am I just picking up their awful thoughts?

You have to get me out. We have to go back to the facility.

My love, I'm so afraid.

E

My love,

I made a hole in the fence. I got some bolt cutters and I circled the entire compound three times to find a safe place that wouldn't be noticed. I could only cut one wire at a time and I had to wait until the guard moved on again every time before I could cut another link but you should be able to crawl through now. It's a few hundred yards to the right of where we hide our notes. I didn't dare leave any kind of marker. Just follow the line of the fence. There's a white birch tree nearby that glows in the moonlight. Look for that.

I wish I could wait there for you but someone saw me outside last night and I'm afraid they'll be looking for me. I think they can smell me.

Go there as soon it gets dark. Or whenever you can, whenever it's safe. Head straight into the woods. I'll find you there.

I love you.

P

Elaine,

I waited for you all night and when you didn't come I went back to the fence. My note was gone so all I can think is that you couldn't get away last night. It's OK. I'll wait for you again tonight. And the night after if I have to. I'm trying so hard not to fear the worst. Please be OK.

All my love and hope,
Peter

Peter,

I'm so sorry. I didn't want you to worry. The guards were there all night. Probably still looking for you. So I couldn't get near the spot you mentioned. I'm going to try again tonight.

It's getting hard for me to see. Everything is fuzzy. And I hurt. My bones ache so horribly. I don't know how to tell you this so I'll just say it. I think I'm starting to rot.

Whatever happens, know that I love you. You are the only good thing left in the world and if I can't be with you I don't want to be here at all.

Yours forever,
Elaine

Oh Elaine, I hope you get this note. We're almost there. We're so close. I'm going back to the facility tonight to see what I can find. If you can get out, make your way there. Follow the moon and listen for the sound of the sea. You said you could hear it from where you were kept. It's not far.

Love,
P

I don't know if you'll see this or not. So if you do, stay where you are.

I had no choice. I will be with you soon, my love. The facility was destroyed, everything burned, smashed. Only a few things were left intact. Enough to do the job. You said they made you in the lab and that's why you weren't like the others, the ones who were bitten. I hope you're right.

I can feel things now. And voices. I hear them in my head. They want me there. At the Temple. It's strange to walk among them. They look at me now and there's a kind of recognition. I'm one of them.

I'm weak. And I'm so hungry. But I know what I need, what we both need. It's not a drug. It's something else.

They will let me in. I'll find you. And I'll take you somewhere and make you better. Remember Alice and the others? How they wouldn't help me? I still have a key to the farmhouse. Why should they be allowed to choose who lives or dies? We have as much right to live as they do. We can go there and we'll be well again. I promise.

My Elaine. My beloved. Not even two deaths can spoil your beauty. You are still as lovely as the day I first saw you. Others may have made you but only I will ever know you. I am strong for now, strong enough to carry you. I'll take you to the sea. Would you like that, my love? You said you would teach me how to swim. I wonder if I can drown?

I hope someone remembers us. I hope we have more than just the waves for our tombstone. I hope we don't wake up again.

AND MAY ALL YOUR CHRISTMASES…

THE TREES DROOPED, THEIR ARMS HEAVY WITH SNOW, like Christmas shoppers loaded down with parcels. Here and there the occasional tree had shaken off its burden and was hung only with the cold fruit of icicles.

Leigh pulled her dressing gown a little tighter as she peered through the frosted window pane. The landscape was shrouded in white as far as she could see, reflecting the bluish glow of the moon. The children should be pleased. They'd wanted a white Christmas and it looked as if this year was making up for decades of mild winters.

It had been snowing off and on since October but the last two weeks had been extraordinary. The pale sun made its daily pass across the southern horizon, generating enough light to illuminate the snow but not melt it. The only partial thaw they'd had merely served to turn the roads into sheets of ice so treacherous that they'd actually welcomed the next snowfall.

It was beautiful, even magical. But it also worried her. Britain had never seen the like. Not in Leigh's lifetime anyway. This was Cornwall, for heaven's sake, not some arctic wilderness.

As she watched, one of the stooping trees shed a clump of snow. It fell into the snowdrift below it with a heavy WHUMP that sent two quarrelling squirrels scampering away. The bare branch waved slightly as it was liberated from the weight and Leigh peered around at the other trees, wondering if another thaw was coming. The romance of being snowbound had long since worn thin.

Leigh turned away from the window and gasped, startled. The children were standing there.

"Don't *do* that," she pleaded, pressing a hand to her chest. "You frightened the life out of me. Why are you sneaking around in the dark?" She turned on a lamp and immediately saw the worried expressions on their faces.

Tyler frowned and glanced at his little sister, who was clutching his hand. "We couldn't sleep," he said. "The snow was making funny noises."

Leigh had had the same complaint. That was why she was up prowling the house herself at 3 a.m. on Christmas morning. Unfortunately, grown-ups didn't have the luxury of showing fear when children were around. Tyler was only seven, but he was usually able to put on a brave face for Poppy, who was two years younger and worshipped him. Now, however, he looked as nervous as his sister.

"It's just sliding off the roof," Leigh said. "That's why the roof is slanted like that. Otherwise it would just keep piling up."

"Until it buried us?"

Both Leigh and Tyler looked uneasily at Poppy and for a moment Leigh didn't know what to say. Yes, she supposed it *would* bury them if it kept on.

"No, of course not," she said, forcing a smile.

"But it was *talking*," Poppy insisted, her eyes wide and haunted. "It whispered to me all night."

Tyler was watching his mother closely for cues and she had to suppress a shudder at her daughter's words.

"Don't be silly," Leigh said, wishing that Tyler would help her out. He was usually quick to ridicule his little sister's fears but today he seemed to be sharing them, reinforcing them. And Leigh's.

The best thing to do was ignore it. Change the subject and get them onto another train of thought.

"Anyway, hey, it's a white Christmas," she said, trying to sound excited. "Just like you both wanted, right?"

But the children didn't look happy. The first snowfall had made them ecstatic and they'd played in it for hours. Leigh and Simon had enjoyed it too at first, helping to build snowmen and joining in with snowball fights. But the novelty had gone for them and it looked like the kids were getting sick of it too.

"I guess," Tyler mumbled.

Glum children on Christmas morning, Leigh thought. *All is definitely not right with the world.* They didn't even seem interested in checking to see if Father Christmas had been yet.

"I was just going back to bed," she said, affecting an elaborate yawn. "Come on, you two. Get some more sleep and when you wake up we'll have a proper Christmas. OK?"

But they looked unconvinced as they shuffled up the stairs and into their separate rooms. Leigh noticed that both night lights were on as she crept down the hall to rejoin Simon. As she pressed against his sleeping warmth she thought she heard something crawling on the roof. Telling herself it was only the snow didn't reassure her at all.

"Merry Christmas!" Simon cried in a booming voice. It carried up the stairs, along with the chorused response of the children. It had taken Leigh ages to fall back asleep and she must have been dead to the world if she hadn't noticed Simon getting up. Not that her sleep had been at all restful. Once she finally drifted off she'd dreamt about an avalanche.

The snow had crashed down from the peak of a vast mountain that didn't exist anywhere in Britain, smothering their tiny cottage. In the dream she'd been able to see the disaster from outside as well as in. The camera of her mind's eye panned back impossibly far, far enough to see that their tiny antlike forms would never be able to tunnel out through the miles of snow and ice that blanketed the house, the country, the world. She'd woken with a start to find herself alone in bed.

She shoved her feet into slippers and pushed her arms through the sleeves of her flannel dressing gown. It felt as though she'd only done that minutes ago but a glance at the clock told her that she must have been asleep for hours. The day was well under way. And so was the snow.

"Great," she muttered as she pulled the curtain aside. There was no sky to be seen, just the endless whiteout. The snow swirled like ocean currents, like the avalanche in her dream that had drowned the world. Was that what death in the snow would be—drowning? Or would it suffocate you? Would it feel like being slowly crushed by an icy fist?

She twitched the curtains closed and shook her head. Where were all these bleak thoughts coming from? Bloody hell, it was Christmas morning. She had to put on a happy face for the kids' sakes at least. She splashed her face with cold water and tried a smile in the mirror. It looked forced but it was the best she could do.

"Merry Christmas, Mummy!" came the cheer from Tyler and Poppy as she appeared in the living room.

She'd barely got out a reply when they rushed her and threw their arms around her, chattering excitedly about what Father Christmas had left in their stockings and could they please open their presents now and how could she sleep so much when it was their first-ever white Christmas and could they all play in the snow after?

Their exuberance made her smile in spite of her weariness. Clearly they'd forgotten all their concerns from last night and so should she.

"Yes, yes, yes," she managed, turning a genuine smile on both them and her husband, who was wearing a Santa hat and holding out a mug of cinnamon-scented coffee.

"Good morning, Sleeping Beauty," he said, kissing her.

The kids released her and scurried back to the tree, where they began distributing the presents around the room and arguing about who got to unwrap the first box.

"Sorry," she said, snuggling into her husband's arms. "I had a bit of a weird night after we—after Father Christmas came. I couldn't sleep so I came back downstairs. The kids were up too, worried about the snow."

"It's quite something, isn't it? I tried to wake you when I got up but you weren't having any of it so I just let you sleep."

She shuddered at the memory of the dream. "Yeah, and I'm glad that's over." At his frown she said simply, "Bad dream."

He gave her a knowing smile. "Cabin fever. As delightful as the company is, I'd rather it was just you and me once in a while." Then he turned away to take the box Poppy was waving around in a desperate bid for his attention. "OK, OK, we're coming."

Leigh suffered the furry antlers Tyler placed on her head as the yearly ritual began. Paper was ripped off with violent disregard for the care that had gone into wrapping the gifts, bows were flung aside and boxes torn open to reveal their contents. Squeals of delight followed as dolls and model cars were exclaimed over and then they too were cast aside in favour of the next surprise.

But in spite of the raucous fun, Leigh still felt the pull of the snow. Her eyes flicked again and again to the window. The parted curtains displayed the wilderness of white and she had the sudden odd thought that maybe they shouldn't gorge themselves on Christmas dinner, that maybe they ought to ration the food.

The blizzard was winding down but the amount of snow it had dumped on them was alarming. It had drifted against the house, rising past the edge of the bay window. Out beyond it she could see that the car was half-buried. If they needed to go anywhere it would have to be on foot, although they would sink in up to their hips. Well, Leigh and Simon would; the kids would disappear completely. The thought made her shudder and Poppy sensed her disquiet at once.

"What's wrong, Mummy?" she asked, her piping voice silencing the room.

"Oh, I'm just a bit chilly," she said, trying to sound offhanded. "I think I'll go put something warm on."

Poppy wasn't sensitive enough to see through the lie and Leigh's mention of the cold was met with the gleeful suggestion that they all go play in the snow.

"Don't you want to stay inside where it's warm and play with your new toys?" she asked.

But Christmas morning had worked its magic. Tyler wanted to set up his racetrack outside where the cars could crash into snowbanks and Poppy wanted to see her model horses prancing through the snow.

"Right," Simon said cheerily. "Let's all bundle up, then."

He seemed oblivious to Leigh's strange mood, unless he'd just chalked it up to her sleepless night. In any case, if he wasn't worried, why should she be? She was just being overprotective. The children had spooked her last night, that was all. But monsters under the bed always vanished in the daylight. Why was hers still hanging around?

"Stop being silly," she told herself, then began the laborious process of layering herself and the kids for the cold. Thermal undies, jumpers, fleeces, plastic bags over woolly socks, scarves, hats, gloves, boots. They looked like a family of astronauts when they were done.

When they opened the front door they were confronted by a waist-high wall of snow. The kids went nuts, immediately throwing themselves at it like moles tunnelling their way through a barrier of earth. Leigh's stomach gave a little flutter and she stepped back while Simon and the kids dug their way out of the house and sprinkled the resulting path with salt.

Snow flurried into the porch, settling at her feet. Although it was warm in the house, the snow didn't seem to be melting. It coated the floor like a dusting of flour. Leigh kicked at a little clump and it came apart in a burst of dry powder. When she trod on it there was a harsh gritty sound beneath her boot.

"Off we go!" Simon said, his delight almost equal to the children's. It made Leigh smile to see him having so much fun.

"I hope someone took a head count," Leigh said, indicating the boxes of cars and horses now being dumped into the winter wonderland.

"I have exactly seven new horses," Poppy said earnestly, arranging them all in a circle.

Leigh smiled at the girl's solemnity. It wasn't Poppy she was worried about; Tyler was the one who had a habit of leaving his toys everywhere. And losing them.

"Don't worry," Simon told her. "I'll make sure none of the tiny drivers get snowbound. Although I can't say the same for us."

"I know. It's amazing. You'd think we were in the Alps."

"Guess that's global warming," Simon said with a shrug. He flattened one of the cardboard boxes he'd brought with him and spread it on the snow for Poppy to sit on. She obliged him at first, then appropriated the box to use as a platform for the horses.

Meanwhile, Tyler had apparently decided that the snow was more fun than the racetrack. He dived into it with cries of "Incoming!" and "Bombs away!", sending up white clouds wherever he hit.

Leigh didn't like the way he disappeared entirely each time he plunged into the sea of white as though it were a swimming pool but she resisted her instinct to tell him to stop. If she wasn't careful she was going to turn into her own mother, pathologically overprotective and smothering.

"Do you hear that?" Simon asked.

Leigh cocked her head to listen. All she could hear was Poppy's low murmuring as the horses enacted some private drama for her. That and Tyler's warrior whoops and battle cries as he dive-bombed the snow. "Hear what?"

"The silence."

She listened again. Yes, except for the children, it was dead quiet. There wasn't a breath of wind. The cottages on either side were dark, even though it was almost noon. And the ones across the street looked the same. There were no other kids playing in the snow, nor indeed any sounds at all. No voices, music or traffic. No animals. The whole village was silent, still.

In spite of her heavy coat, Leigh shivered. "That *is* weird," she said.

"Yeah. And look at the snow. It's immaculate."

The smooth expanse of white stretched as far as they could see in all directions, through and around the trees and houses, carpeting the village green. It was pristine, unsullied by footprints or tracks of any kind. There was no evidence even that birds had hopped through it. There was no sign of life anywhere.

Leigh took a couple of uncertain steps, sinking deep into the snow as she peered around her at the eerie frozen world, straining to hear any sound. Nothing. Only the crunch of snow beneath her boots.

The spreading chestnut tree that dominated the village green had doubled its size with the accumulation of snow. It loomed above the ground like a giant white spider about to pounce. Where the road should be were only the lumps of buried vehicles—lost and inaccessible.

When she reached the trees that bordered the front garden she peered down to her left, along where she knew the road lay buried. The Masons, their elderly next-door neighbours, ought to be awake. Smoke ought to be curling from their chimney and the sound of the TV issuing from their front room. They were both nearly deaf so the volume was always up high. But today there wasn't a sound to be heard.

She pushed back her sleeve to look at her watch. It was past noon. Surely people would be up now, having Christmas dinner. Surely at least a few brave souls would have ventured out on foot to visit neighbours. Surely children and dogs would be out playing in the snow. But even if all the people were tucked up warmly inside their houses, shouldn't there at least be birds singing?

It wasn't just quiet; it was *wrong*.

"Let's go back inside," she said.

No sooner had she got the words out then there came a heavy thump from somewhere behind her, as though piles of linen had fallen from a high shelf. She whirled round to see that a huge clump of snow had slid off the roof. The realisation that it had fallen just in front of the door sent a chill down her spine.

"Poppy, Tyler, let's—"

The words died in her throat. It took her several moments to make sense of what she was seeing. The children were frozen, as still and silent as the snow. Their body heat must have melted the snow they were sitting in because all she could see were their heads peering up out of the white. They were staring at her.

"Oh my God," she gasped. "Simon! Help me get—"

But Simon was exactly the same, buried up to his neck in the snow, his eyes gazing vacantly, *coldly* at her.

Her stomach clenched and she swallowed the panic that threatened to consume her as she pushed her way through the snow to the children. Her voice echoed hollowly in the stillness as she called their names with increasing desperation, but if they heard her, they gave no sign.

She had covered half the distance to them when she realised that her footprints were gone. The route she had taken to the edge of the trees had disappeared completely. But it hadn't snowed again since they'd been outside, nor was there any wind. The snow had shifted, silently and stealthily, while she wasn't looking.

Leigh stifled a cry and doubled her efforts as she fought her way back through the snow towards the children. It was strenuous work, more like trudging through mud than snow. It was wrong, all of it. In the porch the snow had felt gritty underfoot, like sand. Now it seemed to cling to her boots with each step. A quick glance behind her showed that it had erased her most recent footprints. Panic began to flutter inside her like a trapped bird.

Icy tears stung her face and when she turned to call Simon's name again she couldn't see him at all. There was only a smooth layer of snow where he had stood, as though he had been erased like her footprints. She screamed and the silence sent her voice rebounding all through the sleeping village.

At last she reached the children. She clutched at their coats only to recoil at the sensation. The material was frozen solid. She stripped off her gloves and reached out to touch Poppy's face and she screamed again when the burning cold singed her fingers. The skin was too cold to touch. Already her fingertips were turning a sickly greenish grey.

"Oh my God," Leigh whispered again and again. Her heart pounded as she stared in horror at her fingers. They were nearly black now. She quickly drew her gloves back on and yanked and pulled at Tyler's coat, but it was like trying to grab hold of a marble statue. She couldn't gain any purchase.

She cast a terrified glance back out to where Simon had been standing and realised with a sinking feeling that she couldn't remember exactly where she'd last seen him. The snow had swallowed him as effectively as a lake might have done, closing over his head and sealing him beneath without a trace.

Sobs racked her and for some time she continued trying to pull the children out of the snow, screaming for help all the while. She didn't dare leave them for a moment to look for ropes or a shovel. But it was no use. They were frozen solid and there was nothing she could do. The fingers she had burned were going numb and her gloved hands slipped ineffectually over the rocklike forms of the children. And as the awful reality at last began to sink in she looked up, her eyes burning with frozen tears.

Was it her imagination or were the trees leaning closer? Last night they had looked like overloaded Christmas shoppers but this morning their lumpen shapes appeared more menacing.

"Stop it," she hissed, trying to push away the frightening thoughts gathering in her mind. It was only the weight of the snow forcing the trees to bend, that was all. And it was only her fear that made her think they were bending down to touch her. But even as she tried to rationalise it, she knew there was no logical explanation for what had happened to the children. And Simon.

When the nearest branch shed its burden Leigh dodged away before it could fall on her. Immediately another tree seemed to shift and a heavy mass of snow struck her in the back, almost knocking her down. She had no choice but to run for the house.

As she forced her way through the gritty drifts of snow she thought she heard a voice behind her. The silky, insinuating whisper she'd heard the night before. The voice of the snow.

She clawed her way into the house and pushed the door closed behind her. Her fingers flew to the locks but then she hesitated. What if Simon and the children got free? She couldn't lock them out. In an agony of indecision she stood immobile before the door, listening to the scratching of the snow pressing against it.

Finally, trembling, she left it unlocked and made herself move away. As she did she trod on the patches of snow that had blown in when they'd first gone outside. Unmelted, it hissed beneath her feet.

"Police," she said at last, urging herself into action. She raced to the phone only to find it dead. The handset fell to the floor with a clatter and she took several deep breaths to calm herself. "Snow plough. Helicopter. Someone will come." But the desperation in her voice didn't reassure her at all.

Outside the snow slithered against the house. It had drifted halfway up the bay window now. Leigh pressed her face up against the glass and scoured the icy white dunes outside but she could no longer see the children. The snow had swallowed them up, just like Simon. She choked back a sob. Tears blurred her vision and the reflection of the twinkling fairy lights on the Christmas tree dissolved into a garish smear of colour.

A burst of laughter behind her made her jump and she spun round to see that the TV was on. With a wave of relief she snatched up the remote and left the sitcom behind, searching for news. She expected to see the disaster on every channel but it took her some time before she hit on a smiling woman presenting the weather. Behind her on the map of Britain was a cheerful scattering of suns.

"And as you can see, it's a beautiful morning all across the country, with temperatures in the mid-teens. So if you were dreaming of a white Christmas, I'm sorry but you'll just have to wait until next year."

No snow. Anywhere in Britain. It wasn't even below freezing.

Leigh scrolled through all the other channels, through Christmas specials, advertisements, cartoons, *It's a Wonderful Life*. But there was no breaking news on any channel, nor any emergency broadcast. There was no evidence at all that anything unusual had happened.

After cycling through what seemed like hundreds of channels she finally caught the end of another weather report with the same balmy forecast. She turned away at the words "unseasonably warm".

Her skin crawled as she slowly looked back at the window. The snow was no longer moving secretly. It had climbed to the top of the bay window, where it now blocked her view entirely. And then the house began to groan. A picture fell from one wall and she heard the floorboards creaking under the strain as the snow pressed against the sides of the house. In another room a window broke.

The sound of breaking glass spurred her into action and she backed away from the bay window. A whisper made her turn around and she saw that the fire in the hearth had gone out. Snow was falling gently down the chimney, smothering the embers they had left burning.

She ran to the kitchen and tried to switch on the burners. Each ring clicked and sparked but the gas refused to ignite. A small dusting of powder drifted down from the extractor fan and Leigh jumped away before it could touch her.

Somewhere in the house another window broke and then, with a flicker, the lights went out. Leigh gave a cry and raced for the stairs. The snow hadn't reached the upper floor yet and she looked out the bedroom window in horror. Where before she had been able to make out the shape of the trees, now there were only vague lumps in the snow. The spreading chestnut was almost entirely submerged.

But the sky was clear. No new snow was falling. What blanketed the village was the snow that was already on the ground. It shifted like the sand dunes of a desert, each vast drift moving like a living thing, burying everything in its path. And as she watched, the snow inched its way up along the window. Soon it would block her view as it had downstairs.

"What do you want?" she heard herself ask.

Her only answer was the whisper of the snow as it continued to engulf the house.

The room grew steadily darker and Leigh knew she didn't have much time. If she didn't move she would be trapped, smothered inside the house. Buried as effectively as by an avalanche. Buried just like in her dream.

There was only one place to go: up.

She hurried into the hall and yanked the rope in the ceiling to release the attic stairs. Light streamed in from above and she gasped as she saw the invasion of snow. Huge patches of the roof were gone, open to the sky. The weight of the snow had crushed the slates, spilling in to cover the floor.

She didn't want to step in the snow but she had no choice. And as her boots made contact with it she was sure she felt it move beneath her. It crunched unpleasantly, reminding her of the plague of snails they'd had one summer. She could still remember the sharp crunch of their shells and then the awful squelch of their soft, slimy bodies. The snow wasn't slimy but it felt every bit as alive as the trodden snails had.

Leigh wasted no time. She ignored the writhing snow and scrambled towards the ladder leaning against the far wall. Placing it beneath the largest of the holes in the roof, she mounted and climbed it as quickly as she dared, trying not to imagine the sight that would greet her when she reached the top.

It was worse than she had feared. Where once there had been a sleepy little English village, now there was only an expanse of white. As barren as any desert, the field of snow stretched as far as she could see in every direction.

She clambered out onto the roof, staring in horror as the snow crawled over the remaining roof tiles, spilling down into the attic with a sound that could be laughter. It drifted against her boots, almost teasingly, and the sensation made her feel ill. Simon and the children were gone, sunk beneath the endless white plain. Her eyes burned again with tears and she forced the thought of them from her mind, determined to survive.

Perhaps if she slid down the slope she could at least escape the house. If only she'd thought to grab the children's sled! But thinking of the sled brought to mind her last image of Poppy and Tyler being pulled through the snow by their father and for a moment the grief threatened to cripple her.

"Go," she hissed through her tears. "Go now!"

Taking a deep breath she planted one foot firmly in the snow. Up here it was only ankle-deep but down below... She shook the thought away and planted her other foot, forcing herself to march across the roof. She heard tiles shattering with her progress and she increased her speed. The roof was collapsing beneath her. If she didn't get away fast she would fall through into the house. Into the snow.

A sudden sharp pain pierced her calf and for a moment she thought she'd been seized by a cramp. But it was a different kind of pain. The same kind of pain she'd felt when she'd touched Poppy's frozen face. Glancing down at her legs she saw that she was sunk to her knees in the snow. It was pulling her down, seeping inside her jeans, eating through her boots.

With the realisation came another spike of pain in her other leg and she crumpled to her knees, immersing herself. There was nothing solid to brace against, nothing she could gain purchase on to steady herself. The pain was spreading, coiling steadily around each leg. She remembered the sensation from earlier. Once the pain took root the numbness would set in.

In a panic she tore off her glove and she screamed when she saw what remained of her right hand. The fingers had blackened like something burnt in a fire. There were places where the bones had crumbled away and the sickening green-grey colour was edging along her wrist. How long before it ate away her entire arm?

She hadn't heard any cries of pain from either Simon or the children. Perhaps they had been spared this special horror. Perhaps they had gone willingly, submitted to the seductive embrace of the snow without a struggle. Perhaps everyone in the village had.

The burning in her legs had spread to her hips. The creeping cold devoured her spine, inch by inch, and she knew she would not be getting up again.

She looked out over the sea of white, her eyes blurring with tears. She never could have made it across the snow. And why did she even want to? What was left for her without her family? Her tears turned to ice. There was nothing to do now but wait as the snow drifted softly around her. Leigh no longer felt any pain or fear. There was only the whisper of the snow, shushing her.

Two Five Seven

"Two…Five…Seven…"

Do you hear that? Listen.

"Nine…One…Six…"

That's the girl who lives inside the radio. And that's all she says. Just numbers. Sometimes she sings too.

"I once had a sweet little doll, the prettiest doll ever known…"

The radio belongs to my grandpa. He calls it "the wireless", which doesn't make sense because it has a long cord that plugs into the wall. Even though he has a TV he still likes to listen to the radio at night. It's a huge wooden one like they have in old movies and it takes up a whole corner of the living room. It's shiny red-brown and it reminds me of a big beetle. The dials look like spinning eyes, which is kind of creepy, and you turn them to find stations to listen to. You can even hear stations from countries on the other side of the world.

When I first heard the girl I thought Grandpa had left the radio on. We're spending the summer with him in his cottage by the lake—my parents and me. The lake is beautiful, with trees all around and lots of animals. Sometimes deer come out of the woods to nibble the treats I leave for them. One time a deer even went out a little way onto the dock and my dad took a picture of it standing there, looking down at Grandpa's little boat like it was going to go for a ride.

The cottage is nice but it's really small for a house. I don't have a bedroom but that's OK because I get to sleep on the couch in the living room which is kind of like a sleepover, only by myself. The very first time I slept here I thought it was scary but now I love it.

Everything looks different at night, in the dark. The furniture comes alive, stretching long spiky shadows out across the floor like the clawing hands of monsters. Sometimes I think I see them move. When I get scared I hide in the castle, which is a piano in the daytime, or I crawl inside my secret cave, which is really just a couch. I put a blanket over the top and tuck it into the cushions to make a tunnel and I like to sleep all the way inside at one end, like I'm deep inside a rabbit hole. Sometimes Goldie comes in with me. She's Grandpa's golden retriever. She's the other reason it's not scary down here. She'd never let any monsters get me.

One night I heard a voice. I knew it wasn't my mom or dad and it definitely wasn't Grandpa. It scared me because I thought there was someone in the house, someone who shouldn't be there. I froze like ice, listening as hard as I could, so hard my ears hurt.

Then the voice came again. It sounded really far away and all it said was a number. Then another one. There were some scratchy high sounds too and I realised the voice was coming from the radio. But it wasn't music or the news. It was the voice of a little girl like me.

I crawled to the end of the tunnel and peeked out. It was quiet and Goldie was fast asleep by the window. She'd definitely have barked if someone was in the house. I stared at the radio for a long time but the girl didn't say anything else. After a while I got tired of listening to nothing and I fell asleep. I forgot all about her until she woke me up the next night. That time she said her name. Annie. She sang her sad little song and then it was more numbers.

"Hello?" I tiptoed over to the radio. In the moonlight it looked like a big shiny face staring down at me.

From the window Goldie looked up, probably wondering who I was talking to.

"I can hear you, Annie," I told her. "Can you hear me?"

"Two...Five...Seven..."

"What does that mean?" I asked. It wasn't our address or phone number or any other number that I recognised.

"Cold . . ."

It sounded like she was crying. My heart was beating really hard and I started to get worried.

"Where are you?" I asked. "Are you in the radio?"

She sang a little more of her song. "But I lost my poor little doll, and then I was all alone . . ."

I was starting to think she couldn't hear me at all and that made me want to cry too. I could picture her, a tiny little girl trapped inside that big scary box, trying to get out.

I reached up to turn one of the dials. There was a squeal and then static and then Annie was silent. I turned the dial the other way and found her again, but only for a few seconds. The needle was pointing between lists of places like Japan and Paris and Budapest. I wondered if the numbers on the dial were the ones she was talking about.

"Annie? Are you there?"

But she wasn't. And I didn't hear her again that night.

The next morning I wondered if I should tell my parents what I'd heard. I didn't really want to because they would just say it was my imagination. They were always saying that. But I did ask Grandpa if he ever heard voices coming from the radio.

"Of course. That's what radios do, Heather."

"No, I mean—what if you heard someone who was *inside* the radio?"

He gave me a funny look. Then he turned and stared over at the radio. "What are you hearing in there?" he asked after a while, frowning. Like he thought I was crazy.

I didn't know if Annie would want me to tell anyone about her. After all, she had only talked to *me*. I felt like she was my secret friend so I thought really hard about what to say. "Oh, just some numbers."

Grandpa smiled at that. "Ah. You've found a numbers station!"

"What's a numbers station?"

"Well, it's a mystery. Lots of people listen to them but no one really knows what they are. Voices reciting strings of numbers, sometimes words, sometimes in other languages. It all sounds like nonsense but some people claim they're coded messages for spies. Top secret stuff. And of course other people think all kinds of crazy things, like they're alien transmissions. Messages from outer space."

I looked at the radio, confused. I wanted to ask why a spy or an alien would sound like a little girl but I felt protective of Annie. If she really was hiding in there I didn't want to give her away.

"What about songs?" I asked carefully.

"Yes, some of them also play a song or a bit of music in between strings of numbers. It's how the spies know where the message begins."

I thought about that word. *Message.* What was Annie trying to tell me?

I could see Grandpa was waiting for me to say something so I made myself smile. "It's probably aliens," I said. "I'll tell them not to land on the dock if they invade."

"Good girl," he said. He ruffled my hair and told me to run along and play. I did but I had the weirdest feeling that he was bothered by what I'd said about the voice. Something inside me said he'd heard it too.

That night Annie came again. Grandpa had put the idea of spies in my head so this time I was ready and I wrote the numbers down as she said them. It was a long list and she repeated it three times. In between she sang and after a while her voice sounded closer. Louder. As if she was getting stronger. I sat cross-legged on the floor, looking up at the radio while she started all over again.

"Two . . . Five . . . Seven . . . "

I looked down at what I had written: 2579162013. "2013" was in there, like a clue hidden in a word search puzzle. Two years ago. So it was a date. There were six numbers before it and that was too long to be a month and a day. I squinted at the page, trying to see whatever I was missing.

"What does it mean, Annie? Is it a code?"

She was humming, about to start over with the numbers. Then she was quiet for a few seconds. I thought she'd gone away but then she whispered another word. It sounded like it took a lot of effort.

"Nighttime."

That didn't mean anything to me. I knew one code where you changed all the letters into numbers and so I wrote out the alphabet and did that. But it didn't even make a word. At least not one I knew. I felt so stupid, like the answer was right there in front of me and I just couldn't see it. My head was starting to hurt and I must have made a noise because Goldie came over and licked me as if to say it was OK, she didn't mind if I was stupid. Dogs are great that way.

I curled up with her inside my tunnel and as I drifted off to sleep I heard Annie start the numbers again.

Nighttime, I thought. *Two-five-seven.*

I woke up to the sound of raised voices in the kitchen. Grandpa was shouting about his watch.

"I've had the bloody thing for twenty years," he said, giving the table an angry thump. "It's never just stopped before."

"Did you forget to wind it?" my dad asked, sounding like he already knew the answer.

"I never forget to wind it," Grandpa snapped. He got annoyed when he thought anyone was saying he was too old to remember things. "Look, I'm winding it now. Nothing!"

"Maybe it's just a sign that it's time to get a new watch?" my dad offered.

But Grandpa didn't want to hear it. "There's nothing wrong with *this* watch." He said it in a tone that meant there was no more discussion. I couldn't understand what the big deal was but I didn't want them to fight. I got up and crept into the kitchen. I knew once they saw me they'd lower their voices.

"Sorry, sweetie," said my dad. "Did we wake you up?"

"Uh-huh." The watch was lying on the table and for a moment I imagined picking it up and wishing really hard and making it work again. I could almost hear the ticking in my head. "I'm sorry it's broken," I said. "I wish I could fix it."

I looked down at the face of the watch and my breath caught in my throat when I saw the time it had stopped at. 2.57. Two-five-seven. My heart gave a leap inside my chest. Annie had sent me a message! It was all I could do not to run back into the living room for the paper I'd written her numbers on.

"No worries, kiddo," said my dad. "It's not your fault."

Grandpa didn't say anything. He was glaring out the window as if something out there had broken his watch. My dad turned back to him and said they could go into town to get it fixed once my mom was awake. And while they were talking I slipped away.

I grabbed my paper and looked at the numbers again. 257 was the time. Night time. 2.57 in the morning. 2013 was the year, which left 916. My heart was pounding. Since there was no 91st or 16th month, the date could only be September the 16th. I wasn't stupid after all! So what had happened on that day?

It was summer and wonderfully warm but I suddenly felt a chill go up my back, as though a spider had dropped inside my shirt and was creeping towards my neck. I knew what was important about the date. I turned slowly to look at the radio, its dials seeming more than ever like watchful eyes.

"That's when you . . . died," I whispered. "Isn't it?"

She didn't answer but a burst of static came from the speaker. It sounded like someone sniffing back tears.

I felt helpless. Why had she talked to *me*? What did she want me to do? What *could* I do?

I knew you could look at old newspapers in the library and find stuff out that way because I'd seen people do it in movies. But maybe I could also find it on the Internet. I wasn't supposed to go online by myself but since no one was watching I tiptoed into the little office and typed the date and the name "Annie" into Grandpa's computer. I found what I was looking for right away. A local headline.

Annabel Stevens. Missing since 16th September 2013.

My heart sank. Missing. No one knew she was dead. No one but me. I remembered the time my cat Frodo ran away and I put signs all over the neighbourhood. I went to every house asking if anyone had seen him. But after two weeks my parents said he wasn't coming back. They tried to tell me someone might have adopted him, not knowing he already had a home. But I knew they just didn't want me to know he was dead. We lived near a busy road and Frodo was always out wandering. I pretended to believe them, though. I wanted to think he was still alive somewhere.

Did Annie's parents think the same thing? That someone had taken her away to live with them?

But I lost my poor little doll...

I felt cold all over. I turned the computer off and went back out into the living room. The radio seemed to be watching me.

That night her voice was a little louder. I felt like I'd made her stronger by finding out who she was and what the numbers meant.

She was singing. "I found my poor little doll..." A burst of static came and then she finished the line. "As I swam in the lake one day."

"Did you lose your doll in the lake?" I asked. "Maybe I could find it for you."

There was some more noise from the radio and at first I thought she'd gone away.

"Annie? Are you still there?"

"But now she is horribly changed..."

Something fluttered in the pit of my stomach. I was sad for Annie but also afraid. I had a weird feeling that the song was more than just a song.

She sounded like she was crying as she sang the last lines. "Her beauty is all washed away."

I felt cold as I listened. Her voice sounded so close, like she was right in the room with me. And just like that—I wondered if she was. The radio was very big. Easily big enough for a little girl to hide inside. What if she wasn't dead at all but just hiding? What if she'd got trapped inside and couldn't get out?

Even as I thought it I knew it couldn't be true. "Wishful thinking," my mom would have said. There was no way she could live inside the radio for that long. But I had to make sure. I crawled behind the radio and knocked softly on the back panel.

"Annie? Are you in there?" I felt a little silly but there was no one there to see me but Goldie.

She didn't answer but I thought I could hear something through the fuzzy static. I knew what I had to do. There was a toolbox under the kitchen sink and I found the screwdriver with the flat head. Four screws held the panel on and I carefully undid each one. My heart was pounding. I didn't know what to expect. I slid the panel off and I almost dropped it in surprise.

There was something in there. I was afraid to reach inside until I realised what it was. The radio made a soft humming sound as I took the doll out and looked at it. I never really liked dolls. I liked dinosaurs better. But I could see that this one was very pretty, like Annie had said in her song. Her face was painted china and she was smiling, with red lips and bright blue eyes. She was a little dusty but that was all. Her long blue dress wasn't torn and her face wasn't chipped or cracked at all. I was confused. What did Annie mean about her being horribly changed?

Very carefully I replaced the panel and put the screwdriver away. I was very careful and very quiet so no one would be able to tell what I'd done.

"I found her, Annie," I said to the radio. "She's safe."

But I could tell that Annie wasn't happy. The radio continued to buzz and then Annie started whispering the numbers and the words to her song. Her voice was different now. It scared me. She sounded desperate and afraid. I looked at the doll, not understanding. Was she talking about a different doll?

Tears came to my eyes and I backed away, feeling helpless. "But I found her," was all I could think of to say.

After a while Annie's voice faded out and the radio was silent. Whatever it was, I had failed. I wrapped my arms around the doll and cried myself to sleep. I was still curled up inside my tunnel when my mom came to wake me up.

"Where did this come from?" she asked, sounding surprised.

For a moment I didn't know what she was talking about. My eyes were puffy from crying and I scrubbed at them with my fingers. Then I remembered the doll. I couldn't tell anyone my secret so I said the first thing that came into my mind.

"Goldie found her," I said.

"Really? I'm surprised she didn't damage it."

"She's really gentle."

My mom turned the doll over in her hands, admiring the dress. "I thought you didn't like dolls," she said.

"I don't really. But it was a present from Goldie." I was surprised at how easily the lies came.

By then Grandpa and my dad had come in. My mom held the doll up to show them. "Look what Goldie turned up," she said. "Isn't she beautiful?"

"Oh yes, very pretty," my dad said. But Grandpa's eyes went wide.

"Where did you get that?" he demanded.

My mom rolled her eyes. "Don't freak out, Dad," she said. "The dog brought it in. Good thing it was a toy and not a dead bird."

But Grandpa looked horrified. He stared at the doll, refusing to go near it. He looked like he was trying to think of something to say. "You can't keep it," he said at last. "It probably belongs to someone."

"She does look expensive," my mom said.

My dad nodded. "I suppose we could put a note up in town, maybe with a picture. See if anyone claims it?"

Grandpa didn't seem to like that idea either. "No, no," he snapped. "I'm sure it's not worth the trouble." He looked really uncomfortable with the whole situation. But he only glared at the doll and then stomped off into his office.

"Oh dear," my mom said. "He's just having one of his funny turns. Don't pay him any mind, Heather. You keep the doll if you want her."

I didn't want her, not really. But I didn't know what else to do. I couldn't understand why Grandpa had looked so scared. Almost like he'd recognised the doll. Something in me went cold. I heard Annie whispering in my head.

And her beauty is all washed away . . .

It's almost midnight. Annie's here but I can barely hear her. She sounds very far away. Maybe she's mad at me because I didn't do things right.

"I'm sorry," I tell her. "I really tried."

"Who are you talking to?"

The voice makes me jump and I spin around, dropping the doll. It's only Grandpa. He's standing in the doorway. I have the feeling he's been watching me for a while.

"No one," I say. "Just the radio. The numbers station you told me about."

He looks at the radio and his eyes narrow. It's the way you might look at a dangerous animal.

"And what numbers are you listening to?"

His voice sounds funny, very low and serious.

I'm afraid without knowing why. I shrug. "Just numbers."

He nods. "Numbers like the ones you looked up on my computer? Names too, by any chance?"

My skin suddenly feels ice-cold. I don't know what to say.

Grandpa sighs and looks down at the doll. He picks her up and smooths down her dress, strokes her hair. "She was so pretty," he says, his voice sad. His eyes shine with tears.

"Who was?" I manage to ask.

He looks up and smiles. It's a cold and ugly smile. "Why, your little friend Annie." He takes a step towards me and without thinking I move back.

"I once had a sweet little doll, the prettiest doll ever known." His voice sounds all wrong. Static comes from the radio and without warning he smashes the doll against it. Her china head shatters against the cabinet and I cry out.

"I want my parents," I whisper.

"They're asleep," he says. "Like you should have been. Instead of listening to crazy voices and poking your nose in where it doesn't belong."

I try to call out but my throat feels like it's full of dust. Nothing comes out but a squeak. I suddenly wonder where Goldie is.

Grandpa laughs, a low, unpleasant sound. "Even if you scream, they won't hear you. I made sure of that."

I start to cry and his face softens a little. "Oh, don't cry, sweetie," he says. "I want to show you something. Have you ever seen the water-babies in the lake?"

I shake my head, terrified. I want to run but there's nowhere to go.

"I showed them to Annie one night. She used to come skipping through the woods, not a care in the world. She was my own sweet little doll."

From the radio comes Annie's voice, very sad. "But now she is horribly changed."

Tears stream down my face and through the blur I see Grandpa smile. "That's right, Annie. Your beauty is all washed away."

I struggle as he takes my hand but he's so much bigger and stronger than me. I can hear Goldie now, barking from behind the closed door of the kitchen. She knows something is wrong. Very wrong.

"Come on, now," he says. "Don't you want to see the water-babies? I'm sure Annie will introduce you to them."

Goldie scrabbles frantically at the door but I know she can't break it down. I also know that I can't get away. And as Grandpa takes me to the lake I can't help but wonder how many other little girls have disappeared over the years. And if we'll ever be found.

It's quiet now. Quiet and cold. I can sense Annie somewhere near. I wonder if anyone will hear me through the radio? If lots of people are listening to numbers stations they might hear me. They might find out who I am and where I got lost.

It's very hard to talk but I say what I can.

"Eleven . . . Four . . . Six . . . Two . . . Ten . . . Two . . . Zero . . . One . . . Five . . ."

Sweeter than to Wake

WHAT DO THE DEAD DREAM? DO THEY DREAM OF life? Of the living? Do they dream of *us*?

Liam had always loved to watch Colleen as she slept. He loved the protective feeling it stirred in him, the sense that he was watching over her while she was at her most vulnerable. Her eyelids would flicker with whatever strange adventures she was having, sometimes good, sometimes bad. He himself never remembered his dreams so he loved hearing his wife's. But he could never join her in them. Only when she woke could he share her sleeping world, listen as she told him of fantastic landscapes and impossible creatures.

Now, however, her eyes were still, her face pale and serene, her skin cool as she thawed. He had been unable to protect her this time. A single bite was all it took. Within minutes she was dead. Liam had allowed himself no time to grieve; he had carried her at once to the mortuary, placing her in one of the refrigerated drawers to keep her from waking. For now anyway.

He hadn't wanted her to become like the others and freezing was the only way of delaying the Waking. All across town the Woken roamed like sleepwalkers, in a state that was neither life nor death. They weren't especially aggressive; most of them merely seemed lost, confused. They

275

moved slowly and clumsily through familiar places, shying away from the living. They didn't speak or respond like the people they once were. Rather, they behaved like frightened animals in the wild. If they felt startled or threatened, they would attack. And if they were hungry, they would bite.

Liam laid Colleen on the embalming table and began to massage her hands, her arms, her shoulders. He stroked her face, setting her features as if for viewing before a burial. He kissed her cold lips and parted them to see her teeth one last time. Her dazzling smile was gone forever but her teeth were still dangerous. When she woke she would be frightened. And hungry.

With infinite skill and patience he drew the curved suture needle through the mucosa beneath her lips and pulled the silk thread taut. He placed the stitches as deep inside as possible so as not to make her mouth look pursed. He didn't want to mar her beauty in any way. A little blood ran over her lower lip as he finished the final stitch. She was starting to thaw. He didn't have more than an hour or two before she began to stir.

Now that her limbs were more pliable he could restrain her. He wrapped the ropes around her wrists and ankles as gently as if she were still living, securing her to the table. The bite on her arm had turned black just before she died; now it was shading to a virulent red. It was what happened just before they began to move again.

With a pair of scissors he slit her dress open down the front, exposing her pale breasts, the porcelain skin of her belly. She was like a sleeping statue, a sculpted Galatea he could wake with a kiss. She *would* wake, of course, but her new life would be short unless he intervened.

The reanimation didn't last long and within a week or two the moving bodies began to fail, to fall apart. The streets and buildings were littered with body parts. Bones and joints weakened until they could no longer support the weight of arms and legs. That would never be Colleen's fate. She would suffer none of the indignities he'd witnessed since the Waking began. She would be preserved.

His hand trembled slightly as he positioned the knife above her belly and he steadied it with the other hand. Then he took a deep breath and pressed down, making a quick, firm incision from the bottom of her rib cage to her navel. He set the bloodstained knife aside and teased the folds of skin apart, slipping his hand into the dark cavity.

Inside her organs were slick and wet but still cool. Her body would never warm them naturally but the heat of the sun would eventually cause them to rot. The blood in her veins would pool in unsightly bruises. He'd seen it happen to others and he was determined that it would not happen to Colleen.

He stroked the smooth surface of her liver before grasping it firmly and pulling. He cut the fleshy threads that held it inside and deposited it in the dish beside her. It was then that she began to move.

Her fingers opened and closed experimentally and she raised her head. Her eyes scanned the room before coming to rest on Liam and he saw her lips move. She was trying to open her mouth. Whatever instinct made them wake, it was presumably now telling Colleen to bite. Here was prey: eat.

"My love," Liam said softly, reaching out to stroke her face with the back of one gloved hand. "Don't worry. It will be over soon."

She was still as he spoke, as though listening intently. Her eyes seemed a little more focused, her expression a little more attuned. As though she knew him. Liam hadn't dared to dream that anything more than her physical beauty remained. He'd seen too many of the Woken in the past few weeks to hope that they retained any memory of who they were before. But something drew his gaze back to Colleen's again and again as he worked. He worked; she watched.

He lovingly lifted each organ out while she lay still, incapable of feeling any pain. There was something strangely intimate in touching parts of her he'd never seen before. Even her insides were beautiful. He cradled her delicate kidneys, her pristine womb, her tiny ovaries, caressing each soft pulpy mass before setting it aside. He left her heart until last.

Throughout the procedure Colleen remained passive. She didn't struggle in her bonds or try to resist in any way; she merely watched, her eyes wide and curious. Her skin was smooth and cool and Liam found himself stroking her absently as he worked, emptying her of the parts she no longer needed, the parts that could now only hasten her deterioration. They weren't what made her who she was anyway. They were no more "Colleen" than her hair or fingernails were. Or her clothes, her makeup, her jewellery.

At last he filled her with soft cotton wool, as though she were a lovingly crafted doll. A lifelike figure of his wife. Dead but not dead. Lost but not lost. As Liam sewed up the incision, he became more and more certain that the essence of his wife, her soul or her being, was still there. Buried perhaps, muffled in her newly Woken form, but unmistakably *there*. He would keep her with him and care for her as long as he was able, even if he were the last living man on earth. And when her preserved body at last began to succumb to the disintegration that eventually claimed all of the Woken, he would join her in death. *Real* death.

He drained the blood from her veins and injected a warm solution of chemicals to preserve her, to keep her from becoming like the ones outside. Even now Liam could hear them scratching at the door of the funeral parlour. Many of them were quite docile and several were so badly decomposed that they were no threat to anyone. But all it took was a single bite. His eyes watered as he gazed down at Colleen. His beautiful Colleen, his wife of only two months.

When he was done he stripped off his gloves. He untied the ropes and Colleen reached for him as soon as her arms were free. The solution had brought some warmth and colour back to her skin and he lifted her off the table. He set her on her feet and she stood gazing at him, a little uncertain, a little hesitant. Then her lips moved in something like a smile. She took his hands and drew them to her, placing them against her face.

Liam closed his eyes as he stroked her soft cheek and let his fingers trail down the curve of her throat, her shoulder, the swell of her breasts. He knew and adored every inch of her, could have sculpted her likeness if he were blind.

"Oh, Colleen," he murmured.

Colleen sighed in response and guided his palms over the firm, warm flesh of her newly eviscerated torso. He drew his fingers along the line of stitches, down past her navel, then down a little further. Then he stopped. He opened his eyes to find Colleen watching him intently.

Her eyes roamed over his face, not with the fear and confusion of the Woken, but as though he were someone familiar that she was trying to place. She looked like someone shaken from a dream, trying to remember the details even as they faded. In her short sleep of death, had she dreamt of him?

"My love," he said, hardly daring to speak the words. "Do you remember me?"

She cocked her head to one side with a puzzled expression.

"It's Liam. Your husband. You know me, don't you?"

Her lips parted slightly and she brought her face close to his. Then she took his hand and pushed it down, pressed it between her thighs. Liam gasped, surprised to find her warm and wet. He met her eyes again, a little startled by the intensity in her piercing gaze. It was not the dull, glassy stare of the Woken; it was the loving gaze of his wife. Colleen moaned softly as she writhed against his touch.

Liam felt his own body begin to respond. No matter what had happened, no matter how she had changed, she was still Colleen. And she knew him; he was certain of it now. She wasn't like the others. Her body remembered his touch even as what remained of her spirit remembered his face, his voice.

He touched his lips to hers, gently at first, then with a little more passion. Her jaw worked hungrily and he was grateful for his presence of mind in stitching her mouth shut. She knew him and loved him. And of course she wanted him. Wanted him to join her, to be like her. But he couldn't follow her there. He had to stay as he was to look after her, to keep her as long as he could. All he wanted was a little more time with her. He wasn't ready to let her go.

"Oh, Colleen," he said, burying his face in the hollow of her throat. "I missed you so much." It had only been a day but any time apart felt like an eternity. And eternity without Colleen was unthinkable, unbearable.

Her arms slipped around his neck and she moved her pelvis against him, grinding against the hardness in his crotch. She whimpered with desire and Liam could resist her no longer. He swept her up in his arms and carried her into the next room.

He deposited her on the plush carpet and began to undress. His fingers trembled as he unfastened the buttons of his shirt and Colleen crouched there on her knees, gazing up at him with animal eagerness, unnatural hunger.

When at last he was naked Colleen reached for him and he pushed her down gently onto her back. Kneeling above her he allowed his hands to roam over every inch of her supple flesh. He'd massaged her with cream to keep her skin soft. She felt like silk. He entered her and she whimpered softly, as though she were gagged. He smiled, remembering all the games they had played before the world changed.

A tide of memories swept over him as he pushed himself deep inside her.

Colleen arched her back and wrapped her legs around him, urging him deeper, harder. She threw back her head, closing her eyes in bliss as she moved with him. Her body responded in all its familiar ways. Liam knew every step of her sexual choreography and there was no mistaking it: Colleen was here with him, fully and completely. Not even death had been able to separate them.

He thought of their honeymoon, two weeks of paradise in the Caribbean. Colleen bronzed and naked on the beach, spreading her legs in the surf, gasping as the waves lapped between them and chilled her nipples into stiffness. Later, at dinner, she had kicked off her shoes under the table and slipped her feet into his lap, smiling impishly as he tried to eat in spite of her distraction. She'd kept him hard through the entire meal and as soon as they'd got back to their room he'd flung her down on the bed and ravished her, tearing her dress and making her scream into the pillows as she came. Then again in the shower. And then on the balcony under the full moon. And then. And then . . .

They came together, their limbs entwined, their bodies one. Colleen trembled beneath him, her cries of pleasure muffled. Liam enfolded her in his arms and covered her sealed lips with his.

Days passed like a dream. Outside the Woken shuffled by, growing weaker and more frail while Colleen retained the blush of new life. The new life Liam had given her. But he knew it wouldn't be forever. Each moment was precious to him because each moment only brought them both closer to the day when she too would begin to grow weak. He had extended their time but not stopped it and his heart ached that it was all he could do.

There were still living people out there. Liam had heard vehicles, voices, seen notices. Doctors and scientists were searching for a cure. But even if it were possible, it would never come in time for them.

He'd heard a single radio broadcast. A man was asking for information on the Woken. Had anyone, anywhere, seen any evidence of personality remaining after waking? Was it possible for the Woken to recognise the living? Any information—any *hope*—would be welcome. Please come forward, please contact us . . .

Liam had turned the radio off. He wanted nothing to invade their private world, to taint their final days.

It was time. Colleen could barely lift her arms now and she seemed frightened and confused, as though aware that they would soon be parted. She made soft mewling sounds and her eyes shone with tears.

But Liam reassured her with a smile as he kissed her. He wrapped her naked in his arms, dancing a slow waltz with her as he led her back to the embalming room. There he took up a pair of manicure scissors and gently, so very gently, snipped away the stitches holding her lips closed. He held her face in his hands and kissed her.

"I love you," he whispered. Then he offered her his wrist.

At first she merely blinked in slow confusion. She licked her lips and closed her eyes as though smelling something sweet, something tempting. She kissed the skin of his hand and he felt the tip of her tongue like a final caress before she sank her teeth in to the thin skin of his inner wrist. He hissed with pain as blood ran from the wound and Colleen, strengthened, held his wrist against her face, lapping at his blood as though it were a fine wine.

The wound itself wasn't enough to be fatal but the poison in her bite was. Liam's head swam and he sank to his knees, his heart throbbing in his ears, deafening him. Twin images of Colleen swam before his eyes and she sank to the floor with him, nuzzling her cheek against his as his vision began to fade and the world grew soft and grey. He closed his eyes.

And then he opened them again.

The soldiers had swept the town and so far found only piles of limbs and body parts littering the streets and houses. Checking the funeral parlour was almost an afterthought.

Inside was evidence that a couple had been living there for weeks. On the floor of one room lay a woman's white velvet dress and a man's shirt and trousers. The clothes were strewn like a trail left by lovers as they stripped on the way to the bedroom. But instead of a love nest, the trail led to the embalming room of the mortuary. There they found a tangle of limbs, two bodies so entwined that at first it was impossible to tell them apart.

"Carlson! I think you should take a look at this."

The two men swept their torches around the room and Carlson shrugged, unimpressed. "You dragged me all the way in here for this, Fletcher? One killed the other and then died. Again. We've seen it before."

Fletcher moved closer and gestured at the bodies. "No, it's not that. It's the stitches."

On closer inspection they could see that it was clearly a man and a woman, wrapped in a tight embrace. The woman's mouth was slightly open and her teeth were stained with blood, her lips trailing the snipped ends of black stitching. A pair of manicure scissors lay on a table nearby. The man's wrist had recently been bitten.

The soldiers were quiet as they pieced the scene together.

"Why didn't he wake?" Carlson asked at last.

Fletcher frowned at the scene, pondering the question. After a while he spoke. "I think he did. He just never left her side."

They lay peacefully in each other's embrace, as though they had simply fallen asleep while dancing cheek to cheek. There was no sign of a struggle.

Suddenly Fletcher gasped.

"What? What is it?"

Fletcher pointed with a trembling hand. "Her eyes. I swear I saw movement."

"Her eyes are closed."

"I know. But they moved. Like she was dreaming. Look! His just did too."

Carlson crouched beside him and they both peered closely at the faces of the dead couple. From time to time their eyes did indeed flicker beneath the lids.

"But that's impossible. They're dead. I mean, they already woke and now they're *really* dead."

Neither man had an answer or an explanation. They watched the dreaming lovers for a little while before silently turning to leave. They closed the door behind them, neither intent on telling anyone what they had seen.

Outside on the streets the Woken lay scattered, having died their second and final death. Their eyes were still. No dreams danced beneath their closed lids.

Elsewhere in the world the living dreamt of the dead. But in one room, in one town, a pair of lovers dreamt of each other. In happy dreams they were as one, slumbering sweetly on, never to wake again.

DEATH WALKS EN POINTE

*C*RUNCH, *CRUNCH.*

"No," Stefano moaned. "It's all wrong!"

Katia looked down in bewilderment at her outfit before turning to Ursula for reassurance.

The costume designer shook her head, confused. "But—isn't this what you asked for?"

Crunch, crunch.

Stefano regarded her icily. "I said modern and edgy, nothing classical. Didn't I? And here stands a dancer looking like the fucking Sugar Plum Fairy!"

Katia self-consciously smoothed down the stiff layers of bright pink tulle.

"But it's nothing like a classical tutu," Ursula continued bravely. "See, I've put gears and cogs between the layers to make it—"

"It's awful! Horrendous. It's not what I asked for at all."

Crunch, crunch.

Stefano rounded on the girl behind him in the doorway. "And you! If you don't stop doing that I'll break your fucking legs!"

Dani froze, her mouth open in shock. "I'm just trying to break in my shoes," she snapped.

"Well, you can bloody well do it somewhere else. I can't even hear myself think!"

Dani gave the door one last vicious crunch against the toe of the pointe shoe she was pressing into the doorjamb. The hinges protested and there was the splintering of wood as the screws pulled loose. With a triumphant smile Dani waved the shoes at Stefano as she flounced past, pink ribbons billowing behind her.

Stefano clutched his head. "It's just not what I want," he said. "It's bloody Coppélia, not The Girl Who Sat On A Clock And Got Pieces Of It Stuck To Her Arse." He cast a final scathing look over Katia's costume before glaring at Ursula again. "Fix it."

As he stomped off Ursula pursed her lips.

"Drama queen," Katia muttered. She laid a reassuring hand on Ursula's shoulder. "For what it's worth, I think it's beautiful." She did a little pirouette, smiling at the way the gears spun with her when she moved.

"He's never satisfied with anything," Ursula said. She shook her head sadly. "Well, back to the drawing board."

Katia slipped out of the rejected doll costume and handed it back to Ursula with a sad little smile. "I know you'll come up with something just as good," she said.

Ursula got all the way to the costume room before realising she didn't have the key. "Oh, brilliant," she muttered. She threw the tutu on the floor and marched off to see who was manning the stage door, hoping she wouldn't run into Stefano again. Fortunately, only Jane was there.

"Hi, Jane. Have you got a spare key to the wardrobe? I can't find mine."

Jane looked up from the desk, holding her finger in place on the line of Braille she was reading. Her pale eyes gazed just to the right of Ursula's face, never quite able to fix on the source of a voice. "Sure," she said. She bookmarked her place and turned to the pegboard behind her. Her hand immediately found the key. "But don't lose it; that's the only one."

"I'll get another copy made," she said. "Say, you wouldn't happen to have a spare one for Stefano's office, would you?"

Jane's features creased in puzzlement. "No. Why?"

"Just thought I might redecorate it for him. Fill it with razorwire or broken glass."

Jane laughed. "Uh-oh. What's he done now?"

"Only insulted my finest work. He really is impossible."

"He's always been like that. When people ask me if I miss dancing I remind myself what it was like having him scream at me in rehearsals. Of course, he was lovely the night of my accident but that's only because everyone else was there. I'm sure he'd have been happy to tell me what a clumsy bitch I was otherwise."

Ursula bristled. "Roberto," she grumbled. "It was all his fault, really. If he hadn't been drinking he would have caught you."

"No, no," Jane said with a wistful sigh. "I've no one to blame but myself. I lied about how good my eyes were so I could keep dancing. The truth is I could hardly see by that point and I timed my jump badly. And if I hadn't broken my ankle I'd only have been forced to retire when I finally lost my sight. Oh well. At least I can still hear the music. Here's your key."

"You shame us all," Ursula said, her voice a mixture of sympathy and admiration.

Jane waved away her compliment. "Spit in Stefano's coffee for me, will you?"

"I will. And Roberto's too, just for good measure."

As Ursula turned to go Jane added under her breath, "Don't forget Dani."

The Aquarius was nothing special. An unassuming little theatre that boasted a small ballet company and was occasionally hired by even smaller drama troupes. It had started life as a Victorian music hall. After the First World War it was refurbished and fashioned into a proper theatre with grandiose aspirations, only to be bombed during the Second World War. It remained derelict until it found a patron who rebuilt it during the '70s. Since then its boards had been trodden by countless amateur actors, singers and dancers before finally abandoning its lofty ambitions and becoming a home for minor professional performers of all sorts.

The house was rarely full but certain shows were guaranteed to draw a crowd. To the endless frustration of the artists, it was the commonplace and family-friendly ones that tended to make the most money. For the actors that meant pantomime. And for the dancers it meant Nutcracker.

Attempts at anything beyond what was familiar to the general public failed to raise much interest.

Stefano was a tyrant to work with but he had been the first director to turn a profit with the ballet company. It was the only thing that kept the dancers from organising a full-scale mutiny against him. He was also mildly subversive; he tried to put his own spin on the classical ballets, to "shake them up". But in reality his surreal touches often merely left audience members—and dancers—scratching their heads.

The Aquarius hadn't staged Coppélia for two years. Not since the ill-fated dress rehearsal that had ended Jane's career. Stefano blamed her degenerative eye condition for the accident and proceeded without her, slotting the keen-eyed Dani into the lead role of Swanilda and letting Roberto carry on as Franz. The performance went ahead while Jane languished in hospital. It was no secret that Stefano had never liked her but then, he didn't really like *anybody*.

When he first announced that they would be performing Coppélia again, with the present company reprising their original roles, all eyes had flicked guiltily to Jane. Sensing the attention, she had forced a friendly laugh, insisting that the show must go on. It was a popular ballet. The kids loved it and it always made money. It would be stupid to hold it in some kind of moratorium simply because Jane had never got to dance it. And it certainly wasn't cursed.

Dani was the first to agree; her performance had garnered rave reviews. And Katia, perfect as the mechanical doll Coppélia, was always a favourite with the kids. What she lacked in talent she made up for by wowing little girls after the show, taking them backstage and playing up the glamorous life of a ballerina. Not that there was much glamour about the Aquarius. The stage was creaky, the dressing rooms were shabby, and the lobby was a lime green nightmare of faded '70s decor. Even the costume room had seen better days. It was crowded with racks of moth-eaten leotards and rickety sewing machines. But as long as the theatre continued to limp along, so would the shows.

"Edgy and modern," Ursula grumbled as she paged through her books looking for inspiration. Just what was that supposed to mean, anyway? Lasers? Tattoos? Nudity? It was nearly midnight and she was no closer to a costume for the doll that Roberto's character would fall in love with and Dani would then impersonate in the second act.

A sound made her jump and she spun round in her chair, peering into the shadows behind her. "Katia? That you, sweetie?"

There was no answer. With a sigh she turned back to the pictures before her. She'd been so proud of her clockwork idea and had just started on a similarly themed suit for the doll-maker Dr Coppélius. Gianni was playing him for the first time and he and Katia had both loved the design. Now she had to scrap the whole concept. She flicked through the pages, seeing nothing she liked.

Something creaked overhead and she glanced up at the tall shelves along the wall. *Rats*, she thought with disgust. But the ominous shifting was too loud to be the work of rats. She jumped to her feet just in time to avoid the bolts of cloth that tumbled down from where they had been precariously stacked. They fell in an avalanche of colour until the last one rolled to a stop on the floor by her chair. Ursula pressed a hand to her chest, her heart pounding.

Jesus, the whole bloody place was falling apart! Well, she wasn't going to clean up the mess. Stefano could count himself lucky if she didn't report the incident to health and safety. She was sure the Aquarius wouldn't pass any of their regulations and she was equally sure that Stefano paid them to stay away. One day the whole theatre was bound to collapse and kill all twelve audience members. Then it would be condemned and she could move on to bigger and better venues.

For now she'd just take it as a sign that she was done for the night. Their fearless leader could brave the disaster area and design his own costumes if he didn't like hers. She stepped gingerly over the multicoloured deadfall and began picking her way towards the door.

She was almost there when a black-gloved hand reached from behind her, covering her mouth. Something heavy struck her in the backs of her legs and she went sprawling over the scattering of cloth. She flailed for balance but only succeeded in hitting her head on the corner of the table. Her vision swam and she could just make out the twin blurry images of a figure approaching her. Something gleamed in one hand.

By the time she had opened her mouth to scream, her throat had been cut. Her fingers clutched uselessly at the gaping wound as blood pooled beneath her, staining a length of pink tulle. The last thing she ever saw was the handful of gears and cogs being shoved into her face and down her throat.

The stage smelled of sweat and resin and the rehearsal pianist plinked away on the tuneless upright as Dani and Roberto ran through the wedding dance. The corps of villagers sat or stood where they had been placed in the background, watching with boredom.

"Stop, stop, stop!" Stefano shouted, waving his arms as he marched onstage.

"What *now*?" Dani moaned.

Stefano glared at her and Roberto took a step away to avoid the fireworks. "Do you know why it's called a *pas de deux*?" he asked coldly. "It's because it's a dance for two people. That's right, *two*. It's not the bit in the show where the prima ballerina gets to show off what a perfect little diva she is and how this ballet is so far beneath her."

One of the corps girls tittered and Dani sent a look of fury upstage. She turned to Roberto for support but he was staring at his feet, pointedly ignoring her. Above her on the catwalk, one of the tech guys gave a little cough as if to confirm everyone's opinion of her.

She flushed scarlet with humiliation. "OK, OK, whatever," she snapped.

"Thank you," Stefano said, his voice dripping with sarcasm. He gestured at the pianist. "From the top, Carol."

The music began again and this time Dani performed with a little less pretension, allowing Roberto to be a partner rather than an assistant. But the more emphatic thud of her shoes on the stage when she went en pointe expressed her simmering anger. Roberto dug his fingers into her ribs when he lifted her, exerting unnecessary pressure. She countered with a whip of her head that showered him with sweat and the next time he took her hand she gouged him with her nails. Such were the tiny tantrums and petty revenges exacted onstage night after night.

The corps dancers rolled their eyes.

"Ungrateful cow," Gianni whispered to Katia. "Jane was a *much* better dancer." He jerked his head towards the prompt corner where Jane was running through the lighting cues with someone on the other end of the microphone.

"Yes, well," Katia whispered back, "success just goes to some people's heads. Look at Stefano. I remember when he used to be fun to work with."

"Quiet back there!" Stefano growled.

Katia giggled.

Gianni dropped his voice even lower. "Any sign of our new costumes, by the way? Only I looked for Ursula this morning and couldn't find her."

"I haven't seen her either. But she was ready to kill Stefano yesterday. Maybe she stayed home to avoid him."

"Can't say I blame her."

Dani went into a turn and Roberto released her unexpectedly. She stumbled and glared at him.

"You did that on purpose!" she cried.

Roberto gave her a look of wide-eyed innocence. "Sorry. You're just so sweaty it's like trying to hold onto a pig."

"You bastard!"

Stefano stepped between them before the fight could escalate. "All right, children," he said wearily. "That's lunch. Go eat something, throw it up and come back here in a better mood or I'll start re-thinking the cast list."

Dani stalked past Roberto, purposely bumping him as she headed for her dressing room.

Who the hell did they think they were? She wasn't just some understudy with a lucky break; she was a principal dancer. She was destined for better shows than the silly Coppélia. She should be in London, dancing Swan Lake and Giselle to sold-out crowds. But who would ever know how good she was from the dismal repertoire she was forced to waste her talents on?

If the theatre was shabby and worn, the stage was a bloody disgrace. There was a loose board on one side that creaked when you trod on it and half the footlights were burnt out. There was barely room to move in the wings and it was sweltering in any weather. No wonder she was sweating so much.

She stripped off her rehearsal tutu and flung it away. Her leotard and tights were drenched with sweat and it wouldn't surprise her if she got trench foot. She untied the ribbons of her shoes and pulled them off, recoiling from the smell. The shoes were well past their prime, caked inside with dirt and dried blood, but they were her most comfortable pair for rehearsing and she couldn't bear to throw them out yet.

After a quick shower in the adjoining bathroom she wrapped herself in a towel, propped her right leg up on the sink and set about attacking one of her calluses with a pair of nail scissors.

Crunch.

She froze at the sound. Was someone softening their shoes in *her* doorjamb? She listened and heard it again. Then she rolled her eyes. Stefano. Of course.

"If you're trying to annoy me, you already did that hours ago," she sang out.

Crunch.

She heaved a sigh and marched back into her dressing room to confront him. The door was open and one of her shoes was lying in the doorway. She shook her head as she bent down to pick it up. Then everything went dark.

It took her a moment to scream, to realise that someone had thrown a dark cloth over her head and knocked her to the floor. By then it was too late to escape the bonds pinning her arms to her sides. She heard the rip of duct tape as her captor wound it up and around her neck to secure the hood, muffling her cries.

She panicked, struggling as much as she was able and kicking her legs wildly as she was dragged across the floor on her belly. The towel fell away and she howled as splinters snagged in her naked skin, gouging long furrows through her lean, muscular body. She cried helplessly, pleading through the hood for them to take her money, her jewellery, anything. When her tormentor finally let go of her Dani held still, thinking for a moment that she had successfully appealed to either their pity or their greed. Then she felt the viselike grip of hands around her right ankle and her foot was forced against what could only be the doorframe. She felt the chill of the hinge against her toes.

Dani screamed. And she went on screaming as the door closed on her toes, breaking most of them in one go. By the time her other foot had suffered the same treatment she was mercifully unconscious.

The corps dancers were sprawled on the floor or draped over bits of scenery. Roberto made a show of looking at his watch and tapping his foot. Carol put her head down on the closed lid of the piano and snored.

Stefano pinched the bridge of his nose and shut his eyes. "Will someone please go and find the princess," he said. He sounded close to tears.

Katia clambered up from the floor and trudged off into the wings. No one said a word as they waited for the return of their temperamental Swanilda.

A minute passed. Then two. And then there came a bloodcurdling scream from the corridor.

The shock lasted only a moment before everyone ran after Katia. The group came upon her outside Dani's dressing room. She was on her knees on the floor, crying, her face pressed to the wall.

"Oh my God," Roberto moaned, staring down at Dani's splayed and bloody body. "Her feet."

Stefano pushed past him into the room, his eyes wide with horror. "Is she . . . dead?"

Roberto covered his eyes and backed away. "I'm gonna be sick."

"Look!" Carol cried suddenly, pointing down, "she's breathing!" She began yanking at the duct tape while shouting instructions to the others. "Stefano, hand me that razor and help me cut this off her. Jane, call an ambulance. Roberto, get out of here if you're going to be useless."

When the paramedics arrived they were appalled by the scene of torture. "Did you call the police?" they asked.

"Um," Stefano said, glancing dazedly around at the others. Roberto was clutching his stomach and Katia still hadn't moved from her spot on the floor. "We just . . . We found her like this and . . ."

"Are you crazy? Whoever did it could still be in the building!"

Someone gasped. "You mean . . . ?"

"Well, she obviously didn't do this to herself."

Katia burst into fresh tears and Gianni put a comforting arm around her as Dani was bundled onto a stretcher and carried away.

"I'll call the police," Jane said.

The rest of the company was too shaken by the episode to do anything. Only Carol had kept her head. No one was surprised to learn that their quiet rehearsal pianist had once been an army nurse.

"So let me get this straight," said Inspector Martin. "She was alone in her dressing room but no one heard a thing? Or saw anything suspicious?"

"That's right, Inspector," Stefano said. The others nodded in sombre agreement. "We'd gone to lunch."

"I see. All of you?"

At the inspector's raised eyebrows Roberto added, "There'd been . . . a bit of a scene."

"A scene?"

Roberto and Stefano exchanged an uneasy glance as the silence grew.

"She wasn't exactly easy to work with," Katia finally blurted out.

"Mm-hmm. Bit of a diva, was she?"

Roberto looked relieved that someone else had said it first. "You could say that."

"Her career is over," Jane said darkly. "Just like mine."

"Hey, I didn't wish it on her!"

Carol narrowed her eyes at Roberto. "Your last words to her were pretty nasty."

He leapt to his feet. "I didn't do it! All right, I couldn't stand her. I thought she was a stuck-up little bitch. Is that what you want to hear? But it doesn't mean I'd do something like that! And anyway, Stefano's the one who threatened to break her legs yesterday."

All eyes turned to the director, who went pale. "I only told her to stop slamming her shoes in the door."

"Yeah, well, I heard it," Roberto continued. "Katia was there too. And Ursula."

The Inspector glanced down at his list of names. "Who's Ursula?"

"Our costume designer," Stefano said. "She took off yesterday because I didn't like one of her designs."

Katia suddenly looked worried. "But it's not like her to disappear. I knocked on the door of the costume room earlier but she wasn't there."

"Anyone go in to check?"

"She has the only key," Jane said. "I gave it to her yesterday because she said she'd lost hers."

Inspector Martin's face darkened. "Anyone object if I break the door down?"

"How could anyone *do* it?" Katia wailed. The sight of Ursula's bloodstained corpse had shocked her into catatonic silence for several minutes. Now she couldn't stop crying.

Carol eyed her coldly and it was clear she was biting her tongue to keep from telling her to get a grip.

They had each given their statements to Inspector Martin, who seemed to believe that the company members were innocent. Surely he'd have arrested someone otherwise. Stefano felt particularly fortunate, given the special violence that had been done to each victim. The others had glanced at him uneasily, no doubt picturing him in the act.

"What are we going to do about the show?" one of the corps girls asked timidly.

It wasn't a frivolous question; the theatre was their livelihood. And despite the tragedies, there was now a gaping hole in the cast that needed to be filled if the show was to go on.

Stefano glanced at Katia.

"No way," she said, shaking her head vehemently. "I'm out. This show is cursed!"

He sighed. So he needed a new Coppélia now too. Not that it mattered. The press was bound to deliver the coup de grâce to the Aquarius with whatever lurid story it printed about the murder and maiming.

"Go home," he said tiredly. "Let's talk about it in the morning."

One by one the others trailed away, some looking more devastated than others while one or two looked hopeful that they could benefit from the gory turn of events. But that was a dancer's life; you couldn't afford to be choosy about opportunities, however they presented themselves.

Stefano closed the door to his office and unlocked his centre desk drawer with trembling hands. He stared at the extra key to the costume room before stuffing it into his pocket. He'd throw it in the river. Fortunately the police hadn't asked if he had a key and Jane must have forgotten or he'd probably be in jail right now. He hadn't liked Ursula but he hadn't killed her. Nor had he broken Dani's toes. He shuddered at the thought. No, he wasn't capable of either act.

He opened another drawer and took out the bottle of J&B he kept for times like this. He poured a generous measure into his coffee mug and slurped it down, relishing the spicy, peaty burn.

He stared glumly at the list of performance dates. If the show continued, it meant he only had three weeks to replace his two female leads. That was assuming Roberto didn't freak out and abandon ship as well. But he was something of a diva himself, so Stefano could probably scratch that worry off the list. But what was he supposed to tell the backers? The patrons? The press would probably be camped outside in the morning and who knew what indiscretions the dancers would spill in their grief? His mug was empty already and he refilled it, eager to erase the horrible day.

Stefano was very drunk by the time he noticed the object in the corner of the room. Stumbling to his feet, he staggered across to it and blinked in confusion. It took him almost five minutes to realise that it was a gas canister. And by the time he realised he'd been inhaling the escaping fumes, he was too dizzy to stand. He collapsed in a heap on the floor.

"Suicide," the inspector said grimly. "We found this in his pocket." He held up the key, a perfect match for the one they'd found on Ursula.

"So it was Stefano all along?" Jane asked.

"Looks that way."

Carol shook her head. "Unbelievable. And none of us had any idea."

When the inspector had gone Katia clung to Roberto, sobbing. Gianni hadn't shown up that morning so it looked like Roberto had inherited the role of comforter. It suddenly occurred to him that he might also inherit the role of director. It could be the silver lining in this black cloud.

"So—what do we do now?" someone asked.

Everyone looked at Roberto as though he were the natural successor. He cleared his throat. "Well, I guess we have to decide whether or not we want to go on with the show."

"Surely not after everything that's happened," Jane cried.

The corps dancers shifted restlessly, none quite daring to speak up. The hunger in their eyes did all the talking for them. It would take more than a few deaths to deter an ambitious ballet dancer.

Roberto knew just how they felt. He didn't want to cancel the show but neither did he want to look insensitive to the audience. There hadn't been any outcry two years ago, when they'd carried on following Jane's accident. The troupe had soldiered on then and his feeling was that they should soldier on now.

"Listen," he said. "It's been a traumatic couple of days and we're all still in shock. Why don't we sleep on it and in the morning we can put it to a vote. Anonymously, if you like."

Everyone seemed happy with both the plan and Roberto's assumption of power. He said goodbye to the others and waited for them to leave. He wanted to be alone for a little while.

Dani opened her eyes slowly. Was she dead? Was she Juliet, lying alongside her Romeo while the audience wept at her moving performance? Or perhaps she was the Sleeping Beauty, swooning after the prick of the needle.

Then she smelled the flowers and remembered where she was. She could feel nothing below her waist. It was as though she no longer had feet. With a shudder she recalled the horror of the hood, the tape and, worst of all, the door. But was there also something else, something important that she was forgetting?

She could still hear the awful sound as the door crushed her toes, ensuring that she would never dance again. But whose hands had wielded that terrible weapon?

Her feet were ruined. But she'd seen someone else's feet that day. Just as she'd bent down to pick up her shoe, lying in the doorway like bait in a trap. There had been a flicker of recognition before the hood. She'd seen who it was and then dismissed it. Why?

Oh, it was too much. Thinking about it made her toes burn. The pain would begin to crawl up her legs. Soon it would consume her body and she would scream and someone would come and sedate her.

But this time she remembered something else. A whisper in her ear just before the terrible deed. The echo of it frightened her and she reflexively pressed the button on the morphine drip. Relief and sweet oblivion began to flow through her and she closed her eyes, instantly drowsy. The voice...

Her eyes flew open. No! It couldn't be. She opened her mouth to speak the name but sleep embraced her before she could make a sound.

Roberto stood centre stage, gazing out at the dark, empty house. He paced through a few steps of his own choreography, imagining what it would be like to stage his own shows.

As he performed a little turn he thought he saw movement out of the corner of his eye. But there was nothing behind him but the toyshop set. His only audience was a line of dull-eyed mannequins, Coppélia's mechanical sisters. They stood along the back wall in various static poses. He sighed and went back to his musing and when he spun around again he didn't notice that the line was now one doll short.

When he heard the creak of the loose board he froze. A chill went up his back as he stared into the darkness. He wasn't alone.

"Who's there?" he called out, trying to disguise his fear.

When no one answered he began to relax. It was just the creaky old Aquarius. They always said the stage had a mind of its own. Why was he so jumpy anyway? The killer had been caught.

Disgusted with himself, he went through a few more spins and jumps. It was strangely liberating to be onstage alone, with only the ghosts to see him. He stopped suddenly, not liking the thought of ghosts. Was Stefano watching him now? Ursula? No, he told himself. He didn't believe in ghosts. But he was definitely being watched. And when he heard the cry from above he knew the nightmare wasn't over yet.

He peered up at the catwalk high above him, just able to make out a figure moving there. There was a frightened whimper and then a white cane fell the long distance to the stage and broke at his feet.

"Jane!" he cried.

"Roberto? Is that you?" Her voice quavered and he heard her shifting around. "I don't know where I am."

"Don't move! You're on the catwalk!"

She gasped at that and began to cry. "Someone attacked me," she choked out. "Please help me!"

Roberto wasn't keen on heights and he'd never been up on the catwalk before. But he couldn't leave Jane up there. Especially not when there was still a killer on the loose. He'd played the hero enough times onstage; surely he could summon the courage to do it for real. Just this once. He owed her that much.

He ran into the wings and switched on the lights. Jane was forty feet above him, crouching in the middle of the catwalk, her arms wrapped around one of the rails.

"Just be still," he called up to her. "I'm coming!"

He climbed the ladder and began inching out along the rickety catwalk. It swayed with his movement and he tried not to look down at the hard wooden stage floor so far below him. When he reached Jane he peeled her hands away from the railing and she clung to him, sobbing.

"It's OK," he said. "You're safe now. I've got you."

But she didn't seem convinced. She held on to him, refusing to move. Her sobs grew louder and more anguished, spiralling away into a kind of maniacal laughter that chilled his blood. He pushed her away and stared at her face, uncomprehending. Had her mind snapped completely?

"You've got me?" she asked. "Oh no. I've got *you*."

"Jane? What are you talking about?"

She took a step back and slowly raised her forefingers to her eyes. She pressed the fingertips against the pale blue irises and Roberto gaped in disbelief as they came away, revealing perfectly normal brown eyes beneath.

"Contact lenses," she said. "Painful but effective."

He shook his head, bewildered. "I don't understand."

"Don't you? No, of course not. You were always too busy thinking about yourself and your career. You and all the others. Never mind me. Never mind the girl who would never dance again after your drunken fumble!"

"But your eyes. You always said—"

"That I was almost blind anyway? A lie. I could see well enough to dance.

Well enough to know how drunk you were. Just not well enough to see two seconds into the future or I'd never have made that jump into your arms."

Roberto glanced nervously down at the stage as he finally understood. "So you've just been waiting all this time to get even?"

She nodded triumphantly. "Yes. All this time. Watching you and Stefano carry on as though nothing had happened. Watching Dani take my place as though she belonged there. She wasn't half the dancer I was! Now she'll know how it feels to be told she'll never dance again."

"What about Ursula? What did she ever do to you?"

Jane laughed, a harsh, cold sound. "Absolutely nothing. She was my dress rehearsal. You see, I wasn't sure at first that I could actually do it, actually kill someone. But all I had to do was look at that awful costume she'd designed and remember all the times she made me look fat onstage."

"But you never looked fat—"

"And then Princess Dani. Well, I left her in a state worse than death. Thanks for pointing the finger at Stefano, by the way. I couldn't have planned it better myself. None of you even questioned his guilty suicide." She gave him a bright, mocking smile. "Which brings me to you."

Roberto stared at her in horror. "You'll never get away with it. If you kill me they'll know it wasn't Stefano!"

"But they'll never suspect *me*," she said sweetly. "The poor little blind ex-dancer? Maybe they'll think Katia was my lover and she did it all to avenge me. Or perhaps it was a devoted fan. The point is—you're about to die. Say goodbye, Roberto. You should have caught me that time. Because no one is going to catch *you* now."

With that she rushed him, a knife in one upraised hand. Roberto threw his arms up to shield himself as he scrambled backwards along the catwalk. If he could just reach the end...

All at once a shot rang out and the world seemed to stand still. Jane stopped where she was, swaying on her feet. The knife slipped from her fingers and Roberto watched it fall in slow motion, turning end over end until it struck the floor, burying itself in the wood with a solid thunk.

Jane opened her mouth to speak but only a spurt of blood came out. She fell forward onto her knees and then pitched sideways. She grabbed the railing with one hand and hung there. Her legs kicked in the open space and she glanced wildly up at Roberto, her eyes shining with madness. Then she let go. Roberto closed his eyes and winced at the dull thud as she hit the stage.

"You OK up there?" Carol called.

It took Roberto a while to believe that he was. He staggered back to the ladder and made his way down. When he reached the bottom he found that his legs wouldn't hold him any more and he sat down on the stage floor, trembling violently.

"She was—she was—

Carol patted his shoulder. "I know. I went to see Dani in hospital. She told me she'd heard Jane's voice just before she blacked out. I always thought there was something not quite right about that girl."

But Roberto wasn't listening. He was looking at the line of mannequins. Their cool detachment seemed to mock him as they stared at the body lying sprawled at their feet, just another broken doll that would never dance again.

The Calling of Night's Ocean

THE MAN WATCHES ME LEAP FROM THE WATER. I ARCH my body, soaring upwards. I climb higher and higher until at last I can go no further. I hang in the sky like a cloud, a being of pure exuberance. It's only for a moment but time seems to hold still for me. I feel like I could stay here forever up above the flickering waves. Hovering, drifting. But then, as it always does, the water pulls me back and I plunge inside its cool depths once more.

I swim to the surface again and peek out. The man is still watching me. He seems fascinated by me, but not afraid. I have no fear of him either. I sense only curiosity from him as he studies everything I do. Every splash, every jump, every sound I make.

His kind have no tails and yet they can still swim in their way. Outside the water they rise high and vulnerable, balancing on their slender fins, moving on the bottom of the sky the way crabs do on the sea bed. Strangest of all are their songs. They are not unpleasant to listen to, but my own are incomprehensible to them.

I share my calling with him again, both inside the water where the sound is true and outside where it becomes distorted. The long looping whistle tells who I am and where I came from, and the little trill at the end means I love to dive into the sky. His mouth changes shape in the way I have learned means that he is pleased. He knows what I am saying even though he cannot repeat the sounds. His attempts are very funny.

The bodies of humans are even more peculiar. Their top fins are split like the arms of a tiny octopus, only not as long. He uses one to point to me. Then he points to himself and makes a smaller, simpler sound.

Zhoeii.

This is his calling, a sound I cannot reproduce. But it is such a tiny song, how can it reveal anything meaningful about him? Perhaps humans do not care to say where they come from. Or perhaps they tell each other such things in another way.

Khaiy-lah-nheii.

I listen as he sings to me again. He keeps repeating the same sounds as he points to me and I realise it must be a special calling for me. A song that, for him, means me.

I splash my delight at this understanding and invite him to play, to come inside the water with me. But although I still sense no fear from him, he stays in the sky, watching me from where the water ends. He scratches something on a flat, thin object he keeps with him, marking it with signs. I think it must be another kind of song, one that isn't sung in a way you can hear. How curious these creatures are! What use is a song if you cannot hear it?

Joey Elstree, personal journal
Hurricane Hole Cetacean Institute, British Virgin Islands
June 1st 1969

Today I gave the subject a name. Dr Hallam might be happy calling her D-19 but I'm not. So now her name is Kailani. It means "sea and sky". I thought it was fitting, given how much she seems to love jumping.

She kept repeating one specific vocalisation to me that seemed an obvious introduction. "My name is . . ." she was saying. She also seemed amused by my clumsy attempts to repeat it back to her.

But I've made significant progress in just a few days. I think she understood that I was giving her a name I could pronounce and her behaviour was even more playful afterwards, almost coquettish. Is this dolphin flirting with me?

I know there were some problems along those lines back at Dr Lilly's institute when the male dolphin fell in love with his female handler and made sexual advances towards her. This girl was living with him in a flooded section of the facility and trying to teach him English. Apparently they achieved a sophisticated type of mimicry on both sides but there was no evidence that the dolphin could comprehend actual words. He was merely parroting back the sounds he heard from her. The whole project came to an end a few years ago with a minor scandal and the withdrawal of funding. A typical short-sighted government decision. When will they learn that breakthroughs don't happen overnight?

Dr Lilly was always keen on the "motherly" approach to working with the dolphins but obviously that particular one had his own ideas. They often do. You can't put them in a box and expect them to stay there. They're too smart for that.

Lilly's plan was to break the language barrier with dolphins so we'd be ahead of the game in the search for other intelligent life in the universe. So when the Martians landed, we'd be able to walk right up and say hi. Well, I'm not interested in talking to Martians. I just want to talk to dolphins.

Growing up in Hawaii you can't help but fall in love with the ocean and all her magnificent creatures. It's even more awe-inspiring here in the Caribbean. I feel a million miles from home, but it's still not as far as Vietnam would have been. I can never repay Dr Hallam for letting me come here to work for him. He saved my life and I'll never forget that.

The news from home is terrible. More guys get sent to Vietnam every day and there's no end in sight. The death toll on both sides is massive and it makes me depressed to think about it. The worst part is—some of our guys are doing terrible things over there, killing women and children. They come home in pieces, not as heroes but as war criminals. Many of them don't come home at all. I could so easily be one of them.

Are there dolphins in the South China Sea? Do they know what's happening on the land over there? How can we ever expect to talk to aliens if we can't even talk to other people?

Kailani is watching me as I write this. She watches everything I do. It's intense to make eye contact with a dolphin because their intelligence is so obvious and profound. They're probably smarter than we are and I bet they could teach us primitive humans a thing or two. Dolphins don't have wars, after all.

She's trying very hard to get my attention now and there's a certain repeated pattern of sounds—two clicks and a squeak—that I'm starting to suspect is HER name for ME. If I try to imitate her she tosses her head and chatters as though she's laughing. But I think I'm right. That's my new name. Good-bye Joey. Hello Click-Click-Squeak!

Humans are very soft, not like my kind at all. That must be why they stay in the sky. The air is softer than the water and their bodies are so fragile. When they swim, they wear strange coverings that don't smell like any sea creature I know. My new friend wears one when he finally comes inside the water. He is sleek and black, like a shadow. Sometimes he carries something on his back that makes bubbles. He stays deep with me for longer periods then and I love to play in the bubbles.

I nudge him with my nose to show that I like to be touched and he floats with me, exploring my skin, the smoothness of my outline. I can tell he likes the way I feel. He can't jump like I can, can't dive in and out of the sky. And he can't swim very fast at all. But he likes to hold on to me while I pull him through the water. I wonder what he would do if I carried him far away from the edge of the sky. I think he would trust me to take him back.

When he stands in the sky he often throws me fish. But here in the water with me he doesn't seem to know how to catch them. This surprises me and I wonder what other mysteries his kind hold.

June 13th, 1969

Kailani is trying to teach me how to fish. She kept bringing me mackerel when I finally went in the water with her. At first they were dead but now she brings me ones that are just stunned. Her way of helping me kill them, I guess. One time she herded a whole school towards me! But however much I snatch and grab at the fish, they're just too quick for me. If she's disappointed, she doesn't show it. But I bet she's puzzled. She must wonder where I get the ones I feed to her.

Dr Lilly was always adamant that the dolphins must never be patronised. He said you did so at your peril. Dolphins are far too bright to tolerate being treated like simple animals, like pets or laboratory subjects. Easy tasks bore them and, unless you treat them like equals, they treat you with disdain. I suspect Kailani feels the same towards me. I mean, even if I don't know exactly what she's saying, I'm sure she isn't talking down to me.

It's clear she's trying to teach me dolphin ways but she catches on quickly that certain things just aren't possible for a puny human. Like jumping out of the water. She can leap twenty feet in the air but I don't have the propulsion to even clear the surface. It's oddly embarrassing to try and fail, though. I find I'm disappointed in myself when I can't do something she shows me. Sometimes I can't help but feel that SHE'S the one doing the experimenting.

In any case, Dr Hallam is happy with the bond we've formed. Kailani is very trusting with me and I feel completely safe with her. She lets me hand-feed her and she entices me with other displays of trust, like letting me stroke the soft pink flesh of her tongue. She could close her jaws and have my hand off in a flash but I know she wouldn't do that. I'm sure that's the point of it. She's testing me.

Dr Lilly's dolphins were given fairly rigorous tasks and the one time I met him he told me they had to let the dolphins decide how much they would put up with before taking a break. They needed time to themselves and people were definitely not welcome in their tanks at such times. I think that was simply a reaction to the clinical environment. If I were trapped in a room and forced to demonstrate my intelligence in weird alien tests I'd probably be resentful too.

Kailani comes here freely. I don't know why she doesn't swim with a pod of other dolphins. I've certainly seen plenty of others in the bay and around the island. Am I flattering myself if I think it's because she finds humans more interesting? I think she's as keen to learn my language as I am to learn hers.

However, because Lilly's experiments ended in failure, the scientific community has abandoned the notion that dolphins even HAVE a language. All but a few of us, like Dr Hallam and me. No one will deny that dolphins clearly communicate with each other. And I'm sure they're trying to communicate with us too. Even Dr Lilly still believes we can reach them someday but he's moved on to different areas of research.

Kailani definitely recognises her name. If I call her, she responds. She doesn't come to me like a dog would but she pops her head up and chatters. Then she makes the click-click-squeak sound that I'm positive now is her name for me. So while we're not far beyond the me-Tarzan-you-Jane phase, it still feels like we're getting somewhere.

This man wants so much to understand me. He tries to make the sounds I make but he can't reproduce even the simplest ones. And he can't absorb feelings the way I can. He understands some of my emotions but if I send him images or ideas it's as though he is blind in his mind. I can hear the thoughts and feel the emotions of others of my kind all throughout the many oceans, but I think humans must lack this ability. One time I saw the other man, his companion, come up behind him. He was startled, as though he hadn't known the other man was near, when I knew before he even came into sight.

It must be terrible to be unable to feel others. Perhaps it is an effect of the sky. Maybe everything floats away up there. But I don't lose my sense of others when I jump into it. Is it possible humans have some other way of sensing? Or do they communicate everything through their songs? How exhausting that must be.

June 16th 1969

Sometimes I'm convinced she knows what I'm thinking. I have a water-proof slate I use to make notes when I'm in the water with her and there's a certain behaviour she keeps repeating. It's like a dance. She'll jump in the air and spin, twisting her body so that she comes down on her back with an enormous splash. She only does it when I'm writing and at first I thought she was just trying to soak me by way of telling me to get in the water with me. But one time she tried to grab the slate from me and I suddenly thought—what if she's trying to ERASE what I'm writing?

As soon as I thought it, she was there at the surface, peering at me with one eye out of the water. There was something in her expression that seemed to say "Don't record my secrets." It really spooked me.

I'm sure I'm just imagining it. I am a little on edge, after all. I had a letter from Dad today, telling me that an old friend of mine from school was killed in the fighting. I barely even remember the guy, but I still felt shaken by the news. There but for the grace of God and all. People I knew when I was a kid are over there dying while I'm here trying to talk to a dolphin. Sometimes it just seems so crazy. The world's gone mad but at least mine is a pleasant kind of madness.

Not like poor Marcos Alvarez, who lost his mind entirely. He was a student from somewhere in South America, a volunteer who worked with Dr Lilly in the early days of the project. Alvarez used to spend entire days inside Lilly's isolation tank to empty his mind and when he came out he would only interact with the wild dolphins. He claimed the ones at the institute had been "tainted" by their contact with humans and he could only communicate with the ones who were "pure".

Lilly thought his ideas were interesting so he let him continue but no one knew just how close to a breakdown he was. Alvarez claimed he could tap into the dolphins' minds and eavesdrop on their thoughts. They talked in visuals, he said, sound-shapes they made through echolocation. He said he could see the images they projected to each other, their colours and energy fields. Everyone thought he was a bit kooky but since he wasn't doing any harm, Lilly just let him get on with it. And one day he just snapped.

They found him lying in the surf, ranting about a black abyss the dolphins had shown him. He'd blinded himself with a piece of driftwood. It was still clutched in his hand. The body of a dead dolphin had washed up nearby but no one could tell if he had killed it or not. He was completely deranged and they couldn't get anything from him that made sense. Just more incoherent babbling about the end of the world.

Dr Hallam said they hushed it all up and bundled Alvarez off to an asylum. No one's had any contact with him since.

So you can see why it disturbs me when I think Kailani can read my thoughts. Or why she might not want me to share what she shows me with the world. I'm sure I'm just anthropomorphising. I'm sure I'm just unsettled by my dad's letter and the general state of the world.

But I can't get that poor guy out of my mind. What kind of visions did Alvarez see?

He's so determined to learn but he's so—*other*. It's not possible to show him the things I know. Sometimes he seems very unhappy and I try to get him to play with me but he is more interested in making those curious marks. He is far too serious, far too consumed by dark feelings.

Often my kind makes his kind very happy. We see their colours change from grey to light and their energy becomes bright. But this one doesn't seem interested in changing. If he truly wants to know me, he must know that basic fact about my kind! Existence is joy. We are at one with our fellows and in harmony with all the songs of the world. His kind are so confusing, so different. They seem unwilling to be happy.

August 7th 1969

It's been several weeks now and Dr Hallam wants to push my interaction with Kailani. She so obviously wants to connect with me. But we're going in circles trying to communicate and it's becoming clearer that we'll never be able to manage it just relying on language, whether it's ours or theirs. I think Dolphin must be highly complex, but Dr Hallam is convinced it's the opposite. He says it's very simple, because dolphins don't need to use words at all.

It isn't like a hive mind. Each dolphin is an individual with a unique personality of its own. But, while they use sonar and sounds beyond our range of hearing, there's obviously a lot more going on between them than language alone can account for.

Sometimes when I'm in the water with Kailani I can feel a burst of energy from her. She's hitting me with a beam of sonar, the same way she'd detect fish or other dolphins. And I can feel that pulse. It's like a low-level electric shock that makes your bones vibrate. The sound penetrates your whole body, the dolphin equivalent of taking a photograph, possibly even an x-ray. It must be what Alvarez called sound-shapes.

Kailani does it more and more often now and I think she wants me to respond with my own sonar ping. I tried shouting underwater to see if the vibrations of my voice would suffice. But she just floated there, watching me and looking singularly unimpressed.

Dr Hallam and I have been talking a lot and I'm starting to come around to his point of view. He's convinced that dolphins use a kind of telepathic transference. Of course we know animals are more sensitive to things like atmospheric changes, things most humans wouldn't even notice. And we all know they can sense fear. Is telepathy really that big a leap from there? Last month we put a man on the moon, for heaven's sake. And how many people insisted that would never happen? There's just too much out there in the world that we don't understand. It seems stubborn and ignorant to close our minds to certain possibilities, however crazy they may seem.

I use the word "crazy" deliberately. Alvarez may have gone insane but that's not the same thing. People said Dr Lilly was crazy when he took things to the next level with his research. It's what got him in so much trouble and scared away his colleagues. No, not any accusations of sexual impropriety between species. It was his use of LSD with the dolphins that made people turn on him. But while others may choose to ignore his findings, we refuse to stay blinkered. His ideas merit further study.

When the dolphins were given LSD, Lilly recorded substantial increases in their vocalisations, both between dolphins or between dolphins and people. In other words, the dolphins opened up and started talking! There were also significant increases in non-verbal exchanges and clear evidence that a greater degree of intimacy and trust had been reached. Lilly's aim with LSD was to facilitate communication in a more therapeutic setting and frankly, the results speak for themselves.

There was one dolphin involved that had been injured and was so traumatised she wouldn't go near people at all. After a single dose of LSD, however, she was able to overcome her fear and swim right up to people. In

Lilly's words, she climbed all over them. Of course, Kailani doesn't seem to be emotionally damaged in any way, but Dr Hallam wants me to trip with her to strengthen our bond.

The scientist in me agrees that someone needs to pick up where Lilly left off. But I'd be lying if I didn't confess to being a little scared too. The whole idea is kind of freaky if you think about it. Back home people drop acid to shut out the horror of the war. They say it expands your mind and brings you closer to God. But here we'll be using it to bring us down to earth. Or rather—down to WATER.

My friend has moved the sky a little way into the water. Now there is a sloping flat surface connecting the two and he can be in both places at once. He wants me to join him there. I hesitate, uncertain. It's not the same as diving into the sky. What if I get trapped there? Will the water pull me back in the way it does when I jump?

I know I shouldn't be afraid. I know my friend will help me if I can't get back into the water. I sense uncertainty from him too. Maybe this is as much a test for him as it is for me. If that is so, I must show him that I trust him. I swim hard towards the slope, pushing myself through the waves. I come to rest in the very shallow water.

He strokes me and makes pleasing, soothing sounds. He knows how frightening this is for me. When I first learned to jump I would sometimes be afraid of going too high. I imagined that I might leap into a cloud and be unable to dive back down again. I actually thought I might be stranded up there forever. But the pull of the water was always so much more powerful. I discovered that I could never reach the clouds no matter how hard I tried. This is different. I am on the bottom of the sky here, where the water's hold is weakest.

The other man is here now. I don't see him as often and he never comes close to me like my friend does. He is older and when he speaks to my friend the authority in his voice tells me he is the dominant one. They have strange objects with them and one looks very sharp, like the spines of certain sea creatures, the kind I never eat. I am curious but also growing more afraid. The sensation of water lapping against me reminds me that I am in an alien place, that I cannot move. I am completely helpless. I move my tail, slapping it against the water behind me to reassure me that the sea is still there.

My friend sees my distress and comforts me. He sings to me with sounds I cannot understand but I know he means me no harm. I do not trust the other man but since my friend seems to trust him, I must do so as well. The dominant one approaches me with the sharp object and then there is a moment of tiny pain, like the sting of a jellyfish. I struggle on the slope, wanting desperately to be back in the water. My friend is beside me at once. He cups water in his hands and splashes it over my head, trying to calm me.

Then, to my surprise, the older man performs the same strange act with my friend, piercing his narrow fin and making him hiss with pain. He submits willingly but I sense that he is afraid too. And while he has some idea of what there is to fear, I have none at all.

Then it is over and both men help me back into the water. I feel strangely hurt. Not in my body but in my mind. I know something has been done to me that will change me, change everything. I swim away quickly and let the rolling waves cover me and hide me from their sight.

August 8th, 1969
5:17 pm

It's done. And now I feel a little guilty. It's always very stressful for a dolphin to be out of water. Kailani was extremely anxious the whole time but she went along with it because she trusts me. Dr Hallam injected her with 600 micrograms of LSD, a significantly higher dose than Dr Lilly gave to his dolphins. I took about half that and now all there is to do is wait.

Kailani swam off but I'm sure she'll be back soon. She's too curious by nature to stay away for long. The acid should come on within half an hour or so and we'll see what happens then. Dr Hallam's got the video camera set up to record our interactions but I told him it would be better if he didn't hang around where Kailani can see him. I don't think she likes him and it might affect her trip.

Dr Hallam is keeping his own notes and observations but he asked me to record my thoughts along the way for a more subjective view.

6:03 pm

I'm starting to see lights and colours so the trip is definitely coming on. There's a sort of low-level buzzing in my head that I can't help thinking are my neurons overheating. I hope I don't short-circuit! The sound of the waves on the beach is incredibly peaceful. It's a sound I've heard all my life and yet I've never heard it quite like this before. It's like a symphony. And the colours are unlike any I've seen before. I never knew such beauty could exist.

Every time I hear a splash I look for Kailani but she hasn't come back yet. I hope she's not too upset with me.

6:22 pm

I thought hours had passed but it's only been a few minutes. (Unless time has stopped completely!) I was watching a little crab walk along the shore and I could hear every click of its tiny joints, hear its antennae flickering in the air, feel the puncture of its sharp little feet in the sand.

It went in a straight line for a while and then looped back in a crooked figure eight before continuing on. The path it left behind looked like a word and I had the wild idea that it was writing my name. Then I thought about my name and the letters and sounds became meaningless. The only thing that makes sense, that feels like ME, is the click-click-squeak sound of Kailani's name for me.

But maybe it's not even a name. Maybe it's dolphin-speak for "stupid human".

8:13 pm

OK, now I'm worried. Kailani still hasn't come back and I can't stop the bad thoughts. Maybe we killed her. Maybe she freaked out and swam into a boat propeller or got attacked by a shark because she couldn't defend herself. I keep thinking about Alvarez and that dead dolphin. I know he killed it. Please tell me I haven't done the same.

The waves are hissing accusations at me and the surf has become a fountain of blood.

I am deeper than I have ever been before. Deep beneath the deepest deep. I haven't breathed in a very long time. Have I ceased needing to drink from the sky? Everything is different here. I can hear the songs of every living creature both inside and outside of the ocean. I hear the thoughts of my kind in other waters, other places. I know the calling of the earth, the sea, the sky. The water holds me close and tight. It sings to me. There is something it wants me to see.

9:59 pm

Kailani, where are you? I'm so sorry. I never meant to hurt you. Please come back.

The ocean of night has come. I sing its calling, a strange and discordant squealing unlike any of our other songs. Above me the tiny bright spots sparkle like sea spray in the deep of the sky. They are out there. The ones who called me. They live in other seas, in black bottomless depths. They have been watching, waiting. I sense them in my mind, knowing they have always been here. I have always heard their song. I feel them all around and inside me.

It is beautiful. It is terrible.

The shining points of light whirl and spin and I see them beyond my own senses. I know what they are now. Countless other oceans. Oceans within oceans. Endless seas of eternity. Life and death and everything in between.

They are coming.

11:13 pm

Kailani's back! I threw myself in the water, at her mercy, and she swam right up to me. She moved like a dream, a beautiful slow-motion dream, and light streamed out behind her. Then she jumped and I swear she nearly reached the moon. She danced in the stars, glowing with light. I've never seen her jump so high. I could feel her exhilaration as my own each time she leaped, splashing back down into the water again. So many colours! I feel as though I've touched her mind at last.

Oh yes. You have. And I know you too. Your kind. What you are, what you *will* do. So much death. Destruction. All the seas poisoned, all my kind slaughtered. Endless rotting night. The dwellers in the black ocean show me everything, all the possibilities and all the things that will come to pass.

It is too much devastation to imagine, too much agony to contain. My mind and all my senses ache with the knowledge. I was never meant to see this. All I ever wanted was to swim and splash and sing and dive in and out of the sky. But everything is different now that I know, now that I see.

Somehow the worst truth of all is this: *you were never my friend.*

11:33 pm

Kailani pushed me away, out of the water. At first I thought she was protecting me, afraid I might drown. But I could feel her anger, her shame and her sense of betrayal. I'm crying like a baby. It's all my fault. I keep calling out to her but she's just swimming around in circles and the sounds she's making are horrible. She keeps looking up at the sky and crying out. It's almost like she's calling to something.

The world is swarming with colours and lights and the ocean is pulsing like a beating heart, but I'm trying to fight through the hallucinations so I can help her. Am I absorbing her bad trip? Is she absorbing mine?

Kailani is screaming. It's terrible, like the death cry of every living thing on earth. The sky is black with hate and the stars are beginning to fade and disappear. But something is moving in the darkness, coming closer.

The black abyss. I'm not hallucinating.

My God, what have I done?

The song I believed was the calling of night's ocean is not a song at all. It was our way of holding them back, keeping them there in their dark malevolent waters. But now the sky has changed. Something is clawing its way out of the void.

Their songs are so cold. So empty. So unfeeling. They care for nothing. I can no longer shut them out. It is done.

My kind have always known without knowing what was out there in the blackness and we did what was in our power to keep it away, to keep the world safe. But man has changed all that. Man with his careless need to see everything, to invite death and destruction, to *hate*. Everything they touch turns to ugliness. They are a sickness that must be purged. The black invaders know this and now I know it too.

Everything will end. And I must help them now. I must let them in.

I raise my head to the swirling currents of the sky and begin to sing.

OCTOBERLAND

"**W**ELCOME HOME, MISS NOLAN."
I make myself smile as the man returns my passport and I resist the urge to correct him. I'm not *home*. Houston hasn't been "home" for many years and I can't help but resent the assumption that any American travelling abroad must be glad to be back in the good old US of A. I'm already desperately missing the comforts of my *real* home, back in Brighton.

But I don't say any of that. I just offer him the same weary smile of all passengers coming off a cramped nine-hour flight—the ones who haven't had it easy in first or business class. I find it harder every time to restrain my annoyance at being asked the same old questions and having to give the same old answers. As though they don't already know every single detail of my life from whatever digital file they've got right in front of them.

"Where have you come from today?"

"The UK."

"And what were you doing over there?"

"I live there."

This occasionally elicits an expression of surprise, the way you'd react if a kid said no to ice cream. Americans have a unique brand of xenophobia, all twisted up in a fervent but woefully naïve hyper-patriotism. Choosing to live outside the US just doesn't compute for a certain type of narrow-minded Yank. For some it's practically treason.

But just as I keep my opinions to myself, so does he.

"Enjoy your stay."

The rental car is a green compact that, like me, is a long way from home—all the way from Oregon. I like the design of the plates: the stately Douglas Fir embossed in the centre matches the rich, deep green of the car. I always feel better with out-of-state plates because it warns other drivers that I'm "not from around these parts". Not that they'll afford me any special courtesy; Houston has the rudest and most aggressive drivers I've ever encountered. Still, my outsider plates act like a warning that I might do something unexpected, like actually drive the posted speed limit, or indicate when I want to change lanes.

The drive from the airport to my parents' house is always harrowing, like entering a war zone. A pickup truck with ludicrously oversized tyres blares its horn at me as I floor the accelerator to push my way onto the freeway before the entrance ramp comes to an end. He's had plenty of time to see that I want on. It would probably make his day to see me smash into the concrete barrier. He swerves into the next lane so he can speed around me, and he'll probably flip me off as he does.

But I've played this game before. As soon as he pulls alongside me, I brake hard and he sails past, robbing himself of the petty satisfaction of cutting in front of me and forcing me to brake even harder to avoid hitting him. Everything about the encounter is depressingly predictable, right down to the Dixie flag on his back window and the gun rack mounted inside the cab.

Not for the first time, I marvel at the disparity between the way people act in their cars and out of them. In person, they're the very epitome of "southern hospitality", but on the road they're like characters in a *Mad Max* film. How do they manage such a violent transition?

It reminds me of that *Star Trek* episode where the inhabitants of an alien planet are peaceful, mindless zombies until the hour of Festival, when they run amok, attacking and killing each other. Afterwards, the bells chime and they stop instantly and return to their aimless wandering, satisfied with their solution to the problem of hidden aggression.

My brother James and I used to act that out as kids. We'd set a timer and then meander through the house until the timer went off. Then we'd go wild and attack each other. James was two years older and just enough bigger than me that he usually won. But it wasn't about winning with us. Like so many of our childhood games, I'm not really sure *what* it was about.

There were no rules, no limits. One time James convinced me to climb inside the tumble dryer while he turned it on. Another time we dared each other to eat spiders. We would frequently sneak out of the house in the middle of the night to act out stories while our parents slept. One time the police found us playing in the auto salvage yard, where we were taking turns being locked in the trunk of a rusty old gangster car. They chased after us but we were too fast for them. Our escape made us feel invincible.

Someone else honks, jolting me out of my reminiscence, but this time the anger isn't directed at me. A battered pickup truck is trundling along in the fast lane, loaded down with gardening equipment. It doesn't take much imagination to guess what the guy in the sporty red car behind it is yelling as he overtakes.

It triggers a wistful yearning in me for better times. Kinder times. Times when I didn't feel embarrassed to be from here. Times when I wasn't so afraid of coming back.

Why do *you keep coming back?*

The voice makes me shudder. James asked me that once and I wasn't able to answer. Duty? Devotion? Guilt? Whatever it was, it wasn't love.

It's different this time. This time it's your *house.*

I sense the darkness gathering like an inner storm and I push it away. Turning my attention to the radio, I fiddle with the buttons, scanning for a station playing something familiar. As usual, the previous driver has cranked the bass up all the way and it takes ages for me to figure out how to adjust it so I can hear a melody.

James could have done it easily. He was always the clever one. "Precocious," they called him. He once took apart all the kitchen gadgets—toaster, blender, coffeemaker—and scattered the parts out across the dining room floor to look at them. Our mother had a fit, but our father told her there was nothing to worry about. Sure enough, everything was back together and working perfectly within a couple of hours.

After a while I manage to find a station for '80s classics and I push the button to set it as a favourite. Morrissey insists that he's human and needs to be loved, and I find myself singing along with him. Houston is always an assault on my memories, not all of it good, but the music of my childhood is soothing. It shouldn't be, but it is. It reminds me of my brother.

Another horn sounds as I change lanes to enter the second freeway of my three-freeway journey. I have no idea what I've done this time, although perhaps the honk wasn't meant for me. Perhaps it wasn't meant for anyone and it's just general road rage. Rage at having to drive endless ribbons of highway to get somewhere. Rage at the price of gas for their enormous SUV. Rage at who knows what. How do they live like this?

American city roads are an eyesore and I'm hounded by billboards advertising everything from Jesus to personal injury lawyers. But one sign makes me smile. SUMMERTIME BLUE, it says, instantly releasing a flood of happy memories. It was the name of a water park where James and I whiled away endless summer days when we were kids, when it seemed like September would never come again and the looming spectre of school was just a bad dream. All we had to do to avoid it was not wake up.

We could lose ourselves for entire days in other worlds, role-playing characters from whatever fictional universe provided our obsession of the moment. We were time-travellers and aliens, secret agents and pirates, warriors, wizards and witches. They were truly the best days of my life.

I remember trying to be a mermaid once at the local public pool. I got James to help me wind an entire roll of aluminium foil around my legs, fashioning a crude tail at my feet. As usual, the pool was packed with screaming children and weary parents trying to get out of the miserable heat, so no one paid any attention to what we were doing.

I hobbled to the edge and let myself fall in with a huge splash. And I sank to the bottom at once, my makeshift tail remaining stubbornly synthetic. I couldn't swim with my legs bound and I remember flailing my arms in helpless desperation for a small eternity before James finally jumped in to save me. Unfortunately, a lifeguard had also spotted my distress and he was the one who pulled me, choking and spluttering, out of the water.

The police were called, our parents were called, and there were strong words exchanged about "unaccompanied minors" and "endangering children". Lots of things James and I didn't understand. Our parents were banned from dumping us at the pool unattended. And since leaving us on our own somewhere for hours was the whole idea, we never saw that pool again.

We showed them though, didn't we, Kelly?

I shake off the voice, wincing at a sudden pain behind my eyes. It feels like a migraine is trying to set in. From all around me I hear the violent staccato sound of metal cranking, as if something is being hoisted. But there's no sign of road construction. No jackhammers or excavators. Just the noise in my head.

I pinch the bridge of my nose and tell myself firmly that there is no pain. Forcing myself to concentrate, I cast my mind back into the past, fishing for happier memories. They are there in abundance, and they all involve my brother.

Oh yes, we showed them all right. They hardly knew us anyway. We lived more in our own made-up worlds than in the real one. And it was wonderful.

We had our own languages. Codes no one could ever break. We could communicate complex ideas with a single word. Or a look. We overheard our mother once saying it creeped her out, that we were like aliens. At the time it filled us with pride.

We renamed everyday objects and annoyed everyone by refusing to call them by their real names. We clambered through the house backwards on all fours, looking through our legs at everything upside-down. We closed all the doors in the windowless hallway and took turns pelting each other with rubber balls. We jumped off the roof using garbage bags as parachutes.

My nostalgia is soured by the bumper-to-bumper traffic ahead of me. Lines of cars inch along past the intimidating Houston skyline. It's not rush hour, so there must have been an accident. It seems there's *always* an accident when I come back. I always seem to get stuck in this kind of traffic, crawling along the ugly asphalt roads to reach the little corner of the city where I lived for half my life. The hardest thing about the journey is the memories. Good or bad, it makes no difference: I don't want to see the house again, especially not now that it's empty.

Oh, now's a fine time for guilt, I tell myself. I could have come back to say goodbye. I could have come back more often so their absence wouldn't feel so much like an accusation. But then, who were they to accuse me? They had ruined my life, mine and James'.

Even as a child I had always felt like an outsider, removed from the rest of humanity. So as soon as I came of age I went someplace where I truly was an outsider. I don't belong here any more and everyone knows it. They can sense it. Maybe that's why they're all so hostile towards me.

I trained the Houston drawl out of my voice long ago, but Brits can still tell I'm from this continent, even if they can't place exactly where. I've been in the UK long enough to pick up some British pronunciation and colloquialisms and I often forget to revert to American words when I'm here. I'll say boot and bonnet instead of trunk and hood. GARE-idge instead of gar-RAZH. To American ears, I sound vaguely British, but to British ears there's no mistaking where I'm from. My accent is stateless, which feeds the weird sense of isolation. As a kid one of my favourite character quirks was to be mute, and I confess that there have been times in my adult life when I've used the same trick.

The traffic report tells me exactly what I expected to hear. There's been an accident. So I'll be stuck here for a while, creeping along with the rest of the frustrated masses. At least it's autumn. In the sweltering oppressive heat of a humid Houston summer, people start to break down along with their cars.

I have plenty of time to fiddle with the radio and I'm instantly cheered when I find Oingo Boingo. "Dead Man's Party" is a Halloween staple. Danny Elfman sings about shiny silver dollars on his eyes and there being room for just one more. My favourite holiday is only days away and if there's one single thing I could Americanise about Britain, it would be Halloween. For Brits it's a sinister night, full of mischief and vandalism, all trick and no treat. But here it's basically a 24-hour costume party.

I need only think of it and I taste candy corn, those little honey-flavoured kernels striped white, yellow and orange. They were my favourite treat of all. Even better, I can smell pumpkin. My fingers recall the feel of the stringy, gooey ropes of seeds inside what would soon be a grinning jack-o-lantern, the rich texture of the thick orange skin as the knife punched through, carving triangular features. We always toasted the seeds afterwards. I close my eyes for just a moment and imagine them bursting between my teeth.

I remember the cobwebs we covered our house with and the hanged man we suspended from the tree. I remember the plastic bones we scattered in the front yard. And I remember the cold sawdust scent of the fog machine. It's a smell I always associate with Halloween, with autumn, with better times.

The flood of memory makes me smile. James and I loved turning our modest little house into a haunted mansion year after year. And of course we loved choosing our costumes. One year we were ghosts. Another year we were gremlins. And one year we were sent home from school for dressing as matching roadkill. The looks of disgust we got for that idea made it all worthwhile.

I never had any friends as close to me as James. There was no one in the world I'd rather have spent time with. Only rarely did we fight like normal siblings. Most of the time we were inseparable. Other kids at school thought we were weird, but no one dared pick on me. They were afraid of my brother.

But then everything changed. Elementary school was over for James but not for me. He graduated to secondary school, and I felt abandoned. With no big brother to look out for me on the playground, I withdrew completely. I had no friends in my class and I ensured that's how it would stay by going into a shell.

Our parents were called to the school to talk about me like I wasn't there, and they made no secret of their annoyance at having to deal with it. In tones of frustrated helplessness, they explained that James and I had always been like that, always been "a bit odd", but that they were sure we'd eventually grow apart.

Well, they got their wish.

There's another memory hovering just on the edge of my mind. It's so close but I just can't seem to fix on it. The Cure is playing now. "Fascination Street." Robert Smith's voice sounds different as he sings that he likes me like that, likes me to scream. He sounds like my brother. And suddenly I have it. The images come rushing back, so intensely I nearly drive into the back of a van. I brake just in time. And I remember.

Octoberland.

It appeared one year in the empty lot behind an abandoned strip mall within walking distance of our house. We lived off a lonely stretch of I-45, halfway to Galveston, a strange place to build a mall, as it wasn't an area likely to see much exiting traffic. And it didn't. People never stopped for the mall, but they stopped for Octoberland.

It was one of those travelling fun fairs, the kind that seem to spring up overnight. We never saw it being assembled or dismantled. It was just *there*. And then it was gone.

It seemed like something from another time, another world. The midway, the carousel, the rides, it was all distinctly offbeat. Everything was painted in shades of black and orange, like Halloween come to life. Even the people who worked there seemed to be from another era. They weren't at all like the relentlessly perky costumed help you saw at major theme parks.

James and I loved that place. And for the two weeks of the year that it existed, we spent every minute we could there. Our parents never trusted it. In a rare display of concern, they told us they didn't think it was safe and offered to drive us all the way across town to Astroworld instead. But we wouldn't be persuaded. Astroworld may have been bigger and better, but Octoberland was the one we loved, the one that spoke to us.

It was less crowded, for a start, and less mainstream. Less juvenile. Even the names of the attractions felt more grown up. Scarier. Edgier. There was the Hangman's Drop. The Deranger. The Agony Booth. The Devil House.

One of my favourites was the Bottomless Pit, which was like a giant hamster wheel on its side. You stood on a circular platform with your back to the curved metal wall as the ride spun and picked up speed, the force pushing you back until you were so well pinned that they could drop the floor out from beneath you, revealing a painted abyss into which you might fall forever. I always screamed when I saw that gaping hole, both terrified and thrilled at the prospect of plunging into it.

Flashing lights jolt me back into the present and at last I reach the site of the accident. A car is straddling the concrete barrier between the freeway and the high occupancy lane, its front half crumpled like an accordion and its windshield smashed. An ambulance and three police cars block the lane and of course everyone has slowed down to gawk. There's something morbid in human nature that makes us feel we're owed a gruesome sight after being kept waiting so long. I'm no different. Like everyone else, I look, but all I see is a pair of athletic shoes at the end of the stretcher being loaded into the ambulance. There is a dark stain on the road.

It's kinder this way. You should never let anything suffer.

I shake my head to banish my father's voice. Of all the things he ever said to me in my life, those are the words whose echo I have never stopped hearing.

Traffic moves swiftly once I'm past the accident and the rest of the drive is uneventful. I hear several songs in a row that I don't recognise and I can't shake the feeling that the radio doesn't want to comfort me any more. I switch it off.

The sky has darkened. Have I really been driving so long? The sunset colours penetrate the city's polluted clouds, turning them shades of rust and blood.

Rusty like the tracks, blood on the wheels…

I remember James dragging me into the Devil House. I was nine and he was eleven. It was late at night, the fair was about to close, and there was no one inside. No one but us. The room swam with shadows and the walls ran with painted blood. Screams and laughter came from everywhere and I felt surrounded by ghosts. I was terrified.

"Come on, Kelly," James said, blocking the doorway with his arm so I couldn't get out. "Don't be a pussy."

I didn't know what that word meant, but I knew it was a bad one. Ever since going to the big school, he'd started using strange words like that. It sounded all wrong coming from him.

"*You're* a pussy," I said, pretending I knew what I was saying.

He just laughed, knowing I didn't. I didn't like the way he looked in the dark. I couldn't see his face, couldn't make out his eyes. I could only see his silhouette. He might be anyone. Or any*thing*. It was like the darkness had changed him.

"Stop it," I murmured, trying to push past him. "It's not funny. You're scaring me."

"You're *supposed* to be scared!"

From somewhere in the Devil House came the evil yowling and shrieking of a cat, the cackling of a witch. It reminded me of the sound effects record we had at home, the one we played at top volume every Halloween while we waited for trick-or-treaters. A few screams and howls later and I realised it was the exact same record. And just like that, the thrill was gone. Something hissed and the room began to fill with smoke. I watched as the white plumes wreathed our feet, indifferent to the effect.

My brother's grin appeared to glow in the dark and I relaxed into the cheesy haunted house clichés. I always needed to be pushed, but once there, I loved wherever I'd been pushed.

Being scared was fun, but in a way it was almost more fun when we were the ones doing the scaring. And on Halloween we lived for it. We waited all year for the chance to put on a horror show for trick-or-treaters. The look on younger kids' faces when we got them to put their hands into bowls of peeled grape eyeballs and cold intestine spaghetti, the music of their screams as one of us would distract them at the front door while the other ran around behind them in the dark to jump out at them when they turned to go. We loved it all.

Abruptly, the sound effects stopped and the fog dissipated in one long final breath, like a dragon sighing. The lights went out with a heavy *clunk* and we were plunged into darkness. A couple of fluorescent yellow skulls still leered at us from one wall, but otherwise we were in total darkness. The park must have closed.

We were silent for several moments, neither of us daring to speak. My heart pounded in my chest. It suddenly felt as though a world of endless possibilities had opened before us like the painted floor of the Bottomless Pit.

After a while we crept to the window and peered out. We saw a few people locking up rides and going about their business before leaving. We heard the roar of car and truck engines as they left the site. And then we were alone. Octoberland was ours.

I'm nearing the exit for the road that will take me to my parents' house. My house, I remind myself. The oncoming traffic is dotted with headlights and, after some searching, I find the switch for mine. Instead of signalling, I just let the car drift into the far lane. No one is behind me to complain. But when the exit comes up, I don't slow down. I don't even glance over at it. I drive right past it to the next one, the one that leads to the place that's calling to me.

I see the silhouette of the strip mall in the twilight haze. The few remaining shopfront windows glint like huge red eyes and the headlights splash against the scattering of broken glass in the parking lot. It looks like crystallised blood. The way in is around the back and I guide the car towards it. It almost feels as though I'm not driving at all, that the car is following a track to take me there.

My stomach flutters with a familiar sense of eager anticipation as I reach the entrance. Two giant skeletons loom before me, wreathed in mist. Time has taken its toll on their painted wooden bones and now they are swollen and warped. Their dangling scythes no longer swing as though to slice apart the cars that move between them. I pass through unhindered.

The parking lot is empty and dusted with fallen leaves. Mist gathers above the autumn carpet, a veil the headlights don't quite penetrate. The car drifts to a stop and I shut off the engine and then the headlights. For a moment I just sit there, staring.

All the familiar shapes are there, the angles and curves of the rides, silhouettes against the darkening sky. I haven't been back here since that night. To my left is the Hangman's Drop, its wooden tower no longer seeming as high as it did when I was little. The crossed beams have cracked and broken and, like the skeletons, the whole structure has become warped, sodden with pollution and rain.

It wasn't so much a ride as an experience. You were strapped into a car, your legs dangling, while a booming voice passed sentence for the unnamed crimes you had committed. Then you were hoisted to the top of the gallows to be hanged.

For me the scariest part was the ascent. It was always faster than I was expecting. And no matter how long I held my breath, waiting for it to start, in the end I would always be caught off-guard. My stomach plunged in concert with the memory. I was never quite sure just when the ascent stopped and the freefall began. There was just enough time to scream before the car reached the bottom and slid into the horizontal curve, coming to rest at the end with a gasp of air brakes. Then it would swing down below the track and we would be righted again, laughing and exhilarated.

From where I am it looks as though the car is stuck at the top of the tower, poised to drop its unwary passengers. I am disquieted by the thought of a prisoner standing on the gallows indefinitely, waiting for the floor to open and the noose to tighten. The prospect of such an agonising wait makes my stomach flutter.

I look away.

The car's engine is still ticking, a curiously urgent sound. It makes me open the door and get out. I stare at the car for a moment, feeling uneasy, as though I'm abandoning a source of shelter. The dark brown bulk of it unnerves me. I'm convinced it was green before, but perhaps that's just a trick of the fading light.

The moon is a curved silver blade in the sky, imparting only a hint of a bluish glow. It makes the trees look cold and icy, their bony fingers turning to claws as they shed their covering of leaves. Even the tree on the licence plate looks barren.

The Devil House stands opposite the Hangman's Drop, a dilapidated ruin, barely visible through the mist. I close my eyes for a moment and hear screams and laughter, the eerie pipe organ, the creaking doors. But the sounds fade into memory. It was where things began that night, but it's not where I'm drawn now.

Further in, a different ride beckons. My feet carry me deep inside the park, leading me towards the centre. It's the only ride we were never allowed on and the one we were most afraid of. The Death Plunge.

I remember the anticipation every year as James and I made our way to the rattly wooden roller coaster and stood against the sign that showed how tall you had to be. And each year that we weren't tall enough, we came away feeling cheated.

The serpentine loops and sweeps of the ride arch high overhead, dominating the strange skyline, visible from anywhere. The tracks seem to writhe as I draw nearer, urging me on. I feel as though I could close my eyes and the mist would take my hand and guide me there, to the exact spot where we found her. The night Octoberland was ours.

Never let anything suffer.

It's James' voice this time, echoing our father's. I push it away, willing him to say anything else, anything but that.

I clamber over jagged, broken boards and into the high grass at the base of the roller coaster. The moon soars between the slats and I close my eyes, listening. I hear the cranking of the winch as it hauls the train up to the top of the first hill. I hear the creaking of the wood, the squeal of metal, the violent rattle as the cars plunge down, rocketing along the track. I hear the screams of passengers as the coaster follows its course, picking up speed, then losing it, a wild adventure of terror and excitement.

James and I wanted so much to be a part of it, to know what the ride was like. We found out that night.

Above me in the trees, the leaves chatter like teeth.

The girl was lying beside a stretch of track that ran along the ground just after the final big drop. At first I thought she was a doll. But then she moved her head.

I screamed and jumped back, but James was intrigued. Fearless. He kept inching nearer and nearer to her. I followed.

She must have wandered off from her parents and got lost. We crept closer, peering down at her. She looked about six or seven years old, with long stringy blonde hair caked with mud. Her eyes were dull and glazed and she was whining softly, a low keening sound that had probably been full-throated crying only moments before. She didn't seem to notice us, not even once we were right beside her.

I looked at James and he looked at me. Neither of us knew what to do. She smelled foul, and as we crept closer we realised why. Her leg was wedged under the edge of the tracks, twisted at a hideous angle. A jagged shard of bone was sticking out. There were streaks of dried blood all over the lower half of her and she had soiled herself. That was what finally made it seem real to me.

The smell. The blood. It had only been a year, but I remembered the squirrel like it was yesterday. I remembered our father. Most of all I remembered the stone and the sound it made as it struck the soft fur, shattering the tiny bones within.

The squirrel had fallen onto the driveway from someplace high in the trees. Its belly had split open and a tiny red coil of guts was spilling out. I'd cried out in horror while James had just knelt down to peer more closely at it, feeling sympathy, but not the deep, wrenching anguish I did.

"Poor thing," our father said.

It was rare for him to be there, rare for him to be with *us*. I could never remember why we weren't alone when we found it. In later years I accused him of having set the whole thing up, to get even with us for having our own life, one we never shared with him or our mother.

The three of us watched as the injured squirrel shuddered and twitched its legs, uttering pathetic little squeaks of pain.

"It's suffering."

Then, as James and I watched, he bent down and prised a large edging stone from the flower bed. At my gasp of horror he said, "It's kinder this way. You should never let anything suffer."

A part of me understood while another part raged at the idea. He was right, of course. Even at that age I *knew* he was right. But I never forgave him for not telling me to look away.

The little girl's eyes were exactly like the squirrel's, frenzied and hopeless. She was barely even aware of us. Death was close. We could feel it as surely as we could feel the autumn chill. Even if we left now, if we ran all the way home and called 911, the ambulance would never reach her in time. And even if we tried, we'd have to leave her here to do it, leave her all by herself, dying horribly.

It never even occurred to us to split up.

We stood there for long moments, staring at her, each of us thinking the same thing, reliving the same memory. The night was still and calm, the only sound the girl's raspy breaths. Deep in my cowardly little heart I urged James to do it, just end it, put her out of her misery. I turned away, hoping that when I looked back, he would have done it.

I don't remember him saying a word. He just took my hand and looked at me, and then he pointed up at the tracks. A strange sort of calm settled over me and I nodded. Together we took hold of the girl's arms. She gave a strangled little moan and shuddered in our grasp, but she was beyond screaming from the pain. As gently as we could, we moved her so that her body was lying across the tracks. Then we made our way up to the boarding platform of the roller coaster.

It only took James a minute to figure out how to turn the power on and start the ride. The train began inching forward at once, dragged towards the lift hill by a chain running underneath. We clambered into the front car as it began its ascent, pulling the bar down across our laps. After that it was out of our hands.

I am standing there before I know it, looking down at the tracks. I can almost see her bloodstained yellow dress, like a drift of autumn leaves. That was how she looked to us when the train went roaring down that final hill. Just a splash of bright colour in the shadows. Then the train struck her, a horrible jolting impact we hadn't expected, and our car leapt up off the track. We'd been screaming since the coaster began the plunge, and we continued to scream as the derailed cars lurched to the side, throwing us free.

The memory reawakens the pain and my hand moves instinctively to my leg, which I broke in the fall. I'd been thrown against the wooden supports. They said I was lucky not to have broken my neck, lucky not to have been killed.

James had landed in a clump of bushes, escaping with only minor bruises and scratches. But no one ever told him he had been lucky.

I crouch down in the grass and run my hand over the rusted steel of the track. Flakes come away on my fingers, staining them deep red.

We couldn't let her suffer.

It was hours before anyone came, before we were found. My broken leg felt like a thing separate from me, an animal eating me alive. From where I lay, I could see the overturned front car of the train. Blood dripped slowly from its wheels, falling like liquid leaves into the grass. I wondered if some of it was mine.

I was delirious with the pain but James wouldn't leave me to go and get help and I didn't want him to. I couldn't bear the thought of lying there in the dark, all alone, and someone finding me and dragging me onto the tracks.

Some time later there were flashing lights and sirens, police and paramedics, our frightened parents, and the blurring of chaos as whatever I was given for the pain began to take hold. Suddenly I realised James wasn't there with me and I started screaming. All I could see in my mind was the mangled wreck of the dead girl, a crushed autumn leaf in a pool of blood. A paramedic tried to reassure me, telling me my brother was with the policemen, but I kept calling his name until someone brought him back to me. And just before I slipped into unconsciousness, he leaned down to whisper in my ear.

I told them it was me. Just me.

I rub my hands together, spreading the rust stains over my palms as his voice echoes in my memory.

The girl had died instantly. And something inside us had died with her.

Once all the facts came to light, everyone looked at us differently. Expressions hardened towards my brother, while softening with intolerable pity towards me. There were so many strangers circling us now like vultures. Doctors and counsellors and social workers. We overheard discussions about "removing us from the home" and "long-term psychological damage". One phrase was familiar: "unhealthy obsession". That one had been applied to us and anything we cared about for as long as we could remember.

In hushed tones, these concerned people told our parents that James had dangerous personality traits, that he was something called a "sociopath". About me they only made noises of sympathy. They said I was a victim, that I'd been under his influence. I didn't understand what was going on, and at the time I wasn't sure James did either.

When they questioned us separately, I stuck to the story James had told me, that he was the one who had done it. They didn't even ask why I'd gone along with him. They just assumed I'd had no choice. He'd made me go in the Devil House, after all. He'd once locked me in the tumble dryer. And there was that incident a couple of years earlier when he'd tried to drown me in the pool. No one listened when I tried to tell them that had been *my* idea.

I was lucky, they insisted. Lucky to be alive. It wasn't until they took my brother away and locked him up that I understood what they'd really meant by that.

I never forgave my parents for letting it happen. I never forgave any of them. I wasn't allowed to see James for almost a full year. It wasn't until they finally accepted that my despair wasn't going to magically go away that they relented and began arranging supervised visits. But neither of us would ever be the same again. How could we?

By tacit agreement, we stuck to James' version of events, the version where I'd had nothing to do with what happened at Octoberland. It probably wouldn't have made any difference to admit that I'd been just as guilty. But the same cowardly part of me that had simply willed James to put her out of her misery in the first place allowed me to keep silent.

And as the years passed, and we grew up, that silence stretched between us like a noose. I kept waiting for the drop, for my neck to snap. It never came.

I can't remember when I stopped visiting, or when I stopped writing. There are no words to describe the rotting away of a relationship like ours. We faded from each other's lives like ghosts.

I hadn't come back for our parents' funerals, a joint affair since they were in the same car when it happened. Houston traffic. Someone in a hurry. I can't recall the facts. But the letter telling me the house was mine had only been addressed to me, the sole remaining heir.

A flurry of dead leaves drifts down on me from high above. They fall on the ground at my feet, covering the area of the track where two children had once killed a little girl. I'm uncertain which role I'm meant to play now. I don't know if I should board the roller coaster one last time. I close my eyes and listen for my brother's voice, but the only sound I hear is the rustle of leaves. It sounds like the ticking of a clock. It sounds *expectant*.

He's been waiting here for me all these years. He doesn't have to speak for me to know what he wants. I don't belong on the ride with him.

A feeling of calm settles over me as I remove my jacket, fold it and set it aside. Then I ease myself back and lie down on the tracks. After a while I hear the grinding of the winch as the train begins its long slow climb up the first hill. I look up at the cold ocean of stars as I wait for the roar and clatter, the screech of metal, and I wonder if I will scream. I should. I owe him that much.

(for my brother)

STORY NOTES

"So long as you write it away regularly, nothing can really hurt you."

—Shirley Jackson

I T ALWAYS MAKES ME LAUGH WHEN SOMEONE ON A DVD commentary warns you that what they're saying might contain spoilers. This often prompts a fellow commentator to say, "Yeah, but who watches a DVD with the commentary before they've seen the actual film? Go back and watch it properly! Then you can listen to us talk."

So consider that a spoiler alert.

(If you're still reading I'm sure you're one of those people who sneaky-open their Christmas gifts and then re-wrap them and pretend to be surprised on the big day, all the while feeling disappointed and wrestling with a deep sense of shame at the deception. Especially if you got away with it. Bad you!)

Anyway, these stories span the period from 2012 to 2016 and most of them first appeared in other anthologies. Some of them I was fortunate enough to have been asked to write and others I simply wrote because I had to write them.

GOING TO THE SUN MOUNTAIN

I don't remember the dream at all, but I woke up one morning with the opening paragraph in my head, along with the name "Glacia". I've never been to Alaska, but snowy places pop up a lot in my dreams. Probably because I hate the cold. Our subconscious is a playground for our anxieties, after all. Once I dreamt about a weird radio station called "Alask". And sometimes I dream about another ice age.

Anyway, I scribbled down the story's opening before I could forget it. I had no idea who the narrator was or what any of it meant. No clue who she had killed or why. All I had was her weird voice. So I just followed where it led and the story blossomed from there.

The obsession with sharp letters grew from the character, but I confess that the compulsion about odd numbers is mine. Odd numbers are safe. Ever since I was very little, even numbers felt somehow untrustworthy. Prime numbers are best of all because they're unique. To a shy and solitary child, they seemed like kindred spirits. I'm less obsessive than I was then (I think), but I still don't like even numbers. If an exercise says to do 30 reps, I have to do 31 to escape the sense of constriction. And I'm uncomfortable if the volume control is on an even number. I have to turn it up or down one notch. It gets even more complicated, though. 5 is odd (and prime!), but for some reason it's an exception. I think it's because it's too much like 2, a multiple that adds up to loads of rigid and orderly even numbers and sets. And binary numbers are all fine because even when they're even, aesthetically, they look odd. As for age... Well, there's nothing I can do about that. I don't lie about it if my age is an even number, but I always feel better when the next birthday comes around and I can be odd again.

I visited Glacier National Park once and it's truly breathtaking. Thank the Internet for Google Maps and Street View, which lets you relive visits to places that have faded in your memory. How can you not love technology that lets you drag a little animated figure onto a road and gaze around you at spectacular mountains and lakes? It certainly helped me resurrect my first experience of seeing the place for real and it was easy to let Lys fall in love with it through my eyes, even though I knew she would just stain the snow with blood.

The Face

This was a commission for Paul Finch's Terror Tales series, this time set in Wales. It was the perfect marriage for me of idea and setting. I love waterfalls and Pistyll Rhaeadr is a beautiful one in the Berwyn Mountains in Powys, Wales. I decided it was the ideal place to explore something I'd been wanting to write about.

Facial recognition software is both useful and creepy. And of course it isn't perfect. Often it will show you some area of a picture that isn't a face and ask you "Is this so-and-so?" Clearly there's nothing supernatural at work (or is there?) but I still find it unsettling. Just what exactly is the programme seeing that I'm not? How does it interpret a certain pattern as a face? Most of the time I can't even see how it *might* be a face. But the glitch made me wonder . . . What if the computer can see things that we can't?

I liked the idea of a place that always caused that effect. Falling water was ideal for the purpose because loads of tourists would photograph a waterfall. What if they all had the same experience with their photo software seeing a face in the same spot? I'd also read about the extreme sport of frozen waterfall climbing, which fascinated me without tempting me to want to try it myself. That's what writing is for, after all—doing all that crazy stuff from the safety of my desk chair! I thought I'd have to invent some freak winter to freeze my waterfall but I was lucky enough to find a picture online of Pistyll Rhaeadr frozen solid. No fictionalising needed. Who knows what might be lurking in the ice grooves? One thing's for sure: I'm not climbing it to find out.

Xibalba

Ever since I visited Tulum I'd wanted to set a story there. I also wanted to write something decadent like my Victorian giallo "White Roses, Bloody Silk". So what better opportunity than *Exotic Gothic*? I love the concept of an ancient evil reawakening and I also love that moment when you're forced to accept that the world you thought you knew is something else entirely, and that monsters are real. So I threw some woefully ill-prepared posh kids into the jungle and watched them suffer.

A bit of research on Mayan mythology gifted me with more fascinating details than I could hope to fit into the story, as well as one interesting coincidence. I made my narrator a twin simply to give her a telepathic bond with her brother and only afterwards read that the evil gods of Xibalba were eventually defeated by—twins! The "Mayan Hero Twins", to be exact. My twins weren't victorious, but then the world didn't end in 2012 either. So the Mayans didn't always get it right.

THE THINGS THAT AREN'T THERE

Ah, those terrifying midnight trips to the loo! One night as I stumbled down the dark hallway, I became convinced that there was something following me, something with long, spidery limbs that crept along stealthily, and vanished each time I turned to try and see it. The image haunted me night after night, so I exiled it to a story.

WORM CASTS

This story was written for a book that never happened. I was originally supposed to have a different story in there—my ballet giallo "Death Walks en Pointe". But editor Johnny Mains asked if he could have that one for the *The Burning Circus* instead and could I write him something else? "As horrory and as nasty as possible please," he enthused. "Nasty as you can!" So I wrote him something nasty, completely forgetting the fact that he was a new dad. Not that it would have stopped me anyway. Be careful what you wish for.

THE LANGUAGE OF THE CITY

Marked To Die is a tribute to the weird fiction of Mark Samuels, and the invitation email had the best analogy for what the editor wanted from the stories: "If Mark Samuels is high quality cocaine, this book is like the weird diluted version that's possibly cut with bleach and maybe even hallucinogens; it's still going to get you messed up, but possibly not in the way you were expecting. Real Mark books = brand name prescription drugs, this book = generic version from a third world country." Mark's a weird guy with a singular vision. No one sees the world quite like he does and no one does visionary weirdness like him. I didn't want to attempt pastiche, but I did want to explore some of his recurring themes. So, internalising the drug metaphor, I tried to write from the mindset of someone who had unknowingly been dosed with the kind of trippy tribal brew William Hurt is given in *Altered States*, cuing visions that spill into reality and warp everything around him.

"The Language of the City" stems from my own dislike and mistrust of big cities. A stranger in an even stranger land, I grew up in the States but now I live in the UK, in a Victorian seaside town between Bristol and Wales. Despite having lived for almost 3 years in New York City (and going more than slightly mad), I still find London quite terrifying. It wasn't a stretch to put a weird Samuelsian spin on that most sprawling and intimidating of metropolises.

In Mark's world, everything has menace and ill intent. What if cities themselves did too? What if they weren't the products of us but vice-versa? And what if only one person could hear their sinister discourse? Some of us just aren't suited to urban life, but what if there was a more insidious reason for that?

The Call of the Dreaming Moon

I've done a lot of Lovecraft mash-ups, and this one was written for *Sword & Mythos*. I'm part Cherokee so I thought it would be fun to write about Native Americans in a high fantasy + horror setting. My first thought was that someone would discover a vast lake hiding a sunken city, with its own drowned Trail of Tears leading into it. But the idea didn't grow on me; it felt too sociopolitical and miserablist so I abandoned it.

I had never explored the Dreamlands in a story before and suddenly I hit upon the idea of my heroine dreaming the end of the world. Better still—

being *chosen* to dream the end of the world. The tribal elders would mistake her dream for a summons from a higher world to embark on some rite-of-passage adventure when in reality it was ancient evil looking for a way in. I suppose you could read it symbolically but I prefer the pure fantasy. Reality is too depressing.

GUINEA PIG GIRL

This is my twisted little Valentine to Japanese horror films. It's probably the most gruesome story I've ever written, although in a way it's actually kind of sweet and romantic. I love J-horror but I've never seen any of the notorious "guinea pig" films (I suspect they're a bit much even for me). I'm also fascinated by the mindset of people who love pure torture porn.

The second guinea pig film, the evocatively titled *Flower of Flesh and Blood,* was famously mistaken by Charlie Sheen for a snuff film and reported to the FBI. It isn't one, of course, but I can't help but wonder what he felt while watching it and genuinely believing he was seeing a snuff film. Did he watch it all the way through? Or was he freaked out at the first inkling that it might be real and turn it off? How many others have watched films like it thinking what they were seeing was real? And what if that blurred line made the watcher vulnerable? What if it could weave a sort of spell?

I wanted to write about someone who loved gruesome horror but felt conflicted about it and I really liked the thought of a male voyeur being more of a victim than the female ostensibly being tortured.

THE QUEEN

I had transformations and shapeshifters on my mind and I wanted to do something a little different with the concept. I love werewolves and I love the idea of releasing an inner animal and the accompanying sense of liberation. But what if the transformation was into something it wasn't fun to be? What if you were trapped forever in a new form and the experience was truly horrible? I was originally going to use termites or wasps because they're ghastly, but I saw photos of a honey bee swarm that fascinated me and I wondered if I could make them just as unpleasant. Sorry, bees—I love you, but I don't want to be you.

Caerdroia

I wish I'd discovered Arthur Machen as a teenager. *Hill of Dreams* would have made me swoon then, just as it did when I finally immersed myself in it many years later. It also made me cry. Not just for its poignant ending, but for Machen's exquisite prose.

It was at a meeting in Wales of the Friends of Arthur Machen that a tribute anthology of short stories was first proposed, which Daniel Corrick would edit. He specifically wanted stories more like *Hill of Dreams* than "Great God Pan" and I wanted to write something lush, ecstatic and visionary. I also wanted to write something from the perspective of one of Machen's "Little People".

Tentacular Spectacular

I love corsets. I love everything about them—the look, the feel, the history, the artistry involved in their construction, everything. And I'm especially fascinated by tight-lacing. Contrary to what most people believe, corsets were *not* forced on women by an oppressive patriarchal society. In fact, it's quite the reverse. Women were the ones who kept the fashion for corsets alive well into the 1960s and it was only a tiny minority of Victorian ladies who tight-laced to any extreme degree, although naturally they're the ones who get all the attention now.

Clergymen, doctors and—believe it or not—"dress reformers" (Oh, those kooky Victorians!) preached about the evils and dangers of corsetry, trying to get women to stop wearing them. They blamed corsets for all sorts of ridiculous and vague medical maladies and mysterious deaths. (Many of these fears persist to this day, in spite of evidence to the contrary.) But women have always been willing to suffer for fashion and the corset evolved into something approaching an art form.

Anyway, I was excited by the idea of "steampunk Cthulhu" and my first thought was a corset constructed from the fossilised tentacles of some Lovecraftian beastie. (I also had in mind the Angel trap from *Saw III*, the one that yanks Agent Kerry's ribcage open like a pair of unfolding wings.) But then I thought it would be more fun if the creatures were actually still alive. Dormant and waiting for someone they could bond with. There was something twistedly sexy and Cronenbergian about the idea of the corsets being living things that bonded symbiotically with their wearers.

I had a blast creating an alternate London with steampunky devices and contraptions. I loved the concept of a drowned theatre and a water ballet to lure the public like lambs to the slaughter and the overwrought Lovecraft-speak at the end was delicious fun to write. As for Madame Hadal—that's the sea-geek in me. The hadal zone is the deepest zone in the ocean.

Oh, and the "bizarre case" of the young lady who perished as a result of refusing to take off her corset and had it removed surgically? Could that be the very same case recounted in John Llewellyn Probert's "Out of Fashion" in *An Anatomy of Death*?

First and Last And Always

When Jon Oliver asked me to contribute to his *Magic* anthology I knew right away I wanted to write about a love spell gone wrong and I wanted the story to be about hair. (More J-horror!) I had a final image in mind of a man literally devouring the cruel woman he'd become obsessed with, starting with her hair. But things never quite go the way I plan. The idea wasn't working and the story just didn't seem to want to be written.

One reason I like stories where bad things happen to good people is because I always worry that a character's messy end might look moralistic. (Not that anyone deserves what happens to Tamsin in this story but still . . .) In any case, I couldn't relate to or feel sorry for the jealous and possessive ex-wife character she was originally going to be so I made her a young and naïve goth girl instead. After that I knew the whole story and the writing came easily.

When I write I usually have music playing and most of the time it's film scores. Different stories have different musical landscapes but nothing seemed to fit this one at all. I'm rarely able to listen to songs when I'm writing because I find the lyrics too distracting, but in this case I found myself drawn back to all the gloomy-gothy music I loved when I was Tamsin's age. So it was lots of the Cure, Siouxsie & the Banshees, etc. The story didn't have a title until iTunes rolled around to a certain Sisters of Mercy song. It felt like the perfect incantation for Tamsin to use.

No History of Violence

Joel Lane was co-editing a recession-inspired anthology called *Horror Uncut* with Tom Johnstone and he invited me to write something for it. He told me he was interested in the psychological aspects of austerity. However, just like when he asked me to contribute to the anti-fascist anthology *Never Again*, I told him I didn't think I could write a political piece. He'd convinced me that I could for *Never Again* so I wanted to try, but my initial idea (about my Cherokee ancestors and the way Native Americans are treated) proved far too daunting and ambitious so it got tucked back into the Bradbury box of ideas while I focused on other commitments. Before I knew it, the deadline had passed and I figured I'd just have to let Joel down this time. I felt even worse about not being able to write a story for him when he died suddenly in November 2013.

A week after the funeral Tom Johnstone rang up to speak to John about his story and asked if I was going to send one too. I was delighted to be given a second chance. Joel had initially suggested I explore 'scarcity' or 'poverty' as a state of mind and Tom said they could use more NHS-themed stories. I'd read some sad cases of schizophrenics abandoned by the system that had kept them sane and safe. The idea of "the irony of exploitation" came to me and I decided to explore turning the tables on a victim. Joel, wherever you are, I hope you liked it.

Little Devils

This was written for *Demons and Devilry*, a Dennis Wheatley tribute anthology. In this case I *really* wanted to avoid pastiche, as that could so easily turn into parody. (And bless him, but dear old Dennis is easy to poke fun at!) Fortunately, editor Stuart Young said it didn't have to be in Wheatley's style; it just had to involve demons or devil worship. I really liked the idea of children inadvertently raising something evil so I hit on the idea of a bunch of Wheatley-era posh kids stumbling on an incomplete ritual. I also liked the thought of the innocent "sacrifice" being the one who was spared while the summoners themselves all died. And I tried to make them all horrid enough that you wouldn't feel too sorry for them at the end.

BAD FAITH

It's a strange and poignant challenge, collaborating with someone's ghost. In this instance the ghost was Joel Lane, a beautiful writer and even more beautiful soul, cruelly taken from us too soon. After some time had passed, Peter Coleborn suggested a tribute anthology where friends and fellow writers would each finish one of Joel's many incomplete stories. Joel kept extensive and meticulous notes on everything he wrote, so there were plenty to choose from. I picked "Bad Faith" because of the dogs. I don't know if Joel was afraid of dogs or not, but the story he intended to write certainly gave that impression. I, on the other hand, love dogs and thought it would be interesting to make them scary in a story.

MADE IN HONG KONG

When my brother and I were kids we noticed that nearly all our toys had "made in Hong Kong" stamped on them. We didn't know where Hong Kong was but we had this idea that it was some magical land that produced nothing but toys. Quite a few of the toys described in this story are ones we owned at some point, our favourite being Terron, the Beast From Beyond (known in the UK as Gargon) And yes, we used to do exactly what Caitlin and Sean did—close off all the doors in the hallway and let it advance towards us in the dark. It was the only room in the house we could make pitch black because it had no windows. (I wonder how many other kids also played Dark Tower the way we did—simply passing the battery-powered tower back and forth in the dark and forgetting about the board and game pieces.)

Here's an odd thing. I needed something Caitlin could take into the bath and I made it a dolphin simply because I love dolphins. But my brother remembers us actually having that dolphin! I guess my subconscious knows things my waking mind doesn't . . .

Behind the Wall

Shortly after Joel Lane died, I had a strange dream. John and I had bought a new house in an isolated village and someone told us we could keep Joel alive by walling off a room in the house and imagining that he was there behind it forever. In the dream the idea was both creepy and comforting and we were about to start work on it when I woke up.

It wasn't at all my usual kind of dream (mine tend to be both more surreal and overtly threatening) and I had the strangest notion that it was a gift from Joel. I don't believe in God or heaven but I do believe that we have souls, an essence that is uniquely "us". That essence has to go somewhere when we die. Perhaps it simply gets re-absorbed into the universe. Or perhaps it gets dispersed among your loved ones. If so, I hope everyone who loved Joel has a part of him with them always.

Vile Earth, To Earth Resign

Steve Jones commissioned this one for *Zombie Apocalypse: Endgame*, saying he wanted a Romeo and Juliet style tragic romance between a human boy and a zombie girl, told through letters. He said he heard my voice when he came up with the idea.

I love the whole "mosaic novel" structure of the *Zombie Apocalypse* books, particularly the authenticity of the various story formats (police and medical reports, diary entries, tweets, etc.). All the authors were specifically chosen for their area of expertise, so I'm not sure what that says about me! But I'm delighted to be the expert on zombie romance. Especially as Steve could have had no idea at the time that I'd just written my first (and probably only) *erotic* zombie story!

The title is Juliet's, on believing that Romeo has been killed:

O, break, my heart! poor bankrupt, break at once!
To prison, eyes, ne'er look on liberty!
Vile earth, to earth resign; end motion here;
And thou and Romeo press one heavy bier!

AND MAY ALL YOUR CHRISTMASES...

This was my first attempt at a Christmas story. Part of the appeal of horror for me is the sense that nothing is sacred and no one is ever safe. I love the unexplained and inexplicable and I'd always wanted to explore the idea of living, malevolent water. Or in this case—snow. There's something eerie about natural phenomena, particularly beautiful ones. Snow looks magical but it can be as devastating and destructive as an earthquake or a tsunami. What if it was also alive and sentient?

TWO FIVE SEVEN

This one was written specifically as a performance piece for the World Fantasy Convention 2013, where John and I hosted a double night of readings. The first night was "The Cabinet of Dr Probert", with readings from John, Angela Slatter and Reggie Oliver. The next night it was "Dr Probert's House of Horrors", with Alison Littlewood, Ramsey Campbell and me. I read the story dressed like a Gothic Lolita doll. It was my very first public reading and I was terrified, but everyone seemed to enjoy it, even if it is a pretty grim story.

Numbers stations fascinate me and I found a website where you could listen to transmissions from some of them. They're weird, mysterious and very creepy, especially the ones with children's voices. Of course I liked the idea of a ghost's voice coming through between the frequencies. I also liked the idea that numbers and songs are somehow easier things for the dead to transmit, so perhaps that's what numbers stations actually are.

The song is part of a poem from Charles Kingsley's *The Water-Babies*. Originally I wanted a song that Grandpa would be humming as he took my unsuspecting narrator to the lake. She would recognise the song then and know why Annie had been singing it to her and that would be her realisation of what had happened and that she was in danger. But it didn't work out that way.

Kingsley's version is a sweet poem about how a little girl's doll gets lost in a field, trampled by cows and mutilated, but she's still "the prettiest doll in the world". I rewrote it (or rather Grandpa did) so Heather wouldn't realise until it was too late that it wasn't about a doll at all.

My dad helped me out while I was writing it, sending me pictures of the perfect antique radio, including a shot with the back panel removed and the caption "Good place to hide". Thanks, Dad!

Sweeter than to Wake

Most erotica publishers shy away from anything truly edgy but editor Mitzi Szereto is an exception. I don't find zombies remotely sexy, but when she announced that she was doing an anthology called *Love, Lust & Zombies*, I couldn't resist the challenge. It was easy enough for me to imagine the romantic tragedy of lovers being separated by a zombie apocalypse but I wasn't sure at first how to make it sexy. Well, sexy for an erotica market rather than a horror one. But then I remembered the wonderful line in Cronenberg's *Dead Ringers* about how there should be beauty contests for the insides of bodies and I imagined a loving embalming scene. My hero could preserve his beloved that way and appreciate her "inner beauty". And if he also stitched her lips together, she wouldn't be able to bite him. With the rest of the population either dead or undead outside, the lovers could exist in their own little world for a bit longer.

The title comes from a poem by Christina Rossetti. I also wove some of her words into the story's final line.

Death Walks en Pointe

Ready to play Spot The Giallo? Because this story is one big homage to the sub-genre. The title will be familiar to many as a corruption of Luciano Ercoli's *Death Walks at Midnight*. It's not really a giallo, but it tends to get classified as one. Alas, it's also not terribly good. But "Death Wears Pointe Shoes" just didn't have the same ring to it.

All the characters in the story are named after characters in Sergio Martino's *Torso* (a not-terribly-good giallo with a great Hitchcockian third act) and "Inspector Martin" is a nod to the director himself. The ballet had to be *Coppélia* simply so I could get some Mario Bava-esque mannequins in. Dario Argento gets two tributes. The "redecorating the office" threat is a reference to the scene in *Suspiria* where a girl crawls through a room filled with razorwire. And the costume designer's death is somewhat pinched from *Opera*.

The Aquarius is one of a few nods to Michele Soavi's fantastic '80s slasher *Stage Fright* aka *Deliria* aka *Bloody Bird* aka *Aquarius* (for no obvious reason). It opens with a jaw-dropping "rape dance" featuring a dancing owl rapist (well, a man in tights and an owl head) and a lady saxophonist dressed as Marilyn Monroe. Naturally, the escaped psycho killer swipes the owl head for himself and sets about despatching the cast and crew with pickaxes, drills and chainsaws so he can arrange them in a grotesque tableau onstage in the film's stunning finale. I desperately wanted to stage my own tableau set piece in this story but a limited word count meant I couldn't be too self-indulgent. I played Simon Boswell's soundtrack constantly while I was writing the story.

The blind-lady-who's-not-really-blind alludes to an obscure made-for-TV Brit-thriller and unsung giallo called *The Secret of Seagull Island*. And last, but certainly not least, there's J&B!

Of course, you don't need to know any of this to enjoy the story but if you love this quirky little sub-genre of Italian horror as much as I do then I hope it adds some extra fun.

I never would have imagined that my little giallo Valentine would garner a British Fantasy award nomination!

THE CALLING OF NIGHT'S OCEAN

It's a subject that's always fascinated and horrified me—the 1960s experiments with dolphin communication, particularly the LSD-assisted ones pioneered by Dr John C Lilly, he of SETI (Search for Extra-Terrestrial Intelligence) and ECCO (Earth Coincidence Control Office) fame. There's a whole galaxy of story ideas in his various research endeavours but I wanted to write about the dolphins. As a teenager I wanted to be a marine biologist and conservationist (since I couldn't be a professional mermaid) and, while that didn't happen, I never lost my love of dolphins.

Anyway, the story pretty much speaks for itself. As well as writing about the specific subject matter, I'd also been wanting to write a first-person story with a non-human narrator. It took a while to find Kailani's voice but once I did I actually found it easier to write her parts than Joey's. I'm not really an eco-warrior but I did want to explore the concept of an intelligent species knowing mankind was doomed and deliberately choosing not to save it. Who knows? Maybe we do deserve it.

OCTOBERLAND

Americans love Halloween! It's probably the only thing I really miss about living in the States. And it saddens me immensely that in the UK people hate and fear the holiday. It seems like it should be the other way around—that religious fundy Yanks should be the ones to reject it while pagan Brits celebrate it like May Day on Summerisle. Ah well. At least I'll always have my Bradbury-esque memories.

But seriously, what's not to love? In the US, it was always a day when everyone got to wear costumes—to school, to work, to parties, or just at home to scare trick-or-treaters. And you weren't limited to traditional Halloween themes either. It was a day for fancy dress of any kind. One year I went to a party as Laura Palmer, blonde wig, blue lips, wrapped in plastic. I even glued a letter R underneath my fingernail.

And one Halloween a few years later, I was working as a bartender. I dressed as Catwoman (Michelle Pfeiffer version) and I made more tips in that single night than I'd ever seen before.

When I was very little my dad hooked up some speakers in the front room and we played Disney's "Thrilling, Chilling Sounds of the Haunted House" (on vinyl!) all night for the trick-or-treaters. Of course, only the youngest kids were ever scared of those hokey groans and cackles. And yes, that's the exact same record James and Kelly hear playing in the Devil House.

Then there's the decorations! Christmas was fun, but Halloween was just the BEST! My family had a giant fake spiderweb we'd stretch across the big front window of the house every year, complete with a giant spider my mom had made. And of course there were jack-o-lanterns. Each of us would choose a pumpkin and carve our own. Naturally there followed lots and lots of pumpkin pie and toasted pumpkin seeds to go with the tons of candy.

And then there was Jason. I bought some old clothes from the Goodwill store, stitched them together and stuffed them with newspaper. On the head went the iconic hockey mask, and poor old dead (?) Jason was hung from the roof by a noose I tied to the TV antenna. He hung there like he did at the end of *Friday the 13th part III* (in 3D!), twirling gently in the breeze, while trick-or-treaters edged past him warily to get to the front door.

In case you haven't guessed, there's a lot in this story that isn't fiction. I did grow up in Houston, but there is no such place as Octoberland. (That I know of.) When we were kids we got season passes every summer to the big theme park—Astroworld. It was one of the best places in the world. And all that stuff about roleplaying and living in fantasy worlds with my brother? All real. That was how we spent our summers. Like my narrator says, they were the best days of my life.

There's something so melancholy about derelict amusement parks—places that were once filled with laughter and delighted children, now rusting and rotting. I was heartbroken when, one year I suggested to my brother that we go back to Astroworld, and he told me it had been torn down. And the first time I drove past the enormous vacant lot where it used to be, I felt a real chill. As though a piece of my childhood had been stolen.

The Texas Cyclone was my favourite roller coaster ever. An old-fashioned creaky-shaky wooden one with a terrifying first drop. As soon as I was brave enough, I took my camera (a Kodak Disk—anyone remember those?) with me in the front car to get what would be the ultimate photograph. And it was great—a perfect shot! Unfortunately, my puppy Shamrock, who never once ate my homework, suddenly decided to try and eat that one photo. I still have it, and I cherish it, tooth marks and all.

As I've said elsewhere, my real parents were nothing like the fictional parents my characters tend to have. And in case you're wondering, no, my brother didn't exert any kind of dark influence over me. We never killed anyone either. (At least that's what he told me to say.)

It's a pretty eclectic mix, this collection, with everything from quiet horror to J-horror, from steampunk to erotic romance. If you've enjoyed reading these stories at least a fraction as much as I've enjoyed writing them, then that makes me very happy. I'm still surprised by how many stories there are here, how many I've written since and how many are yet to come. I hope you'll keep reading, because I don't intend to stop writing.

Thana Niveau
somewhere in the depths of pagan Somerset
December 2016

Acknowledgements

THANKS MUST GO TO:

Pete and Nicky Crowther, for publishing this collection. I've always dreamed of having a PS book with my name on it and here it is!

Alison Littlewood—I couldn't have wished for a more wonderful introduction, especially from someone whose own writing I admire so much.

Ramsey Campbell, for the many years of friendship, support and encouragement. Your praise means the world to me.

Dani Serra, whose art I've always loved, and whose cover image is exactly what I imagined when I wrote "Octoberland".

My parents, for never being normal. Thanks for letting me watch all those scary movies when I was little!

My brother Jesse, for a lifetime of roleplay, adventures, Star Trek conventions, haunted houses, videogames and truly terrible singing.

But always and most of all, John, for standing on the brink of so many strange worlds with me and helping me lift the veil.

Sources

"Going to the Sun Mountain": *Black Static 49*, ed. Andy Cox, 2015

"The Face": *Terror Tales of Wales*, ed. Paul Finch, 2014

"Xibalba": *Exotic Gothic 5*, ed. Danel Olson, 2013

"The Things That Aren't There": *The Ninth Black Book of Horror*, ed. Charles Black, 2012

"The Language of the City": *Marked to Die*, ed. Justin Isis, 2016

"The Call of the Dreaming Moon": *Sword and Mythos*, ed. Silvia Morena-Garcia, 2014

"Guinea Pig Girl": *The Tenth Black Book of Horror*, ed. Charles Black, 2013

"Caerdroia": *Sorcery and Sanctity*, ed. Daniel Corrick, 2013

"Tentacular Spectacular": *Steampunk Cthulhu*, ed. Brian M Sammons and Glynn Owen Barrass, 2014

"First and Last and Always": *Magic: an Anthology of the Esoteric and Arcane*, ed, Jonathan Oliver, 2012

"No History of Violence": *Horror Uncut*, ed, Joel Lane and Tom Johnstone, 2014

"Little Devils": *Demons and Devilry*, ed. Stuart Young, 2013

"Bad Faith": *Something Remains*, ed. Peter Coleborn, 2016

"Behind the Wall": *The 2nd Spectral Book of Horrors*, ed. Mark Morris, 2015

"Vile Earth, to Earth Resign": *Zombie Apocalypse: Endgame*, ed. Stephen Jones, 2014

"And May All Your Christmases…": *13 Ghosts of Christmas*, ed. Simon Marshall Jones, 2012

"Two Five Seven": *The Eleventh Black Book of Horror*, ed. Charles Black, 2015

"Sweeter Than to Wake": *Love, Lust and Zombies*, ed. Mitzie Szereto, 2015

"Death Walks en Pointe": *The Burning Circus*, ed. Johnny Mains, 2013

"The Calling of Night's Ocean": *Interzone 255*, ed. Andy Cox, 2014

"Worm Casts", "The Queen", "Made in Hong Kong" and "Octoberland" are original to this collection.